COURTING CALAMITY

4 Historical Stories

Amanda Barratt, Gabrielle Meyer,
Jennifer Uhlarik, Kathleen Y'Barbo

BARBOUR BOOKS
An Imprint of Barbour Publishing, Inc.

LADY AND THE TRAMPS

∽

by Jennifer Uhlarik

Dedication

*To my husband—my hero on so many levels.
A man who bravely served his community
for twenty-six years in law enforcement,
who selflessly adopted his eldest son and
also raised mine like his own,
and who healed my wounded
heart with caring, gentleness,
and understanding.*

Chapter 1

Near Salinas, California
September 1874

Jake Hicken tugged at his shirt collar. Almost every seat in the Southern Pacific Railroad's passenger car was full, and the sun hit the windows just so, augmenting the heat to a near unbearable level. Usually on the train, the *click-clack* rhythm of the wheels would settle his mind and help him focus on his job.

Today was different.

Why in heaven's name had Ben Figueroa summoned him to Salinas now? Such an incident had never happened. Jake had considered ignoring the summons, but—well, curiosity won out. That and the fortuitous fact that he'd learned Wells Fargo was looking for someone to act as one of the guards overseeing the transport of a money shipment going to Monterey, twenty miles west of Salinas. He'd tried not to overlook his train fare being paid by his employer, which would allow him to satisfy his curiosity. Would Figueroa finally give Jake some acknowledgment and respect—or would their eventual visit take a darker turn? These and other questions pounded his mind until his Stetson ratcheted tight around his skull like a vise.

Lord God, all this pondering and worrying isn't doing me any good, is it? He removed the offending hat and wiped perspiration from its band. *I s'pose I'm not trusting You if I'm fretting so much.*

The silent admission did little to allay his concerns. But then, he shouldn't be preoccupied with such things at the moment. Until the $25,000 Wells Fargo shipment was delivered, he must focus—make sure no one slipped past him to get into the next car where the safe held their valuable cargo. The two guards inside the safe car—Mel Engvall and Carden Smits—were well seasoned, but it was his job to be sure no one made it to them.

Jake tugged the Stetson in place and straightened. Unbuckling his saddlebags, he removed his leather-bound journal then rose and walked toward the back of the car.

Out on the platform, wind whipped around him. He secured the door and, enjoying the cool air, leaned a hip against the metal railing. The loud, rhythmic clatter of the rails finally calmed his spinning thoughts, allowing him to discreetly look through the windowed door and take stock of the rear-facing passengers.

He opened the journal's cover. Modeled after Wells Fargo detective James Hume's mug book, the pages contained pictures and descriptions of known thieves and outlaws. Taking a casual stance, Jake alternated between looking over a few pages then perusing the car. Of the passengers facing him, none matched the descriptions. Of course, that was only half the car's occupants, since the rest faced forward. After several minutes of comparing the pictures to the train's occupants, he secured the journal's flap and reentered the car. Pacing toward the front, he'd just passed his seat halfway down the car when a quiet voice spoke.

"You remind me so much of my dear Wilbur."

Startled, Jake stopped. The words had come from the white-haired woman he'd been sitting across from. "Pardon?"

"My husband. He's been gone for several years now, but with your light brown hair, dark eyes, and strong, bearded jawline, you could have been his twin."

Next to her, the young man—all of about twenty—flushed pink at her comment. "Grandmother." He laid a hand on her arm. "Leave the man alone."

Ignoring him, Jake sat and offered a smile. "Is that so?"

"Surely is. Both of you, handsome as the day is long."

Grandson's cheeks flamed red. "Grandmother, please."

Jake's own cheeks warmed. "Thank you kindly, ma'am."

"And unless I miss my mark," she continued, "you're thinking of someone special. I can all but see your thoughts churning. You've the look of a man pining for his woman."

Oh, his thoughts were churning, all right, but *not* over a special woman. "Do I?"

Her grandson's mortified expression stirred mirth in Jake's chest. Poor fella. The young man clamped a hand about his grandmother's wrist and whispered in her ear.

"Not to hear my grandson speak," she whispered. "Eddie says you've the look of an outlaw." She flicked a gaze toward the Colt Peacemaker tied against Jake's leg. "To me, you look far too refined to be of such ilk."

He chuckled and shot Eddie a reassuring glance. "On the contrary, I've worked since I was eighteen upholding the law."

"See?" Grandmother patted grandson's hand, the young man looking like he might sooner crawl under the train than continue the conversation.

"Are you heading to see her now?" The grandmother seemed unaffected by poor Eddie's discomfort.

7

"See her? Oh. . ." Right. His supposed woman. He cleared his throat. "No, ma'am. I'm attending to some business." He'd not taken the time to find a woman with whom to settle down, and he doubted he would.

Her brows arched. "Oooh, you're on the job," she whispered. "In pursuit of someone?"

"Grandmother, leave this poor gentleman alone." Eddie shot him an apologetic, if embarrassed, look.

"It's fine." Truth was, the good-natured woman reminded him greatly of the nuns who'd helped raise him. "No, ma'am. Something much more mundane." Best if no one knew of the valuable contents in the iron safe one car back.

A wistfulness flashed in her expression but was quickly replaced by a twinkle in her eye. "A word of advice, sonny—something I learned from nigh on forty years of marriage. Let your business keep you from her side only long enough she'll miss you. Not so long she'll worry." She patted his knee with a weathered hand. "It makes the reunions that much sweeter."

The crimson flush of Eddie's face as well as her pointed words made Jake chuckle. "Thank you, ma'am. I aim to return home as quickly as I can."

"Good, good. That'll please her."

"Yes, ma'am." He grinned broadly. "Now, if you'll excuse me, please, I've been sitting too long. I think I'll walk the aisle a little more."

"Oh, of course." She nodded. "I didn't mean to interrupt."

"It was a pleasure talking to you." Jake touched his hat brim and rose, continuing his circuit.

As he neared the front, his gaze strayed to the first grouping of seats across from the privy. On a previous trip up the train car's aisle, the seats had been occupied by two men, each sitting sideways, legs stretched across the benches. Their clothes were dusty and trail-worn. Their dark, bushy beards were all he could see of their faces because they'd kept their hats pulled low as they slept, one using his fancy tooled leather saddlebags as a pillow. In an otherwise full car, they'd stuck out for so rudely taking up valuable space, though Jake wasn't aware that anyone had challenged the men.

Those seats were now empty.

Had they stepped out onto the front platform? Or maybe one was in the privy and the other—*where?* One thing was for certain. They hadn't slipped past him and out the back door.

As he reached the front, he pulled at the door to the forward platform. It didn't budge. An odd tingle clawed his spine. Looking out the window, he noted a rope extending from the area of the doorknob to the platform's railing.

The two space-hoarding men were gone, and the door was secured after them. *Not good.*

Mattie Welling eased her position between several small bodies scattered across the hard boxcar floor. Oh, how she envied the youngest ones, slumbering nearby. She'd not slept a wink. The jarring clatter of the wheels had long ago grown tiresome, every jolt and bump rattling her teeth. Riding in the boxcar was a far different experience than being on the orphan train where, hardly the height of luxury, at least they'd had real seats. Before they'd stowed away in this car, she'd watched the passenger car two cars ahead fill, wishing she could provide that for her children again. But that wasn't to be.

Despite their humble accommodations, it wouldn't be long before they reached Salinas—and soon after, their final destination in the mountains west of the town.

These children, the unfortunate souls left unclaimed at the end of a long orphan train, had waited only days to arrive in Salinas. Mattie, on the other hand, had waited almost a decade since her brother turned eighteen and aged out of the Children's Aid Society orphanage. On the last of his birthdays they'd spent together, he'd promised to head west, set up a place, then send for her. Owlie, dreamer that he was, vowed it would be open and spacious, where they would raise livestock or crops, where each could raise a family. With those promises on his lips, he'd taken up the small chest holding his scant belongings—the one on which the other orphans had carved their names as a remembrance—and departed. It was the last she'd seen of him.

A part of that dream was nearly a reality. She and the orphans would soon take up residence on the sizable property her brother had secured. But Owlie wouldn't be sharing it with them. Heart aching, she opened the carpetbag and removed the now-tattered letter. Despite having the message memorized, she reread the brief words for the thousandth time.

Dear Miss Matilda Welling,

I have the regrettable duty of writing to inform you of Owlie's passing. Your brother died on February 2, 1874, of an extended illness. Before his demise, he expressed his heartfelt regret at letting you down and asked me to convey that he loved you dearly. Among his last effects was a deed to some land in this area (though I'm not sure where), a deck of cards, and two pennies. I am certain he would want you to have the enclosed items.

With sincere condolences,
Dr. Richard Preston
Salinas, California

The tearful shock of the letter's contents had long ago waned, but the haunting loneliness of Owlie's passing still remained. Her beloved older brother—the only family she'd had since she was eleven—was gone. Thank God for Dr. Preston's honesty, or the deed could easily have disappeared without her being any the wiser.

She flipped the page to stare at the deed.

"Again, Miss Mattie?" Fifteen-year-old Derry Beglin glowered at her. "You're reading that blasted letter again?"

She glared back at the cantankerous young man. "Why does that bother you?"

Her eldest charge's dark eyes flashed. "For one, it says the same thing as it did the day you got it. And for another, that stupid deed would stay a whole lot safer if you weren't pullin' it out every two minutes to gawk at it."

"Watch your tongue, young man. I'll not abide your disrespect." Mattie shook the paper. "This *stupid* deed is the key to our futures. Yours, mine, all of ours." She motioned to the seven children around them. "And I'm unsure how to make you understand the compulsion I feel to re-read this letter. I suppose I'm hoping to find some clue into Owlie's life since he left. He wasn't the best about writing, and the few letters I did get were brief, more describing the land and house than about himself and his life. Or maybe I'm trying to remember all the wonderful things he told me about where we're going." Her throat knotted. She folded the worn letter and deed, tucked them into the special interior pocket she'd sewn into her carpetbag to hold them, and cleared her throat roughly. "The truth is, I miss my brother, and that letter makes me feel some little connection to him."

A loud thump sounded on the far end of the car's roof, followed by another. An instant later, angry voices argued for a moment before something slammed against the narrow door at the end of

11

the car. The door burst open, and the two youngest MacGinty children awakened with frightened wails. The other children stirred at the sound.

Mattie and Derry both shot to their feet, the carpetbag tumbling from her lap as a tall, muscular man swung into the car. She gaped at the masked figure when he stepped to the side and, seemingly startled himself, drew his pistol.

Oh Lord! Protect these children!

She inched forward, discreetly motioning her charges behind her. Derry moved to her shoulder, though she shot him a glare. "Stay with the littles," she hissed. "Please."

A second form swung from the roof into the boxcar. Just as his companion had, he drew his pistol.

Mattie's heart pounded. "Please don't hurt us."

The first man spoke to his companion. *"Cierra la puerta. ¡Rápidamente!"*

At the foreign words, twelve-year-old Augustina Garza rose as the second man shoved the door shut. The girl took a couple of steps toward them, expression perplexed.

"Augustina, stay," Mattie hissed and darted a look to nearby Sam Beglin. The second-oldest caught the Mexican girl's arm and herded her and those children nearest him into the corner.

"What do you want with us?" Mattie demanded.

The first man stepped toward her. "Nothing, except I could make use of that bag." He nodded to the carpetbag.

"There's nothing of value in it. Only clothing." And the deed.

"Then it will suit our purposes quite nicely." He leveled the gun at her head. "Give it to me."

The second man turned, stepping farther into the car. *"Es hora, mi gemelo."*

"The bag. Now!" The first beckoned for it then cocked the gun.

Derry's crowding presence disappeared, and an instant later the carpetbag sailed into view, landing in front of the men. "Take it. Just don't shoot her."

Mattie shook as the first man grabbed it then holstered his gun and rushed toward her.

"Get down. Now!"

"What? Why—" Before the word could fully form, the men dropped to their bellies. In the same moment, a deafening explosion roared. The concussion stole her breath and pitched her backward, tumbling into little bodies. The door the men came through slammed open, and the terrifying grind of metal against metal filled the air. Their boxcar teetered on its wheels. All around her, children screamed.

As suddenly as she was blown backward, all momentum shifted toward the front. An unseen force hoisted Mattie like a marionette in unskilled hands and threw her toward the other end of the car. Pain jolted her as she tumbled. The metallic scream grew louder, more ear-piercing as the train braked. She skidded across the wooden floorboards, past the two men, as two tiny children slid past her toward the door.

Instinctively, Mattie reached for the kids, latching onto one's arm and grabbing the other by her dress. She barely had time to pull them to her before her right side slammed the front wall and her head cracked hard against the doorframe, sinking her into blackness.

Chapter 2

His gut churning, Jake kept to a respectful pace as he headed toward the back of the passenger car again. No sense alarming anyone by hurrying. If he could just find the men, he'd stop whatev—

Beneath him, the floor bucked as cacophonous thunder tore through the car. A force like a mule kick sent Jake reeling. His shoulder blade smashed into something solid, and he hit the floor with a grunt. Chaos ensued.

Passengers tumbled from their seats. People screamed. Bodies streamed into the aisle, shoving and crowding to escape the deafening noise at the back of the car. Feet pounded the floor around him, some stepping on him in their haste. Pain coursing through him, Jake pulled himself from the aisle to escape the crush.

An instant later, an ear-shattering screech overcame his senses as the engineer reversed the wheels to slow the train. The car pitched hard toward the front again. He pulled himself into a tight ball, covering his head with his arms to block even a bit of the metallic shriek. The car groaned and shook. Panicked screams grew louder.

Once the train evened out and the immediate pitch toward the front tapered off, Jake pushed to his feet, pain coursing the length of his body. He gulped several breaths and fought to clear his thoughts. Finding a bit of his mental equilibrium again, he took a good look around.

Scenery blurred past the windows more slowly as the train's speed tapered off. Passengers littered the car, few still in their seats. At the back of the car, one bloodied man stood at the door to the platform, struggling to open it.

If the engine had hit something, surely the impact and sounds would've come from the front. But everything had come from the direction of the safe car.

Oh God.

That mule-kick was likely an explosion rigged to blow open the safe. He had to check on Engvall and Smits!

The train coasting now, he scrambled over seats and around passengers, reaching the back door and the man attempting to open it.

"Hey, fella." He tapped the man on the shoulder. "Why don't you try to help the injured folks up ahead."

"I gotta get out of here." The big fella's eyes were huge with panic. "I'll die if I stay. They're shooting the cannons again."

Understanding came. "You're not gonna die. The war ended about ten years ago now. Remember? It's over."

The fella panted. "Over?" His shifty glances toward the door lent no assurance that he was getting the picture.

"Listen, I need your help." He couldn't afford anyone trampling evidence in what he expected was the scene of a robbery. "I need for you to go that way and help anyone you can." He flashed the badge pinned to the inside of his vest. His job as a Wells Fargo Special Agent afforded him no special powers or privileges with the train, but perhaps the sight of a badge would make the man listen.

"You gotta get all these people off the train. Ain't safe." He attempted to reach around Jake for the doorknob.

"I know." Hang it all! The longer he stood jawing, the more likely the disappeared men were making off with the Wells Fargo shipment. "Go that way. Understand me?"

After a slight hesitation, the fella obeyed.

Jake turned toward the door. The window was spider-webbed with cracks, obscuring his view. He turned the doorknob and pulled, but it didn't budge. Drawing his gun, he broke out the cracked glass.

A rope from doorknob to the platform railing held the door fast. He'd *just* used that exit moments before, so he had to have barely missed the culprits.

Jake drew the knife at his belt and cut the rope then stepped onto the platform. As the train finally lurched from its last crawling movement to a final stop, a loud clatter from the right side of the safe car drew his attention. He crept to the platform's steps to peer down the side.

"God, no." A good portion of the wall was gone, blown away. Several jagged boards hung by threads, rattling against the remaining wall.

His gut knotted. There was no way Engvall and Smits could've survived such an explosion. If only he'd paid the passengers more mind, rather than worrying about Ben Figueroa.

Jake hurried to the left side of the platform and, stepping onto the stairs, peeked out. At the far end of the safe car, two masked horsemen waited, each with a spare horse. One called something in Spanish while looking toward the back platform of the safe car. The other, obviously spotting him, attempted a pistol shot. Jake ducked back as the ill-aimed bullet struck the corner of the safe car. Wood splinters showered the air. More shouting ensued.

They were still robbing the train!

Anger boiled from the pit of Jake's belly, and he lunged to the far side of the platform. Ignoring the inner voice that screamed for caution, Jake scampered up the ladder attached to the platform's railing and jumped onto the damaged roof. Crawling to the rough opening, he peered inside.

One masked man, holding a large bag open, shook it.

"¡Rápido!"

"I *am* hurrying!" The other pitched stacks of money into the bag.

Just as Jake drew down on them, the edge of the hole gave under his weight. He reeled through the air, body tumbling, and landed hard on his right hip. Lightning tore through him as he fought to bring the Peacemaker to bear.

The one with the bag grabbed for his gun, but the other stumbled up and shoved his partner toward the door. Jake managed a single shot as they barged through the back door, the bullet taking a piece from the top of the nearest man's ear.

Breathless, he waited for returned fire, but all he heard was pounding hoofbeats. At the gradually disappearing sound, tension dissolved, and he sagged, head lolling to the side. He gulped a couple of breaths before he opened his eyes.

When he did, he jerked in surprise. There against the base of the blown-out wall, two bodies lay twisted and unrecognizable, but for the size of their frames. One tall and burly. The other compact and wiry.

Engvall and Smits.

Lord, they were good men. Please let them be with You in glory.

How easily it could've been *him* in this car, with one of the other men acting as the outside guard. But, used to working together, they'd encouraged him to take the passenger car position. The decision saved his life.

His gaze fell on the rack of rifles Wells Fargo kept in the corner. Holstering his Peacemaker, Jake limped toward the rack and grabbed one. He'd try to get a shot off at the men who murdered his friends. After checking to see it was loaded, he hobbled toward the door. Easing the rifle barrel through the door, Jake checked first to the right then the left. As he stepped onto the platform, a movement directly ahead drew his attention to a strange door at the end of the next boxcar.

An odd place for a boxcar to have a door. Normally, they had only a sliding door in one or both sides. He'd not seen such a thing before.

Framed in the opening, two very small children—both with white-blond hair—hovered over the body of a woman. The little boy, all of maybe three, squatted to pat the woman's cheek. "Get up. Please?"

Jake lowered the gun and limped to the left side of the platform. Peeking out, he found four mounted riders—one sagging in his saddle—retreating at a gallop. Too far off for a shot. He glared after them as they followed the tracks a short way then arced west.

Gaze drifting back to the boxcar door, his nerves pinged. Who were these people, and why were they there? Jake hurried toward the next car's side door and, hovering at its edge, risked a look inside. Several kids huddled at the back while the two towheaded children cried over the woman at the front. As he hoisted himself into the opening, he took a mental count. Eight plus the woman.

"I'm here to help," he called, flashing his badge. "Are any of you hurt?" He nodded to the huddled kids at the back.

A dark-haired young man struggled to stand, a wide trail of blood dripping down the side of his face. "We're fine. Move along."

Jake crossed toward him. "How bad are you hurt?"

"Ain't nothin'. Like I said, move along." He jutted his chin in the direction of the door, but the motion made him sway on his feet.

"Sit down, kid, before you fall. I'll be back to check on you and the others in a minute."

As Jake turned, the young man caught his left arm. "I told you to go—"

Nerves firing, Jake shouldered the rifle and spun, the barrel thumping the unsteady young man in the chest. "Don't!"

Startled gasps and a few frightened cries sounded from around the boxcar.

The fella's eyes rounded and he lifted his hands.

"Sit down. Understand me?"

"Derry!" a voice from the corner shouted. "Do what he says."

Jake flicked a glance to a slightly younger boy in the corner, hands splayed in front of him. "Please don't hurt my brother, mister."

He looked back at Derry. "You gonna sit, or—"

"He'll sit," the younger boy called. "Won't ya?"

Derry nodded. "I will." He took two steps backward before he turned. The young man barely made it to the wall before he collapsed.

"Kid." Jake settled the rifle in the crook of his elbow and turned to the other boy. "What's your name?"

"Sam Beglin."

"All right, Sam. I'm Jake Hicken. Starting with your brother Derry, check on all these kids and make sure no one's hurt bad. Understand?"

"Yes, sir."

Jake scanned the other faces. They were all a fair bit younger than the two boys. He paced toward the front.

There, the towheaded boy and girl still crouched over the woman, but as he neared, they both drew back, fear etching their tearstained faces. Jake smiled. "I'm Mr. Hicken. Do you mind if I try to help your ma?"

19

"That's Miss Mattie." The boy whimpered.

"She's sleepin'," the girl said. "She do not want to wake up."

Jake's smile deepened. "Maybe I can wake her."

The girl—the older of the two—pulled the boy a couple of steps toward the center of the car. "Come with me, Paddy."

Jake took a knee beside the still woman.

Lord, please don't let her be dead. He'd already have to bury two friends. The thought of adding this woman to that list turned his stomach.

Thankfully, it took only an instant to find a steady pulse, setting his heart at ease.

A mop of light brown curls webbed across her face. He gently pushed the hair away to reveal a pretty oval face, high cheekbones, and small lips that naturally rested in a smile.

"Ma'am?" He touched her cheek, the smoothness of her skin startling him. "Can you hear me? Miss Mattie?"

She stirred.

"Miss Mattie, please open your eyes."

After an instant, she stirred again, her hand straying to the right side of her head. Her eyelids pressed tight.

"Ma'am, you got a passel of kids here who need you to wake up." And he'd feel a whole heap better once the pretty gal opened her eyes. "You hear me?"

She brushed his hand away with a sloppy gesture. "I hear you fine. Now who are you?"

⟲

Oh Father, don't let those men have returned, please.

Mattie forced her eyes open, but it wasn't the masked men who hovered. Instead, it was a handsome bearded man with kind brown eyes.

20

"Wells Fargo Special Agent Jake Hicken, ma'am."

"Pardon?" His words resisted absorption into her addled brain.

Patrick squatted near her. "You waked up."

The children! Mattie lurched into a seated position, pain cascading through her midsection. Overcome, she braced a hand against the floor.

"Easy now." The man steadied her with a firm hand. "You all right?"

Mattie attempted to inhale, but she groaned instead.

"Where are you hurt?" The man's soothing baritone calmed her.

She leaned back against the wall, her legs jutting toward the back of the car. Mattie extracted her brother's hand-monogrammed handkerchief—one of a new set she'd never had opportunity to send before his death—and dabbed at her forehead. Meeting his concerned gaze, she touched her right side. "My ribs," she whispered. "And my head."

He gave her a once-over glance. "You don't appear to be bleeding, but you could've broken some ribs." He nodded toward the side of her head. "May I?"

Mattie smiled awkwardly. "Yes."

With a delicate touch, the man sank his fingers into her hair. When he prodded a tender spot, Mattie sucked in a sharp breath.

The gentleman cringed and withdrew his hands from her hair, but cupping her chin, held her gaze, unmoving. "Pretty. . ." He released her then, almost like he'd been stung. ". . .big. . .bump." His face flushed. "I'd, uh, caution you to take things slowly."

Had he just called her pretty?

She brought the handkerchief to her mouth to hide her flustered smile. "Of course." Mattie looked around at the children. "Patrick, Moira." She looked at the youngest of her charges. "Are you hurt?"

The children showed her scraped elbows, a bruised knee, a torn stocking. Thank goodness, nothing of real concern.

"Ma'am," the man said. "Who are you? Why are you and these children in this boxcar?"

Instantly, her caution heightened. How had the handsome stranger introduced himself? He'd given a title along with his name, though both escaped her. If he was an employee of the train, he'd detain her and the children until they could pay train fare. A ridiculous thought. Once detained, she'd have no chance to earn money for anything. And if she'd been able to pay the fare, they'd have ridden in the passenger car.

"Derry?" She crawled to her feet, but as she straightened, her surroundings pitched violently and her handkerchief fluttered from her hand.

"Whoa, there. I said to take it slow, didn't I?" The man scooped the fabric and was at her side in an instant, his solid form becoming the wall on which she leaned until her world righted itself again. He glanced at the kerchief. "Miss. . .Owl?"

Mattie braced a forearm against his chest and willed the dizziness away. "Miss Owl?" What was he talking— Oh! "O.W.L. From the handkerchief."

"Yes. Is that your name?"

Her world still swimming, she leaned her forehead against the back of her hand, which was still firmly braced against his chest. "My brother's monogram. Oliver Lucas Welling. In my favorite style of monogramming, the last initial goes in between the first and middle ones." Her memories traveled over the years. "The first time I ever monogrammed a handkerchief for him, we laughed at that. O.W.L. I teased him, started calling him Owlie instead of Ollie. The name stuck."

Regaining her bearings, she straightened and met his gaze, realizing how close they stood. Her breath caught, and she pulled away.

"I have to check on my kids." And what in heaven's name had possessed her to tell him all about Owlie?

"So they *are* your children?"

"They're orphans, and I am their guardian. We're trying to reach my brother's property east of Salinas." Not Owlie's anymore. *Hers.* Only. . . She scanned the boxcar again, finding no sign of the men, nor her carpetbag. *Oh Lord, without the deed, is it really* my *property?*

"And you're riding in a boxcar because—?" His brows arched.

Lord, how much do I tell this comely stranger?

The truth was always best. Oh, how many times the Children's Aid Society workers had encouraged the orphans with those words. But could she trust this man?

Mattie breathed as deep as her aching side would allow. "My name is Matilda Welling, and I was a chaperone on an orphan train coming from New York. I came on this particular journey as a means to get to my brother's home. However, upon reaching San Francisco, these eight hadn't been placed in homes, so I took them. Unfortunately, money is tight, so. . ." She ducked her head.

"So you all stowed away."

"I suppose you'll arrest me for that." She waited for the inevitable.

"No, ma'am."

"You won't?"

He almost laughed. "Arresting stowaways isn't my job."

It wasn't? Oh, thank God.

"I do need to ask you whether you saw anything unusual before the chaos ensued."

"Unusual?" Perhaps it was the realization she was safe—at least from him—or maybe it was her painful ribs, but fatigue stole through her. Mattie steadied herself against him once more. "What do you mean?

He cupped her elbow, lending her strength. "Are you all right?"

She was tired. Sore. Overwhelmed. "I think I should sit."

He nodded. "Down there, or here?"

"I'd like to be with the children, please."

"Of course." He looped his left arm behind her back and guided her toward her unusual family.

"Patrick, Moira. Go sit with the others, please."

As the children fairly skipped past them, her handsome helper cleared his throat. "Not to pressure you, Miss Welling, but did you see anything unusual before the train got rocked?"

Oh did she. "I found it quite unusual that two men near broke down that door behind us moments ago."

"Two men? Can you describe—"

"Hey, Mr. Hicken." Sam trotted over then. "Everybody's bruised some. Owen's wrist is swellin' up pretty bad. Derry's got that cut on his head. Annie and Fiona are crying, and neither me or Augustina can tell why."

Hand straying to the *pretty. . .big. . .bump*, Mattie rubbed at the pain. "I'll check on the girls."

She angled toward Ann Beglin, Fiona MacGinty, and Augustina Garza, but before she could reach them, voices sounded outside the car.

Footsteps clanged on the next car's platform, and in an instant, Mr. Hicken was gone, limping badly toward the opposite end of the boxcar. Limping? She'd not noticed that before. Halfway there, the man loosed a shrill whistle.

"Stop!"

A man on the platform turned.

"Don't go in there," Mr. Hicken continued. "It's a Wells Fargo car. No one enters it without my permission."

"I was checkin' for injured. And I got to see whether we can pull it to Salinas."

24

The Wells Fargo agent motioned toward the sliding side door. "Come around, and let's talk."

Mattie's heart seized. No. The train worker would see them. Heart pounding, she settled near the crying girls and pulled Ann into her embrace.

As Mr. Hicken hobbled toward the freight door, she looked at Augustina. "What happened to the men who broke in here?"

The dark-haired girl nodded toward the door at the end of the car. "They jump."

"To the next car?"

Augustina gave a solemn nod.

Taking her carpetbag with them, no doubt.

The Southern Pacific worker didn't notice them until Owen sneezed. Then, his brow furrowed, the man spun on Mr. Hicken, who'd exited the car.

"You stowin' folks away on the train, mister?"

"I'm doing no such thing."

"Then them kids are stowin' away of their own accord?" The train worker acted as if he'd confront them.

"Settle down there." Mr. Hicken caught the man's arm. "They might've been, but now they're witnesses to a robbery." He hobbled several steps, yet his quiet words still reached her ears.

"Wells Fargo will see to it their fare is paid."

Chapter 3

While the train workers ministered aid to injured passengers and assessed the viability of each train car, Jake stood outside and considered what he knew. Two men disappeared from the front two benches of the passenger car. The engineer and others confirmed the missing fellas hadn't been up front in the engine. So they must've gone toward the back of the train.

He stared at the side of the passenger car, visualizing the men in the front seats. Both doors were secured with rope from the outside, the back one within minutes after Jake had accessed it himself. So they had to have slipped out one, tied it shut, walked across the roof to the other, and tied that one. He shot a look toward the back end. The men hadn't walked to the back door to go out, so they'd left through the front.

Jake hobbled to the front of the car and climbed the ladder built into the platform's railing. On the roof, he crossed to the far end, descended, and pretended to tie a rope around the door.

From where he'd sat in the car, he hadn't seen anyone try to access the front safe car door. Stepping onto the adjoining car's platform, he turned the knob. Locked.

"So they didn't get in that way, which means. . ." He descended the steps to the ground and traced a line with his gaze. *Up the ladder, across the roof.* Jake limped down the length of the car. *Down to the back door.* And somehow they'd gotten into the car.

He studied the doorframe. No sign of it being kicked in—and Engvall and Smits would've shot the instant they thought anyone tried to rob the shipment. No, the thieves would've had to enter in a quieter manner, or they'd have been dead before crossing the threshold. Crouching, he examined the lock. No apparent signs of tampering.

"How in the name of all that's holy did they get in?" Jake mopped his face with his hand. It made no sense. The guards wouldn't have opened the door for anyone, including him.

"Mister," someone called from behind him.

Gritting his teeth, Jake pushed to his feet and turned, finding the brakeman. "Yeah?"

"We're about to get under way." He jutted his chin toward the safe car. "It don't look like the wheels and undercarriage are dam-aged, but I wouldn't recommend you riding in there."

"No. I'll ride in the passenger car." His friends' bodies had been moved to the caboose for protection, and several passengers who'd been injured badly in the explosion and ensuing stop of the train had been carried to the boxcar. "Do you know, have the woman and her eight kids been moved to the passenger car?"

"Yeah. Ain't none of us Southern Pacific men happy about it though. We don't take kindly to stowaways."

"They aren't stowaways any longer. They're my witnesses." Maybe the best he had. "As I said, once I get word to the company, Wells

Fargo will pay their fare."

"It's the principle of the thing, you know." He motioned Jake toward the passenger car with what looked like a rolled piece of leather. "C'mon."

"What'cha got there?" Jake nodded toward the item.

"Something I fished out from under there." He hooked a thumb at the safe car. "Sometimes stuff along the tracks gets hung up in the wheels or undercarriage."

Ahead, the engine began to chug smoke.

"You best get aboard and take your seat."

Jake thanked the man and lumbered toward the passenger car. Upon entering, he immediately found Miss Welling and her passel of kids in the nearest seats.

She rose, wide-eyed, as he pulled the door shut beside her.

"Mr. Hicken, I haven't had the opportunity to thank you." She scarcely breathed the words. "The children and I very much appreciate what you've done for us."

"You're welcome." He smiled. The kids did seem grateful, except for the eldest, Derry. He wore a sour expression and eyed Jake with distrust. Focusing again on the pretty woman, he cleared his throat. "I'll need to speak with you and your kids at some point, but I'm going to interview the other passengers first, if that's all right."

"Whatever you need. We'll wait."

At the front of the car, the train's conductor had cordoned off the first pair of benches for him. Jake took the rear-facing seat and called the nearest passenger to sit across from him. Over the next hours, he interviewed every passenger—all but Mattie Welling and her eight orphans—particularly those who'd occupied the benches around where the pair of suspected thieves once sat. Not that anyone had noticed much.

"If they spoke, it was to whisper in Spanish," one woman said.

"But they mostly just slept."

"They got on at the San Jose stop," a gentleman had offered.

Descriptions of their clothing had varied. Some said light-colored pants, others said dark. He'd seen enough from the safe car's roof to know one had worn light brown pants and a darker shirt, and the other wore dusty black pants and a faded chambray shirt. The passengers' descriptions told him absolutely nothing.

Everyone agreed the men had dark beards, though no one could offer an eye color, the shape of their faces, any visible scars. With the robbers wearing masks, he'd seen no details of their features. All he had was the fact he'd clipped the one, taking a piece of his ear.

That and the fact they'd boarded at San Jose were the only helpful details. Clothes could be changed. Beards shaved. But it would be hard to hide a wounded ear.

It was precious little to go on.

By the time they arrived in Salinas, darkness had fallen. As the passengers filed out, he closed his eyes and removed his hat, wiping sweat from the band inside.

"Sir?"

Startled, he found a woman he'd interviewed earlier facing him. "Yes?"

"I thought of one other detail," she whispered as she sat across from him. "One of the men got up to use the privy, and I noticed his feet."

He furrowed his brow. "His feet? Do you mean his boots?"

"No, sir. I mean his toes. They turned inward, like this." She shifted her skirt and nodded toward her feet.

Jake leaned forward, hip screaming. At seeing her toes turned toward each other and her heels apart, he met her eyes again. "Pigeon-toed?"

"Yes. My niece had that issue as a small child, but she outgrew it.

29

I've never seen a grown man afflicted by the condition."

Nor had he. "Thank you. That may be helpful."

Jake scribbled the information into his mug book as the remaining passengers exited, leaving only Miss Welling and company. As she sat cuddling the smallest boy in her lap, Jake cursed himself roundly. He was an idiot. What had possessed him to say Wells Fargo would pay train fair for nine?

A pretty face. Real pretty. His cheeks warmed afresh as he recalled looking at her eyes and saying as much.

Him and his big mouth. There was no telling if the company would pay their train fare. If they didn't, he'd be on the hook for it, and it would take all he had saved.

He mopped a hand over his face. "You really are an idiot."

A sharp knock at the window startled him from his musing. Squinting, he found fellow Wells Fargo agent Tom Abendroth—a man with unruly black hair and a tobacco-stained beard. He'd met the detective only twice, but he had an impeccable reputation. The man darted onto the car's front platform and entered.

"Abendroth, what're you doing here?" Surely nothing to do with the theft. There was no way anyone could've known of it, since Jake hadn't notified the company yet.

"I live just outside of town. When the train got to be hours behind schedule, the sheriff was mountin' a search party, but—" He shrugged. "You look like you tangled with a bear."

Jake blew out a breath. "Hasn't been my best day. Did you see the next car?"

Abendroth nodded. "What's left of it. Dynamite?"

"Yeah. They got away with a sizable amount of money."

"Any chance you got a look at 'em?"

"Yes and no." He stood, pain jolting down the right side of his body. Jake braced a hand against the window. "I almost had 'em.

Crawled up on the safe car roof and was about to get a shot off whilst they were unloading the money, but the roof gave under me. Missed 'em."

Having caught his breath and his balance, he slung his saddlebags over his shoulder and limped into the aisle.

Abendroth eyed him. "You look plumb stove up."

"I been through worse." He owed it to Engvall and Smits to keep going. There was no reason the robbers needed to kill them. If it was the last thing he did, he'd make those blasted thieves pay.

"What can I do to help?"

"Right now?" He chuckled. "I don't even know where to start." He took a limping step down the aisle, detailing what he'd pieced together about the pair's movements. "I don't know how, but some way they got through the door without bustin' it in, took out the guards, and set the dynamite to blow the safe." He pinned Abendroth with a hard look. "I'm also not sure how the two of 'em got clear of the blast."

At the back of the car, Miss Welling handed the sleeping boy off to Sam Beglin then rose. "I think I can shed some light on that, sir."

Mr. Hicken faced Mattie, his brows arching to reveal eyes full of exhaustion and pain. "Oh? What can you tell me, miss?"

The unruly-haired man beside her rescuer whispered under his breath.

"Forgive me. Introductions first. Miss Welling, meet Tom Abendroth." Mr. Hicken motioned to his friend. "He's a Wells Fargo Special Agent like me. Abendroth, meet Miss Mattie Welling. She and her eight kids were riding in the boxcar two cars back when the explosion went off."

She exchanged pleasantries then met Mr. Hicken's gaze. "I began to tell you earlier. . .we were in the boxcar when two men forced their way through that door at the end."

"I remember that."

"The men spoke both Spanish and English. They came in, said they needed my carpetbag, then told me to get down."

Mr. Abendroth folded his arms with a thoughtful expression. "So you gave them the bag?"

"Not willingly." Mattie shook her head. "When one leveled a gun at my head, my oldest boy, Derry, threw it to them, trying to protect me. Then they both lay down on the floor and. . .*boom*. In the ensuing melee, I hit my head and passed out. My girl, Augustina"— she nodded to the child—"she said the men jumped from one car to the next, taking my bag with them."

"Did it contain anything of value? Money, or. . ." Mr. Abendroth arched a brow at her.

"Clothing for myself and eight children." And the deed, but until she knew she could trust these two, it was best not to mention that.

"They took *your* bag." Mr. Hicken wore a thoughtful expression. "Didn't either of them bring one?"

Didn't they? Searching her memory, she didn't recall seeing any. She looked back at the orphans. "Children, do any of you remember whether those men in the boxcar carried any kind of bags?"

Augustina spoke up. "They carry no bags, *señorita*. They take ours instead."

Several of the other children confirmed her recollection.

Mr. Abendroth shook his head. "What fool comes to rob a train but doesn't bring a bag to stash the goods in?"

"One of 'em had saddlebags. Real distinctive ones." Mr. Hicken straightened. "Tooled leather. He was using them as a pillow."

"But they didn't have saddlebags when they went into the boxcar." Mr. Abendroth seemed to complete Mr. Hicken's thought.

"What does that mean?" Mattie glanced from one to the other.

"It means they lost 'em somewhere between this car and the time they entered the boxcar." Mr. Hicken smiled at his friend. "Abendroth, you want something to do, then find the brakeman and ask him for what he found hung up in the undercarriage of the safe car."

The fellow trotted down the aisle to the door.

Once he was gone, Mr. Hicken turned to her again. "What do you say. . .shall we get you and your kids out of here?"

"Yes, please. I know there's a doctor in town. Would you help me find him?"

"Of course."

She pinned the handsome Wells Fargo agent with a concerned look. "I can see you're in a fair bit of pain as well. Please don't try to pretend you're not."

A sheepish expression crossed his face. "Doubt anyone'd believe me if I tried."

"No, sir. They wouldn't." How refreshing. A man filled with so little pretense he could actually admit the truth. "You should probably let him look at you too."

She led the way back to her kids.

"Children, we're going. Please gather your belongings." At Sam's side, she reached for the still-sleeping Patrick. However, when she picked him up, he roused, his knee lodging against her sore ribs. Pain flared, and her legs grew weak. As she went down, Patrick tumbled from her grip, his startled cries filling the car. Strong arms caught her, circling her waist and keeping her upright.

"You hurt?" Mr. Hicken's voice rumbled near her ear, his strong presence just inches behind her.

Urgent calls erupted from Ann, Augustina, Moira, and Fiona across the aisle. In front of her, Sam and Owen crowded around

Patrick, who sprawled on the bench next to Sam. Only Derry was focused elsewhere, glaring at her as if ready to fight.

As the wave of pain abated, she straightened, her cheeks warming furiously. "I think I'm all right," she whispered over her shoulder.

Mr. Hicken's arms disappeared from her middle, and his hovering strength pulled back as well. "You sure?"

She turned, glad to see that his face looked just as warm as hers, then gave her full attention to Patrick.

Sam and Owen almost shouted at Patrick to draw his attention from his wailing. Behind them, the girls pressed in to minister to the little clan member's scrapes or injuries.

"Boys, quiet down. Let me get to him. Please."

Derry nudged her arm as he leaned in. "Don't you let that fella touch you like that again, Miss Mattie," he grumbled under his breath. "Ain't appropriate."

"What?" She gaped at the young man. "Are you accusing me of some—"

"No. Him." He flicked a discreet glance in Mr. Hicken's direction.

A shrill whistle split the air, and everyone but Patrick stilled. Startled, she spun.

Mr. Hicken removed his fingers from his mouth after providing the ear-piercing silencer. "Kids, wait on the benches outside while we calm the little one." He nodded toward benches lining the depot's outer wall then met her eyes. "That all right?"

"A fine idea. Children, please do as Mr. Hicken says. We'll follow directly."

The children exited, all except Derry, who stood in the doorway, eyeing Mr. Hicken.

"Derry. Go sit with the others, please."

"I don't trust this fella, Miss Mattie."

She turned a firm look his way. "I do." At least to a point. He'd proven himself trustworthy enough to help with this situation. "Go. Now."

The young man huffed but obeyed. Once he was gone, she hurried to the crying boy.

"I'm so sorry, Patrick. Tell Miss Mattie where it hurts."

The boy rubbed the curls at the back of his head, big tears brimming in his eyes.

Mattie attempted to look at Paddy's scalp, but his fidgeting made it difficult. She shook her head in Mr. Hicken's direction. "I can't see anything."

"Let me look," Mr. Hicken said, sitting across from them. "I bet I know where it hurts."

"Where?" Patrick whispered the question.

"I bet." He leaned toward her little charge. "Right...about...here." He lifted the boy's arm and gave the child a little tickle.

A smile and a pout warred on the boy's face, and Patrick drew his arm back to his side. "No."

"Hmm. Then maybe here?" The man leaned nearer still, pain flashing in his eyes as he tucked a finger under the boy's other arm. This time his attempt elicited a sound somewhere between a giggle and a snort, and Patrick pushed the man's hands away with a shy grin. "No."

"How about here?" Mr. Hicken brushed his fingertips along Patrick's neck, and this time the boy laughed. Mr. Hicken turned to her. "This is *very* serious. We'd better get this boy to the doctor." At that, the man offered a discreet wink and pushed himself up, leg obviously paining him.

Admiration flooded her heart. She'd not known many grown men who seemed so natural with kids, particularly small ones like Patrick. "Then we'd best get on with it. C'mon, Paddy." She beckoned the child.

The boy shook his head. "I go with Mr. Hiccup."

She struggled to hold back her laughter. "Hick-*en*. Not Hiccup."

"Haven't I told you? Hiccup is what my special friends get to call me." He hoisted Patrick onto his left hip and limped toward the door. "C'mon, friend."

Patrick wrapped chubby arms around the agent's neck and snuggled close, seeming completely at ease.

Chapter 4

"Found ya!"

Jake glanced up as Tom Abendroth entered the doctor's yard from the street and stalked up the moonlit path toward him.

"What're you doin' here, Hicken?"

"I was waiting for Mattie Welling and her eight kids to be seen by the doctor."

Confusion etched Abendroth's features.

"Didn't want to lose track of her. I haven't fully questioned her yet."

"Ahh. I understand. Took me a while to track down that brakeman. Here's what he gave me."

Receiving the item, Jake unfurled the roll to reveal the flap and decorative buckle of a tooled-leather saddlebag, now torn, beaten, and covered in grease. He turned it toward the lamplight for a better look then grinned at Abendroth. "I'm just bettin' this matches something lying along the railroad tracks near the blast site."

The other agent returned the grin. "I'm bettin' you're right."

Jake peered up at the sky, thankful for the full moon that was painting the landscape in silvery light. "I figure I've dallied around here long enough." He pushed up from the rocking chair he'd parked himself in. "I'm gonna limp on over to the livery and see about getting a horse then ride out to—"

"I can ride out and search the tracks. If you're willing to let me help, that is. That way, you can stay and question the lady."

Jake hesitated.

"Look," Abendroth pushed on. "There's a lot to be done and not a lot of time. If I go to the tracks and find the rest of that saddlebag, maybe pick up on the robbers' direction, it'll free you to question witnesses, look over the safe car, see to the burial of your friends. If I'm gone more than two days, I'll send word where you can catch up to me."

It wasn't ideal—far from it. This was *his* investigation, after all. But how often did he have a second agent with whom to split the duties? Not allowing Abendroth to go when the other man was able and willing was pure foolishness.

Jake blew out a big breath. "All right—but do keep me apprised."

Abendroth nodded. "I will. While I'm gone, if you need anything, you ask Sheriff Roy White. Tell him I sent you. He's a good man, good enough I let my baby sister marry him."

"That's high praise, I take it?" Jake's was an odd upbringing, the only child of a woman who'd never married, and who'd lived his entire life in the sanctuary of a San Francisco convent. He didn't profess to know what having a sister, much less allowing her to marry someone, might feel like.

"The highest." Abendroth thrust his hand at Jake. "I'll be in touch within two days."

He departed, leaving Jake to stare at the remnant of the saddlebag.

Jake held the torn flap toward the lamplight. The top edge was jagged where it had been ripped away from the rest. The once beautiful leatherwork was now so scuffed around the edges that the intricate design was unrecognizable. Toward the center, near the mangled silver buckle, the design was clearer, but for the grease that covered it. He retrieved a bandanna from his saddlebags and scrubbed at the leather to remove some grease then turned the flap toward the lamplight again. Better. He studied the design more closely. There on the medallion that secured the buckle were letters carved into the floral motif. He held the leather closer to the lamp. *R.F.* The owner's initials maybe? He turned the flap over to study the back side, only to discover a small design branded into the leather. Squinting, he attempted to make sense of it. A V-shape with a cross extending from its center and an odd flourish over the top. Was that an artisan's mark, perhaps? Or—

At that moment, Miss Welling and her orphans exited the office. Dropping the leather flap, Jake lurched from the chair, his hip jolting fire down his leg.

"Miss." He braced a hand against the doorframe, giving himself a moment to catch a breath. "Anyone hurt bad?"

"It appears not. I have a few bruised ribs and a *pretty. . .big. . .bump* on my head."

A foolish grin crossed his lips.

"Owen has a sprained wrist." She patted the stocky blond boy's shoulder then motioned to the eldest boy, still glaring distrustfully in Jake's direction as he held the littlest boy. Jake glanced around, finding the littlest girl—Moira was it?—drowsing in Sam's arms. "Derry needed a few stitches for a cut on his scalp, and the doctor said he may have a headache for a few days. Thankfully, although the rest of the children were jostled and bruised, they don't have any serious injuries."

He looked at each of the children then back to her. "I'm real glad. I think the Lord was watching over you all." He'd considered just how badly any one of them could've been injured, especially weathering the explosion in the boxcar like they did. It could've been far worse.

"I believe that very much, Mr. Hicken, and it pleases me to hear you say so."

For some unknown reason, her statement set him awash in sheepishness. What in heaven's name was *that* about? He cleared his throat. "What're you planning to do now?"

She shrugged. "I suppose that depends on you. Are we free to go?"

"I might have a few more questions to ask you and the children, but they can wait until you all have slept some. I don't see why, by tomorrow afternoon, you can't be on your way. . .wherever."

"As I think I told you, we're trying to reach my brother's property outside of Salinas."

"But Miss Mattie, what about the deed?" Owen blurted. "Don't we—"

Miss Welling clamped a hand over his mouth, cutting off the boy's question. For one flustered moment, she stared at Jake before an awkward smile crossed her lips. "Pardon me for a moment."

She bent to face the boy. "Owen, don't interrupt, please. I'll answer your questions in a bit." She looked around. "All of you, please gather your bedrolls and wait near the gate." She nudged the nearest children toward the stack of rolled blankets at the corner of the porch.

"I'm tired, Miss Mattie," one of the girls whined.

"Can we just sleep here?" another asked.

"No, we can't sleep here. Bear with me another few minutes, please. It won't be long."

Once they'd toddled off, she gathered the last of the bedrolls and straightened. "Forgive me. Sometimes they forget their manners."

"In my estimation, they're quite well behaved." He had to admire an unmarried woman with the grit to take in eight orphans with only the help of her brother.

"Thank you. Given all that's happened today, I'm very proud of how well they've done."

Jake grinned. "What did the boy mean—about the deed?"

Her eyes widened an instant before she shrugged and shook her head. "Oh, we're all so exhausted, it's a wonder any of us are making sense at this point."

Jake nodded, but something he couldn't quite lay hold of tugged at his exhausted thoughts. "Where exactly is your brother's place?"

"Southwest. In the mountains."

Jake's brow furrowed. "Is he coming to pick you up, or—"

"No. We'll be walking from here on."

"Into the mountains?"

She shrugged. "We haven't the money to hire someone to take us. By Owlie's description, it's a sizable property with a beautiful home and vineyard. I know we can find it."

Frustration gnawed at him. "You're sure your brother can't come to pick you up?"

"Unfortunately, no." Her light eyes clouded, and when she spoke again, her voice cracked. "He passed some months ago. Consumption. Doctor Preston was with him as he died." She shook her head, a distant look in her eye. "He never mentioned his illness in his letters. I guess that explains why he kept asking for handkerchiefs these last several years." She extracted the one from her sleeve and fingered the delicate stitching in its corner. "I thought he enjoyed the fanciness of my monogramming them, but no. I suppose the request was far more down-to-earth than that."

Jake gawked. She'd come all this way, knowing her brother was dead? "Meaning no disrespect, but. . .are you daft? You're a woman completely alone except for a bunch of young kids following you like ducklings. You've stowed away on a train, lived through a dynamite explosion, and were robbed to boot, and now you think you're gonna *walk* yourself up into the mountains, find your brother's place, and live up there? What on earth are you thinkin'?"

Her pretty features hardened. "Hmm. Let me explain. Just like these children, I am an orphan. I have been since I was eleven. Owlie and I lived on the streets in New York City after our parents' deaths until we were taken in by the Children's Aid Society three years later. We were given a home, love, and an education by Charles Loring Brace and others." Her voice ratcheted up a notch.

"Derry, Sam, Owen, and Ann Beglin have a similar story. Orphaned, they turned to the streets for a couple of years until we brought them in and gave them a place to stay. The MacGinty children—Fiona, Moira, and Patrick—were all brought to the Society's door after a neighbor found them in a rat-infested apartment alone. Their mother had died, and their father abandoned them. They were starving when they were brought to us."

She dashed away a stray tear then continued, her voice shaking. "And Augustina? Her uncle—the only relative she had—brought her from Texas to New York City. She isn't sure why. But her uncle was killed in front of her on the streets, we suspect because he was one of the few Mexican people in that city. She sat crying over his body until Derry and Sam found her and took her with them. She too lived on the streets for at least a year before we took her in."

Jutting one foot out, Miss Welling folded her arms and tapped her toe. "These children have been through quite enough in their lives. They've traveled from New York to San Francisco, hoping for placement in a permanent home. None of them were chosen. So, what on earth am I thinking? I'm thinking that for all of my brother's many faults, he left me with a sizable piece of property, and if

I can provide these eight children a stable home, love, and room to grow, then I will do that. But we have to get there first, and if that means walking, then we shall walk. Now, if you'll excuse me, we need to find somewhere to sleep tonight." She stalked toward the children.

Jake stared, mind spinning to digest everything she'd just thrown at him.

"Wait." His hip protested as he stepped off the porch and tried to hurry after her. "Please." Hang it all. If she was determined to find that place, then she'd do it with *him* along. But only *after* he wrapped up this robbery.

Miss Welling stopped short, back still to him, but before he could catch up, the door opened.

"Anyone else waiting to see me?" the doctor called from behind him.

Mattie Welling spun then and stalked back up the path. "This gentleman has injured his hip, Doctor."

"It's nothing," he groused.

But when she met him on the path and pushed him back a step, his leg nearly gave way with the sudden change of direction.

"See, Doctor Preston?" She glowered at Jake. "It pains him visibly."

The man stepped off the porch to meet them on the pathway. "What did you do to injure it?"

Stuck between Miss Welling's pushing and the doctor's pulling, Jake balanced on one foot and struggled to know where to focus. "I fell off a train car roof. But I'm fine."

The doctor shook his head. "A hip injury is nothing to play around with. At least let me take a look."

Hooking Jake's arm, Dr. Preston escorted him back to the porch and in the door before he was any the wiser.

The audacity of the man! Did he think she had an endless supply of greenbacks, perhaps a pouch full of coins? What else could she and these children do but walk? And while the doctor reiterated what was in his note—that he didn't know where Owlie's property was—they'd come this far. She'd find it.

Arms full of bedrolls, Mattie herded her children from the doctor's gate and down the middle of the street. They would need to find somewhere secure to sleep. She'd seen the livery stable not far away as they'd been transported to the doctor's home. Perhaps they could sleep there for the night.

Come morning, she'd have to find a way to feed the children and herself. They'd demolished the last of their food not long before the robbery. It was surprising that no one had complained too loudly about their stomachs rumbling. Hers certainly was. Maybe Derry and Sam could catch them a few fish from a nearby stream, settle their bellies for a bit.

Lord God, if there's a better plan, please show me.

The memory of standing on New York street corners begging for food as a child flashed to mind. Of hearing stories of Derry and Sam stealing from—and being chased by—street vendors from whom they'd pilfered apples and other food items. Or the three MacGinty children so gaunt and weak the Children's Aid workers had feared they may not survive.

Oh Father, we are so near our new home. Please see us through to the end without any of us having to do something that would cause us to lose our Christian witness in the process.

Mattie paused, taking stock of their location. "Let's hurry, children. The livery stable is only another block or so, I believe." She turned to smile encouragement to her kids—encouragement she was too exhausted to feel just then. However, the line of her charges stretched out down the street for more than a block.

"Sam! Derry! Why aren't you keeping the children corralled?"

Derry shifted Patrick, who'd fallen asleep on his shoulder, and cursed. "Why aren't *you*? You're the one who signed for us, took us all in. It's *your* job."

Anger and irritation stirred in her chest. "Young man, I've told you a thousand times that I won't abide your disrespect. Nor will I let you teach these children such foul words. You watch that tongue."

"Or what?" He glared, almost daring her to react.

Father, what do I do with this dreadful behavior?

"Shut up, Derry." Sam, holding drowsy little Moira, gave his older brother a shove. "Miss Mattie's doing the best she can. And we *did* say we'd help out."

Owen came up, dragging leaden feet. The boy flopped onto the ground as if he couldn't take another step.

"Help out, yes. But I never agreed to do it all for her. Feels almost like I'm the adult here. . ."

Just as Ann and Fiona rejoined the group, Mattie smacked Derry hard across the cheek, the sound loud in the stillness.

"Don't you dare speak to me that way, young man. I am working as hard as I ever have in my life. I'm the one making the difficult decisions. And not once have I asked you to do more than your fair share." Her heart thudded like a herd of galloping horses.

Derry's face turned the color of beets, and his jaw firmed. "If you weren't a woman, I'd—"

"Oh, leave off, Derry!" Sam stepped between them. "We're all tired. Miss Mattie's doing her best for us, and once we get to her brother's place, it's gonna be even better."

Ann, Fiona, and Owen all added their agreement to Sam's words.

Panting, Derry looked at them all, gaze finally settling on her.

"Won't be nothin' unless she gets that deed back. And she'll be doin' it without me. I'm done with all this." He pushed his way past the younger children. "Take this brat—" Derry forced her to drop the three bedrolls she carried and take the sleeping boy.

Mattie's own anger stirring, she hoisted Paddy to her hip. "Where do you think you're going?" Her ribs ached with the added weight.

Standing nose to nose with her, he growled. *"Anywhere but here."* He kicked one of the bedrolls past her then walked after it. "Sam, Owen, Annie. . ." Derry scooped up the blanket and turned. "Let's go. Now."

"You're not taking these children with you. Caring for them is *my* job."

"They're *my* brothers and sister. I was takin' fine care of 'em before this."

Owen shook his head, and shy little Ann tucked herself against Mattie's leg.

"We're staying here, Derry." Sam shifted Moira in his arms. "You should too."

"No, thank you." When the others didn't join him, he huffed. "Fine then. I'm done." He stalked off across the street.

Mattie's heart lurched as the young man disappeared into the shadows. What in heaven's name had gotten into him?

Father, help.

"Idiot." Sam shook his head.

"This isn't good," she groaned, wholly unsure whether to follow him.

"Don't worry, Miss Mattie." Owen patted her arm. "He'll come back eventually."

Her stomach knotted in fear. "Let's get you all settled. Maybe I can find him after that." She motioned to the next cross street. "Sam, you lead. Turn up ahead. The livery should be a short way down on the right. Girls, please pick up the bedrolls and carry those for me."

As they each walked past, she counted heads. Sam and Moira. . .two. Owen, Ann, and Fiona made five. Patrick. . .six. She flashed a look toward the spot where Derry had disappeared. *Seven. Lord, please protect that boy!* And Augustina made—

Her heart stalled.

"Where is Augustina?"

The children looked around, though no one answered.

"Augustina?" The girl's name echoed in the empty street as Mattie scanned shadows. "Honey, where are you?" A wave of panic washed over her. "Augustina! Answer me!"

Oh God. Please. . .where is she?

"C'mon, Miss Mattie. We'll all go look for her," Owen said, stumbling in the direction they'd just come.

"No," she said after an instant. "Owen, can you carry Paddy with your hurt wrist?"

"Yeah." The boy came near.

"Then you take him. Sam, get them to the livery and settle them in an empty stall or the loft. I'll find Augustina and meet you there."

"I will." Sam gave a serious nod. "And once they're settled, I'll come help you."

"No!" Mattie handed the sleeping child to Owen. "Stay with the children. I'll find our girl and join you as soon as we can."

Sam's displeasure at the order was obvious, but he led off, the other children falling in with him.

Once they disappeared around the corner, Mattie darted down the street, scanning shadows and benches for her last charge.

"Oh God, please, where is she?" Mattie made a slow circle. "Show me, Lord."

A shadow at the edge of the nearest alley caught her attention, and lunging toward it, she found a bedroll. Snatching it from the ground, she looked down the dark, narrow passageway then darted into it. Mattie swept down the path, searching.

As she drew toward the back corner of the building, her heart stuttered. There Augustina hunched over a pile of precariously stacked crates, peering into the adjoining alley.

Oh, thank You, Lord! But I may just kill her.

Mattie marched up to the child and grasped her upper arm, dragging the girl off her perilous perch. The crates tumbled into the adjoining alley.

"Child, do you have any idea how much you frightened me?"

In the tight confines, almost no moonlight reached the alley. In spite of that, Augustina's eyes grew so round, the whites showed in the darkness. She drew back, though Mattie held her tight.

"What possessed you to run away from me?"

"Por favor, señorita." Augustina barely breathed the words, drawing her index finger to her lips in a plea for silence.

Mattie opened her mouth to answer, but before a sound escaped, a man's form stepped into the opening, gun trained in her direction.

"You are listening to our conversations, why?" he said in a thick Spanish accent.

A second man, cloaked in shadow, appeared from around the corner, his gun also pointed in their direction. After an instant, he uttered a bitter-sounding word in Spanish. "These are two of the ones from the boxcar."

Chapter 5

Jake roused, fatigue pulling at his mind. He could roll over and go back to sleep.

For the briefest instant, he succumbed to the thought. But when he rolled onto his right side, lightning jolted through his hip and stole his breath. He sagged into the hay, fighting for air as a flood of thoughts rushed to mind.

He was in Salinas. In the livery's loft. The doctor had looked at his hip the previous night and deemed it badly bruised, told him to stay off of it, and recommended copious amounts of whiskey for the pain. He'd consumed only enough to dull the pain then crawled into the hay and slept fitfully until now.

Fighting through the pain, he clamped a hand over his eyes.

"Keepin' you awake too, huh?" someone said from a few feet off.

Jake turned. "What?"

A grizzled old fella, wiry and tan, clamped his hands over his ears. "Some blasted idiot dumped a bunch of kids here overnight.

Up and left 'em sleepin' in a stall down there." He jutted his chin toward the ladder. "One of the little ones ain't quit bawlin' for a couple hours."

The distant mournful wail of a young child filtered into his consciousness—the same wail as when Mattie Welling tried to lift Patrick to depart the train.

Gritting his teeth, Jake lurched into a sitting position. "It's just kids, you say?"

"Yeah, like five of 'em."

Five? "How old?"

"I don't know, little. Ten and under, maybe."

Five kids ten and under. . .

Jake loosed a quiet oath and pushed to his feet. After donning hat and gun belt, he draped his saddlebags over one shoulder and eased down the ladder. Following the wails, he turned down the third row of stalls.

"Mr. Hiccup!" Patrick raced out from behind an open stall door, past a couple of men at the stall's entrance, and wrapped himself around Jake's leg.

The men, probably stable hands, turned his way.

"You know these kids?" one of them asked.

Jake hoisted the boy into his arms and limped to the open door of the stall. Inside, Moira, her older sister, and two of the other children whose names escaped him, huddled inside. "I know 'em."

"And you are. . .?" the other questioned, voice distrustful.

"Wells Fargo Special Agent Jake Hicken." He fumbled to remove the badge pinned to the inside of his vest. Freeing it, he held it out for the men to see.

One fella eyed it then him. "They yours?"

"No. They were witnesses to the robbery on yesterday's train. Them, three older kids, and a woman. Miss Mattie Welling.

Have you seen her?"

"No sir," the same fella answered. "Ain't seen anyone old enough to be responsible for this bunch. Not till you walked up."

The pair exchanged glances, and then one clapped him on the shoulder. "Good luck figuring out where their ma is, mister." His tone was suddenly jovial.

Both hurried away.

"Hey, wait!" Jake stared after them, though neither man stopped.

Of all the dumb luck.

He turned toward the stall. Settling Patrick's backside on the top of the stall door to take some weight off his bum hip, Jake pinned his focus on the eldest of the children and beckoned the boy. "You, c'mere."

The stocky boy rose and crossed the short distance. "Yes, sir?"

"What is your name?"

"Owen Beglin."

"Owen. Right. Can you tell me what's goin' on, son?"

The boy shrugged. "I don't know, sir. We left the doctor's place last night, but before we got here, Miss Mattie and Derry got in a bad fight, and Derry stomped off. Then Augustina disappeared, so Miss Mattie went after her. Sam brought the five of us here to sleep. He laid down too, but we woke up this morning to all of 'em still bein' gone. Even Sam disappeared sometime in the night."

What in blue blazes? Miss Welling and several of her orphans, missing. And, of course, him with a robbery to investigate.

Lord, this is the last thing I need, getting sidetracked with trying to find Mattie Welling and half her brood.

Patrick's belly growled loud enough that Jake heard it. "I'm hungry, Mr. Hiccup."

Mattie Welling said their bag had been stolen. They'd carried nothing away from the train other than their bedrolls. So unless

they each had a stash of jerky or something in their pockets, then. . .
"When's the last time you ate?"

Owen hung his head. "Yesterday."

"Before the robbery?"

"Yes, sir."

He rolled his eyes heavenward. "All right. Get those blankets rolled up. I'm going to ask where we can get some food around here, and once I return, we'll fill those bellies."

Mattie woke to the *clip-clop* of horse's hooves. A strong arm circled her waist from behind. Mr. Hicken?

Mr. Hicken! Heat blanketed her. What in heaven's name. . . Why was she secretly hoping the handsome stranger was once again holding her as he had on the train? She fluttered her eyes open and blinked at her surroundings.

Oh Lord.

She was on horseback with nothing but mountainous terrain around her. She glanced behind. Her heart pounded at the glimpse of a dark-haired man with a scruff of a beard, close-cropped and patchy, darkening his jawline.

"Turn around, señorita."

Mattie continued to eye the man. "Explain yourself. Who are you, and where are you taking me?" And how in heaven's name had she gotten here.

"Turn around." He spoke with more force.

Oh Lord Jesus, what happened? She scrambled through her jumbled thoughts of the previous day. Stowing away in the boxcar, the men barging into the car, the explosion, Mr. Hicken. . . Her thoughts ordered themselves until—

She'd gone searching for Augustina after the girl disappeared, and the two men in the alley had grabbed them. In her struggle, one of them struck her bruised ribs with such force, she must have passed out again.

"Augustina?" She called the name loudly. *Lord, please let her answer!*

"Quiet!" the man hissed. "Stop moving."

"Señorita?"

At the girl's frightened cry, Mattie twisted to see her. The man drove his hand into her tender ribs again. Pain flared, and Mattie sagged, gripping the saddle horn to keep from losing her balance.

Before she could regain her composure, they rode over a rise into a meadow containing a tiny shanty. The man guided the horse toward the front door.

Lord, protect us. And the other children. What might they be waking up to this morning?

The man drew the horse to a stop outside the hovel. As he slid from the bay's back, a second horse came into view, this one ridden by Augustina and a second man.

"Get down." The man growled the command as he pulled at Mattie's elbow.

Belly knotting, she obeyed and pulled Augustina close once the girl had dismounted. The man Mattie had ridden with gave her a gentle shove toward the door. "Inside. Sit over there."

The simple room, maybe ten feet by twelve feet, contained a fireplace and hearth spanning one wall. A blanket-covered steamer trunk sat on some kind of wooden blocks to form a makeshift table. A lone cane chair sat beside it. And on the far end, a cot balanced out the room. Empty whiskey bottles littered the corners, and half-empty ones sat on the fireplace mantel, hearth, and the makeshift table. A thick layer of dust covered the surfaces, and spiders had taken up residence in the upper corners of the room. It had the look of a place long unused—even abandoned. Mattie moved toward the hearth, pulling Augustina with her. As they sat in the corner, the man who'd ridden behind Augustina crossed to the bed and nudged a shivering form huddled in a blanket.

"Mi gemelo, sit up. Por favor."

The man complied, drawing his blankets around his shoulders. His ear and hair were caked with blood. As the heavily bearded man looked at the wound, Mattie studied the three. They were all around the same age, each with dark beards. All three favored each other. Brothers? Almost certainly. The two with the heavier beards might even be twins.

The one with the lighter, scruffier beard crossed to the fireplace, grabbed a coffeepot, and exited. Augustina nudged Mattie and shot a discreet glance toward the blanketed steamer trunk. Mattie followed the look with her own. There, half hidden by the blanket, sat the carpetbag! If she could just get to it, with one quick reach inside, she could have her deed.

Father, that's all I want. To get the deed and leave these men alone. They can have whatever else is in the bag.

Only, if these were the train robbers, then Jake Hicken was likely looking for the bag's other contents. He'd been kind to her and her children. Had he not helped her calm Patrick after the boy had fallen from her arms the previous evening? A Wells Fargo detective who, despite his own injury, pulled away from what *must* be a difficult investigation to help her calm a crying child in one of the most endearing ways. The least she could do was repay the favor.

But. . .

But calming a fussing child was a far cry from risking her life to return what armed thieves had stolen!

"What do you want with us?" she asked as the man returned with the coffeepot and two pairs of tooled-leather saddlebags.

He shrugged. "You were the ones listening to our conversation in the alley last night. What did *you* want with us?"

She scrambled for an answer that would pacify them. "We weren't listening. I was trying to get my children to the livery stable to sleep. Augustina lost her way, and I came to collect her. That was all."

Father, let them believe me. It is the truth, after all.

The heavily bearded one inspecting his brother's wound spoke. "Javier, *el agua.*"

Patchy-bearded Javier tossed the saddlebags onto the cot and poured some water from the coffeepot into a mug on the table. He shook his head. "I wish I believe that you tell the truth, señorita, but I cannot. You saw *mi hermanos* on the train, and you follow us into the alley."

Hermanos. Brothers. She understood that much Spanish. "I didn't. *We* didn't. I promise you."

Mattie ached to elbow Augustina and tell her to confirm the story but thought better of it.

Javier handed the cup to his brother, who retrieved a folded cloth from a stack on the windowsill, dipped it in the mug, and dabbed at his brother's swollen ear. "Promise all you want. It does not change anything."

Her muscles knotted. "Then I'll ask again. What is it you want with us?"

"We do not decide this yet." Javier shook his head. "But when we know, you will know."

Chapter 6

By the time the five orphans had put away the flapjacks and scrambled eggs Jake had ordered, he'd discovered that Owen was a watchful young man, quiet and thoughtful. His younger sister, Ann, was painfully shy and rarely spoke, though he'd managed to elicit one skittish smile from her. Fiona, the elder sister of Moira and Patrick, was also shy, though less so than Ann, and she was fiercely attached to the girl. The youngest two, Moira and Patrick, were both curious and friendly, with good senses of humor.

No wonder Miss Welling loved them. They were a good group of kids.

Lord, where is she? Please let her and the rest of her kids be safe.

He couldn't explain it, given he'd only known the woman half a day, but her going missing stirred anxiety in his chest that he'd never experienced before. The knot it formed made breathing hard, and his mind raced. She hardly seemed the type to lose interest and walk away. So where in blue blazes was she?

A bell over the door jingled, signaling someone's entry. A tall blond man stopped just inside the door, looked around and, eyes locking on Jake, sauntered their way.

"You the one asked for the sheriff?"

Good to see the stable hands had tracked down the lawman as he'd requested. Jake rose. "Yes, sir. The name's Jake Hicken."

As he flashed his Wells Fargo badge, Patrick shook his head. "No. Him's Mr. *Hiccup!*"

The table erupted in giggles, and even he couldn't help grinning.

"Hiccup, huh?" The sheriff eyed him, a lopsided smile spanning his face.

"Apparently so, leastways if you listen to this little fella." He laid a hand on Patrick's white-blond curls.

"Sheriff Roy White." The lawman extended his hand, and Jake shook it. "Tom told me you were in town before he rode out. What can I help you with?"

He glanced around the somewhat busy restaurant then at the kids. "Owen, take this up front and pay for our meals, would ya?" He fished a coin from his pocket and pressed it into the boy's pudgy hand. Feeling something sticky on Owen's palm, he glanced at Patrick and Moira. Those two were probably sticky from head to toe. Jake fished out his handkerchief and poured water from his glass onto it. "Ann, Fiona, can you get the young ones' hands wiped whilst I step outside for a moment?"

At the girls' somber nods, White led the way, and Jake limped after him. Once the door shut behind them, Jake positioned himself where he could keep an eye on the children through the window.

"Before you ask, they aren't my kids." As quick as the words departed his tongue, regret struck him. That sounded as if he didn't like them, and that wasn't the impression he intended to give. He wouldn't mind laying claim to any of 'em. He'd always thought if he ever married. . .

His cheeks warmed at the rambling progression of his thoughts.

"I was wondering. Ain't usual, dragging a young family along with you on a job like yours."

"Of course not. Too dangerous." He drew a deep breath and plunged in. "These are five of eight orphans a woman named Mattie Welling took in at the end of an orphan train." He explained about her trying to reach her brother's property outside of town and ended with her and three of the kids missing. "You haven't found 'em, have you? It's her, two boys—both dark haired, about so tall." He indicated Derry's height then Sam's. "Both about age fourteen or fifteen. And a Mexican girl, maybe this tall." Again, he indicated Augustina's height. "Age twelve or thirteen."

White thought a minute then shook his head. "I haven't seen the woman or girl, but I might have the boys. One of my deputies found two young men knocked out cold near one of the saloons in the middle of the night. Looked like they'd been fightin'. Black eyes, busted lips. We weren't sure if they'd slipped into the saloon and found trouble or whether they were fightin' each other. Either way, got 'em locked in the jail. You're welcome to come see if they're the two you're talkin' about."

The anxiety in Jake's chest eased at the possible good news, but as he glanced inside, his heart stalled at finding Moira standing in her chair, both hands and one knee braced on the table top. Beside her, Ann shook her head and pulled at the younger child, to no avail. Moira wiggled free and tried again to climb on the table.

"Pardon me a minute!" Jake lurched for the door.

Amused, the other man called out. "Take care of that. Then meet me in my office. Three blocks down on the left."

Jake caught the words as he slipped inside and ran to the table in time to catch Moira as she stood on the tabletop.

"Oh no you don't." He pulled her into his arms then sat, his hip screaming at the sudden movements. He settled the giggling girl on the chair next to him. "Hasn't Miss Welling taught you not to climb on the furniture?"

"Miss who?" the wee girl asked.

Right, the children didn't know her by her last name. "I mean Miss Mattie."

Owen returned, holding out several coins to Jake. "There's the change."

"Thank you." He received the money and looked at each of the faces surrounding the table. "C'mon. We gotta go to the sheriff's office." But first he needed to send word to Wells Fargo of the robbery and request payment for the train fare he promised they'd pay.

Gritting his teeth against the pain, Jake stood again, plucked his saddlebags from the back of his chair, tucked the damp handkerchief inside, and herded the children through the door to the boardwalk. "Fiona and Ann, will you girls please take Moira and Patrick's hands while we walk?"

Fiona did, but Ann looked at him with a tiny shake of her head. "Please?"

Again, the girl declined with a jiggle of her head.

He arched his brows. "Why not?"

The girl's face reddened, and she wouldn't meet his eyes.

Fiona whispered something to Owen, who in turn looked Jake's way. "My sister thinks she did wrong in there because Moira climbed on the table."

Lord, I've got a train robbery to investigate—and Mattie Welling and three kids are missing. I don't have the time to deal with this.

But the instant he saw the sadness in the diminutive girl's eyes, something tugged so hard at him, he couldn't *not* address it. He beckoned Ann to the nearby bench and sat. "Did you try to stop her?"

Head hanging, the girl nodded.

"I know you did, because I saw you try."

The girl risked a glance his way but quickly lowered her gaze again.

"Moira's a little girl. You're a little bit bigger girl. Right?"

Ann's head bobbed.

"Sometimes little people like Paddy and Moira don't listen to bigger people. I'm not upset with you because she didn't listen. Sometimes they don't even listen to adults like me. That doesn't mean you did anything wrong. It means she doesn't mind very well sometimes. Understand?"

The girl swallowed. "You're not mad?" The words were so soft, he nearly missed them.

Jake grinned. "I'm not mad. In fact, as soon as we find Miss Mattie, I'll tell her just how grown-up all of you were whilst she was gone."

The tiniest hint of a smile graced the girl's lips.

"So do you think you can help me with Paddy and Moira?"

Still unsure, she finally nodded.

"Good. Then let's go."

He rocked to his feet, taking an instant to find his balance, then herded the kids down the street. Half a block down, Paddy—firmly held by his eldest sister—moved up alongside Owen and slipped his free hand into the older boy's grip. Only steps beyond that, a small hand slid into Jake's big mitt. Startled, he found Ann smiling shyly at him.

Heat cascaded from his head to his toes, and he tightened his grip around her hand, wobbling a smile at her in return. Facing front again, he blew out a breath.

Lord, help me keep my focus. I've got to find the train robbers and return the money. I can't afford to get distracted.

Only he *was* distracted—by a handsome specimen of a woman

and her eight sweet kids.

And for heaven's sake, he liked it.

Thankfully, the men showed little interest in either Mattie or Augustina, and that realization allowed Mattie time to fight through the tangle of fear that threatened to overtake her. In the hour since they'd arrived at the shack, the men had cleaned the injured man's wounds—what looked like a nasty tear to his ear as well as a scalp injury of some kind. The man was up and around, watching over them, but he was obviously moving slowly, and his eyes had the glassy, distant look of fever. The other two were much sharper, watchful, patrolling outside the tiny cabin periodically.

At one point, the three stepped outside and talked among themselves. Mattie strained to hear, but their words were lost in whispers. All she was able to glean was their tones, which started out calm but slowly climbed until the two healthy men traded sharp words. Arguing, but for what reason—and for how long? Hopefully long enough to get in the carpetbag and at least see if her deed was still inside.

"Go." She gave Augustina a nudge. "Sit on the other end of the hearth and watch. If they look like they'll come inside, tell me."

The girl moved, and Mattie hurried to the covered trunk. There she unfastened the bag and pawed through the money inside. More money than she'd ever seen. She shook off the thought of taking a little. If she and Augustina could get away, she'd try to take it all. Return it to Mr. Hicken.

Seeking the special pocket she'd sewn inside, she felt for the deed. Empty. Mattie's heart sank. Had the men found it?

As the tension abated outside the door, Augustina waved furiously. Trembling, Mattie refastened the bag and tucked it under the blanket then rejoined Augustina on the far side of the room. In the same instant, the injured man entered. He halted inside the door, gaze darting until he found them.

"What are you doing?"

Mattie nodded toward the other corner where they'd been sitting moments before. "The sun is coming in the windows over there, and it's too warm, so we moved."

He scowled but walked to the cot, grabbed one pair of saddlebags, and returned outside. There he handed them off to the one who looked like his twin. The other man tied them behind his saddle.

Augustina inched nearer, watching.

"Señorita, why he stands that way?" she whispered.

"Stands what way?"

The girl slid nearer still, until they were inches apart. "His feet. . .they are not straight."

Mattie turned to see what the girl meant. The man standing beside the horse had toes that pointed quite prominently inward.

"I'm not sure. I haven't seen that before."

They both watched in curiosity until he mounted his horse. The sparsely bearded man and the injured one watched him ride away.

Augustina laid her head on Mattie's shoulder. "*Lo siento*, señorita. I am sorry." She dipped her chin to her chest in hopes of hiding their discussion.

"Sorry for what?"

"For we get caught."

Mattie slipped an arm around the child. "I know you didn't mean for us to get caught."

"No, señorita. I hear the voices between the buildings. One. . .how you say? I hear it before. On the train."

"You heard a familiar voice from the train."

"*Sí*. The voice says the words *mi gemelo*."

Mattie had heard one of these men speak the same phrase. "What does that mean?"

"It means. . .my twin."

So the two were twins, and Javier was their brother.

"I do not hear many people say to each other these words. So I go between the buildings to see who it is. But they hear us."

It was an unusual endearment. Understandable why the precocious girl would be curious and go to investigate. "Don't lose hope. We'll get out of this. Now, shhh."

Lord, please don't make a liar out of me. We will get out of this, right?

"Por favor. There is more for me to tell, señorita."

Javier entered. "No talking."

Mattie swallowed hard and boldly met his gaze "What are we waiting for, sir?"

"Mind your own business, señorita." He looked through the door as his brother entered and collapsed onto the cot. "It is nothing that concerns you."

"As long as you're holding us captive, what happens here concerns me very much."

This time Javier only glowered at her.

She wouldn't have expected him to answer her query, but it was worth a try. "Please. We're hungry. Might we have a bit of food?"

Again, the man turned. "I told you to keep quiet."

The injured man perked. "¡*Basta*, Javier! Enough. It is a small thing she asks. Give them some jerky."

Turning to his brother, Javier spat harsh words in Spanish.

Augustina inhaled sharply, burying her face against Mattie's shoulder.

She snugged her charge against her side. "What is it, child?"

"He says it does not matter, that. . ." She gulped. "Once *she* arrives, we will likely be dead."

Chapter 7

Jake waved the five young ones through the door to Sheriff White's office. As he did, Sam Beglin, sporting a large bruise along his jaw and a split lip, bolted up from the cot inside one of the two jail cells at the back of the room.

"Oh, thank God!" The young man gripped the cell bars with bruised hands.

In the second cell, Derry Beglin sat up, his demeanor as dark and sullen as the bruise that had swollen his right eye shut.

Sheriff White sat on the corner of his desk and shoved his hat back on his head. "These the boys you mentioned?"

Jake nodded. "That's them. Derry and Sam Beglin."

The lawman removed a set of keys from his desk. "Reckon I'll release 'em to you, unless you tell me otherwise."

"That's fine. Let 'em out." *Lord, I already don't know how to keep track of five children* and *investigate a robbery, much less find Mattie Welling and the other missing girl.*

Once the sheriff unlocked Sam's cell, the kids crowded around the young man, and he greeted them before turning Jake's way. "Mr. Hicken, where are Miss Mattie and Augustina? Didn't they come back last night?"

"Looks like she's slacking off, as always." Derry spewed the bitter words as the sheriff stepped up to his cell door to unlock it.

"Oh, don't start with that again, Derry!" Sam growled. "Have you lost your ever-lovin' mind all of a sudden?"

White looked over his shoulder at Jake. "You *sure* you want this one let out? He sounds like trouble to me."

"You better let me out, old man." Derry paced to the door. "I haven't done nothin' wrong."

"Old man?" White balked. "Boy, I'm thirty. That's—"

"Old."

The sheriff flashed another look at Jake, his irritation evident. Truth be told, Jake's annoyance was growing as well, yet he nodded for the sheriff to unlock the door.

Owen shook his head at his older brother. "You disrespected Miss Mattie somethin' awful last night, and then you walked out on us. Seems pretty wrong to me."

"And me." Sam stepped up alongside Owen. "That knot on your head's playin' tricks with your brain, I think."

As Sheriff White unlocked the door, Derry shoved his way through it, deliberately bumping the lawman's arm in the process.

"I told you all to come along." He lodged his index finger against Sam's chest. "It was your choice to stay, so don't make it sound like I did you so dirty."

Jake's ire stirred. "Derry Beglin, shut up, or I'll have Sheriff White lock you back in that cell after all."

Derry's eyes narrowed, and he pushed past the children to face Jake. "What gives you any authority to go bossin' me around, mister?

You ain't my father."

"You're right. If I was, I'd have taken care of that attitude long before now. As for what gives me the authority, I'd like to think Miss Welling would consider me a friend—"

"Friend." He huffed. "Is that what you call it?"

Jake stared. "Is that what I call *what*?" He shook his head. "You know what—never mind. Like I was saying, as Miss Welling's friend, I suspect she'd welcome me putting you back in line when you need it."

The boy gave him a contemptuous glance. "You ain't got the spine to try, Hiccup."

"Don't I?" Jake shrugged out from under his saddlebags, and they hit the floor, unheeded.

Derry rolled his eyes, but not before the barest spark of fear flashed in them. "I'm done with all this." He tried to move past Jake toward the door.

"Oh no you're not." Sliding in front of the kid, Jake settled his palm against Derry's chest. "You just called me spineless, boy. You aren't walking away without an apology. . .or a fight. Which do you want?"

Again, the young man gave him a once-over, his breathing coming a little faster. "I'm not fightin' you. You're wearing a gun."

"Then you'll apologize."

The kid was silent. Hopefully thinking—doing some figuring in his head, just as Jake was. All things being equal, the odds weren't in Derry's favor. Jake was several inches taller and outweighed him by a good thirty pounds or more. While the boy had lived on the streets and might have some fighting skills, Jake had bested plenty in his eight years of wearing a badge—with both guns and fists. But with his bruised hip, the odds were closer to even—and Jake would tire quickly. Not to mention what that would do for his ability to investigate the robbery and find Mattie Welling after the fight was done.

But he couldn't simply ignore this disrespect. Not for his own sake, Derry's, and especially Mattie Welling's.

"I'm not hearing an *I'm sorry*, so. . ." He removed the gun belt. "White, you mind holding this for me?" Jake held the belt out as the lawman approached. Once he'd taken it, Jake shucked his jacket, hat, and badge.

As each piece came off, Derry's eyes widened.

Sam stepped nearer. "Derry, you fool. What's gotten into you? Just apologize."

"Shut up," the eldest Beglin hissed back.

Sheriff White stashed the gun in a desk drawer. "Take it outside if you're gonna fight."

Derry's Adam's apple bobbed.

"One last chance, boy." Jake arched his brows. "Either apologize or we can step outside and settle this like men."

Derry's expression hardened, and he batted the hat off his head and shoved past Jake for the door.

Resignation filling him, Jake met the lawman's gaze. "Will you keep the young ones inside, please?"

"They'll be safe with me."

Jake turned for the door.

The sheriff called out. "Do me a favor and blacken that brat's other eye for me."

Jake hesitated before opening the door, expecting Derry was likely waiting in ambush. Sure enough, as he exited, the kid threw his arms around Jake's chest and upper arms, trying to drive him into the street.

Ready for the tactic, Jake drove toward the nearest post supporting the wide porch roof. He slammed Derry into it, and the kid's grip loosened. A second time, Jake slammed him. This time, Derry's grip popped free with a loud *oof.* They both stumbled, off balance, into the street.

Derry caught himself against the hitching rail while Jake stumbled several steps beyond it. When he righted himself, Derry approached, fists balled and dancing like he was spoiling to fight.

The kid swung. Jake dodged the blow and drove his shoulder hard against Derry's chest. Arms flailing, the boy sprawled in the dirt but scrambled up. When he did, Jake swung again, connecting solidly with Derry's nose.

The kid sagged, blood spouting from both nostrils. Half senseless, he touched his upper lip then stared at the red stain on his fingertips for a long time.

Jake used the lull to catch his breath. A crowd had formed along the boardwalk, and people also approached on horseback or in wagons, crowding to see the excitement. Scanning the faces around him, a warning flared in his gut.

"I think you broke my nose, Hicken!" Derry bellowed.

"I might have."

As he faced the kid again, a tall, muscular fella with a dark, heavy beard dismounted his horse nearby. Something snagged Jake's attention, and when he swiveled back, the bearded man's eyes widened in recognition. Jake's focus landed on the horse's brand. A V-shape with a cross growing out of its center and some kind of flourished cap.

In the same instant, Derry caught Jake at the waist and drove him several feet before he tackled him. Pain exploded through Jake's hip and torso, stealing his breath.

Derry reared up and struck, though Jake twisted, the blow glancing off his shoulder rather than connecting with his chin. Gasping, Jake shoved his foe off and rolled to his feet. He stumbled sideways, his surroundings weaving.

Gritting his teeth, he scanned the crowd for the man. The horse still stood where his rider had dismounted, but the fella was gone. Widening his search, Jake caught a glimpse of him skirting the growing crowd just before he ducked into the alley beside White's office.

A force like a stampede struck him square in the back. Jake hit the ground face-first, mouth smashing the dirt. He tasted blood as he struggled to push up on all fours. As he did, Derry drew back to kick. Jake dropped again and rolled, missing the kid's foot. Summoning all his strength, he got his boots under him and stood, teetering, as Derry waded toward him again.

"That's enough, kid." He panted the words. "I don't have time to finish this now." Not when one of the robbers might've disappeared down that alley.

"You ain't gettin' off that easy, Hiccup." Derry stepped in and swung.

Jake dodged the punch, caught Derry's arm, and clamped it tight between his own ribs and his bicep. Grabbing the boy's shirt, Jake smashed his forehead into the kid's noggin. Derry's knees went soft, and Jake carefully lowered the half-senseless kid to the street.

All was silent for a moment then, "Move along! Fight's over," Sheriff White bellowed, exiting his office. "Walk on, folks. Nothing to see."

The crowd thinned.

Sam darted through the dissipating people to come to his brother's side. After one wide-eyed look at Derry, he turned to Jake. "You all right, Mr. Hicken?"

He waved at Derry. "See to your brother, would ya?"

White walked up and, latching onto Jake's elbow, guided him off a couple of steps. "Think you got your point across?"

"Time'll tell." He turned toward the horse the bearded man had ridden, still standing in the middle of the street. "Do you know that brand or whose horse it is?"

The lawman squinted. "That's the Figueroa brand. Why?"

Jake furrowed his brow. "*Figueroa?*"

White nodded. "Benicio Figueroa. A *Californio* man. Owns a sizable ranch with a vineyard outside of town."

"Ben Figueroa?"

A gunshot rang out, and something slammed Jake hard in the left shoulder, twisting him around.

"Eat, child." Mattie brushed the hair back from Augustina's face then offered her some of the jerky their injured captor had given them.

"I am not hungry," she whispered, fear and sorrow coloring her words.

It had taken time to calm the child after the overheard threat that they might be killed. And who on earth was the *she* whose arrival might signal her and Augustina's demise?

Mattie cupped the girl's chin in her hand. "We *must* keep our strength up." She smiled, willing Augustina to understand. They would run once an opportunity presented itself, but she dared not risk whispering that plan aloud. "It's very important."

Whether the girl caught her meaning or only meant to silence Mattie's nagging, Augustina reluctantly took the jerky and nibbled the corner.

"Good girl." Mattie also took a bite from her own half-eaten strip.

Lord, show me a way of escape. Or show Mr. Hicken where these men are hiding. Something, Father, so Augustina and I can get back to the other children. Please.

And what about the others? She'd failed them. Failed to protect and care for them. The other orphan train workers had discouraged her from taking so many children at once, but how could she choose? She loved them all. If she could get free from these men and reach Owlie's property, they'd be able to build a life.

First, she must get Augustina away from this awful shanty. Then she would find the rest of her children. She could *hope* that Derry had returned. Between him and the more levelheaded Sam, they would take care of the younger ones until she returned.

And hopefully by now Mr. Hicken was in pursuit of these men. Dare she wish the man would show up and rescue her? Wish it, sure, but she wouldn't count on the handsome detective. Her life and Augustina's depended on finding the first opportunity to run. Thankfully, the injured man looked like he might fall asleep, which left only Javier to outwit. And she might have an idea for how to outfox him. A very simple one.

Mattie cleared her throat. "I hate to bother you, but we need to relieve ourselves."

It wasn't only a ploy. They'd not thought to allow them such opportunity since they'd arrived.

"You'll have to wait, señorita."

"We *have* been waiting—all morning. Unless you expect us to address this issue here inside the cabin, we'll need to use a privy."

His displeasure obvious, Javier mumbled something Mattie didn't catch.

The injured man roused at his brother's murmuring. "Why do you complain? You are the one who brought them into the camp, Javi."

"No! *Era tu* gemelo. That was Ignacio's decision. I did not want any part of this plan."

"So you remind us." The injured man spoke in exasperation. "You are the oldest, the righteous one, better than the rest of us."

"No, Rafael. This is not what I mean." Dragging Rafael from the bed, Javier escorted him toward the door "This plan. . .it grows out of control." They stepped outside. "We agree to kill one man."

Javier pulled the door closed, leaving it slightly cracked.

Mattie lurched to her feet. "Warn me if they seem ready to come in," she whispered then crossed to the nearest window.

Javier's voice carried through the mostly closed door. "But to make it look like an accident, we are told to rob the train. This is two crimes."

Mattie tugged gently at the window. Stuck. She darted a look toward Augustina. The girl waved her on, so Mattie rushed to the next window. It wouldn't budge either.

"We agree to kill one, but there are two men guarding the money."

What in heaven's name was he saying? The robbery—securing the contents in the Wells Fargo safe—was *not* their main focus? Rather, killing someone was?

"Now, two men are dead, and we do not know whether either of them is the right man."

Mattie hurried to the window over the bed and, moving the stack of folded cloths to the table, tried it as well. It gave a quiet *pop* and slid up a couple of inches. Heart pounding, she looked toward Augustina. Wide-eyed, the child glanced toward the door then nodded encouragingly at Mattie.

"You were injured," Javier continued. "If the man's aim was an inch closer, you would be dead. Your saddlebags slip from the train, leaving something to tie us to the robbery. Diego should have been back from looking for them, but he does not come."

Mattie pushed the window higher. Opening it fully, she pinned Augustina with a look.

"Get the carpetbag and come. Quickly!" She mouthed the words, overenunciating and pantomiming as she did.

The girl darted up to obey.

"And while Nacio and I go to town last night, these two find us. We are forced to take them captive. How many crimes is that now? Two murders, a train robbery, and kidnapping."

Augustina dashed over and, setting aside the bag, slipped through the window with Mattie's help. Mattie then passed the carpetbag out to the child and climbed onto the cot. Putting one leg through the opening, she started to wiggle through.

"Four crimes, mi hermano, and we still do not know whether Jake Hicken is dead or alive."

Chapter 8

The thinning crowd scattered at the gunshot. Jake and the sheriff both went for their pistols—only Jake came up empty.

He swore. His gun was stashed inside.

"Go." The lawman gave him a shove. "Get those kids inside, Hicken!"

Jake hobbled to Derry's left side and, with Sam's assistance, hauled the older Beglin up. Getting his good arm around Derry's torso, Jake dragged the stunned kid toward the sheriff's office, Sam aiding from the other side.

"C'mon, kid." Jake hefted Derry through the doorway, his hip screaming with the effort.

Inside, Derry all but collapsed on the floor.

"Can you get him to one of the cots?" Jake nodded to the cells.

"Yes, sir." Sam guided his brother to the back of the room, and Jake turned toward the sheriff's desk. He sat in the chair and peered across the room. Fiona huddled with Moira and Patrick in the far corner, the two young ones looking upset. Owen headed into the cell to help Sam and Derry. Ann, her dark eyes huge, came around the desk to stand beside him.

"You're bleeding." She whispered the words as she touched his blood-stained sleeve.

"Yeah, but I'll be all right." He tried to reassure her with a smile.

"Do you need help?"

His smile broadened. "No, darlin' girl. But thank you." He tugged the damp handkerchief from his saddlebags, which White must've set on his desk. He pressed the wadded cloth against the wound under his shirt, fighting to keep the smile in place in spite of the pain. "I'll be fine. I promise."

Ann gave a somber nod and moved away a few feet. Jake fished his gun belt from the bottom drawer of White's desk and stood to buckle it around his waist. He fumbled a moment to fasten it then sat again to tie down the holster. Fingers clumsy, that took some doing.

When he looked up, Ann had moved to his right side.

"You're going out there?" Tears pooled against her lower lids.

Jake nodded, her emotion tugging at him. "I have to. It's my job."

Hesitating, she took his hand with a grim nod. "Please come back, Mr. Hiccup."

The request, spoken in the tiniest of voices, stole his breath. *Lord, what're You doing to me?*

He attempted a smile as he squeezed the girl's fingers. "I will." He stood, reluctantly releasing the child's hand. As he limped from behind the desk, he grabbed his hat and badge. Just inside the door, Jake pinned on the badge, tugged the Stetson in place, and through the window, looked up and down the street. The horse bearing Benicio Figueroa's brand still stood in the middle of the road, but neither its rider nor Sheriff White was in view. Removing the thong from his gun's hammer, he slipped through the doorway and around into the alley where the man had disappeared, inching toward the back.

"Put the gun down, Nacio," White's voice rang out.

Jake eased his gun from the holster and peeked around the corner. Part of the way down the back of the building, Sheriff White faced the bearded man.

"I do not look for problems with you, *señor*."

"Then why are you shooting people in my streets?"

The man, facing White, backed up a step. "I do not know what you mean."

"Oh, I think you do." White stepped forward, hooking a thumb toward a cast-iron downspout attached to the back wall. "And I think you'd better explain why I caught you shinnyin' down the drainpipe from my roof just now."

Jake ducked into the alley, positioning himself behind the man.

The fella shrugged as he again shuffled backward. "There was a fight. I climb up high for a better view."

"If that's all you were doing, why is your gun drawn?" White asked.

Jake stepped up then and lodged the barrel of his own gun against the base of the other man's skull. "Drop the pistol."

The fella stiffened, hands coming up in surrender. His Peacemaker slipped from his grip to dangle by the trigger guard around his index finger. Biting back the pain, Jake reached for it with his injured arm.

Once Nacio was secured, White shoved the gunman, face-first, against the building. "That was wise of you, Nacio." He settled his forearm against the man's neck and relieved the fella of the Bowie knife at his belt. White handed the blade to Jake then continued to search for other weapons. Finding nothing else, White turned the man around.

"Here's your rider, Hicken. Ignacio Figueroa, one of Benicio's sons. He and his twin, Rafael, are the middle of the four boys."

Figueroa glared first at White then shifted toward Jake.

Ignacio's light-colored pants and darker shirt matched some train passengers' descriptions, as well as his own quick glimpse. The beard matched descriptions as well.

"Stand him up straight for me."

White jerked the man into the middle of the alley, holding him by the arm, his pistol leveled at his spine.

Jake's gaze landed on his feet. "Pigeon-toed. One of the passengers mentioned that."

When Ignacio spat in Jake's direction, White smashed him into the wall again. "You're gonna behave better than that, Nacio. Hicken's a guest in our town."

"Jake Hicken is the illegitimate son of a gold miner dog—"

For a moment, Jake's mind clicked over the man's words. Then, leveling his gun at Ignacio Figueroa's face, he cocked the hammer. "Say that again."

"Hicken!" The sheriff painted the air with salty words. "Don't you shoot him."

"Trust me, Sheriff. I just want to hear him say that again."

"That's what worries me."

A wicked smile sprouted on Nacio's lips. "I said, your mother is a gold miner dog, and you are an illegitimate cur. If my aim was only slightly better, you would be dead, mongrel."

Jake stood, stoic for an instant before a smile tugged at his lips. "If your aim was better." He lowered the Peacemaker's hammer then locked eyes with White. "Sounds like a confession to me, Sheriff. Attempted murder?"

The lawman, visibly relieved, gave a grudging nod. "I think so." He shifted to Nacio. "Let's go." He marched the man up the alley, gun still trained at his back.

As White herded Nacio inside, Jake limped to the bay horse that someone had finally tied to the hitching rail. The fancy tooled-leather bags tied behind the saddle were similar to the piece of leather recovered by the train's brakeman. Emblazoned on the medallion above the buckle was a set of initials—I.F., surely for Ignacio Figueroa. Holstering his own gun then balancing Nacio's pistol and Bowie on the saddle, Jake untied the bags. Fire tore through his shoulder with the movements. Retrieving the weapons, he hauled everything inside and set it on White's desk.

"You tangle with another bear, Hicken?"

Jake turned to find Tom Abendroth standing beside his brother-in-law as White closed the left-hand cell door where Derry had been moments before. Inside, Nacio Figueroa glared out. In the right-hand cell, another man, younger and smaller but with similar facial features, stood.

"Where's Derry?"

"I got another cot in the back room. I told the other two boys to help him in there."

As the pulse-pounding energy of the past several minutes waned, fatigue stole over Jake. Shaking, he stepped behind White's desk and collapsed in the chair.

"I think I did tangle with a bear." Derry had put up a decent fight.

The sheriff crossed to him and looked at his shoulder, front and back. "Looks like the bullet went through. We need to get the bleeding stopped."

Jake looked across the room. The MacGinty children and Ann huddled in the corner, all staring with forlorn looks.

"Sheriff, is there a woman in town who'd be willing to look after these kids until I can sort out where Miss Mattie is? Preacher's wife or something? I'll pay her." He touched his blood-soaked vest then held his fingers out for the sheriff to see. "They really don't need to see all this."

Tom and White answered in unison. "Pru."

"My wife, Prudence," White continued. "You don't have to pay her though. She loves kids."

"I'll walk 'em over there if you want." Tom motioned, though Jake didn't notice in what direction.

"Thank you." Far better they go before they were forced to witness the treatment of a bullet wound. The young ones especially might have nightmares of what they'd experienced in the last day.

The sheriff carefully pulled Jake's shirt aside to see the entry wound. "I don't assume you've got a horse, do you, Hicken?"

He shook his head, wishing to close his eyes, but he didn't dare. The minute he stopped, he'd be down for hours, perhaps a day.

White caught his brother-in-law's gaze. "Do me a favor and saddle Spitfire and Chase before you return."

Jake shot a look at the back room. "Before I send Derry to your wife, I think I oughta have a talk with him, make sure he'll mind his manners." The last thing he wanted was to unleash Derry's possible anger on an unsuspecting woman.

"Probably wise. Tom, take the rest of the kids to Pru. We can get Derry over there once we're done here."

Once Abendroth and the kids departed, White hooked his thumb at the backroom door. "We'll do this in there, away from prying ears."

He locked the front door as Jake stood and collected Nacio's saddlebags. The back room was the size of two jail cells, with a second desk, the cot where Derry rested, and a potbellied stove. White motioned to the chair, and Jake gladly collapsed on it. While the lawman lit a lantern on the desk and gathered a few supplies, Jake eased out of his bloodied vest and shirt. Returning, White dropped several mangled pieces of leather on the desk beside Nacio's saddlebags.

"Tom found Diego, the youngest of Benicio Figueroa's sons, combing the railroad tracks north of where the explosion occurred, collecting up that pile right there." White nodded to the desktop then pressed a clean cloth to each of the holes in Jake's shoulder.

Jake spread out the pieces. The size and shape of the remnants looked like that of a pair of saddlebags. Probably the same ones from which the badly beaten flap had been torn. Surely the wheels of a full-speed steam train would cut through leather like butter.

"There were four men in on the robbery. Two on the train and two who brought horses for their getaway." Diego, scrawny and small compared to his elder brother, didn't look at all like the second man from the train. While he'd not gotten a glimpse of the riders, the fact Diego was collecting leather from the tracks was a good indication he was one of them.

Jake removed his hat and, setting it in his lap, wiped the band inside. "I want to talk to Benicio Figueroa next."

"All right. We'll get you patched up then take a ride out there."

Nacio's slur—that Jake was the illegitimate son of a gold miner dog—drove home two points. That at least *one* of Benicio's sons was aware of the indiscretion their father had had with his mother twenty-five years ago. And that Benicio's summons was a ploy to draw Jake out where they could kill him.

But why had Ben Figueroa waited until now?

"What is it you suggest, Javi?"

Mattie's ears perked to the injured brother, Rafael's, words.

"How do we get out of this trouble?"

As she ducked her head through the window, a shot of pain lanced her bruised ribs. Swallowing a cry, she locked eyes with Augustina. "Go. Run." She mouthed the words, shooing the girl away.

"No, señorita! Not without you." Augustina kept her voice to a whisper.

"I do not know, hermano. I fear we are too far into this to stop now."

She gave the child a shove. "Go. Find Mr. Hicken. I'll be right behind you."

Augustina's eyes brimming, she backed away a step then another. Finally, she turned and ran, carpetbag in hand.

Lord, please keep her—us—safe!

Balanced on her left leg, Mattie carefully twisted to extract her right. However, her stocking caught on the window frame and, unable to free it, she toppled into the dust. Again, pain flared though her middle. Heart hammering, she glanced toward the front corner. Had the men heard? When they continued to talk, she loosed herself and pushed off the ground.

Mattie ran, tracing the same path Augustina had taken. Already the girl had disappeared over the next rise. Thank God! She too started up the hill, but as she surged toward the top, a shot split the air. Dirt kicked up to her right. With a yelp, she shifted left, her shoes slipping on the grass. She went down hard and slid, clawing the ground to stop herself. When she finally halted, she pushed onto her hands and knees, far more slowly than before. A second shot scattered dirt in her face.

"Stay, señorita. If you run again, I will not miss." Javier's voice came from somewhere all too close for comfort.

She shook her head and eased her hands into plain view. "I won't run." *Lord, get Augustina far from here, please!*

The grass rustled as the two brothers came alongside her. Javier jerked her off the ground by her arm and shoved her into Rafael's grip. "Where is the girl?"

"I don't know." Her whole body shook.

Javier's face twisted with anger, and for a moment, he glared. "Take her inside and watch her. I will find the child—and the money."

Rafael gave her a shove toward the house as his brother moved to the top of the rise.

Prayers bubbled through her thoughts, and her stomach knotted. Would Augustina be able to evade Javier? She, a young girl, wouldn't have anywhere near the experience or ability that he would. Yet she was smart and quick-witted. *Lord, be with her.*

Rafael walked her to the door and shoved her inside. "Do not give me any more trouble."

Stumbling, Mattie's feet tangled in her petticoats. She braced her hands against the steamer trunk's top, but the blanket skidded off and sent her tumbling over it, landing in a heap on the other side.

"Get up." Rafael glowered at her. He sank onto the cot. "And put everything back like it was."

Ribs aching and hope waning, it took a moment to find the will to move. Would Augustina return with help before it was too late for Mattie?

Hand braced against her side, she tottered up. The trunk had overturned, so she righted it, centered it back on the wood blocks it sat on, then picked up the blanket. The folded cloths which she'd moved to the tabletop had scattered in her fall, so laying the blanket in a ball on the trunk's surface, she squatted to retrieve them. Once more she stacked them, one by one, but she paused partway through and squinted at the one in her hand.

There in the corner was the familiar monogram—O.W.L. She picked up another and turned it over, checking the corners. It too had the delicate stitching. One by one, she checked the remaining cloths. They *all* contained her deceased brother's initials. Turning, she brushed the wadded blanket from the top of the trunk. Long worn into the patina of the old wood were the carved names of every orphan who'd lived in the Children's Aid Society's care the day of Owlie's eighteenth birthday.

Mattie eased into the nearby cane chair, barely able to breathe. Was *this* Owlie's home—this tiny shack that would hardly withstand a gust of wind? He'd *said* the place he was preparing for her was sizable. Plenty of room for both her and him—and families as they grew them. Her stomach soured. This wasn't suitable for one. What in heaven's name would she do with herself and eight children—*if* she managed to survive this ordeal and return to them.

The distant *pop* of a gunshot roused her, and she rushed to the back window. Breathless moments passed before Javier reappeared, pistol in hand and carrying the carpetbag.

Augustina wasn't with him.

Chapter 9

While the sheriff staunched the bleeding and cleaned the wounds, Jake quietly filled him in on the robbery and what he'd pieced together thus far. As Jake looked at the beaten leather fragments, White gave him a gentle nudge and cast a discreet look toward Derry. The young man stood several feet back, craning his neck to see what Jake was doing.

"You good at puzzles, Derry?" Jake called over his shoulder.

The kid feigned disinterest. "I'm good at a lot of things."

"A smart fella like you, I just bet you are. I'd welcome the help piecing this mess together, if you're of the mind." Maybe the olive branch would help smooth things over with the kid.

Derry hesitated then parked himself on the corner of the desk. "Fine. I'll do your job for you." Pawing through several pieces, he began to lay them out.

Jake watched him a moment then turned again to White. "The thing that's got me worried is, where are Mattie Welling and her other orphan girl?"

"Augustina." Derry kept his focus on the leather fragments.

White picked up a roll of bandages and pressed a clean dressing to the entry wound. "Hold that a minute." When Jake did, he applied a second to the exit wound and began to roll out the bandages. "Tell me again what you know about their disappearances."

"Not a lot. Last I saw Miss Welling, she was leaving Doc Preston's place late last night to find a place to bed the kids down. Maybe Derry can tell us more."

As the sheriff bandaged Jake's shoulder, the boy darted a shifty-eyed glance between them then focused on the puzzle again. "Not much to tell. We were heading to the livery stable, and all the littles were draggin' their feet. I was already carrying Patrick. Got so they were stretched out across a block or more, so Miss Mattie started barkin' at me and Sam about it." He stiffened his spine. "A man ought to get more respect than that, so I told her I wasn't having it. When she slapped me like I was a child, I walked off. I don't know what happened after that."

Understanding flared in Jake's thoughts.

White tied off the bandage. "That'll hold for now. There's a spare shirt in the bottom drawer to your right."

Derry set the last two pieces of leather in place. "You're missin' the flap on one side, but beyond that, there's your puzzle."

Itching to talk to the sheriff alone, Jake nodded toward the other room. "If you would, fetch my saddlebags off the other desk, Derry. I got the last piece in there."

The kid eyed them then eased from the desk, and jerking the door open, marched into the other room.

Jake and the sheriff turned to each other.

"He fancies himself a man, Mattie's equal," Jake whispered.

White nodded. "He's smitten with her."

It explained a lot. The bluster when he'd found them in the box-car, the angry glares when Derry was told to sit outside at the train depot. Even today, in his insults toward Jake and not being willing to apologize.

Jake pulled open the drawer and extracted a blue shirt. "Thank you for this." He tugged the garment on as White cleaned up the mess.

Derry returned and passed the saddlebags to Jake, who unfastened one side and handed the rolled flap back to Derry in turn. The young man shook it free and, turning it the correct direction, set it in place.

"Look there, Hiccup. A perfect match."

Perfect, indeed.

"You mind if we leave this here for now, Sheriff?" Jake nodded to the torn saddlebags.

"I don't mind. Consider it your desk for as long as you're in town."

Jake smiled his thanks, and as the lawman exited to dump the bowl of dirty water, Jake turned to Nacio's saddlebags. Opening the first flap, he looked on the back side. Then he turned over the torn flap they'd just set in place. Both were marked with the Figueroa brand. The letters on the medallion of the intact saddle bags read I.F., he guessed for Ignacio Figueroa. The torn ones said R.F. What had White said the other brothers' names were? Ignacio, Diego... A thought struck.

He swatted Derry's knee. "You do me another favor, kid?"

"What do you want?"

Jake picked up the torn flap and showed it to Derry. "There's likely a horse tied somewhere out front wearing this brand." He tapped the mark. "Look to see if there's a pair of saddlebags that look similar to this. If the medallion says D.F., bring me the bags."

Once Derry exited, Jake set the torn flap back in place and

proceeded to extract the contents from Nacio's kit. Nothing of much consequence in the first pouch. Paper and pencil, some jerky, a box of ammunition. More typical supplies in the second.

As Jake picked up a small fabric-wrapped bundle about the length of his index finger and twice as wide, Derry reentered, toting the requested bags.

"Here you go, Hiccup."

Jake verified the initials. "Check inside the flap for a brand like these others."

As the kid obeyed, Jake loosed the rough twine that knotted the small bundle he'd pulled from Nacio's bag.

"Same brand." Derry showed him the flap.

He grinned at the boy. "The puzzle pieces are coming together." Four brothers—and of the two they'd captured, both carried the same style of saddlebags. A third set was destroyed along the train tracks near the site of the explosion, and Mattie had said they'd demanded the carpetbag from her when they entered the boxcar. So perhaps a third Figueroa brother had lost his while moving about the train.

He unwrapped the bundle.

"Keys." Derry peered over his shoulder.

"Yep."

"*They* important to your case?"

Was the boy truly interested? "Not sure. Six keys of varying sizes." He looked at the post and bit of each. "Looks like all of them are masters."

Derry leaned against the desk and snatched up the cloth they'd been wrapped in. "You mean they'll fit any lock?"

"Maybe not *any*. . .but they'll fit a lot of locks." Was *that* how they'd gotten in the door to the safe car? He'd not been able to ferret out that detail as he'd pieced together their movements on the train. Both Engvall and Smits were too wary to let anyone kick in the door, and he'd seen no evidence of that anyway. Nor had he heard gunshots before the explosion. He'd have to take a ride over to the station and look to see if any one of the keys might fit the safe car door—if the explosion hadn't so mangled the lock that it wouldn't operate, that was.

"Give me the cloth." He beckoned for it, but Derry pulled the lamp nearer, turned a corner of the cloth toward the light, and squinted. Jake rocked to his feet and peered around Derry's head to see what had caught his interest.

Ornate stitches in white thread.

O.W.L.

Jake plucked the material out of Derry's hands and smoothed the cloth out on the desk.

"That's Mattie's!" Derry blurted.

Jake's mind spun. A handkerchief just like the one he'd seen her use in the boxcar among Ignacio Figueroa's belongings. . .

He grabbed the cloth again and hobbled out to the cells. Locking gazes with Nacio, he shook the handkerchief. "Where did you get this?"

Derry settled at his side.

Nacio turned disdain-filled eyes in Jake's direction then looked away. "You are not worthy to dignify with an answer, mongrel."

When Sheriff White entered, bowl under his arm, Jake nodded to the back room again. The lawman followed them inside, shutting the door.

"I found these keys wrapped in this handkerchief among Nacio's things. I'm guessing they used them to get into the safe car during the robbery, but the cloth. . ."

"It's Mattie's," Derry piped up.

Roy White took it and turned it toward the light. "That's *Owlie's.*"

"You know him?"

88

"I did. He died of consumption about six, eight months ago. Odd fella. Never gave us a last name. Just *Owlie.* Likable enough but stayed drunk most of the time. Had big dreams of buyin' property, but he was too inclined to the faro tables to ever make that happen."

Jake's heart sank. Owlie was not at all who Mattie had described.

Derry snorted and rolled his eyes. "Don't that figure. . . . She's dragged us all out here, and for what?"

White looked at the kid then Jake. "What's he talking about?"

"Owlie was really Oliver Lucas Welling, Mattie Welling's older brother."

The sheriff folded his arms, his brow furrowing.

"Mattie had one of these handkerchiefs with this monogram when I found her in the boxcar yesterday." He blew out a breath. "Why would Nacio Figueroa have it now? Do he and the other brother have her?"

White shook his head. "Don't go jumpin' to conclusions, Hicken. Owlie suffered from tuberculosis for years. He coughed into those fancy cloths all the time. Musta had fifty of 'em—and every last one had pretty stitchin' in the corner."

The argument was sound, except— "Let's say it's not the same one Mattie Welling was carrying. I still want to know where Nacio got this."

"Valid question. Owlie's old place ain't but a mile or two from Figueroa's ranch. To my knowledge, no one's been up there to clean the place out."

"You know where it is. . .his place?"

"I know it well. Took Owlie out there a few times across the years. Usually when he'd gambled away his horse or some such."

It was entirely too big a coincidence that Nacio Figueroa was carrying one of Owlie's fancy handkerchiefs. "Something just isn't setting right with me. As soon as Tom gets back, I want to ride out there and see it for myself."

"We need to gather a posse first. Three fellas ain't much."

"A woman and a little girl's lives may be at stake. How much time are you talking about?"

"Depends on who I can find."

Derry pushed his way in. "Don't forget about me. That makes four."

❧

Oh Lord. Augustina is dead, isn't she? How did this happen?

Mattie sat on the hearth, her stomach knotting so tightly, it threatened to expel the bit of jerky she'd eaten.

The little girl had gotten away, over the rise. Mattie had hoped she'd get free—make it back to Mr. Hicken with the money. But Javier had pursued her, and minutes later, he fired a single shot and returned. When he'd come, he bore only the carpetbag, not Augustina.

Surely he wouldn't have let her go. She was a loose end he'd want to tie up.

If she'd truly escaped, he'd not been gone long enough to do a thorough search for her, and he wouldn't give up easily if the child was missing.

The conclusion was obvious. Augustina was dead—killed by his lone bullet, her small body left for the predators that roamed these mountains.

Oh Lord Jesus, no!

Chapter 10

As they rode over a rickety bridge spanning a small creek, the ache in Jake's hip and the throbbing of his shoulder were only slightly dulled by the three healthy gulps of whiskey he'd downed before leaving Salinas for the western mountains. If his hunch paid off, the pain would be a small price to pay.

Sheriff White slowed his pace, and Jake, Derry, and Tom came alongside.

"Owlie's place is beyond that ridge." He nodded to it. "The cabin sits in a little hollow. Once we cross the rise, there's only one direction we can approach from without being seen—if there's even anyone there. The right side of the house has a fireplace but no windows. Every other direction has at least one."

"All right."

"One of my part-time deputies is gathering a posse. We got some extra fellas coming if you're willing to wait."

"Señor Hicken?" a small, shaky voice called from behind him.

He reined his horse around, hand near his gun, only to find a sodden Augustina Garza.

"Oh, thank God." He nudged his mount forward and, at her side, slid from the saddle, dropping straight to his knees. "Are you all right?" He took her by the shoulders and looked her over. "You're drenched!"

Flanking him, the other three approached.

The girl's face contorted. "Two mans. . .from the train. . .take me and Señorita Mattie. We try to get away, but the one man, he follow and shoot at me." She shuddered. "I do not know what happen to Señorita Mattie, but there was other shooting."

His heart stalled, and he spun her little frame and checked her for blood. "Are you hurt?"

"No, señor. He miss me." She turned to face him again. "I fall in the stream when he shoot at me, so I pretend I am dead. The water carries me here, so I hide under the bridge. I plan to walk to town, but you come here first."

Jake pulled the sopping child into his arms, and she clung to him, shivering.

"You're freezing."

She nodded against his chest. "The water is cold."

And surely fear didn't help matters. He pulled back from her then stifled a groan as he eased out of his jacket.

"Wrap this around you until we can get you some dry clothes." He draped the jacket over her shoulders.

She tucked her arms into the sleeves. "Lo siento, señor. I am sorry. I lose your money."

"What do you mean?"

"Señorita Mattie. . .she give me the bag with the train money and tell me to find you. But when the man shoot, I do not hold on to the bag. Lo siento, señor."

He chuckled as he again pulled her into his arms. "I'm not worried about the money right now. You and Miss Mattie are what's most important." He gave her back a vigorous rub to work some warmth into her.

"Hicken." White nudged his horse into easy view. "This is your investigation. How do you want to do this?"

"I'm not looking to take over, Sheriff. You know the house, and you know the men. I'll follow your lead. But given we know Mattie's inside and they've taken shots at Augustina, I think we need to get her out now."

"I can see your point."

A thought came to Jake's mind, and he held Augustina at arm's length. "Tell me. . .is one of the men injured?"

"Sí. Here." The girl touched the top of her ear.

Jake looked at his companions. "I managed one shot while they were robbing the train—right after I fell from the roof of the safe car. Clipped one of 'em in the ear as they escaped." They were closing in.

Grabbing hold of his saddle's stirrup, Jake pulled himself up. "Derry, I want you to stay with Augustina while the three of us go up ahead."

The young man pinned him with a stern glare. "Don't you think *you* oughta stay, given you can barely walk, Hiccup? You're half a man right now."

Irritation clawed through his chest, but he forced a grin. "Truth is, Derry, you're right. Between my hip and my shoulder, I'm not at my best. And that's exactly why I'm asking *you* to stay with Augustina. You proved yourself a fierce man to contend with in our fight, and right now I need a good man on the most important job. Will you please stay and protect her?"

The kid sat up. "Well, when you put it like that. . .'course I will."

❦

Mattie looked across the tiny shack at the two brothers. Javier occupied the chair, drumming his fingers on Owlie's blanket-covered trunk. Rafael sat against the wall beside the window she'd opened earlier, head back and eyes closed. By his even breathing, he seemed to be asleep.

"Please," she whispered, drawing Javier's attention. "I told you before, I need the privy." She hadn't lied earlier, but things were more urgent now.

"Did you not see when you tried to run? There is no privy."

She glanced out the back window. No outhouse. "That doesn't change the fact that I need to relieve myself. Please?"

Javier shook his head in frustration then swatted Rafael's knee.

The injured man came awake. "What?"

"The lady needs to go outside."

"You take her, Javi. It is a simple task." He cupped a hand over his swollen ear.

Javier stood. "We both will take her. I do not trust her after she ran."

Stomach roiling, Mattie stood. Javier crossed to her and, drawing his gun, plunged his free hand into her hair. She yelped as he drew her head back, close to his shoulder.

"You try to escape again, señorita, and I will kill you, just as I did the little girl."

A sob tore from her throat. *Oh Lord, help me.* Augustina *was* dead.

"I won't run," she whispered.

"Come, Rafael."

As the injured man pushed off the cot with a frustrated grunt, Javier walked her toward the door, hand still twined in her hair. Just before they reached it, a sharp knock came.

"Javier and Rafael Figueroa, it's Sheriff Roy White! Open the door. We need to talk."

At her back, Javier stiffened, and Rafael's hand strayed toward his hip.

"What do you need, Sheriff?" Javier's voice was loud in her ear.

"Why don't you two step outside, and we'll talk."

From the corner of her eye, a slight flutter of movement near the open window caught her attention. Mattie shot a sideways glance to find Jake Hicken crouched there, barely visible.

"This will not end well, Javi." Rafael's voice dripped fear. "We should give ourselves up."

"If we do, we will hang. We must escape. After all we have done, it is the only chance we will keep our lives."

"You hear me?" the voice from outside rang again. "Come on out, and we can talk."

"The lady and I will go first. Stay close, hermano."

Every muscle quivering, Mattie twisted to catch a better view of Jake. He mouthed something.

Get down.

She whispered a prayer then drove her elbow hard into Javier's ribs. With a grunt, he doubled, and Mattie dropped to the dirt floor, hair pulling free from his grip. Two gunshots sounded. She pulled herself into a ball and tried to stay out of the way as the door flung open and people rushed in. For a second time, someone tumbled over Owlie's trunk.

"Mattie!"

Past the struggle ensuing feet from her, Jake Hicken beckoned her. She darted up and threw herself, head-first, through the window. As she emerged, Jake caught her under the arms and pulled her free.

Once her feet touched the ground again, he stood her upright and gave her a push. "Run to the trees and wait for me."

Too overcome, she fell against him and hung on. Inside, two men—Mr. Abendroth and a second she'd not seen before—wrestled Rafael into submission. Near the door, Javier lay unmoving, blood trailing from a spot above his eye. At the sight, she buried her face against Jake Hicken's shirt and cried.

His arms circled her shoulders, and he pulled her close. "Are you hurt?"

It took a moment for her to answer. "No, but Augustina is dead."

The men inside dragged Rafael to his feet and walked him out of the house.

"No, she's not."

Mattie turned on him, wide-eyed. "She's not?"

"No. When she was shot at, your very intelligent little girl fell in the stream and played dead until she floated to safety."

She pulled away to get a better look at him. "She's not hurt?"

He gave her a tired smile. "She's wet and cold, not injured."

Her breath hitched. "Where is she? I have to see her."

"Give me a minute, and I'll take you to her. She's not far, but—" The smile dripped off his lips. "I need to tell you something first."

Fear wound around her chest, making it hard to breathe. "What? The other children?" *Oh God, please, let them all be safe.*

"They're all fine. Derry's watching Augustina just over that rise. The rest of your kids are safe with the sheriff's wife. We'll get you to 'em soon."

A relieved chuckle bubbled out of her. Her little ducklings were safe and would soon be tucked under her wings again for safekeeping. "Then what?"

Mr. Hicken's handsome but exhausted features turned serious. "I don't know how to tell you this, other than just to say it. Owlie lied about his place. He didn't have a big home with lots of property like he described."

Mattie's throat knotted. "I know. This is what he left me." She patted the wall behind her as a shadow crept over her heart. "A far cry from the sprawling two-story home and acres upon acres of grapes he said he was growing." Her cheeks warmed. "I should've known something was wrong when all Owlie had on him at his death was a deck of cards and two pennies."

Leaning against the wall, he took her hand. "I'm so sorry. What will you do now?"

She shrugged. "I can't very well raise eight children here."

"No."

"I have no money left." Mattie shook her head. "I suppose we'll all find jobs, take in laundry, or. . ." Again, she shrugged. "We were orphans on the street once, and we made do. We'll make do again, Mr. Hicken."

Slipping a gentle hand around the back of her neck, he tugged her to him. "Don't worry. I don't know how yet, but you and your children are *not* gonna be homeless. I'll promise you that."

She weaved her fingers into his shirt and held her breath.

Lord, I staked my life and the lives of eight innocent children on Owlie's lies. Dare I trust that this man is telling the truth?

Chapter 11

Not long after her rescuers had pulled Mattie to safety, Sheriff White's reinforcements showed up. The men helped secure Rafael and wrap Javier's body before the ride back to town.

Jake turned from the happy reunion between Mattie, Derry, and Augustina and crossed to Sheriff White and Tom Abendroth. "You said Benicio Figueroa lives not far from here?"

"A mile, maybe two. Why?"

"I need to see him."

"For what? You said there were four men in on the robbery, and we've got four. Two here and two in the jail. Case closed, right?"

"Not exactly. Ben Figueroa wrote me about two months ago, asked me to come down here and meet with him."

"You *know* him?" Surprise colored Tom's voice.

Jake paused. "No. I don't know him."

The sheriff glared. "Hicken, you're not makin' much sense."

Heat washed through him. "I've never met him, but according to my mother, Ben Figueroa is my father."

All movement in the yard stopped, and every eye turned his direction, including Mattie's.

"What?" White growled.

"You heard me," he growled back. No way he would repeat the embarrassing statement.

White waved at Javier and Rafael. "So these four are—"

"My half brothers."

"And your ma is. . .?" White's brows arched.

"Dodie Hicken. Nobody of any consequence." He scrubbed his face then dropped his voice to an even more confidential tone. "Twenty-five years ago, my mother was the daughter of a prospector. Figueroa went up north for several months that summer, where they met. Over time, one thing led to another, and. . ."

"You don't have to expound." White looked as uncomfortable as Jake felt.

He shot another look Mattie's way, but she'd turned her back, rubbing the blanket-wrapped Augustina, as if to warm her. All around the cabin, men pretended to mind their own business, though their interest was piqued for sure.

Exactly the reason he didn't share his questionable heritage—with anyone.

The sheriff indicated for Jake to follow. Abendroth joined them some feet away.

"Ma's had no contact with him since then. After her father disowned her, she went to live under the care of nuns in a convent in San Francisco. I've always known who Ben Figueroa is, knew roughly where he lived, but I never made contact. Figured it was best for everyone just to leave well enough alone. Up until two months ago, he never contacted me. Then a letter came. Simple. Cryptic. Asking me to come."

"Roy, wasn't it about that long ago that Figueroa had that bad spell?"

Jake turned on Tom. "Bad spell?"

White nodded. "Took real ill. His heart, I think. Pru overheard his wife, Lupe, tell someone in town he'd almost died."

Jake considered. "That might make some sense then, with what I'm thinking."

"What *are* you thinkin'?" Abendroth questioned.

"I've been pondering why Ben would send for me. I'm twenty-four. He's never shown a lick of interest in me. So why now?"

Tom folded his arms. "Facing death tends to make a fella rethink things."

"That's true." White rested a hand on the butt of his pistol.

He'd had the same thought. "Maybe, if Ben had a brush with death, he started thinking he should be sure his legitimate sons had sole claim to any inheritance."

White and Abendroth looked at each other.

Tom spoke first. "I've heard of such things happening, but Benicio Figueroa doesn't strike me as the type. He's lived an unsullied life."

Perhaps, but the man's one indiscretion with his mother had sullied her life plenty.

"Are you even sure your mother's telling the truth, Hicken?" White scowled.

Jake's ire sparked, but before he could answer, Abendroth barged on.

"This was a simple train robbery. Four rich, foolhardy boys did something stupid."

"No. I sent word to Benicio that I was coming, and I told him on which train. I mentioned I'd be on a job, so it'd be a day or two after that when I'd arrive." He cast a glance toward Rafael, who watched from some distance away. "You can't tell me that Figueroa's four sons decided to rob the exact train I was working on by pure dumb luck."

White and Abendroth exchanged another glance.

"He knew when you were coming?" White pursed his lips.

"He knew—"

"I don't mean to intrude, but. . ." Mattie pushed her way into the circle. "Augustina and I overheard these two talking. Jake is right. They were trying to kill him, not rob the train."

Riding behind Jake, Mattie considered all that had happened. When the posse had arrived at Owlie's, the lawman had insisted Mattie, Augustina, and Derry return with them to town. But the idea of being anywhere close to Rafael and Javier had frightened her. She'd pleaded with Jake to allow her and the two children to come along on the mile-long trek to Benicio Figueroa's home. He'd finally relented.

"You didn't seem very inclined to let me stay with you." She spoke the words softly.

He turned his ear to catch her words then shook his head. "Could be dangerous."

"Is that all?"

"Isn't that enough?"

She fell silent a moment but, unable to hold back her thoughts, spoke again. "It's just that. . .it seems like you're upset with me." Under normal circumstances, she'd not consider speaking so directly to a man she'd known only a day, but nothing had been normal since meeting Jake Hicken. "Since that first moment in the boxcar yesterday, you've been nothing but kind, attentive." Almost doting. "But in the space of moments, something changed, almost like you were trying to get rid of me. It was all when you shared about your parents."

He mumbled something under his breath.

"What did you say?"

"Doesn't bear repeating."

"I think it does."

He heaved a breath and glanced over his shoulder at her. "I said, I figured you'd want rid of me, given what I shared."

"Jake Hicken, nothing is further from the truth. Outside of my children, I think you're the only constant in my life right now."

He snorted. "Real constant. Since yesterday."

She held him a little tighter. "Very constant since yesterday. You rescued me on the train, kept us from being detained for stowing away, got us to a doctor, took care of my kids after I was taken, tracked Augustina and me down, and saved us from two very bad men." And that didn't begin to explain how he'd calmed her heart when he pledged she and her eight charges would not be on the streets after discovering Owlie's lies. "We've been through a lot together—and apart—in the last day."

He chuckled at that.

"I'm learning you're a man I can count on. I need that right now." She needed it a lot longer than *right now*, but one step at a time.

The line of riders turned down a path, and as they came around a bend, a beautiful scene unfolded before them. In the distance, a sprawling, two-story hacienda with adobe walls and a tile roof sat atop a high hill. Between them and the stately house lay acres of grapevines growing in neat rows, workers scattered throughout them. She drew a sharp breath at its beauty.

"This is what Owlie used to write about. He didn't write often, but on occasion, he'd describe a large, beautiful home and the rows of grapes. He'd tell me about the beautiful place he was preparing, and he described it so vividly, I could almost see it." Had her brother ever once thought she might reach California—or had he simply thought he'd string her along, promising a life he could never deliver? She shouldn't be surprised. Owlie was a dreamer, and some part of her knew his grandiose descriptions were too good to be true. "I am either naive or stupid to have believed him. Unfortunately, I staked not only my life, but the lives of eight innocent children on his writings."

"I'm sorry. It must feel like a betrayal."

"Yes." Very much. She leaned her head against his back, careful of his injured shoulder. "In time I'll find a way to forgive him."

Jake was silent for a moment before he cleared his throat. "I like that about you."

She pulled back to see his face. "You like what?"

"After everything I suspect you've been through in your life, you've managed to keep an innocence about you. Innocence and love. Those are rare qualities."

Once more Mattie leaned into him and tightened her grip. "You couldn't pay me a higher compliment, Jake Hicken."

Chapter 12

While approaching the hacienda, Jake watched a man leave the vineyard where he'd been talking to one of the workers, mount a nearby horse, and arrive in time to meet them at the front of the stately home.

"Sheriff." He half-nodded, half-bowed in greeting.

"Señor Figueroa."

Jake's heart pounded. Was *this* Ben? Tall, about Jake's own height, with a kind face now etched with concern.

"Might we have a private word with you, sir?"

Figueroa took in the line of riders, numbering about ten, including Mattie and the two kids. "There is something wrong?"

"I'd prefer to have that conversation in private, if you don't mind."

He hesitated a moment then nodded. "Sí, of course. Come inside, por favor."

While everyone dismounted, White instructed the posse members to wait outside. Meanwhile, Jake escorted Mattie, Derry, and

Augustina inside the cobblestone courtyard with Tom.

He led Mattie and the children to an out-of-the-way place not far from the courtyard's entrance. "Wait here," he whispered. "If anything happens, duck outside and get yourselves to safety." Truth was, he should probably leave them with the posse, but after their earlier ordeal, he didn't want Mattie or Augustina out of his sight.

Derry stood tall. "I'll keep watch over 'em, Hiccup."

"I'm countin' on that."

White entered, and Jake followed to a shady spot where Figueroa waited.

"What is this about, Sheriff?"

A door across the courtyard opened, and a lovely dark-haired woman swept out, sashaying toward the group.

The lawman motioned to Tom. "You might know my brother-in-law, Tom Abendroth."

Again, Figueroa offered his half-bow in greeting. "Señor."

Jake held his breath and focused all his attention on Ben as White made his introduction.

"I don't think you would've met Wells Fargo special agent Jake Hicken before."

Ben's movement stalled halfway into his bow, and behind him the woman inhaled sharply.

Figueroa straightened, wide-eyed. "Jake Hicken?"

Jake could only bring himself to nod.

"Then you *did* receive my letter."

His brow furrowed. "Of course I did. Why would you think I hadn't?"

"When I did not hear from you, I did not know what to think." He shrugged. "Perhaps the letter did not arrive, or. . .you did not wish to meet with me." Sadness crept across his face.

Confusion blanketed his thoughts. "I responded to you. Sent a telegram two or three weeks ago, said exactly when I'd be coming. When to expect me."

Figueroa's lips parted slightly. "Forgive me. I did not receive this correspondence. I was not aware of your arrival."

Was the man lying? If he never received the telegram, how had Jake's half brothers known to rob the train he'd be on? Hadn't Mattie overheard—

"You must excuse my rudeness." Ben drew the dark-haired woman into the circle. "This is my wife, Lupe. If I had known that you were coming, I would have been sure that our sons were here as well. Unfortunately, they are all away at school. They attend Santa Clara College in San Jose."

San Jose. Hadn't one of the train passengers said the two robbers boarded there? He would have to check his mug book to be sure, but that rang a bell.

As the men extended greetings to Lupe Figueroa, Ben looked toward Mattie and the kids. "And are these your wife and children?"

"I haven't married." *Yet.* He beckoned the three over from where they stood. "They're new friends from the train ride yesterday."

Mattie grinned shyly as Jake made room in the circle for them.

"Mattie Welling, Derry Beglin, and Augustina Garza, this is Benicio and Lupe Figueroa." Jake hesitated. "My *father* and his wife."

After a momentary silence, Mattie broadened her smile. "A pleasure to meet you both."

Benicio greeted them each personally, taking a moment to speak to Augustina in Spanish. Mattie made no claims to understand the language, though she did understand *bonita.* Pretty. By the way the girl beamed, Mattie guessed she'd been given a compliment.

Sheriff White cleared his throat. "Speaking of the train, Señor

Figueroa, were you aware there was a robbery on board yesterday's train?"

"I did not know this."

"Happened between the Pajaro and Salinas stops."

Lupe stood dutifully beside her husband, though her throat worked up and down several times.

"You were on this train?" Benicio looked at Jake then Mattie.

He nodded. "Miss Welling and her children were passengers. . ."

Thank God. He hadn't called her a stowaway.

". . .and I was helping guard the Wells Fargo shipment that was stolen."

White continued. "The thieves blew the iron safe with enough dynamite to about tear the car in two. The guards inside were both killed."

Lupe clasped her hands so tightly, her knuckles blanched. "It sounds dreadful. Why do you tell us this story?"

"Because I've had to arrest several of your sons for the two murders, robbery, and kidnapping."

Silence filled the air before Benicio shook his head. "This cannot be. I told you. My sons are away at school in San Jose."

Lupe's eyes flashed as she looked at the lawman. "You lie, Sheriff. *Mis hijos* do nothing wrong."

As Lupe shifted toward Jake, Mattie backed up a step, herding Derry and Augustina away from the tension.

"And you." She jabbed a finger toward his injured shoulder.

Instinctively, Mattie batted the woman's hand away before she could connect. Lupe glared but, undeterred, focused again on Jake.

"You say you ride the train to guard the money. How is it *you* do not die in the dynamite blast? What lies are *you* telling?"

"Lupe! What are you saying?" Thrusting his arm out, Benicio blocked his wife from coming any closer.

Jake glanced over his shoulder. "Stay back, Mattie," he hissed.

Heart pounding, she returned to the children.

"We should be thanking God Almighty for my son's safety, no?" Benicio turned to the lawman. "Do not listen to her. She is distraught. She doesn't not know what she says, señor!"

"Everyone calm down!" The sheriff nearly bellowed the words. "Quiet!"

An uneasy silence fell. As White let it linger, Benicio mopped sweat from his brow while his wife only glared.

"I'm real sorry to have to deliver such a blow to you both. I'm even sorrier to say that, as Hicken pointed out to me, it's a mighty big coincidence that your four sons would rob the exact train Hicken said he'd be coming in on."

"But they have not done anything like this before. They are good boys! And how could they have known when he was coming if they are in San Jose?"

"That's why I'm here." Sheriff White exhaled. "I know your sons attend college out of town, but Jake assures me you were the only one he sent word to about his plans. That means there's a connection back to you. I'd like for you to come into town where we can talk."

Benicio's shoulders slumped, and he swayed a bit. "If this is what you need to clear my sons' names, then I will come." He pinned Sheriff White with a firm look. "But I say again, I did not receive the message."

"Are you normally the one to handle your household's affairs?" Jake asked in a gentle tone.

"Of course. It is a man's job."

"I understand." Jake nodded. "But I understand you've been sick."

"Sí. My heart grows weak." He laid a palm across his chest. "It is why I ask you to come. I did not want to die without meeting my other son."

Beside Mattie, Jake shifted awkwardly. Whether from his injured hip or something else, she couldn't tell.

After a momentary silence, he pressed on. "How long have you been recuperating?"

Benicio shrugged. "It has been only a few weeks since I have been back to some of my duties. Perhaps half my normal effort."

"During that time, who managed your household affairs? Picking up mail or messages, paying bills, buying supplies."

His cheeks reddened. "With all of our sons gone, Lupe had to step—" He swung to face his wife. "Did you receive the message of his arrival?"

Lupe's face turned stony, and her palm connected with Benicio's cheek. "Sí! And I kept it from you. Happily. I have endured twenty-four years of marriage to you, and I will not let you steal away any of the money I am owed for that union. Nor will I let you steal away any part of my sons' inheritances, you vile, wretched—"

"They are my sons too!" Benicio bellowed. "And you corrupted them. You put them up to robbery and murder. Why? For money? I have long known you do not love me, but I hoped you knew me. That you trusted me. If you did, you would know I would not leave my sons without." He looked at Jake. "Not any of them."

As Sheriff White took Lupe in hand, Benicio rocked backward a single, stumbling step then heaved a breath.

Mattie rushed to his side and guided him to a nearby chair. "Sit, sir. Please."

Benicio collapsed into the chair, his gaze distant as he rubbed at his chest.

"Jake!"

Feet away, Jake shifted from watching the sheriff and Tom tie Lupe's hands and lurched into motion. Limping to them, he pulled two chairs over.

"Are you all right?" he asked Benicio.

"The sheriff said he has *several* of my sons. Who does he have, and where are the rest of my boys?"

Settling his elbows on his knees, Jake took one of Benicio's hands between his own. "He has your three youngest in jail."

Sorrowful eyes turned on them. "And Javier?"

When all Jake could muster was a silent shake of his head, Mattie settled on the corner of his chair and pulled him into her arms. "I am so sorry."

The man sobbed.

Epilogue

Two months later

Late afternoon sunlight fell on the Figueroa vineyard, casting a golden glow on the plants. Mattie had grown to love that time of day when the sun lit the acres of vines in one last explosion of color before nightfall.

In one of the nearest rows, Benicio walked beside Derry, the two talking in what appeared to be some depth. The young man had taken a shine to Jake's father in the months since they'd met, and it seemed to be a healing experience for Benicio to have a boy on the cusp of manhood to mentor. Ben's influence had calmed Derry, toned down his cantankerous nature, allowing Jake to befriend him on a deeper level as well.

As the two walked among the grapes, Moira and Patrick darted out from the next row. Her heart lurched. What in heaven's name were they doing playing out there *now*?

"Sam? Owen?" She stepped out from behind the courtyard gate.

The two boys stood not far from where the children played. "Yes, Miss Mattie?"

"Why have you taken the littles out where they can get dirty? I don't want them playing out there right now. Jake and I are getting married as soon as he returns, and I'd like everyone clean."

"We got eyes on 'em," Owen called back.

"No, bring them inside, please. I want them to stay clean until—"

Off in the distance, movement flashed, and Mattie's heart fluttered as a buggy turned down the winding path.

"They are here!" Augustina shouted from inside the courtyard where she'd been reading while Fiona and Ann played with their dolls. The three burst out into the yard to wait beside Mattie. The rest filtered up from among the rows of grapes to join them.

Mattie's heart raced as Jake drew the buggy to a stop only feet from them and climbed down, hurrying around to their side of the conveyance.

On the front seat, Dodie Hicken grinned at them.

"Aren't you all pretty!" she declared as Jake offered her his hand. She climbed down, and for one dumbstruck moment, no one spoke.

"Ma, this is Mattie Welling. Mattie, my mother, Dodie Hicken."

She offered the woman a broad smile. "It's so nice to finally meet you. Jake's told me much about you."

"I could say the same about you."

From there, Jake went down the line, starting with Derry, and introduced each child by age. When he finally reached Patrick, Dodie returned to her and cupped Mattie's cheek. "On the train ride down, he told me what a big heart you have. I see now what he means. You all will make a beautiful family."

Dodie pulled her into a warm embrace, and a knot swelled in Mattie's throat. The warmth, the genuineness, the unabashed acceptance reminded her so much of her own mother, what little she could remember from so many years ago.

Lord, You have blessed me. Thank You.

The woman released her, and casting a glance around at the faces, she turned back to Jake. "Where is Ben?"

Jake peered around the group, then craning his neck to see over the courtyard wall, he smiled tenderly. "He's sitting inside. We'll give you two a moment, if you'd like." Jake opened the gate for her.

Mattie couldn't pull her gaze away from the scene as Dodie quietly approached Ben. Not only was it her first time meeting Jake's mother, but it was the first his parents had seen each other in twenty-five years. Their reunion might take a bit of time—and it deserved its privacy. Turning, she glanced around for the preacher but realized that not only had Reverend Stanton climbed from the back seat of the buggy but so had Judge Abel Pierce.

Mattie slipped into Jake's arms. "Don't we need just one of them to get married?" She grinned.

"To get married, yes. Just a preacher. But I figured while we were getting hitched, it would be a perfect time to make these kids officially ours together, and for that, we need both."

Her lips parted, and the telltale sting of tears burned her lower lids.

Jake shook his head. "No crying. Not today." He planted a gentle kiss on her forehead.

"That's not fair, Jake." She brushed away the tears then held him a little closer. "By the end of tonight, I'll be a wife *and* a mother. I'll be living in this wonderful place that Owlie and I dreamed of for so long." She glanced back into the courtyard where Ben and Dodie also stood in what appeared to be an intimate embrace. "And I'll have a mother and father again. You can't give a woman everything she wants and expect her *not* to be emotional."

He looked at her in all seriousness. "Is it too much all at once?

Do we need to slow down?"

She grinned. "Not on your life. Just don't be surprised if a few happy tears are shed—and not just by me."

"All right then. We *must* have a few handkerchiefs around here. . ."

She couldn't help giggling but quickly sobered and stood on her tiptoes. Brushing her lips against his, she lingered there a moment before pulling back to meet his eyes. "I love you, Jake Hicken."

An odd look came over him. "About that. . ." He left the words hanging.

Her heart stalled. "About what? Me loving you?"

"No. The Jake Hicken part." He cleared his throat softly. "Ben asked me a few days ago if I'd consider taking his name. What do you think?"

Her smile broadened. "I think that while we've got a judge here, we ought to make that happen."

"You do?"

"Yes." This time, gripping his suit coat's lapels, she tugged him down to her. Tipping her face toward his, she hovered near his lips. "I do."

His lips curved into a broad smile, and he kissed her again, much more soundly this time. Warmth flowed through her, and she sank into his embrace.

When he finally broke the kiss, he pulled her head against his chest and held her tight. "I love you too, Mattie Welling, soon to be Mattie Figueroa."

Jennifer Uhlarik discovered the western genre as a preteen, when she swiped the only "horse" book she found on her older brother's bookshelf. A new love was born. Across the next ten years, she devoured Louis L'Amour westerns and fell in love with the genre. While at the University of Tampa, she began penning her own story of the Old West. Armed with a BA in writing, she has won five writing competitions and was a finalist in two others. In addition to writing, she has held jobs as a private business owner, a schoolteacher, a marketing director, and her favorite—a full-time homemaker. Jennifer is active in American Christian Fiction Writers and is a lifetime member of the Florida Writers Association. She lives near Tampa, Florida, with her husband, teenage son, and four fur children.

THE SECONDHAND
BRIDE OF POLECAT CREEK

by Kathleen Y'Barbo

*And the L*ORD *shall guide thee continually, and satisfy thy soul in drought, and make fat thy bones: and thou shalt be like a watered garden, and like a spring of water, whose waters fail not.*

ISAIAH 58:11

Chapter 1

Polecat Creek, Texas
Friday, April 25, 1890

Abigail Cooper might have been born beautiful, but Lizzie was born smart. She cast a glance across the counter of Cooper Mercantile to catch her younger sister once again primping in the mirror over in the men's hats department.

"Keep that up and you'll crack the glass," she called.

In response, Abby stuck out her tongue.

"Girls," her father called from upstairs. "Must you continue to behave as if you're still children?"

"Sorry, Papa," Abby said in that sweet tone she reserved for Papa. "Lizzie is just jealous again."

"Of you?" She snorted in a most unladylike fashion. "That would require me actually wanting to be anything like you. Which I do not."

Not completely true. She might have enjoyed knowing what it was to have allowances made for any deficiencies or transgressions just because your eyes were such a pretty shade of blue, your hair curled just so, and your smile apparently caused perfectly normal

119

males to act the fool.

But of these things, Lizzie had no idea. Nor, she tried to convince herself, did it matter that she didn't.

While the younger Cooper sister had been the center of attention practically since birth, Lizzie had happily enjoyed the anonymity that remaining in the shadows allowed. Of course, in a town like Polecat Creek, it was nearly impossible to find someone who did not know who she was, but every single one of them knew her as Abigail's sister.

And that was all right.

She had other plans. Another purpose other than stealing any glory from her sister or fending off the attentions of men.

Indeed, Lizzie would soon be leaving Polecat Creek behind and the mercantile where she'd been born and raised. Again. And this time for good.

Though she loved this town, it just was not where she was meant to be. Unlike her parents, who had loved tiny Polecat Creek and chosen to make their lives here, she had been born to this place but had never felt tied to it.

She had already responded to Mr. Ludlow to tell him she would be pleased to accept his offer of employment, and requested thirty days from the date he received the letter in which to arrange her return to Galveston.

Now all she had to do was make sure Abigail didn't leave first.

The bell over the door jangled, and she looked up in hopes it was him. The one she had pinned her hopes onto.

It wasn't.

Lizzie sighed and went back to her work while Abigail charmed a pair of cowboys into purchasing new hats to go with the boots they didn't need. By the time the men were done shopping, she'd outfitted them in enough clothes to last a lifetime.

Yes, Abigail was good at what she did. And what she did was make money for the mercantile. Of course she was the one who should remain behind.

Just yesterday Lizzie had received a letter from Mr. Ludlow at the telephone company, welcoming her to return to Galveston and resume her employment as a telephone operator as soon as possible. The company was expanding again, the need for new hello girls, as they were called, was urgent, and Lizzie was the one employee he regretted losing though he understood her need to leave back in December to care for her parents.

The letter had given Lizzie hope that she would soon return to the life she had lived before. At the same time, his use of the word *urgent* had both caused her to worry that her plan wouldn't work as quickly as she needed it to and to congratulate herself on coming up with such a brilliant plan at all.

Abigail's sparkling laugh followed the cowboys out the door. As soon as the door shut behind the men, however, her sister's usual surly expression returned.

"Why are they all so stupid?" the younger Cooper sister asked as she sashayed toward Lizzie. "I could've sold them twice what they walked out with, but I got tired of talking to them."

This she said at a whisper. Abigail wouldn't dare let Papa hear her admit she hadn't done her best in selling to the customers.

The regulator clock in the small office situated in the back room chimed twice, reminding Lizzie that she had missed her lunch. Though it was a simple matter just to make a sandwich from the remains of last night's ham and the bread Abigail had made the day before, going upstairs to the kitchen would likely mean Papa would want to continue the discussion that began over the breakfast table.

Lizzie had no intention of returning to the topic of her lack of a husband. Thus, she cast a backward glance at her sister on her way out the door.

"I won't be long," was the only explanation she offered.

If Abigail heard, she gave no indication. At least not before the door slammed shut.

Lizzie set out across the street, picking her way around the muddy mess that was Polecat Creek's main street. The weather was warm for late April, and the sun felt good on her face after too many hours spent indoors.

Her options for a late lunch were limited to whatever was left over from the lunch crowd at Ruby's Café or whatever she could find remaining among the selection of smoked sandwich meats at the butcher shop. Not much of a choice.

Horace Martin, the town's only butcher, was on her father's preferred list of husbands. Lizzie therefore veered to the right once she arrived on the opposite side of the road and headed toward Ruby's Café.

The screen door protested with a loud squeal as she opened it and then slammed with a loud thud after she stepped inside. Though the lunch rush was long ago over, the scent of pot roast—the Friday special—lingered in the air.

Lizzie glanced around and spied two of the two dozen tables still occupied. One of the tables was filled with the same cowboys who'd just bought half the mercantile from Abigail, and the other contained two of the biggest gossips in town.

Miss Nellie Anderson looked up from her conversation with her lunch companion and grinned. Erma Bright, known as Widow Bright as long as Lizzie could remember, swiveled in her seat and waved.

Every Wednesday and Friday, the two women came together for lunch and an update on the town. There was an unsubstantiated rumor that their twice-weekly meals were paid for by Junior Gibbons at the *Polecat Creek Gazette*. Whether that was true or not, the fact was the *Gazette* came out on Thursdays and Saturdays, which gave Junior enough time to transcribe his notes and turn rumors into published articles.

Today Junior wasn't at his table beside the pyramids. Unusual, for Lizzie could set her clock by the reporter's ritual of locking the door at the newspaper office next to the mercantile and crossing the street to Ruby's place just as the clock over the city hall struck the quarter hour before noon.

Eager to add a touch of class to what had been a rundown dining establishment before she took ownership, Ruby Fuller had decorated the walls with paintings of famous landmarks from all over the world. Thus, to Lizzie's right was a small watercolor of the Acropolis situated beside an oversized painting of the Sphinx.

Lizzie returned the greetings just as Ruby appeared from the back. "Sit down over by the Eiffel Tower, Lizzie. Pot roast is all we've got left, so that'll have to do. And a coffee too?"

"Yes, thank you," she told her host. "If it tastes as good as it smells, I'm happy to have it. Where's Junior?"

"Went to check on a two-headed calf that was born out on the Plager farm. He made sure to tell me not to hold his table today." She nodded to the two widows. "I hope he doesn't expect me to take notes for him."

"You poor dear," Miss Nellie called as if she'd known they were talking about her. "Are you here alone, Elizabeth?"

Ignoring the instant attention that question drew from the cowboys seated beneath Buckingham Palace, Lizzie nodded. "I am."

"Come and sit with us, dear," Widow Bright said.

"Yes, please do," Miss Nellie agreed. "I've been meaning to pay your daddy a visit. I understand he's feeling poorly." She made a *tsk-tsk* sound to emphasize her concern.

"Your dear mama is sorely missed right now, I'm sure," Widow Bright offered with a shake of her head. "I know the heavy burden of loss, and I confess I too am guilty of ignoring my social duty to come and pay my respects."

Considering they'd lost Mama six weeks ago come Thursday, it seemed unlikely that either of these women were too concerned about her father. However, Abigail had told her she'd overheard a conversation two Wednesdays ago at the church social whereby these same two ladies along with several more were discussing the alarming dearth of bachelors of a certain age in Polecat Creek.

When Papa's name was mentioned, Abigail's ears perked up. The consensus among the old biddies was that not a one of them wanted to take over the running of a mercantile that was on its way to ruin.

Lizzie let out a long breath and managed a smile. She didn't blame them a bit. If her father hadn't taken up residence upstairs and refused to come down since Mama died, she would be avoiding the man too.

The two of them had never quite seen eye to eye. Mama used to say it was because they were too much alike, but Lizzie knew it was because she was the complete opposite in almost every way of his dear, sweet, favorite daughter, Abigail.

Though the thought of joining these two was high on her list of things to avoid, neither did she want to take her lunch back over to the mercantile. So she sat, carefully choosing a spot where she could watch the door and the goings-on in the street rather than be a captive audience to the women's dialogue.

"I'm so glad we got to see you, Elizabeth," Widow Bright said. "Your mother certainly did miss you once you went off to work for the telephone company." She paused to shrug. "Not that she would ever have told you, I'm sure. She was so proud when you got that position in Galveston. Imagine, she would say to us at choir practice, my little girl all grown up and working with the telephone company."

"She was proud indeed," Miss Nellie said. "But she worried."

"Oh yes, she did," her companion echoed. "Vivian imagined you would never find a man, what with your insistence on being a working woman. And your sister, well, she worried that Abigail wouldn't stop finding men."

A disturbance went up from the table of cowboys, something about which of them the pretty girl at the mercantile had preferred. "Too late for the rest of you," the dark-haired fellow bragged. "I claimed her and I'll win her."

"She said the same to me," another said. "And I'll win her if I want to. Just haven't decided if I do."

"Just being polite, she was," the first man declared. "She's mine, and I will fight the first man who tries to take her from me."

While the argument about her sister and her flirting was poorly timed on the one hand, on the other it did serve as a distraction and a reason for Lizzie not to have to answer either of these women.

Ruby stepped out of the kitchen with a plate in one hand and a cup of coffee in the other. She gave the cowboys a harsh look. "That'll be enough," she told them, and quick as that, the rowdy men were tamed. "Whatever she told you, she says that to all the men who shop the mercantile. Nice hats, gentlemen. Now remember your manners and take them off while you're at the table."

She delivered the plate of pot roast, thick with gravy covering the meat, potatoes, and carrots, and then stepped back to regard the trio. "Ladies, will you be having another round of coffee?" she asked the other two. "Or were you planning on getting home before supper, seeing as you've been here since noon?"

"Just a smidge," Miss Nellie said.

"Two smidges for me," Widow Bright said.

"Three smidges it is." Ruby walked away shaking her head and returned with the coffeepot. Ignoring the women's requests, she filled each cup to the top and then turned and disappeared back into the kitchen.

Lizzie took a bite of roast and savored it. Then another. Oh, this was delicious. And eating kept her from talking, which meant these two had to talk to each other.

Which they did, at least for a few minutes.

Until Miss Nellie fixed her with a smile.

"You know what I'm going to do?" Miss Nellie exclaimed after a sip of hot coffee. "I'm going to pray the Lord brings you someone to help out over at that store. Goodness knows your sister would rather look at herself in the mirror than do anything useful, and your poor father is just overcome with grief, of this I am certain."

"Isn't there a Wyatt boy who might be a good candidate?" Widow Bright asked. "They were always such nice young men." She paused. "Well, all but Ezekiel. He certainly didn't turn out like the rest, did he? I heard he was in prison."

"Oh no, silly," Miss Nellie said. "Remember? He's seeing to the family's ranching interests in Dallas. Almost as bad, though. I never did like Dallas." She looked over at Lizzie.

"You don't mind living in Dallas, do you?"

"I'm afraid Zeke has an interest in my sister, not me," Lizzie said before she thought better of it. "They have an understanding."

Two sets of eyes fixed on her. "Do tell," Miss Nellie demanded.

"It's an arrangement, of sorts," Lizzie said, knowing Abigail would be furious that her secret was out. That's what she got for leaving her letters where just anyone could see them. "They're to be married when he returns to Polecat Creek."

"They are?" Widow Bright said, her thin brows shooting skyward. "I wonder if your mother knew of this arrangement. I know

126

Pearl didn't, or she'd have mentioned it."

Pearl was wife to the eldest Wyatt, the Harvard-trained lawyer who split his time between Washington, DC, and the family's Polecat Creek Ranch not far from town. She and Lizzie had become fast friends ever since Miss Nellie had begun a diatribe, while standing over Mama's freshly dug grave, on Lizzie being a working woman with no time for her ailing mother.

Pearl had stepped in and said just the right thing to Miss Nellie, reminding her that Lizzie had given up that job to take care of her mother, and thus sealing the two of them in friendship forever. Unfortunately, Pearl and the children had joined her husband in Washington, DC, yesterday afternoon, so she was not here to hush up the gossip again. At least this time the topic was Abigail and not her. Still, the conversation grated on her.

Lizzie reached for her coffee cup and focused on the empty lot between the mercantile and the newspaper office. She'd always thought that would be a nice place to plant trees and a garden. Papa always did like to have his hands in the soil, or so he claimed, for she only ever saw him run the mercantile and lament the fact he hadn't been born a farmer.

Perhaps she'd speak to Junior about it, as he was the owner of the lot. Yes, once she'd returned to Galveston and had a little extra money, she would purchase the lot as a surprise for Papa. Perhaps a memorial garden to Mama would be the way to approach the matter.

"Elizabeth? Are you woolgathering?" Widow Bright asked.

Ignoring you wasn't a polite response. So she elected to answer, "I don't know whether Mama did or did not know about my sister's arrangement with Zeke Wyatt. That would be between her and Abigail, I suppose."

"Well, I doubt Vivian had any idea," Miss Nellie said. "Had she known, she certainly would have put a stop to it. That boy is trouble. Always has been."

So is Abigail, she longed to say. Instead, she remained silent, enjoyed her coffee, and planned out the garden across the street while the ladies talked about the man her sister would soon be marrying.

That is, if Lizzie had anything to do with it.

"You said he was seeing to his family's ranching interests?" Lizzie dropped casually into the conversation. "I wonder how he might be found. If Abigail were to be looking for him, that is."

Miss Nellie grinned. "Are you looking to play Cupid for your sister, Elizabeth?"

She was, but she would never admit this to either of these ladies. "I'm just curious. But if my sister were to want to find the man she loves, then what kind of sister would I be to not find out how to help her?" After a brief pause, Lizzie added, "Hypothetically, of course."

"Oh, of course," Miss Nellie said, nodding. "We understand about young love, don't we, Widow Bright?"

"Do we?" She shook her head. "Nellie, I've long forgotten what that was like."

"I'm sure the ranch has someone who collects mail," Miss Nellie said. "Perhaps your sister should write to her beau."

"I think she should, indeed." Lizzie finished her lunch and paid Ruby. When she left, the two old ladies were still sipping on their coffees, their conversation now moved on to other topics.

Lizzie, however, still had her mind firmly on that letter her sister would soon write. An idea occurred as she passed the telegraph office. Why send a letter when a telegram was so much faster?

Chapter 2

Polecat Creek, Texas
Friday, May 2, 1890

Lizzie shuffled the empty plates from the small table that served as their dining table to the sink. As was his practice since Mama died, Papa ate his breakfast in silence and then retreated behind his newspaper.

She missed the discussions they used to have. The spirited debates about anything and everything, and the stories he would tell of his childhood and theirs. The compliments on her cooking and the admonishments to Abigail to appreciate her sister more.

Lizzie had heard none of these things in far too long. Nor had Abigail joined them at the table in months.

Thus, nothing seemed out of the ordinary as she made her way downstairs to the mercantile. She found the store empty with no visible evidence that her sister had been here this morning.

"Abigail!" When only silence greeted her, Lizzie tried again. "Where are you, Abby?"

Again, there was no response.

Panic rose slowly but surely. "No," she whispered to the darkened space. "No, I will *not* be the one left here to take care of things. Not when a job is waiting for me in Galveston. Oh no, I absolutely *will not.*"

Her heart pounding and her mind reeling with the possibilities of where her sister might be, Lizzie turned to hurry back upstairs. If Papa heard her return, he gave no indication of it.

"Have you seen Abigail this morning?" she asked her father.

"No," he muttered without moving the paper to spare her a glance.

An inspection of Abigail's bed in the room they shared offered no clue other than to serve as a reminder that her sister did not value neatness when arranging her bedcovers. From the mess she left behind, it was impossible to tell whether Abigail had spent any time there at all last night.

She returned to the table. "She's not here," Lizzie told Papa. "Are you certain you haven't seen Abigail today?"

The paper lowered. Her father scowled. "Not since last night at supper. She'll turn up."

He returned to reading, signaling that his part of the conversation had ended. Lizzie opened her mouth to complain and then closed it again. Nothing she could say would draw Papa from his newspaper for more than another moment or two.

Not even the possible disappearance of one of his daughters. Lizzie frowned. No, she wouldn't consider Abigail had gone. Not yet.

She couldn't.

A rattle and a slam from downstairs sent Lizzie scurrying down to see what it was. She found her sister heading toward her through the store.

"I don't want to hear whatever speech you have prepared for me, Lizzie," she said. "I'm exhausted. You'll have to manage the store by yourself for a while. I need a nap."

"A nap?" She watched Abigail make her way up the stairs and then called after her. "It's not even half past seven. How is it possible that you need a nap?"

Abigail paused on the topmost stair tread and glanced over her shoulder. "It is possible, Lizzie. That's all I plan to say about that right now."

She turned and disappeared upstairs. If she spoke to Papa, Lizzie never heard it. Then a door closed, presumably to their bedchamber.

Anger washed over her. Lizzie traced her sister's path up the stairs and past their father. She threw open the door and found Abigail lying on her bed, her eyes already closed.

"Who is he?" she demanded.

Abigail rolled over onto her side to face the wall. "Go away, Lizzie."

She crossed her arms over her waist and fixed her sister with a look that told her exactly what she thought of the request. "Not until you tell me what you've been doing. Papa may not care to keep track of you, but as your sister, I care."

Her sister turned over to face her. "You care because you don't want to be stuck here in Polecat Creek running the mercantile any more than I do."

She glanced over her shoulder at their father. He hadn't moved. And yet surely he hadn't missed what Abigail said. Moving inside the room, Lizzie closed the door.

"Why did you do that?" Abigail asked.

"Papa will hear you."

"He might," she said, "but he won't care. He doesn't care about anything since Mama died. Not the store, and certainly not us."

"He just needs time to grieve. Then he will be his old self again," she said. "Once that happens, he will take over the store and we will both be free of the responsibility."

Even as she said the words, Lizzie knew they were made more of hopes than any sort of reality she actually believed would happen. The loss of Mama had sent Papa into a despair that even time would not remedy.

"You left once," Abigail said, the unmistakable tone of accusation thick in her voice. "Now you think I might leave first and ruin whatever escape you have planned."

Lizzie's expression must have given away how close to the truth Abigail was, for the younger Cooper sister laughed. Then her expression sobered.

"You'll be happy to know that I had a plan to leave too. Unfortunately, it failed, and here I am. So go open the store and do whatever it is you want to do to manage without me today."

What she *wanted* to do was scream in frustration, stomp her feet, and make a scene. What she *needed* to do was keep her wits about her and think carefully.

It was slightly possible that Zeke had returned, made plans with Abigail, and then let her down. She let out a long breath as she contemplated what she would say.

"Fine," she finally said, her voice even. "I can do without you today, but don't make a habit of this." She paused just long enough to make her sister think she was leaving. "Oh, since we're talking about escaping, I hope your failed attempt did not involve Zeke Wyatt."

Abigail sat bolt upright. "Why do you say that?"

Lizzie lifted one shoulder in a casual shrug as she rested her hand on the doorknob. "I heard he might be returning to Polecat Creek, and I figured the only reason he would come back would be for you. You two are engaged, aren't you?"

"Engaged?" Her laughter held no humor. "Hardly. Zeke had

nothing to offer me when he left, so he wouldn't commit to anything so serious as an engagement. That is exactly what he said to me. Can you feature it? 'I won't marry you because I don't deserve you'?"

She sighed. Actually, she could.

"I think that's very honorable," Lizzie finally said. "So was it him?"

Abigail shook her head but said nothing further.

Lizzie moved back to settle on the edge of the bed next to Abigail's. "Zeke will be back. Why not wait for him?" She let the question settle between them a moment then continued. "Don't you love him?"

"Girls!" Papa shouted. "Door's opening downstairs, and neither of you are there to help customers. Finish your conversation behind the cash register before whoever's down there robs us blind."

"Well," Lizzie said, "I haven't heard Papa say that many words since Mama died. Maybe he's improving."

Abigail snorted and then rolled back over, dismissing Lizzie and the possibility of any improvement to either her or their father. Lizzie shook her head and went to the door to open it.

Striding past Papa, who was still reading his newspaper, Lizzie grabbed an apple from the sideboard and went downstairs to greet the first customer of the day. As her footsteps echoed on the stair treads, she lifted a prayer that the Lord would send help soon.

Help in the form of a man named Zeke Wyatt.

Every time the door opened, she hoped it would be him. Unfortunately, she was disappointed each time. With the apple serving as her lunch, Lizzie arrived at the end of the day too tired to complain about hunger.

The last weak rays of evening sunlight streamed through windowpanes that could use a good cleaning. Perhaps another day. She was too tired to take on the task tonight.

Apparently Abigail hadn't budged from the bed, for there was no evidence of a meal being prepared. Papa had moved his chair from the table to a spot by an open window in the corner of the room.

He looked back at her when she stepped into view, and she saw tears in his eyes. "I tried to talk her out of it," he said.

Lizzie hurried to his side and retrieved her handkerchief to dab at his wet cheeks. "Papa, what's wrong? What happened?"

His shoulders heaved. "She's gone."

Mama. Of course.

"Yes, Papa," she told him. "I miss her terribly, and I know you do too."

"No." He shook his head furiously. "Your sister. She's gone."

"That's impossible," Lizzie said as her heart lurched. "I've been downstairs all day, and she never came downstairs. I would have seen her if she had, whether she'd left through the front door or the back."

"Abigail climbed out the window." He gestured to the open window. "He was waiting down there on the sidewalk for her. She scampered down and met up with him, and then off they went. I sat right here and watched them walk down the street until they got to the train station. I'm sure they're gone by now."

"Who did she leave with?" Lizzie asked, not knowing whether to panic or celebrate. "Was it Zeke Wyatt?"

Her father looked up sharply. "Wyatt? No. Wasn't none of those boys. I'd know them. This one was a stranger. Cowboy-looking fellow, but he sure did have on a smart hat and a new suit of clothes. I believe we've sold both in our store. Perhaps he got them from us."

"I'm sure he did," she said bitterly, her mind reeling. "Did he happen to have dark hair?"

"He did," Papa said. "Why? Do you know him?"

"No," she said with what breath she had left. "I don't."

Lizzie sank down on the nearest chair and tried to focus. Tried to breathe. Tried to think. Then tried not to think.

She would find Abigail. Yes.

Papa looked over at her and smiled. "I don't know what I would do without you, Elizabeth. Your mother would be so proud of you."

"No," she said softly, "she wouldn't. Not at all."

⌒

Monday, May 5, 1890

Four days after he made a safe exit from the Dallas County Courthouse, Zeke stepped off the train in Polecat Creek. Unlike the day he left town almost six months ago, there was no one waiting at the station for him. No one to watch as he hoisted his bag over his shoulder and walked away.

He might have had any number of relatives there to greet him, but Zeke preferred to make a quieter return. Had he told any one of his brothers of his imminent arrival, there would have been a party.

And then questions.

He wanted neither. Not until he'd achieved what he came here to do.

Zeke patted the pocket where he'd stowed the telegram to remind himself he wouldn't be catching Abigail by surprise. Then he tucked his hat low on his head and stepped out of the station with his destination in full view a few blocks away.

The streets were nearly empty at this early hour. Exactly why he'd chosen the morning train and not the one that arrived mid-afternoon. Though there was no reason for it, Zeke stuttered to a stop.

The plan that had formed in the courtroom just a few days ago was just one question away from being complete. All he had to do was follow the sidewalk to Cooper Mercantile, step inside, and ask Abigail Cooper to be his wife.

Nothing to it, especially since she'd gone to the trouble of sending him a telegram to let him know he ought to do just that, and quickly.

He took a deep breath and let it out slowly. Until that moment, marriage to Abigail Cooper had seemed like the perfect solution to a problem he ought not have had. After all, hadn't he gone off to prove himself worthy of becoming her husband?

Why the hesitation now? Was marrying Abigail to keep himself out of jail the right thing to do?

Now that that very thing was so close to happening, it did not seem so right after all. In fact, marrying Abigail now seemed. . .

Yeah, it seemed wrong.

Like he was using her as a means to a more favorable end for himself rather than walking into town to claim a bride he was ready to marry. Which was exactly what he was doing.

Someone grabbed his shoulder, and instinct kicked in. Zeke whirled around, ready to punch the offender, only to find his brother Eli standing there with a grin as big as Texas.

The middle child of the five Wyatt boys—now men—Eli had been the one to patiently allow Zeke to follow him everywhere he went. The one he'd looked up to from childhood.

Though he'd long ago stopped being Eli's shadow, Zeke had missed this brother the most when he'd gone off to the ranch in north Texas. He had also relied on Eli's wisdom and the letters they'd sent back and forth when he was tempted to give up and give in to the belief that he was the black sheep of the Wyatt family.

The only thing he hadn't told Eli about was the hot water he'd gotten into with Evelyn. Looking at him now, he wondered why that was, and immediately knew it was because taking up with a woman like her had been exactly what Eli had warned him about.

"You attract the wrong sort most of the time," Eli had told him. "Guard your heart and save it for the one you love."

And now here he was. And here was Eli. Right again.

Chapter 3

"Welcome home, Z," Eli said with a grin.

"How'd you know I was coming?"

His brother shook his head. "I didn't. Which means you didn't tell anyone. Which also means you've got a reason for not telling anyone." He paused. "So what's wrong? Are you running from the law or someone else?"

Several responses came to mind. He decided to go with the most truthful. "Neither yet."

Eli laughed but sobered quickly when he saw Zeke hadn't joined him. "What did you do?"

"The real question is what did I not do," he said, studying his boots before meeting his brother's gaze once more. "And that's complicated. It's also the result of me not heeding your advice."

"Okay, how can I help then?"

Of all his brothers, Eli was always the most perceptive and the first to step in and offer help. He was also the last to rush to judgment about anything or anyone, a worthy talent when it came to dealing with Zeke and his escapades over the years.

"I don't know," Zeke said. "Probably the best thing right now would be to forget you saw me here in town."

Eli shook his head. "Can't do that. What else?"

"Just like that?"

"Just like that."

"Okay." Zeke let out a long breath. "Look," he said as he glanced to the right and left before returning his attention to his brother. "We can't talk here. The fewer people who know I'm back, the better, at least for now."

"It's a small town, brother," Eli said. "I don't think you can keep yourself hidden for long."

"I know, but I could use your advice before I let anyone know I'm here." He shrugged. "Or before I leave without anyone finding out. I haven't decided which it will be."

Eli nodded to the building beside the train station where Deacon ran his law office when he wasn't running other things up in Washington, DC. "I have the key. Let's go."

A few minutes later, they were standing in the eldest Wyatt brother's office. Though the morning air outside was crisp, it was downright cold in here. Eli went to the business of laying a fire in the fireplace. Zeke dropped his bag at the door and then stayed out of his brother's way while he took in the surroundings.

Fancy by Polecat Creek standards, the room was sparsely furnished with their father's wooden desk that had been out at the ranch until recent years, along with the two red upholstered chairs that had to have been contributed by Pearl, Deacon's wife.

Over the fireplace opposite the desk was a white flag with the image of a cannon, which Pa always claimed had flown over the battlefield at Gonzales back in 1835. Whether it was true or not, the flag was old, frayed at the edges, not much to look at, and yet well loved all the same.

Pa said it reminded him of himself. Zeke couldn't understand at the time, but he was beginning to now.

With the fire now warming the room nicely, Eli took a seat in one of the chairs by the fireplace and waited for Zeke to join him. Rather than sit, he placed both hands on the back of the empty chair and thought about what he wanted to say.

"I really stepped in it, Eli," he finally admitted. "I got myself in a fix up in Dallas."

"Then why are you here?" his brother asked. "Doesn't seem like coming here will fix something you did in north Texas."

"Oh, but it will." He shrugged. "I just don't know if I can go through with it."

"Pace or sit down, but spill it, little brother. Start at the beginning."

Zeke walked over to the window and looked out. A few more citizens were out and about now, but the sun still hadn't climbed high enough on the horizon to remove the purple nighttime shadows and illuminate their faces.

"It all started with good intentions," he told Eli. "A young lady by the name of Evelyn Prince ran flat into me on the sidewalk and nearly fell into a mud puddle. I saved her from the fall."

"So you did a good deed. That's commendable."

"I guess," he said with a shrug. "But that's where it should have ended, given the, well. . ." He paused before picking up the thread of his statement a moment later. "Given the arrangement I had—or have, rather—with Abigail Cooper."

He hadn't told a soul, not even Eli, about his promise to Abigail to return for her. Nor had he mentioned that he'd wanted to make something of himself so he could be worthy of a woman like her.

So Zeke let that hang in the air between them for a minute. Eli nodded but said nothing.

"You knew?" Zeke asked, incredulous.

"I suspected," Eli said.

Zeke ducked his head. "All right, well, I guess I should have told you, but she and I had this agreement that we wouldn't say anything." He looked up. "That woman Evelyn? She set after me hard. Every time I came to town on an errand for the ranch, there she was. After a while I seriously wondered if she had lookouts posted at the edge of town. And I'm willing to admit I enjoyed the attention."

"You always were plagued by charm." Eli shrugged. "It's what you do with that charm that matters."

"I paid her more attention that I ought to have," he admitted, "and I didn't tell her about my arrangement with Abigail until it was too late. By then she was in love with me and determined we ought to get married. When I told her that wouldn't happen because there was someone else, she didn't take it too well."

"No woman would," Eli said.

"No, that's true. I never sought her out, but she was good company, and I hate to admit I enjoyed being with her."

"If that's the case, then maybe Abigail isn't the one for you." He shifted positions. "Have you considered that?"

"I have, actually. More so since I came back to marry her."

"Then don't marry her," Eli said. "Simple as that. She wouldn't want a husband with a divided heart anyway, would she?"

"I reckon not, which is probably why I'm having such a hard time just walking into the store and claiming Abigail for my bride." He turned to run his hand down the edge of his father's desk. "But if I don't present my wife to Judge Winslow in the Dallas County Courthouse in a little less than a month, he's going to throw me in jail."

"Why and for how long?"

Zeke's eyes narrowed. "You're pretty calm about this, Eli."

"I'm just trying to gather all the facts. And depending on why he's tossing you in jail and how long you'll be there, that sentence might be preferable to shackling yourself to someone you don't love for the rest of your life."

"The why of it is simple. When Evelyn demanded I marry her or else, I had no idea that her 'or else' involved a lawsuit for alienation of affection and fraud that would involve two other women I supposedly left at the altar in addition to her."

"So she's the one committing fraud," Eli said. "Tell the judge and be done with it."

"It isn't that simple," he said. "I might have led her on, though I didn't ever offer marriage. And I did spend a little time with one of the other two women she dragged into the case as coplaintiffs."

"Zeke, really? You did?"

"Just a little fun," he said. "Nothing that would make either of them believe I was in love with them. And I swear on my life I never met the brunette. I found out in court that her name is Matilda. Beyond that, she's a total stranger."

"That is complicated," Eli agreed. "So this Evelyn woman is essentially blackmailing you into marriage."

"She was, yes. But all three women had their fathers and their lawyers there, so there are a half dozen people besides them who are now part of things."

"I see. And none of the others realize there's blackmail involved?"

"The other two women do, else I don't think they would have become involved in the legal proceedings."

"So this woman Evelyn wants you bad enough to force you into marriage using blackmail. Could you be happy with her? It seems like that may be a solution."

"I'm sure she'd make me pay the rest of my life. Apparently

Daddy is a widower and pretty well off, so spoiling Evelyn was his favorite hobby. She told me she'd never heard the word *no* from anyone about something she wanted until she met me."

"Surely not."

"I thought she was joking. I believe it now." He paused. "I can't say any of that sounds like the makings of a happy marriage, but then showing up here and swooping Abigail off her feet only to tell her I'm doing it because the judge is making me doesn't bode well either."

"So here we are," Eli said.

Zeke moved over to the empty chair and sank into it. "Yes," he said on an exhale of breath. "Here we are."

"What are you going to do?" his brother asked.

Lifting one shoulder to shrug, Zeke turned his attention to the crackling fire. "I have no idea."

"How long is the jail sentence?"

He returned his attention to Eli. "I asked Judge Winslow that same question."

"And?"

"Best estimate of the sentence I could expect from him if I don't provide a bride in thirty days is that he would lock me up and throw away the key." He shrugged. "Maybe I deserve it. I sure don't deserve Abigail Cooper."

Eli's brows furrowed. "Why do you think that? She'd be lucky to marry into the Wyatt clan."

"The Wyatt clan, sure." He nodded up at the flag then gestured to the chair where Deacon sat when he was in town. Then he focused on Eli, who was the best man of them all in Zeke's estimation. "There are plenty of Wyatt men, past and present, who are worthy. I'm just not one of them."

"And you are the only Wyatt man who believes that." Eli held up his hand as if to ward off any protest from his younger brother. "I guess you heard Abigail's mother passed."

"No." His brow furrowed. "When?"

"Just about six weeks ago. I thought I wrote about it in my letters, but maybe I didn't."

"I would have remembered," Zeke told him. "Now I feel worse about just showing up to take her away."

"You're assuming she'll go," he said. "Her pa has been in a bad way. I don't take much stock in rumors, but if I did, I'd tell you that it's been said he hasn't come downstairs from their apartment above the store since they put his wife in the ground. What I do know is, the few times I've been in the mercantile, I've not seen him there. Just the girls."

"Girls?"

Eli nodded. "Her sister, Lizzie, came back a couple of months ago to help with the care of her mother and the running of the mercantile."

"I thought she had some sort of employment in Galveston." He paused. "I guess I figured once she left Polecat Creek, she wouldn't come back."

"Could be she thought that too, but situations change. When family needs you, it causes decisions to be made that might not be what you want but are what you need."

Zeke nodded. "I suppose so."

"I can see you're conflicted about what to do, Zeke. And you've told me as much. Between these women in Dallas and Abigail here in Polecat Creek, you've got more women in your life than you know what to do with. I guess I'd like to hear you say whose fault that is."

"Mine," he said quickly. "I own up to it, and I told the judge and those ladies as much. I'm the reason I am where I am. I won't shirk back from that responsibility."

"No, I didn't expect you would." He met Zeke's gaze. "You never have. In fact, I think you take on more than you ought to sometimes."

Zeke shifted positions. "Not this time."

A log shifted in the fireplace, and a shower of sparks drifted upward to disappear into the chimney. The fire crackled, filling the silence between them.

"If you say so." Eli shrugged. "What are you going to do?"

He thought a minute. "I ought to talk to Abigail about this, but I'm not sure I can. I know she wants me married to her, what with the telegram and all, but I can't figure out what's stopping me. It's certainly the obvious solution."

"Telegram?"

Zeke produced the telegram from his pocket and handed it to Eli. His brother took the paper, unfolded it, read it, and then folded it back again.

"Well?" Zeke finally said. "She's pretty clear there that she's put me on notice she's ready to be a bride."

"She is." He handed the telegram back to Zeke. "Only I'm wondering why she wrote that. If Abigail has been waiting six months, why now, especially when she's grieving her mother's death?"

"You're asking me to understand why a woman does something, Eli." He tucked the telegram back into his pocket and leaned forward to scrub his face with his hands. "Why in the world do you think I would be able to answer that?"

From somewhere behind him, the door flew open. Then came a squealing sound. Before Zeke could bolt from the chair, the heavens opened and he was caught in a torrential ice-cold downpour.

Only after he came to his senses did Zeke recall he was indoors and there was no reason he should be soaking wet and shivering. He jumped up and turned around.

There stood the reason.

And she was stunning.

"Zeke," Eli said slowly. "You remember Elizabeth Cooper, don't you?"

Lizzie Cooper? Abigail's sister. Not possible. The Lizzie he remembered wore her hair pulled back in a severe style and walked around looking like she'd just tasted something sour.

"Zeke?" his brother said again. "Are you all right?"

No. Not at all. But he didn't mind a bit.

Chapter 4

If Lizzie hadn't been too mortified to move, she might have run. Unfortunately, that thought didn't occur until it was far too late.

She stood very still and gave thanks there was a chair in the space between her and the poor man she had just drenched. Eli had made an introduction, but the words he said escaped her.

All she could do was stare at the fellow who had been on the receiving end of the bucket of water she'd thought would be used to put out the fire.

A fire in an office that was supposed to be empty.

But wasn't.

Lizzie's gaze landed on the man she'd soaked. Though he favored his brothers in the chiseled features and dark hair they all shared, this one had a way of looking at her that told her he was different than the others. Water dripped off dark curls that brushed his broad shoulders and sluiced down wet shirtsleeves plastered to muscled arms.

He crossed those arms over his chest and leveled her with an even look. Was that the beginning of a smile she saw? And a dimple?

The man she'd summoned on Abigail's behalf was standing in front of her. So close. So. . .handsome. So. . .soaking wet.

Lizzie cringed.

The men were staring at her, so Lizzie said the first thing that came to mind. "No one is supposed to be here."

As soon as the words were out, she cringed.

"No, you're right. Deacon and Pearl are in Washington, DC." Eli Wyatt picked up the wooden bucket she'd brought with her, the bucket that had flown out of her hands when her foot met whatever impediment had been placed in her way. "But that doesn't explain the water."

Embarrassment rose warm on her cheeks. "Fire," came out like the squeak of a mouse.

"Oh," Eli said. "You saw the smoke in the chimney and thought there was a fire." He looked at his brother. "See, it all makes sense, Zeke."

Zeke's gaze collided with hers. After what seemed like an eternity, he nodded to the fireplace. "Fire's over there."

"Yes," she said, her voice more nearly approximating something that sounded human.

"You missed," he continued, never breaking eye contact.

"Yes," she said again. "I tripped."

His eyes narrowed. Then they widened. "Left my bag by the door."

Lizzie looked down at her feet and then back at Zeke Wyatt. "Found it."

Eli walked over to stand beside his brother. "Do you have any dry clothes in that bag, Z?"

Zeke appeared not to have heard, his attention instead on Lizzie.

Though she should have looked away, she did not.

When the younger Wyatt did not respond, Eli tried again. "Dry clothes?" He nudged Zeke with his shoulder hard enough to knock him slightly off balance.

"In your bag," Eli added when Zeke jerked his attention in his direction. "The clothes you're currently wearing are wet, brother. You're probably cold—not that you've noticed."

When speaking to Zeke produced no result, Eli looked over at Lizzie. "Was there something else you needed here other than to put out a fire that didn't need putting out?"

His question jolted her into action. "No, I, that is—" She took a step backward and collided with the wall. "Nothing else. I'll just go now."

Somehow Lizzie managed to make it all the way out the door and onto the sidewalk without doing anything else to make herself look more foolish. She raced back to the mercantile as quickly as she could manage it and then fumbled with the key before finally letting herself inside.

Slamming the door behind her, she leaned against it and closed her eyes, her breath coming in short gasps. *What in the world is wrong with me?*

"What in the world is wrong with you?"

Eli's jab to his shoulder was strong enough to get his attention this time. Zeke shrugged away from his brother and then turned to face him.

"Why did you do that?"

His brother returned to his seat and looked up at him, grinning. "I repeat, what is wrong with you, Z? You've known Lizzie Cooper since you were a kid, but you just acted like a tongue-tied fool."

He shook off the comment and moved closer to the fire. "I'm just cold, that's all."

"Put on some dry clothes then we'll see if that's the cause of your behavior." Eli's grin rose. "My guess is that it isn't."

Zeke walked around the wet chair to find his bag where he'd left it just inside the door. "She tripped over it." He lifted the bag. "That's why Lizzie dumped water on me."

"I figured that out pretty early on. Guess it took you longer than me," he said with a wink. "But you were busy looking at other things that interested you. Or should I say a person who interested you?"

That got his attention. Zeke made quick work of changing clothes then draped his wet things over the chair. Moving to stand in front of the fire, he turned his back to Eli.

What had happened to him? He'd come back to ask Abigail Cooper to marry him and then found himself speechless in the presence of her sister.

Gradually the chill left him. He turned around to look down at Eli. "What am I going to do?"

Eli shrugged. "I don't think you're going to propose to Abigail Cooper, brother, that's for sure."

"No, you're right. I can't marry her, even if it keeps me out of jail."

"I'm glad that's settled. Now, what are you going to do about her sister?"

He shook his head. "I have no idea."

Eli rose to slap Zeke on the back. "Let's go home. We'll figure something out. And in the meantime, with Deacon gone, there are plenty of chores I'd be happy to share with you."

How long Lizzie remained leaning against the door, she couldn't say. By degrees, however, she became aware of the scent of bacon cooking.

Abigail. She was home.

Leaving the door unlatched in case early arriving customers came in, Lizzie hurried up the stairs.

"Abigail, you're back! I have the best news! You don't have to—" She stuttered to a stop and the top of the stairs when she spied her father at the stove, not her sister. "Papa, what are you doing?"

It was a miracle, to be sure. Not only did she not realize Papa knew how to cook, but she also hadn't seen him be interested in doing anything except read the paper and look out the window since Abigail left.

He glanced back over his shoulder at Lizzie. "I got hungry."

Another miracle. He'd also not been willing to eat much of anything.

"I didn't know you knew how to do that," she said as she moved to stand next to him.

"I didn't either until I tried."

Though the fire was a bit too hot for her liking, Papa had done a decent job of frying up four pieces of bacon without burning them beyond what was decent for eating. Now he had four more in the pan and was turning them way too soon.

"Would you like me to take over?" she asked, her fingers itching to take control of the meal preparation before he ruined this batch.

Papa gave her a kiss on the cheek. "You know, I used to have to fend for myself before I married your mother. I did pretty well, I think. And in my day, most of the meals were cooked outside on a campfire."

The bell jangled downstairs, indicating a customer had come in. Lizzie reached around to turn off the fire to the stove's burner. "Why don't you go ahead and have your breakfast? I'll come back up and finish cooking mine when I'm done with the customer."

He gave her a grateful look. "You don't mind?"

"Mind?" She shook her head. "Of course not. Now go enjoy your bacon and your newspaper. I'll be back as soon as I can."

Lizzie walked down to find a man shopping in the menswear department. She went over to the counter and stepped behind it to wait.

"Let me know if you need any help," she called after a few minutes.

"Actually, I do," a familiar voice said.

The man turned to walk toward her, and she recognized him immediately as the man she'd just doused with water. Heat returned to her cheeks.

"Well, I'm completely out of water, so I hope you don't have a fire," she said with a grin.

Zeke shrugged. "I think I can squeeze enough from my other set of clothes to put out a decent-sized blaze."

She ducked her head. "I'm so sorry. I don't think I told you that. Or maybe I did. I saw smoke coming out of the chimney, and it was too early for anyone to be in Deacon's office, plus I knew he and Pearl weren't in town. So I just, well, I did what I thought would help by grabbing a bucket of water from the livery."

Lizzie paused. "I was—am—just horribly embarrassed about the whole thing. If I hadn't tripped over your bag, I promise I wouldn't have spilled the water. I did realize once I stepped into the room that there was no fire."

"Don't be embarrassed." He rested his palms on the counter. "You were looking after my family's interests. I would have done the same thing under those circumstances. I assume you and Pearl are friends."

Lizzie nodded. "I haven't known Pearl long, but I like her very much."

"As do I." He grinned. "Did she tell you about the time my brothers and I—minus Deacon—kidnapped her during a train robbery?"

Her eyes widened as she tried to determine whether he was serious or not. "No," Lizzie said slowly, "I haven't heard about this."

"It's true, I promise. You can ask any of my other brothers. They were all in on it." He shrugged. "It all started with a bet that one of us could stop a train, and, well, it went downhill from there."

"You robbed a train though? And kidnapped Pearl?" Lizzie gave him a sideways look. "I don't believe it."

"I guess you'll just have to wait until Pearl can tell you her version. Let's just say we were all pretty embarrassed." He paused to grin. "And Deacon was furious."

"Are you trying to make me feel better?"

Zeke upped his smile. "Is it working?"

Lizzie matched his grin. "Maybe a little."

"Good, because I'm also looking for a few things, and since I know the owners, I may be asking for a discount."

She laughed. "Sorry, no discounts at Cooper Mercantile. Even family members pay full price."

"You drive a hard bargain, Lizzie Cooper," he said, "but I suppose that's fair. Now come show me where the men's footwear is. I'm in need of some new boots, and not just because mine are wet."

Lizzie walked over to the shoe department and then turned to face him. "Zeke, did you come to see my sister?"

His dark eyes searched her face. "No, I told you. I came to buy boots."

Time to press the subject. Lizzie let out a long breath and tried again.

"I don't mean right now. I mean in general." She gave him a direct look. "Zeke, did you return to Polecat Creek to marry my sister?"

He frowned. "You don't waste words, Lizzie Cooper."

"I try not to. Unless I've just dumped a bucket of water on someone. Then I'm not so good at speaking. Or thinking clearly." She eyed him with curiosity. "In case you're wondering why I asked, Abigail told me about your plans to marry."

"I figured she had." Zeke took a pair of brown boots off the shelf and examined them. "It'd be hard to ask me about it if she hadn't."

"Well, true."

"I like these." He held them out in her direction. "I'll need a hat too."

"Hey," she said, gathering the boots into her arms. "I didn't get your hat wet."

He grinned but said nothing further. Instead, he walked over to the hat department and stuck a Stetson on his head.

"Don't you want to try these on to see if they will fit?"

He glanced over at her, the hat cocked to one side on his head. "They look fine. What do you think of this one?"

She gave him an appraising look then walked over to retrieve one she expected might look better. "Try this," Lizzie said, handing him the black one.

Zeke did as she asked and then stepped back from the mirror to look at himself. "You're right. This is the one." He turned around to remove the hat from his head and balance it atop the boots in Lizzie's arms. "All right, ma'am. I'll take all of this."

Arms full, she stood firmly in place.

"Something wrong?" he asked.

"You didn't answer me." Lizzie shifted positions, and the hat slipped. Zeke caught it and returned the hat to the stack.

"I don't suppose I did." He paused. "Will you still sell me these things if I don't answer?"

"Probably." She thrust the stack toward him, and he grabbed it. "But I'll make you carry them."

Chapter 5

Lizzie turned around and walked back to the counter with Zeke following a step behind. He unloaded the boots and hat then let out a long breath. Time to get to the purpose for his shopping trip at Cooper Mercantile.

She was busy at the cash register and not paying him any attention when Zeke spoke. "What do you know about a telegram from Abigail asking me to come back here?"

"I sent it," she said without looking up.

That admission seemed to take the bluster out of her demeanor. She met his gaze.

"Not Abigail?"

"Unfortunately, no, so if you've come to marry my sister, you're too late. Abigail is gone."

Gone? His heart lurched. He knew her mother had passed, but Eli hadn't mentioned anything about Abigail. Maybe he didn't know.

"What happened?"

Lizzie shrugged. "She ran off with a cowboy a few days ago."

"Oh." Relief crossed his face. "I thought you meant she was gone. Like. . ." He shrugged. "You know. . .gone."

Her eyes widened. "No, nothing like that. I guess I should have been clearer."

Lizzie retrieved the receipt pad and tallied up the cost of the items. Then she tore the paper off and handed it to Zeke.

"I had a reason for sending that telegram that made sense at the time. It still does, in a way. But I owe you an apology for that too. I shouldn't have sent it." She met his gaze once again. "It was deceitful and wrong, and I regret it."

So his future bride was out of his future. Zeke let out a long breath, surprised to discover he felt relieved that this decision had been made for him. There was just one question that had to be asked.

"Why did you do it?"

"Selfishness," she told him. "I wanted to be sure she would stay here, so I thought if I could bring her intended home and cause him to marry her, then they would be the ones to stay here and run the store and take care of Papa."

"But that didn't work out." A statement, not a question, for obviously it hadn't. "So what's your plan now?"

"I don't have one," she admitted. "Although my father did seem to be doing better this morning."

"Not well enough to handle the store alone, I assume?" he said as he put the money on the counter between them.

The door opened to admit a young woman and her little boy. Lizzie bid them good morning then watched the pair make their way over to the housewares department before returning her attention to him.

"No," she said as she made change and gave it to him. "Not at all."

He tucked the money into his pocket. "Tell me about what you did in Galveston. My brother said you had employment there."

"Do you really want to know?" At his nod, she continued. "I was a hello girl for the telephone company. I accepted incoming calls and connected the caller with the person or business he or she requested to speak with."

"It sounds very technical. You must be smart, Lizzie."

"I enjoyed it and being in Galveston. I was hoping to return there soon," she sighed. "But the Lord has His plans, and apparently they are not the same as mine. So here I am. I am grateful my father is still with me, and anything else just sounds selfish."

Lizzie closed the cash register and offered him a smile. Unless he was mistaken, there was a sadness in her eyes that hadn't been there just a moment ago as she busied herself with returning her receipt book to its place beneath the counter.

He considered what she'd said. "Something tells me you have a chance to go back to Galveston but you're not taking it."

She looked up sharply. "What makes you think that?"

"Fire!" a child screamed from the back of the store.

"Oh no." Lizzie bolted around the counter and headed for the stairs with Zeke on her heels. "I turned that burner off and told him not to worry about cooking for me."

As he reached the stairs, he could see a haze of black smoke billowing from something that had to be a fire on the second floor. "Where did you get that bucket of water?" he demanded.

"The livery," she said. "But we've got water in our sink as well as behind the store."

"I don't think you can get to the sink," he said. "Is your father up there?"

"He is," she said as she continued toward the second floor.

"Go shout out a call to the fire brigade then get as many water buckets as you can carry and fill them from the pump behind the store. I'm going to see if I can find your father and bring him down to you."

Lizzie looked as if she might argue. Zeke shook his head.

"Listen to me. You cannot carry your father down these stairs. If he's been overcome by smoke, he wouldn't be able to walk down them. I'm the logical choice to go up there."

She appeared to consider the statement for just a moment and then raced back down. "Fire brigade first then fill the buckets," he shouted to her retreating back.

When she was gone, he turned around to face the billowing smoke. Crouching down, he made his way toward the source of the flames. It appeared something had been left on the stove.

Zeke found a quilt draped on the edge of a chair, folded it, then headed for the stove, trying hard not to breathe. The smoke stung his eyes, but he kept moving toward the amber flames.

When he'd come within reach of the stove, he used the quilt to beat back the fire. After what seemed like an eternity, the flames disappeared.

With all the smoke still hanging in the air, it was impossible to tell whether the fire was out or just temporarily beaten back. Thus, he knew he had to hurry and find Mr. Cooper.

Zeke dropped to his knees and crawled beneath the thick layer of smoke as he called out to Lizzie's father. "Mr. Cooper, where are you?"

No response. He tried again.

Then he heard coughing and made his way toward it. He found an elderly man curled up in the corner of a small bedroom, clutching an old tintype photograph of a woman.

"Had to save this," Mr. Cooper told Zeke when Zeke spied him crawling in his direction. "Then I got lost and couldn't find my way out."

"I'll get you out," he said. "Is there a fire escape up here or another exit we can use?"

"Just the stairs down to the store," he said. "That's all we have."

"Then that's how we'll get down." He offered his hand to Mr. Cooper, and the old man took it. "Hang on tight, stay low, and don't let go."

They got as far as the kitchen when a roar went up from the vicinity of the stove. Whatever he'd managed to beat back had returned with a vengeance. If that fire was being fed by a gas line, their time was seriously limited before the whole place went up.

He yanked on Mr. Cooper's hand. "Sorry, sir," he said when the old man yelped in pain, "but I've got to get you out of here."

They made it almost to the stairs when coughing overtook Zeke. Ignoring it as best he could, he hauled Mr. Cooper toward the exit with the flames climbing up the wall behind them.

"Get out," he shouted when Lizzie's face came into view. "I've got him. Have you alerted the fire brigade?"

"Yes, they're coming, and the water buckets are full. I've left one here at the top of the stairs."

"Then go!"

Lizzie disappeared down the stairs. Faced with a decision on the best way to move the old man to the first floor, he glanced back to see he was not going to manage alone. Nor would a bucket of water do anything for the fire that had climbed the kitchen wall and was now creeping across the ceiling.

Zeke stood and hauled Mr. Cooper onto his shoulders then made his way down the stairs. By the time he reached the ground floor, the fire brigade had burst through the front door and was heading his way.

One of the men shifted the burden of Lizzie's father to himself then nodded to the door. "I'll get him down the street to the doc, and

I'll see that his daughter goes with him. Best get out while you can."

Zeke looked around the mercantile and then shook his head. "Not yet."

Grasping a bandanna neck scarf from the display at the end of the counter, Zeke tied it around the lower half of his face then took off toward the departments with items that he figured were the most valuable. Armload after armload, he carried merchandise to the wagon Eli had left for him before going on back to the ranch on a horse borrowed from the livery.

After a few minutes, several others had joined him in his effort to save what they could. He recognized most of them but was too busy to do more than offer a nod of thanks. Someone brought another wagon up when Zeke's was full, and they began loading things into it.

When it was full, he shouted to the driver. "Take it all out to Polecat Creek Ranch and ask for Eli. We'll store as much as we can in one of the barns until the Coopers decide what to do with it."

The man took off. Zeke didn't bother to watch him go. He was too busy filling the next wagon. And then the next.

Then a noise echoed through the building and the firemen scampered down the stairs. "Get out now!" one of them shouted. "That gas line is going to blow. And move your wagons. This whole block could go up if we can't get the gas shut off."

Zeke was almost to the door when he realized no one had retrieved the cash register. He turned around and raced to the counter. The register was big and old and heavy, but Zeke was determined.

The last of the firemen passed him as he attempted to wrangle the metal monster onto his shoulder. "Get out now!" the fireman shouted. "Leave that thing here."

But he couldn't. He wouldn't. If Lizzie and her father were going to start over, they would need everything he could salvage.

So with one last heave and a prayer lifted skyward, Zeke hauled the cash register into his arms and bolted for the door. He'd just stepped onto the sidewalk when a blast from upstairs catapulted him into the street and everything went black.

Chapter 6

Tuesday, May 6, 1890

Lizzie pinched the spot at the bridge of her nose and closed her eyes. She'd lost count of the hours she'd been awake, but sleep was the last thing on her mind. Had it been just yesterday morning that she'd dumped a bucket of water over Zeke Wyatt's head, thinking there was a fire?

Apparently he'd gone in and out of the store, along with many of their friends and neighbors, and filled wagons with merchandise salvaged before the flames took over. He'd even hauled that ridiculously heavy cash register out of the building just before the gas ignited into a fireball that threatened the whole block.

She'd heard tales of how the explosion had propelled Zeke into the street. How the cash register he'd been carrying on his shoulder flew all the way across the road and landed inside Ruby's restaurant. How, as of this morning, Ruby was still finding coins and adding them to the amount on deposit in the Cooper Mercantile account at the First National Bank.

Last night—or perhaps it was this morning—Papa had accepted the Wyatt brothers' offer of temporary lodging at Polecat Creek Ranch. They'd been greeted by a woman named Rosa who Eli said kept not only the house but all of the Wyatts in line.

Thin and wiry, Rosa wore her pale silver hair twisted into a knot on the back of her head. Lizzie watched out the window as Rosa worked hanging the sheets on a clothesline that stretched from the wash house to an oak tree a short distance away.

She hadn't seen Zeke since she followed the fire brigade officer over to the hospital. The last Eli had heard, he had refused treatment and was helping the brigade put out the last of the fire. If he'd come back to the ranch, no one had seen him.

The doctor who'd seen to Papa told him that Zeke had a head injury, and if he continued to refuse treatment, he might die. Or, the doctor had continued, he might be just fine. One never knew for certain in these cases.

After failing to find anything productive to do in the house, Lizzie went out to join Rosa.

Without a word, the housekeeper nodded to the basket of wet clothes. Well versed in this exercise, Lizzie helped her finish the job in short order.

"You've done this before," Rosa said as she gathered up the empty basket.

"My mother was sick for a while. My sister was the cook, so the cleaning fell to me." She shrugged. "This part I didn't mind."

Rosa studied her for a moment. "You're the one Vivian always bragged about," she said.

"She did?"

"The hello girl, yes?"

Lizzie smiled "Yes, that's me. Or it was me."

They walked toward the wash house in step. Once the basket was put away, Rosa turned to her. "It can be you again, Elizabeth, but only if the Lord allows. It is not yours to decide such things."

Lizzie ducked her head. "I know."

And she did. The Lord had His plans, and He certainly did not need her approval. But that didn't make any of this easier to accept.

The mercantile was gone. What would she and Papa do?

She lifted her head, pressing away the question. "How else can I help, Rosa? Surely you need assistance with something."

The housekeeper shook her head. "If you help too much, Mrs. Pearl will give you my job when she returns. I cannot have that." She punctuated the statement with a wink and then nodded toward the back porch of the home. "You are wanting to stay busy until Ezekiel returns and you can see for yourself that he is fine, and that is good. You also want answers as to what will happen to you and your papa, yes?"

Lizzie looked at her in surprise. "Am I so obvious?"

"It is what a daughter does, dear. But do not try to hurry the Lord, Elizabeth. Just sit still and wait for Him. I understand Ezekiel is to be commended for his efforts to save your father's merchandise. The old smokehouse is filled with things that were saved."

"Yes," she said. "I owe him much."

Rosa patted her arm. "You tell him that when he returns. It will be soon and he will be just fine, of this I have no doubt."

"But the doctor says. . ."

"Pish posh on the doctor." Rosa shook her head. "The doctor, he guesses and hopes." She paused. "Mark my words. The Lord is not finished with Ezekiel Wyatt, and Ezekiel is not finished helping after the fire, or he would be here. He's fine, Elizabeth."

She offered the housekeeper a smile. "I hope you're right."

"Of course I'm right. But there's something else. God has you here for His purpose, of that I am certain, but I do think just maybe

He has you here for Ezekiel too."

Frowning, Lizzie shook her head. "I don't know what you mean."

"When a man is in need of settling down and he is willing to allow the Lord to choose for him, then the Lord will arrange it."

"I don't think that applies to Ezekiel and me," Lizzie protested. "I hardly know him anymore, and he certainly doesn't know me."

"No," she agreed. "But the Lord knows both of you. Now you're keeping me from my work. Go on with you."

Lizzie parted company with Rosa at the back door and went inside to find Papa. When he wasn't in the bedroom assigned to him, she located him in the library where he was propped up on pillows in a chair by the window. A copy of the newspaper sat in his lap but did not appear to have been read.

Pasting on her brightest smile, she walked toward him. "There you are. I wondered where you'd gone."

Papa made a harrumphing sound. "Can't go far with that woman fussing over me." He nodded out the window toward the garden where Rosa was now surveying what appeared to be newly planted crops.

"Rosa?" Lizzie shook her head. "Don't you complain about her, Papa. She's taking good care of all of us." A thought occurred. "Has she treated you poorly?"

Her father tore his gaze from the garden to focus on Lizzie. "She does feed me well and she's certainly cheerful, but she's taken away my pipe and said I cannot smoke in the house nor can I leave the house until I am well enough."

"I see." She suppressed a smile. "Good for her."

He reached toward her and grasped her hand. His expression sobered. "I just wanted to fix your bacon for you. I don't know what happened. Now I've ruined everything. I caused all of this, and I will fix it. I am so sorry."

"Oh Papa, no. Don't talk like that. We'll be fine." She forced a brighter tone. "Much of the inventory has been saved, and Zeke even managed to bring out the cash register. We can start over somewhere else."

The question of where and how hung between them.

"All right, Mr. Cooper," Eli said from the door. "Are you ready to play?"

Lizzie swiveled to see that her host held a box under his arm. He grinned when he spied her.

"I have it on good authority that your father is a master chess player. I intend to either beat him or learn how to beat him."

Papa's laughter dissolved into a fit of coughing. When he could manage to speak, he grinned at Eli. "I don't suppose I mind teaching you a thing or two, young man. Set up the board, and we'll see if I'm in a mood to share my secrets."

Lizzie took the newspaper her father handed to her and then stepped back to watch Eli move a small table and chair over next to Papa. He opened the box to reveal a chess set and then began to set it up on the table.

"Do you know if your brother has returned to the ranch?"

He looked up from the chessboard. "If he has, I haven't seen him, though I understand the doctor isn't happy with him. I know he's got a hard head, but I may send a couple of the ranch hands to check on him if I don't see him soon."

"Papa and I would like to thank him," she said.

"We would indeed," Papa echoed. "Your brother is a brave man. Now let's see what kind of chess player you are, Eli."

After a moment, with the men talking about the intricacies of chess moves, she realized she'd been forgotten. Or at least dismissed.

She escaped the library and, snatching up her father's newspaper, walked down the hall to her bedroom.

Lizzie settled the chair beside the window and lifted the newspaper to read. After just a few minutes, she folded the paper and set it aside. What her father saw in reading newspapers was beyond her. Give Lizzie a novel any day.

She sighed. Unfortunately, all her novels were ash now.

She rose and went back to the library to retrieve a book. Though Papa and Eli acknowledged her when she arrived, by the time she had made her choice, they were too busy with their game to notice her departure.

Tucking the book under her arm, she headed outside. Rosa said the old smokehouse was filled with their merchandise, so she decided to go and see for herself. After peering into several outbuildings, she opened the door to a structure that smelled strongly of smoke.

Whether the scent was from the smokehouse or the items inside, it was unmistakably the place where the merchandise had been stored. There was no light inside, but the sunlight flooding the room through the doorway illuminated a space filled to the rafters with pots, pans, clothing, and all sorts of items that had been for sale in the store yesterday morning.

The tears that had failed to fall until now slipped from the corners of her eyes and streamed down her cheeks. All this ruin. And so many dreams gone, not just for Papa but for her.

"I knew I should have posted a guard here."

Lizzie whirled around to see Zeke standing there. The bandage the doctor had wrapped around his head was slightly off-kilter and so was his smile.

"You're here," she said on a rush of breath as she swiped at her cheeks. "The doctor said you. . ." Her words faded away.

"Might not survive the head injury if I didn't come home to the ranch and rest," he quoted. "I know. He was wrong."

"I'm glad."

"Well, so am I."

"Are you hurting?"

"I'm fine." He shrugged. "So, about the conversation we were having yesterday before we got interrupted. I never did get to find out if I was going to get the family discount."

She laughed and clutched the book to her chest. "I told you no."

Zeke shrugged. "The doctor said I might have gaps in my memory. So maybe I just forgot."

Lizzie shook her head. "You did not. You're just impossible." She sobered. "Thank you."

"For being impossible? According to my brothers, that's pretty much how I've been my whole life. But you're welcome."

"No." Tears threatened again as she thought of what this man had done for her and Papa. "You're a hero. Thank you."

Zeke's expression soured. "I'm no hero, Lizzie." He pressed past her to stand in the doorway and then surveyed the scene. Lizzie moved beside him.

"You're a hero to me."

"We tried to get it all," he told her, his attention still on the merchandise. "We just ran out of time." Then he gave her a sideways look. "How's your father?"

"He'll be fine. He has a cough that might be of concern, but the doctor thinks it will go away eventually. When I left him, he was playing chess in the library with Eli."

Zeke turned away. "Abigail ought to be told about all this."

"Abigail ought to have told us where she was going and with whom," Lizzie snapped. Then she sighed. "If there was a way, I would let her know. I have no idea how to reach her."

He nodded. Silence fell between them.

"Should you be out here?" she finally asked.

Zeke grinned, his eyes meeting hers. Oh, but those dimples.

"Probably not, but the man who advised me to stay put in bed is the same one who didn't think I'd live just because I landed on my head in the street." He shrugged. "I'm thinking I won't take his advice. He tends to be wrong."

"Good point." She allowed her gaze to sweep the distance, taking in the lush beauty of her surroundings before returning her attention to Zeke. "I lived in Polecat Creek all my life until I moved to Galveston, but I grew up in town over the mercantile. This is just so different. It's so pretty out here."

He nodded again, but his eyes were on her and not the landscape. "Yes, beautiful."

Lizzie made the mistake of looking into those eyes a heartbeat too long. With very little encouragement, she could fall in love with this man.

Maybe it was the image of him carrying her father out of the burning mercantile. Or perhaps it was the fact that once Papa was safe, he'd gone back in that burning building to gather up merchandise and even the cash register so that the Cooper family would have something to start over with.

Then there was the thought of his expression when she'd doused him with water and the way he'd made a joke of the whole thing so she wouldn't be quite so horrified.

Despite his protests, this man was a hero. And a hero was a very attractive man to have around.

What was she thinking? She had nothing but the smoky remains of a store, the merchandise that littered an outbuilding on Polecat Creek Ranch, and an offer of employment in Galveston.

There would never be a worse time.

With a roll of her shoulders, Lizzie shrugged away any thoughts of falling in love. With anyone. Especially not this man.

"Lizzie," he said gently. "You've asked about me, but I haven't asked about you."

"Me?" His comment took her by surprise. "I'm fine. It may take some time to get the smell of smoke out of my hair, but otherwise I can't complain."

"No," he said thoughtfully. "You don't seem like the kind who would complain."

She shook her head. "I might be. You don't know. It's possible I'm saving it all up and preparing to present you with a long list of my complaints. Unfortunately, my writing paper has turned to ash and my pens are melted, so I've been delayed."

Zeke studied her for a second. Then he smiled. "Well now, that is a problem." His expression sobered. "Have you thought about what you're going to do?"

"I'm going to take care of my father," she said. "I haven't worked out how just yet. Once he's well enough to travel, I'll take him back into town and rent a room at the boardinghouse for us until we can figure out how to get the mercantile open again." She paused. "Or maybe I'll just take him with me to Galveston. That is always an option."

"You have time to decide."

"I don't, really. I'm grateful for your hospitality here, but Papa and I cannot stay. We need to make other arrangements."

"I wish you wouldn't hurry," he told her. "This place is way too big for Eli and me, and there are several houses on the ranch that are empty. Why not just move into one of those if you don't feel comfortable in the ranch house?"

"Because it isn't ours." She looked past him to land that rolled on toward the horizon. What a temptation to stay, and yet she couldn't. "But thank you, Zeke. You and Eli are far too generous."

"No, you've got it all wrong. I'm being selfish, Lizzie. See, if you and your father aren't here, then I'm stuck with Eli. He's not very entertaining, and he's certainly not as pretty as you are." He shrugged. "You see my predicament."

She laughed. "I bet you use that line with all the ladies."

"Just you," he said with mock seriousness. "Is it working?"

"Not at all."

And yet it almost was. If she'd allow herself, Lizzie knew she could learn to like spending time with Zeke Wyatt.

She decided right then and there to find another place for her and Papa to stay as soon as she could.

Chapter 7

Wednesday, May 7, 1890

Though he'd only spent a short time with Lizzie Cooper yesterday before she made an excuse to hurry away, the way she looked at the land in the same way he did had taken his breath away.

So had the way she was determined to care for her father, which made him want to look out for both of them.

And then there was her beauty. She was nothing like the women who usually attracted his attention, and yet she was everything he couldn't get out of his mind.

He'd told her none of these things. Rather, he'd ignored her poor excuse for fleeing and let her go.

Tomorrow, however, he would be ready. And he had all night to figure out what to say.

No.

Zeke shook his head.

What was wrong with him?

He might have landed on his head, but his brains were still intact. Mostly.

The woman was halfway to the house now. He'd never catch her unless he spoke up.

"Lizzie," he called.

She ignored him. Or maybe she didn't hear.

"Lizzie," he continued, louder this time as he hurried toward her.

His head pounded—it had been that way since he opened his eyes in the middle of the street—and the shouting didn't help. But he kept at it, finally giving up to press his fingers to his lips and whistle.

That did it.

Lizzie turned around.

"Wait," he called.

"Why?" she responded.

Zeke frowned. *Now what?* He hadn't thought that far ahead.

"I forgot to ask you something," he said as he picked up his pace. "Something important."

Okay, now she looks interested. What he would follow up with, Zeke had no idea.

Yet.

He reached her side. Opened his mouth. Watched her eyeing him expectantly.

And not a thing came to mind.

She gave him a sideways look. "Zeke? You were going to ask me something important?"

"Yes," he said, buying time. "I was."

Silence fell between them. What was wrong with him?

"Actually, what I was going to ask is, would you let me show you something?"

"Where?" she asked, obviously confused.

174

Zeke gestured to the horizon she had been studying not so long ago. "Out there."

"Out there?" She paused as if studying him had become much more interesting than anything else. "Zeke, I'm going to need a little more information."

"You said you were a city girl and had never experienced anything like this." Zeke swept his hand around to indicate the pastures and hills behind him. "I just figured it was time you did."

Was that the beginning of a smile he saw?

"And that's the important thing you wanted to show me?"

"Other than my family, Polecat Creek Ranch is the most important thing in my life. It's where my grandparents put down roots, and their parents before them. My father added to what was already ours, and my brothers and I aim to do the same thing."

He'd said too much, of this Zeke was certain. Lizzie was staring. Unless he missed his guess, she was about to turn around and walk back to the house, leaving him standing where he was wishing he'd said something clever.

And then she smiled. "As much as I would like to see it, I don't think that's a good idea."

Zeke grinned. "Which is why it will be so much fun."

Lizzie shook her head. "Yesterday you were blown out of a burning building. Do you really think you're ready to go for a buggy ride?"

"And I survived." He shrugged. "So yes. I am certain. Besides, there's nothing that can be done to clean up after the fire today. The brigade said no going in yet. So, after today, who knows when we will get another chance?"

She seemed to consider his question for a moment. Then she nodded. "Sure. All right. I suppose it wouldn't hurt to see what I've been missing by being a city girl."

A few minutes later, she sat next to him in the buggy with the ranch house disappearing behind them as they headed for the hills.

Literally.

Though it was early May, the trees were budding and the prairie grass was thick. A month ago this pasture had been rife with bluebonnets, a carpet of blue that reached from the ranch house to the copse of trees on the horizon.

He took the winding path up the side of the hill, carefully guiding the buggy around a corner to arrive at a wide low-water crossing on a tributary of Polecat Creek. Lizzie squealed as he guided the buggy into the water.

"What are you doing?" she demanded, though she sounded more interested than afraid.

He should have explained that this was a crossing that looked much deeper than it actually was. Should have. But didn't.

Instead, he urged the horse forward at a trot and shouted, "Hold on, Lizzie!"

Her laughter mixed with the sound of the rushing water as they splashed their way to the other side. Once the buggy was on dry ground again, he dared a look at his companion.

Pretty pink color had risen in her cheeks, and the bonnet she'd been wearing was hanging down her back. Free from their restriction, her curls fell down her shoulders.

Zeke had never seen a more beautiful sight.

"Are you okay?" he asked when he realized she hadn't said anything.

Lizzie nodded. Then she grinned. "That was fun. Can we do it again?"

So they did. Twice.

Finally, the horse had enough and refused to cross again. Unfortunately, they were on the opposite side of the creek from the ranch house.

"Let's hope she forgives us and is willing to take us home later," Zeke said. "How about I show you the spot with the best view on the ranch?"

Lizzie laughed. "That sounds wonderful."

He guided the buggy up the path through the trees that lined the edge of the creek and then headed east toward the hills. After a few minutes, they emerged into a clearing.

The sun shone on her skin and cast a golden glow on her hair. She smiled and his heart did a flip-flop. And in that minute he knew he'd lost his heart to this woman.

This stranger.

It was ridiculous. It was nothing he had ever wanted or considered.

And it was certainly the worst timing he could imagine. The clock was ticking on the amount of days of freedom he had left for a while.

And yet there it was. He was sunk. Smitten.

Done for.

Tomorrow he would keep his distance. That would be the best thing for both of them. Because even worse than leaving Lizzie Cooper was the thought he might have to tell her where he was going when he left here at the end of the month.

Oh, but today he intended to enjoy every moment of their time together.

Every single moment.

"My Grandfather Wyatt grazed his longhorn cattle here," Zeke told her just when she thought he might not speak at all. "Every year about this time the men would gather to take the cattle up the trail. It was something to see."

Lizzie looked past him to the lush grassland and tried to imagine what it must have been like all those decades ago. She'd lived in the very modern city of Galveston for long enough to grow used to conveniences like telephones and electricity.

The wind lifted the ends of her hair—which was certainly a mess—and made the grasses wave. The effect was of an undulating carpet of gold stretching off into the distance.

"I cannot imagine," she told him. "Were you ever allowed to go with him on a cattle drive?"

"I went a few times," he said with a chuckle. "There's nothing better than wearing the same suit of clothes for a month, sleeping under the stars, and chasing ornery cattle halfway across Texas."

"Zeke, that sounds absolutely terrible."

"That's because you're a woman."

"No," she corrected, "that's because I like clean clothes, soft beds, and warm baths. Anyway, you said you went a few times. Is that all? I mean, if you're having that much fun. . ."

"My father had a great plan for his trail drives. A few weeks before the drive, he would send Mother on a shopping trip somewhere. Usually New York or Philadelphia, but sometimes he would send her to London or Paris."

Lizzie tucked a strand of hair behind her ear and tried to imagine. "He was very generous."

"Oh, it was worth it. When the cowboys started gathering, it went better for everyone if Mother wasn't anywhere near Polecat Creek Ranch." He paused. "Then she found out and put a stop to it."

She shook her head. "I don't understand."

"Mother was from solid upper-crust stock," he said, affecting an accent befitting the description. "Her people were mostly bankers and lawyers. She'd had such high hopes that her sons would follow suit."

Lizzie thought of sweet Mr. Wyatt who used to frequent the

mercantile. From his cowboy hat to his well-worn boots, the old man was every bit a cowboy. "Obviously she didn't marry a banker or lawyer."

"Hardly. My father was a cowboy through and through, though he did have his own money and was much smarter with it than he ever let on."

Zeke stretched his back and looked up at the sky then gave her a sideways glance. "But that is why she doubled down on her efforts on her sons, I guess, though she loved my father with all her heart. My brothers and I were awfully happy when Deacon went off to Harvard. Then we figured out that she expected the same from the rest of us."

"Which meant she didn't want her sons on the trail," she offered.

"Exactly."

"Oh. Well, I guess it was difficult not to be included in the drive anymore."

His grin was swift and absolutely devastating. "I never said I didn't go. I just said my mother put a stop to it." Zeke shrugged. "Once I promised to go to Harvard like my brother, she relented. I didn't miss a year on the trail after that until Pa started turning his cattle over to companies that did the driving for him."

She laughed as she tried to imagine this rugged cowboy at college in Boston. "Right."

He frowned. "I'm serious."

Then she felt terrible. "You are? You're a lawyer who went to Harvard too?"

"I made a promise to my mother, and I kept it, but I never promised to make a career out of the law. Too many courtrooms and not enough outdoors." He paused. "My brothers were sworn to secrecy, and my mother rarely bragged about me outside her social circle up north, so it wasn't common knowledge here."

"Zeke," Lizzie said slowly, "let me get this straight. I just rode through the creek in a buggy with a Harvard-educated lawyer who prefers to. . ." She paused. "To do what?"

"Ride through the creek with you," he said. "But yes. I also do some ranching now, although I had a few years between university and ranching where I didn't do much of anything that was worth telling anyone about."

Lizzie swiveled to face him. "My sister was engaged to marry a Harvard lawyer, and she slipped out of town with a cowboy. How like Abigail."

"I never proposed marriage. I did like the idea of having a girl waiting for me back home, but I'm not disappointed that she found someone else. At least not personally, though it does put me in a bind with another issue. But there's no need to go into that." Zeke lifted a shoulder in a shrug. "I have been plagued by charm. Apparently it is a common mistake to assume I want a wife."

Lizzie laughed. "I cannot believe you said that, Zeke."

"No? Then you must be immune."

She wasn't immune at all. Not that Lizzie would let him know this. She reached over to touch his shoulder. "Be serious."

Zeke sobered. "The truth is, Abigail did me a favor in finding someone else before I had to figure out how to tell her to do that. Okay, your turn. Why did you decide to leave Polecat Creek to be a hello girl?"

"I needed a job."

"That's a partial answer," he said. "What's the rest?"

She sat back and shook her head. "You ask hard questions."

"You don't have to answer." He snapped the reins and set the buggy into motion again. "I promised you the view from the hill, and I intend to deliver."

They rode in silence, which was fine by Lizzie. Between the

beautiful scenery and the nearness of the man beside her, conversation was not necessary. Finally, Zeke negotiated a tight turn and the buggy emerged into another clearing. This time the edge seemed to drop off on the other side of a pile of rocks.

Zeke pulled the buggy to a stop then got out to help Lizzie down. "Come with me. I'm going to deliver on that promise."

She followed him as he led her toward the rocks. When she reached them, she gasped at the sight.

Farmlands and pastures unfolded below her as far as she could see. Here and there homes dotted the landscape, as did horses and cattle.

"Come and sit."

Lizzie did as he asked, taking a place next to her host on a flat rock the size of a table. "Zeke," she said under her breath. "It's beautiful."

"You are."

She tore her attention from the view to look at him. "What?"

His eyes studied her face as the beginnings of a smile rose. "You're beautiful, Lizzie Cooper. I wonder if anyone has ever told you that."

Her lack of an answer did not seem to bother him. Instead, he turned toward the view. "Well, they should have."

"Is this what you mean by being plagued by charm?" she asked him, hoping to divert him from their current topic. Though she found him more than just a little attractive, she did not want to encourage him to think there could be anything between them.

"Lizzie," he said gently. "If you have to ask, then my charm isn't working."

Oh, but he was good. "I'm not going to be here long enough to fall in love. Just so you know."

Chapter 8

W ell that works with my schedule," Zeke said. "I've got to be somewhere else by the end of the month, so I would be looking for more of a quick fling."

She frowned. "Why do you do that?"

"Do what?"

"Pretend to be a flirt, Zeke."

He grabbed his chest as if he'd been shot. "Ouch."

"You know what I mean." Lizzie shifted positions to return her attention to the view. He, in turn, studied her for a moment.

"You hardly know me, Lizzie. Why do you think you understand me?"

She gave him a sideways glance. "I'm probably getting this all wrong, but I think you are a lot like me. Not the favorite child or the one who got all the accolades. You worked hard, made that hard work look easy, and made a career out of convincing other people you're less than what you really are."

Oh.

Zeke closed his gaping mouth. How could she understand him so easily and so well?

"No," he finally said. "You didn't get any of it wrong. How did you do it?"

"Guess your secret?" Lizzie shrugged. "Because we are far too alike than you'd ever expect."

"No, I don't think so."

Her laughter held no humor. "Then you're wrong."

He swiveled to face her. "You're not going to offer any proof of that?"

"Look at me, Zeke. I'm no Abigail, and that's all right. I still love her even though I find her completely impossible to understand. And she would probably say the same about me. I can take care of myself—and plan to—but I'm not the one who got the attention. I went off to Galveston where I wasn't compared to my sister and could be a success in my own right. My guess is you've done the same thing."

"North of Dallas to a ranch property the family has up there," he admitted. "I've been using what I learned at Harvard to turn around some of the land issues they were having with the state, and I hope to do some more of that here in Polecat Creek someday. Seriously though. How did you know?"

She offered him a dazzling smile. "You're not just plagued with charm, Zeke. You're also plagued with siblings, and that is a situation I know too well. Fortunately, mine had the good sense to run off with a cowboy. I'm looking better every day now. Too bad you're still stuck with yours. Oh, and while you're at it, be glad you're not also stuck with mine."

Lizzie leveled him an even look. Then, by degrees, her pretty lips began to turn up in the beginnings of a smile. When a giggle emerged, he joined her, and soon they were laughing so hard they nearly slid off the rock.

"You're good for me, Lizzie," Zeke said after a while. "You make me laugh, but you also make me think."

"Think about this, Zeke. You're a hero. You saved my father's life and went over and above to get as much of our merchandise out of the store as you could. You did that. No one else."

"I did have help with getting the merchandise out," he said.

"I'm making a point," she told him. "You don't have to flirt. Just be yourself."

He settled back and gave that some thought. "It has gotten me in more trouble than I care to admit."

Her brows rose. "Oh come on, why not admit it to me? I'll be gone by the end of the month. What kind of trouble has your flirting gotten you into?"

"All right." Zeke turned toward her again. "How about a jail term?"

"Jail?" Lizzie shook her head. "You've got to tell me the whole story."

"I'll give you the highlights. There was a blond, a brunette, and a redhead. The judge gave me a choice of picking one of them. I told them I had someone waiting back home." He shrugged. "Only it turns out I didn't."

"I don't see where any of this leads to a jail term," she said.

"I'm getting to that. Judge Winslow, up in Dallas County, has given me until the end of the month to bring my wife to his courtroom, or he plans to toss me in jail for an unspecified term."

"For flirting?"

"For perjury." He shrugged. "I told him I had someone I had promised to marry so I couldn't be forced to pick one of the three women whose daddies were prompting them into suing me. That was true. In a way. But the judge took it a step further, and I didn't correct him, and, well, the result is I'm going to spend time in the Dallas County Jail come June 1."

"That doesn't seem fair."

He shrugged. "Sometimes charm is a plague."

Zeke waited for her to laugh. Instead, she watched him intently, her brows furrowed.

"What?" he finally asked her. "You look like you're thinking hard on something."

"I am." She turned to face him and pressed her palms to her knees. For the first time since they sat down, Lizzie looked as if she was hesitant to speak.

"Well, out with it. We're way too far down the honesty road to stall out now."

"Okay. You're a hero. I owe you a debt for saving my father's life. I want to pay that back to you."

"Lizzie—"

"No, listen to me. Take me with you to Dallas to meet with the judge. I'll tell him all about your heroics."

"And if that doesn't work?"

She shrugged. "Then I'll marry you."

Zeke climbed to his feet and looked down at her. "No," he said. "I cannot allow any of this. Let's go, Lizzie."

He walked away and heard her scrambling to catch up. "Suit yourself," she told him when she fell into step beside him. "But it's not like we would really be married. I would go on with my life in Galveston, and you can go back to doing whatever it is you do in north Texas. Simple as that."

"Until you fall in love with someone," he told her. "Then what?"

"Or you do," she said. "I guess we figure it out if it happens. I'm sure there are ways to dissolve a marriage if. . ."

"If?"

"You know," she told him. "If we haven't tried to be really married."

"Oh." He sighed. "Let me think about it."

"The situation won't change," she said. "But here's what I'm willing to do. You think about it. I'm going to town tomorrow to make arrangements for my father and me. If you decide to take me up on the offer, I'll need an assurance that someone will look after Papa should I need to be away with you in Dallas for a few days."

He stopped when they reached the wagon. Zeke was watching her, smiling and studying her all at the same time. Something about his expression, about the way his eyes followed her and his lips lifted in the slightest smile.

"Lizzie, are you sure you realize what you're offering to do?"

"Did you realize what you were offering to do when you went into that burning building to save my father?" she asked him.

"I did."

"And so do I."

✺

The letters were mailed and plans were set. Only a few details remained, but the Lord would take care of them.

Lizzie stood very still on the sidewalk in front of the charred pile of wood where Cooper Mercantile had stood. The destruction was complete.

There was nothing left of the business her parents had built on this spot. The dark clouds on the horizon portended rain that would wash away what the fire didn't take. Her eyes and nose burned from the acrid smell of smoke, but she wouldn't cry. Not today. Not anymore.

Last night she'd cried enough tears to fill Polecat Creek. Today

THE SECONDHAND BRIDE OF POLECAT CREEK

she'd awakened with the vow that her crying was done and now it was time to get to work. That's when she wrote the letter accepting her old job back in Galveston. A second letter went to the land-lady at the rooming house on Twenty-Third Street, asking if her old rooms were still available.

Dropping the letters into the mailbox was terrifying. Now that it had been done, she felt. . .what? Fear? Sure. But also relief. Her course was set. She just had to navigate the time between now and when she could leave this life for her old one.

The real trouble, she knew, would come when she told Papa that he was going with her.

That would be nothing in comparison to the reaction she knew he would have should Zeke Wyatt decide to take her up on her offer to help him. He'd spent half the ride back to the ranch yesterday trying to talk her out of her proposal—pun intended—and the other half of the time proving if she had to be tied to anyone, Zeke Wyatt was a companionable man who knew enough about the land to keep her entertained.

They'd also talked about the fire. Gave thanks it wasn't any worse than just the loss of one building.

She looked to the right and then the left. Only the fact that the mercantile was on the corner and there was an empty lot between the store and the newspaper office kept the whole block from going up in cinders.

God had indeed been merciful. No one else's livelihood was gone, and that was blessing number one. For she'd determined to count her blessings today. Blessing number two was the fact that the Lord had spared her and Papa. And, by default, Abigail.

The fact that her sister wasn't here to see this might have been blessing number three. However, Lizzie wasn't feeling that generous this morning.

Someone snaked an arm around her waist, and she turned to see who it was. Ruby. Lizzie offered the older woman—who was near to Papa's age—a smile.

"Come have some breakfast, child," she said gently. "Or at least some coffee."

Her stomach churned, but it was hard to tell whether that was from hunger or dread of the task ahead. "I couldn't."

"You ought to though." Her smile brightened. "Besides, it's Wednesday. Widow Bright and Miss Nellie will be here for lunch today. The coffee might not hold out until suppertime, and I know you don't want to be there when they're drinking their smidge of coffee."

Lizzie grinned in spite of herself. "You make a good point."

"All right, honey." Ruby withdrew her arm to pat Lizzie's hand. "I'll leave you alone then, but if you or your daddy needs anything, you let me know."

A thought occurred. "Do you know of a room for rent for a few weeks?"

"I sure do. I've got a whole floor above the restaurant that used to be where my mama lived until she passed. The apartment there has been empty going on two years, but it's nice, it's furnished, and I hear the neighbor upstairs is a pretty good cook."

"I'll take it," she said. "I don't even care what it costs. You've been such a help to us. I'm glad to pay whatever you ask."

"Oh honey, don't you worry about all that. I'm still finding coins that belong to you. I'll start a jar for me, and we'll pay the rent out of them."

She laughed. "I don't think that's a fair rent, Ruby."

"Just bring your daddy when he's well enough. The door to the apartments is in the back alley, and the key will be under the mat." She paused. "In fact, if you want to go look at it, you can."

Lizzie offered a smile as tears stung her eyes. "I don't know how to thank you. It'll just be two weeks. Three at the most."

"It's yours as long as you need it." Ruby shook her head. "And that smile is thanks enough, Lizzie. Now don't forget about breakfast, you hear?"

With a wave she was off, heading back across the street to disappear inside the restaurant, and Lizzie was alone on the sidewalk again. Alone on a busy sidewalk with wagons and horses and buggies clogging the streets, and the remains of Mama and her childhood erased in front of her.

Lizzie straightened her spine and called on every bit of willpower she had not to give in to the memories. There would be time for reminiscing once she and Papa were settled in Galveston. And if Zeke did go through with their plan, then she could leave Polecat Creek knowing that she had properly thanked the man who saved Papa's life.

Thunder rumbled and the wind kicked up. The rain would come sooner than she expected. She could have taken cover in Ruby's restaurant, but the solitude of the apartment above beckoned.

Chapter 9

There she was.

Zeke reined in his horse and watched Lizzie scurry across the street against the wind to disappear behind Ruby's restaurant. He'd been worried when he found her gone from the ranch.

No, that wasn't quite right. Not worried. He just missed her.

It was crazy, and he had no explanation for it. He certainly didn't know Lizzie Cooper well enough to think about her as much as he did.

And she surely wasn't his type.

Yet she'd pegged him completely yesterday. Knew him like she'd been reading his diaries. If he were ever the type to keep a diary, which he was not.

And she had offered a solution to his problem. A way out. A payback for what she called his heroics.

It felt wrong to take her up on that.

Wrong even to consider it.

And yet it was all he could think about last night.

He'd still been debating it this morning. Finding her gone set a panic in him that propelled him onto his horse and down the road toward Polecat Creek before he'd had time to manage a decent breakfast.

He had to see her. Had to talk to her.

So he delivered his horse to the livery to keep her safe from what looked to be a powerful rainstorm and then followed Lizzie's trail to the stairs leading up to the apartments above Ruby's restaurant.

Acting on instinct, he stepped inside and knocked on the first door he saw. He wasn't surprised when Lizzie opened it.

"What are you doing here?" she asked.

"Accepting your offer," came out of his mouth before he could stop it.

She nodded, her expression stoic. "All right. If we were to leave on Monday for Dallas, would that be all right? I want to give Papa a few more days of healing time before I leave."

"And a few more days before you tell him?"

Lizzie's gaze collided with his. "Isn't that what you would do?"

Zeke chuckled. "We are far too similar, Lizzie. This doesn't bode well." He paused to look around and then returned his attention to her. "You and your father can stay at the ranch as long as you like, you know."

"Through the weekend will be fine for me. And if you could speak with Eli about Papa remaining his guest while you and I are in Dallas, that would be perfect."

"Anything for my wife." He punctuated the jest with a wink.

"I like to think of myself as the woman who will convince the judge that you're a hero, thus avoiding the need for you to take a wife."

Zeke shook his head and said nothing. She hadn't met Judge

191

Winslow. But then Judge Winslow hadn't met Lizzie Cooper.

✧

Dallas, Texas
Monday, May 11, 1890

That certainly hadn't gone as planned. Lizzie looked at the man sleeping on the seat beside her and let out a long breath. She was exhausted. Beyond exhausted.

Maybe that's why she hadn't allowed her mind to wrap itself around the fact she was married to Zeke Wyatt.

Married.

Outside the window, darkness fell heavy as the train's wheels click-clacked along the tracks. Inside she sat very still and tried to sleep.

They'd been up since well before dawn, arriving in Dallas sometime after lunch. The meeting with Judge Winslow, held in his chambers in the Dallas County Courthouse, had been short and sweet.

"Miss Cooper?" she recalled the older fellow saying.

"I am, sir. Elizabeth Cooper."

Then he'd turned his attention to Zeke. "You've brought the bride. Where's the license?"

"Actually," Lizzie interjected, "I wonder if I could have a word with you first, Judge Winslow. I want to tell you about how Ezekiel saved my father when our business burned to the ground only a week ago. He was—is—a hero."

"A hero." The judge's harrumph told her how much of that story he believed. "Then produce a license, hero."

"Technically I have until the end of the month," Zeke reminded the judge.

"And technically I didn't have to let you go in the first place. All three of those women's daddies were livid when I let you slip out without them getting a chance at their pound of flesh. And their lawyers were none too happy either. I have it on good authority there are suits being filed this week against you. If you're not married to this woman here, it appears you'll likely end up with one of them. My money is on the pretty blond."

"Then marry us," Lizzie blurted out, unsure if it was the threat of Zeke landing in jail or the idea of him marrying a pretty blond that had her most upset. "Just like it said in the telegram. You're a judge. You can do that, right?"

A half hour later, they walked out of the courthouse into the twilight as husband and wife. Mr. and Mrs. Ezekiel Wyatt.

Lizzie ought to feel something, but what? Disappointed that she didn't have that sweep-me-off-my-feet moment? Hardly. She wasn't the type. Relief. Yes, that was it. And a sense that she had done something right. Something helpful.

Something to pay Zeke back for what he had done for her and Papa.

Polecat Creek, Texas
Tuesday, May 12, 1890

The dawn had not yet broken, but Zeke was wide awake. He'd feigned sleep last night, and then, when Lizzie finally gave up and closed her eyes, he'd gathered his wife into his arms and held her the rest of the night.

His wife.

Zeke let out a long breath. It wasn't what he'd planned. Or even what he'd hoped.

The whole way up to Dallas he'd prayed that the judge would

listen to Lizzie and turn him loose with a stern warning and a congratulatory handshake over earning such a stellar friendship. He'd also tried to convince her to stay behind at the train station and not go to court with him at all, but she refused to hear him on the matter.

Instead, Judge Winslow slapped him on the back and wished them well in their new life together.

"Wait, what?" Zeke had stammered.

Judge Winslow looked up sharply from the papers on his desk. "Your new life together." Then he paused, his gaze never leaving Zeke's face. "Miss Cooper has said she sent the telegram and that she came here with a willingness to keep you out of jail." He shifted his attention to Lizzie. "Were those not your exact words, Miss Cooper?"

"Yes, Your Honor," Lizzie told him.

"And you stand by those words?" he asked her.

"I do, sir."

The judge had then returned his attention to Zeke. "Your brother has asked for leniency in your case."

"Eli contacted you?"

"Deacon," he corrected. "I had a chance to speak to him on another matter last week when I was in DC. He speaks highly of you and says you are invaluable to the family, especially in the running of the ranches."

"That was kind of him."

"Well," Judge Winslow said slowly, "what I want to hear from you is whether you believe it was truthful of him."

"I would have no way of knowing that, Your Honor. Deacon speaks his own mind, but I wouldn't know his thoughts until he tells me what they are."

The judge studied him for what felt like an eternity. "That's a good answer, son. You're going to make Miss Cooper a good husband. Now let me find that license I took out for you in case you showed up."

"Can you do that, Your Honor?" he blurted out. "Take out a license in my name, I mean?"

Judge Winslow laughed. "I'm a district judge in Dallas County, son. Of course I can. Now sign here, both of you, and let's get on with it. Mrs. Winslow is serving pot roast, and she will be most displeased with me if I'm late."

Five minutes later, all charges against him were dropped, and Zeke walked out of the Dallas County Courthouse a free man. Well, not completely free, because now he was a married man. After a celebratory dinner, courtesy of Judge Winslow, where neither of them ate much or spoke, they boarded the train back to Polecat Creek.

The train blew a whistle at a crossing, rousing Lizzie. Her eyes opened, and she looked up at him. By degrees, she became aware that her head rested on his shoulder, and she sat bolt upright.

If a man had to have a wife, and apparently he did, Zeke could do no better than the woman beside him. Not only was she beautiful, but Lizzie Cooper loved her family enough to sacrifice her freedom to pay a debt only she believed she owed.

Lizzie Wyatt, he corrected.

"We'll be stopping in Polecat Creek soon," he finally told her just to end the uncomfortable silence.

She looked out the window into the pale light of dawn and appeared to be considering her words. "Zeke, I'll be leaving for Galveston in a few weeks and taking my father with me. I accepted the offer of my old job back." She turned to look at him. "I start work on June first. I didn't want you to get the impression I'm staying."

Zeke exhaled a long breath. "I'll be heading back to the ranch north of Dallas about the same time, so I won't be staying either."

She nodded but said nothing further.

"Lizzie, thank you," he said as the train slowed to a stop at the station. "I'm sorry how it turned out."

"Don't be." Lizzie swiveled to face him and leaned her head against the window. "We'll get this sorted out. You'll go back to the ranch and I'll go to Galveston. Once I'm settled in my job, I'll file for an annulment, and that will be that. No one will know we were married but us."

Zeke looked out the window behind her and then shook his head. The last thing he thought he would see when they returned to Polecat Creek greeted him out the window.

"Uh, Lizzie, I think it's too late for that." He nodded toward the glass behind her. "It looks like half the town has come to greet us. Oh, and there's a banner congratulating us on our marriage too."

Chapter 10

Lizzie stepped off the train and into her father's arms. Zeke was right. Half the town had come to greet them and to congratulate them on their marriage.

"My little girl is married," her father said with tears in his eyes. "I am so happy for you. Finally, something good has come of all the terrible things that have happened lately."

"Oh Papa," was all she could manage as he pressed her against him.

Then he held her at arm's length. "You've made me so happy, Lizzie. And your mama would be happy too, rest her soul. I only wish you had confided in me of your love for the man who saved my life."

"Papa, can we talk about this later in private?"

"Yes, you're right." Her father motioned for Zeke to join them. "I understand you are family now," Papa told him when he stood at Lizzie's side.

"About that, sir. If I could do it over again, I would ask your blessing before I married your daughter," he said.

"And yet you weren't going to ask my blessing when you married Abigail?" Papa shook his head. "You didn't think I knew you had an arrangement with my younger daughter before you married Lizzie, did you?"

"No, sir," Zeke said. "Nor am I proud of that."

"Look here," Papa told him. "I am happy because my daughter is happy. I owe you my life, and for these reasons I will give you and Lizzie my blessing."

"And I second that," Eli Wyatt said as he joined them. "You sure surprised me, brother," he said to Zeke.

"And you surprised me," Zeke responded. "How exactly did this welcoming party come to be? I know neither of us said a word to anyone, did we, Lizzie?"

"I certainly didn't," she said.

Eli clasped Zeke's shoulder. "You can thank Deacon for this."

"How did he find out?" Zeke asked.

"The judge who married you called him," Eli said. "He wanted to be sure you two had a proper welcome. And you have."

"And we have," Zeke agreed.

"Speech!" someone in the crowd shouted.

Lizzie cringed. It was time to leave. *Now.*

Zeke shook his head. "Thank you all for coming out to greet us. This has been a memorable day, and it's barely getting started. Now if you'll excuse us, I'm going to take Lizzie home."

A whoop went up from the crowd.

Papa leaned in to speak over the noise. "I'll be staying in town a little longer. I have some things to do."

She gave him a worried look. "Are you sure?"

"Lizzie, I am certain. And I'm fine. I've coughed the smoke out of my lungs and have come to my senses. Stop worrying about me and focus on your husband. He's your concern now, not me."

"You'll always be my concern," she told him. "I didn't want to tell you this now, but I've secured rooms for us over Ruby's restaurant. Why don't you go take a look while you're in town?"

"If I look, and I like the place, it will be mine alone and not yours. So if you've paid Ruby anything, I'll see that you're reimbursed."

"Papa, no! I—"

"Daughter, do not make plans that include me," he interrupted. "I know you, and I know you will do that." Papa nodded toward Zeke. "Your home is with your husband. Thanks to him, I'll be fine. There will be money enough in the register and the sale of the goods that were salvaged to set up shop in a smaller place. I'm rather excited about the prospect."

To her complete surprise and delight, he did appear to be excited. In fact, she hadn't seen this much happiness on her father's face since Mama was alive.

Lizzie considered arguing then thought better of it. Instead, she hugged her father and watched him walk away. There would be time enough later to discuss this topic.

Zeke moved in to take Papa's place beside her. "Smile for the folks," he told her. "You look concerned."

"I am." She looked up at him. "My father just told me to make plans that don't include him. He's even considering opening a smaller store here. And he's going to go and look at the rooms over the restaurant for himself."

Her husband laughed. "Honey, these are good things."

And they were.

"All right, Mrs. Wyatt," Zeke said loud enough to be heard over the crowd. "Let's go home."

Another roar of approval went up. The cheering continued until her husband helped her into the same buggy they'd driven through the creek just the other day, and only faded when they were finally out of sight.

After a few minutes, Zeke slowed the buggy to a stop and swiveled to face her. "I've had time to think about this since we said our vows in front of the judge, and I've got something to say. I know why you agreed to marry me, and it didn't have anything to do with love. Nor did I ask for you to do what you did, though I'll never finish paying you back for it if I live to be a hundred years old."

Lizzie shook her head. "It is I who owe you, Zeke. My father would be dead if you hadn't saved him."

He looked away and seemed to be considering his words. "I said vows, and I thought I could walk away from them as soon as we could undo what we did. But I'm no longer willing to do that."

"What?" came out on a rush of breath.

"You heard me, Lizzie Wyatt. I haven't spent a whole lot of time with you, but a man doesn't need much time to know when a woman is the right one. I can't tell you how I know, except I know. We were meant to be together, and together is what we will be."

"That's ridiculous," she told him, even as she felt the slightest twinge of something she preferred not to think about. An interest that went beyond friendly, a feeling that would soak into her heart and lodge there if she would allow it.

"It's not, and I can see on your face that you feel it too." He reached out with his free hand to place it atop hers. "Lizzie, I want to be your husband in more than name only. I know you're not ready for that, but when you are, I'll be here."

"But I'm going to Galveston soon, and you've got the ranch in north Texas to see to." She paused and hoped that alone would be enough to cause him to come to his senses.

Instead, Zeke shrugged. "I guess we have a thing or two to work out then."

He returned his attention to the road and flicked the reins to set the horse in motion. They rode the rest of the way back to the ranch in silence, which is exactly what Lizzie preferred.

When the ranch house came into view, Rosa was waiting on the porch. "I baked a cake," she told Zeke, though she said nothing to Lizzie. "I moved her things into your bedroom."

"That wasn't necessary." This earned her a look from the housekeeper and a frown from Zeke.

"She's right," he said. "We could have done it ourselves. Now I hope you've made breakfast, Rosa. I'm starved. What about you, Lizzie?"

Lizzie shook her head. "Thank you, but I'm not hungry."

Zeke climbed down from the wagon then reached for her. His hands spanned her waist and his eyes met hers as he lifted her to the ground. A moment passed between them, something akin to an electric charge.

"I keep my promises, Lizzie." Zeke released her to take a step backward.

That night Lizzie slept in Zeke's bed, but she had no idea where he went. The latch on the door kept him out, but unless she slept through any attempts on his part, her husband never tried to open it.

She'd only just finished dressing the next morning when the sound of a horse approaching sent her to the window. Papa grinned up at her, and she hurried to him.

"I have the best news," he told her. "You know how Ruby said she keeps finding money from the cash register in her restaurant?" At Lizzie's nod, he continued. "Well, there's a reason for that. It seems as though the citizens of Polecat Creek have been making a game of hiding money in the restaurant for her to find so's to increase the balance in our bank account. A few of them have gone to the bank and made donations. Daughter, there's enough in the bank to rebuild the store right where it used to stand and to fill it with merchandise again. I'm still pinching myself, but it's the truth."

"Papa," she said on a rush of breath. "That's wonderful."

"It is." His expression sobered. "I'll need to thank the Wyatts for all they've done and arrange for the merchandise they've been storing here to be removed. But moreover, I need to set you free, sweetheart."

"Set me free?" She shook her head.

"You need to live your life now, Lizzie. I told you yesterday, and I will say it again. You've married, and, yes, I was told the story behind it yesterday when Eli broke the news, and now you'll keep those vows. You might think you were helping him out of a jam because he hauled me out of a burning building, but I think we serve a creative God who just happened to use a large dose of his creativity in putting you two together."

"Ah," was all she could say.

"So I'm setting you free from worrying about me, and sending you off to Galveston and that job you want so much. Or to wherever you and your husband wish to be. Just as long as it is decided without consideration of what will happen to me. I'm fine. And I have it on good authority I'll be well fed."

He reached over to embrace her in a hug and then held her at arm's length. "Your mama and I were always so proud of you. I still am, and she would be as well if she were here. What I want to be proud of now is what a good wife you are to that man."

"That's not fair, Papa. I barely just married him."

"Yes, you've married him, but have you started treating him like a husband yet?"

She blushed at the question and then bristled. "With all due respect, Papa, I'll consider that none of your business."

He shook his head. "You've given me all the answer I need. Be a wife to a good man, Lizzie. That's your papa talking. Now, I'm off to handle a few other details in regard to rebuilding, else I'd stay and talk."

His challenge remained long after he was gone. *Be a good wife to a good man.*

Lizzie sighed. How in the world was she going to manage that?

Zeke watched his wife as she bid her father goodbye from his unintended hiding place in the hayloft. He'd gone up to find a harness that Eli swore he'd stored up there last fall, and only realized the benefit of delaying that search when he heard the conversation down below loud and clear.

Be a good wife to a good man.

He let out a breath. He had a long way to go before he would ever consider himself a good man, but he was willing to try for her.

Zeke had meant what he'd told Lizzie yesterday. He intended to keep the vows he'd made. If she wanted to go to Galveston, he'd follow. He meant that too. More than she knew.

Inching closer to the window, he spied her looking up at him.

"How long have you been up there?" she demanded.

"How long would be too long?" he asked with a grin.

"Come down, please. I need to speak with you."

Zeke shook his head. "Unless you want Rosa to hear us, you might want to come up here."

He shifted his attention from his wife to the housekeeper who had been dusting the same piece of furniture in the window behind her for as long as Lizzie and her father were conversing. Rosa frowned at him and closed the curtains.

Lizzie traced a quick path into the barn then looked up at him. "Come down, please."

"I could," Zeke agreed. "Or you could come up here. You never know who would be listening down there, but up here? Well, let's just say you can see anyone who might want to eavesdrop before they can get close enough to hear anything."

His wife gave him a doubtful look. Then she pressed her palms on a rung of the ladder. "Is it safe?"

"Very," he told her. "Men twice your size use that ladder, and it never has so much as wobbled. See, it's nailed down and won't move." He paused to shift positions. "And I'll be right here to help you up." Another pause. "Unless you don't think you can do it."

That did it. Lizzie made a face at him that he knew as determination. He'd seen it in the mercantile during the fire. Then, without so much as another word, she scaled the ladder to climb up into the hayloft.

"Look at you," he told her. "Welcome to the best hiding place at Polecat Creek Ranch." He nodded to the spot by the window. "From there you can see all the way to the hills, and if the curtains are open, you can look into the parlor or into the upstairs windows."

Where she was last night.

Zeke must have read her thoughts. "And no," he continued, "I was not up here last night, so your modesty is safe."

Lizzie shrugged off the statement to move toward the window and settle down in the hay beside it. Even from here he could see the stain of heat rising in her cheeks, showing him he'd embarrassed her.

"You're right," she said as she craned her neck to look out. "I can see all the way to the hills. From here they look so close, but when we were sitting on the rock, the ranch felt so far away."

The view from where she'd chosen to sit was one of the best on the ranch. But right now the view Zeke had was better. How was it possible that Lizzie had no idea how beautiful she was?

He sat down beside her, catching her attention. "What was it you wanted to talk to me about?"

Lizzie appeared to consider the question. "Our marriage," she finally said. "And what we're going to do about it." She shook her head and dropped her gaze. "No, that's not right. What I want to do about it."

Zeke sat back and rested his elbows on his knees. "Go ahead then."

"I don't know how much of the conversation with my father you overheard, but he gave me some advice, and I plan to take it," she said slowly. "I just need to figure out how."

He leaned forward. "How to what?"

Lizzie lifted her eyes to meet his. "How to be a wife to you."

Zeke held out his hand to her, and she took it. "Sounds like we're in the same boat. I need to figure out how to be a husband to you, Lizzie."

"You could start by kissing me."

He shook his head, uncertain he'd heard her correctly. "Kiss you?"

Her lips turned down in the slightest imitation of a pout. "Does that sound so awful?"

Zeke slid his hand up her arm and around the back of her neck as he leaned forward. "Not kissing you," he said, inches from her lips, "is what sounds awful, Lizzie."

The kiss was slow and sweet and everything he thought it would be. When he lifted his head, Lizzie pulled him back toward her.

"Could we try that again?"

This time, he pulled her gently against him and smiled down at her first. "As many times as you want, Lizzie."

"I think I'm going to like being the wife of a hero," she whispered.

"I'm no hero, Mrs. Wyatt, but I am very glad you're my wife." Then he paused and lifted his head. "Hold on a minute. We have some details to work out."

"Details?" She looked up at him. "About kissing?"

"No. About where we will live. Do you still want to go back to Galveston?"

"I like it there," she said on an exhale of breath. "But no, I don't have to go back there."

He kissed the tip of her nose. "That's not what I asked. Do you want to go there? I'll make the answer easier. I have some interest in a piece of ranch land at the end of the island, so I'm not averse to moving there."

"You're not?" She smiled. "Well, I'm not either. Galveston it is." Then he kissed her again. And again.

"Do you care if I work at the phone company for a while?" she asked him after a few minutes. "I enjoyed being a hello girl."

"Then be a hello girl." He kissed her again. "Whatever makes you happy, wife."

She wrapped her arms around him. "Kissing you makes me happy. We should do more of this."

"Now?" he said.

"All the time," she responded. "But yes, now. It's what a husband and wife do, isn't it?"

"It is," he said. "Come here, wife."

Epilogue

Polecat Creek, Texas
December 24, 1890

Lizzie did as Zeke asked and closed her eyes as he led her from the train station into a buggy. It was their first time back in Polecat Creek since they moved to Galveston seven months ago.

Papa's letter asking his eldest daughter and her husband to spend Christmas Eve with him was an easy one to answer. While she loved living in Galveston with Zeke, she did miss her father.

She wrote him regularly, and he answered occasionally. It wasn't that he didn't love her, but Papa just wasn't much of a letter writer.

The buggy slowed to a stop almost before it got moving. "Are we here already?" she asked her husband.

"We are. Now sit still until I help you out." She felt his arms around her, and then his lips on hers. After he'd kissed her twice, she giggled. "I hope we aren't being watched, Zeke."

"I'm afraid we are."

Instead of helping her out of the buggy, Zeke removed her blindfold to reveal they'd stopped in front of an unfamiliar building with a very familiar name emblazoned above the doors: Cooper Mercantile.

Papa stood beneath that sign with half of Polecat Creek cheering. "Welcome back, daughter," he told her as he walked through the crowd to help Lizzie from the buggy. "What do you think of the store?"

She hugged her father then looked past him. "I think it's beautiful, Papa. I can't believe you got it finished so quickly."

"Come in and look at everything," he said as he offered her his arm.

After a tour of the store with Zeke following a step behind and greeting everyone he knew and likely some he did not know, Zeke paused at the counter. "Mr. Cooper," he called to Papa. "You kept the cash register."

"I did at that," Papa said. "I figured it survived just fine—thanks to you—and there was no need to replace it." He paused. "I had hoped that I might show you something else. Or rather. . ."

The door opened and Papa grinned. "Yes, there she is now."

Lizzie turned around to see Abigail stepping inside. "Everything is ready over at—" She squealed. "Lizzie! You're home."

"No, *you* are home," she called to Abigail through the crowd. "Papa didn't tell me."

"I asked him to keep it a secret. Well, that and this."

Abigail stepped out of the crowd. Following in her wake was a dark-haired cowboy. Lizzie took note of her sister's obviously pregnant condition.

They hugged, and then Abigail stepped back. "Lizzie," she said, "meet my husband, Michael."

After they exchanged a greeting, Lizzie nodded to Zeke, who was fielding questions from Miss Nellie and Widow Bright. Junior Gibbons stood nearby trying to look like he wasn't eavesdropping and failing miserably.

"That's her husband, Zeke," Abigail told the cowboy. Then she turned her attention back to Lizzie. "I told Michael all about Zeke and how bad I felt leading him on. I'm glad he's happy. He wouldn't have been happy with me."

"And I am glad you're happy," Lizzie told her. "Where are you living now?"

"Here," she said. "Michael has been a big help to Papa in getting the store built and up and running. I've done what I can, but with the baby coming, I'm afraid I'm not much help."

Lizzie hugged her sister again. "I'm so glad to hear all of this. When you left, I was worried I would never see you again."

"Attention everyone," Papa said, quieting the crowd. "I want to welcome you to Cooper Mercantile's Christmas Eve celebration." He nodded to a stack of small wrapped gifts next to a basket of sweets on a table near the door. "There are presents for the children, so please don't leave without taking one."

"Thank you," someone called, and soon a chorus of appreciation went up.

After a moment, her father waved his hands to silence those in attendance. "As much as I love having all of you here, I'm going to have to send you to your homes soon to await Christmas morning while I enjoy my daughters and their husbands. So before you leave, could we sing a few songs?"

Papa led off with his beautiful baritone, and Ruby stepped up to sing harmony. After they'd gone through a few familiar numbers, her father called for Lizzie's favorite. Soon the citizens of Polecat Creek were lifting their voices to sing "Silent Night."

After the last chorus, Lizzie wiped the tears from her eyes and leaned into Zeke's embrace while Papa shook hands with each person and wished them a Merry Christmas as they left. Finally, there was just the five of them.

"I thought we could move our celebration over to Ruby's

restaurant," he said. "Do you mind that our Christmas Eve meal won't be home-cooked? At least not in my home."

"Papa is still living over the restaurant," Abigail supplied. "Michael made sure his quarters over the store were comfortable and nice, but he likes his little place across the street."

"He insisted we move in above the mercantile," Michael said. "I suspect it was so we could be easy to find if he needs help in the store."

"Michael is teasing," Abigail said. "He puts in as many hours as Papa."

"More," her father said. "I'm coasting toward retirement and letting Michael run things someday."

Lizzie grinned. "I like the sound of that. With Abigail and Michael in charge of Cooper Mercantile, you can come and visit Zeke and me in Galveston."

"I'll make sure he does," Abigail said, "though it might have to wait until our little one comes."

"All right, girls," Papa said. "Let's move this party across the street."

Over at the restaurant, Ruby had decorated her restaurant for the holiday, covering the pictures of exotic locations with drawings of Santa and Christmas trees made by the local children.

A table had been set for six in the middle of the room, and Papa led them there. All sorts of delicious foods were situated in the center of the table, but Lizzie looked away.

Once Lizzie had taken her seat beside Zeke, she looked over at her father. "Is someone else joining us?"

"Yes," he told her. "In the months you've been gone, I've found a friend who has come to mean very much to me."

"Oh," Lizzie said. "I'm so happy for you, Papa."

"Are you?" He shook his head. "I wasn't sure how you would feel, what with how close you were to your mother."

"She wouldn't want you to be alone, Papa," Lizzie said.

"I'm glad you think so." He rose. "I'll just go get her. She felt it was important that I tell you myself before she joined us at the table."

Papa stood and disappeared into the kitchen, returning a moment later with the owner of the establishment. Lizzie grinned. "Ruby?"

The cook returned her smile. "Your father is a charmer."

"Living over the restaurant has been the best thing that's happened to me in a long time. I haven't eaten so well in years—sorry, Abigail, but it's true—and Ruby here was always there to offer friendly conversation and to let me win at checkers."

"I didn't realize you knew I was letting you win," Ruby said.

Papa shrugged. "So now that my daughters know I love this woman, I just have one more thing to say to you, Ruby." He dropped to one knee in front of her. "Will you marry me?"

"Stand up," she told Papa. "You know I'll marry you. Why wouldn't I?"

"I don't know, but I'm happy you're saying yes. Now if one of my sons-in-law will just help me stand up, I'll be even happier."

Michael was the closest, so he jumped up to assist. Papa offered his thanks and then pulled back Ruby's chair to help her take her seat.

Papa offered a blessing, and they all said, "Amen."

Lizzie reached for Zeke's hand under the table. "Before we eat, could I just say something?"

Zeke gave her an astonished look but remained silent. Papa nodded. "Go ahead, Lizzie."

"I'll keep this brief." She paused, took a deep breath, and promptly forgot the perfectly practiced words she planned to say. Instead, Lizzie blurted out, "Zeke and I are going to have a baby."

"We are?" Zeke said, his eyes wide.

"We are," she told him.

Her husband let out a whoop and then hugged her tight. Then he kissed her. "We're having a baby? Us?"

"Well, yes," Lizzie said. "Us."

After a rousing round of congratulations, Papa passed the food. Later that evening, Lizzie and Zeke made their way to the Polecat Creek Ranch where she was introduced to some of the other Wyatt brothers, Ben and Matthew, and their wives.

Finally, it was time for bed, and the two of them went off to Zeke's old bedroom. It was a clear night, and the air was crisp but not cold. Having lived in Galveston all these months, she'd grown used to warm weather most of the time, so a slight chill in the air felt good.

"I'm not sleepy yet," she told Zeke once the door closed behind them.

"That's because you slept on the train the whole way here." He came to stand beside her. "A baby, Lizzie. I can't tell you how happy I am."

"I'm thrilled. You have no idea how difficult it was not to tell you." She paused. "But I wanted it to be our Christmas surprise."

"It's the best Christmas surprise I've ever received."

Then he kissed her, and she melted into his embrace. Oh, how she loved this man. How she loved his kisses. "Zeke," she said slowly, "let's go up in the hayloft."

"Tonight?" He shook his head. "Whatever for?"

She grinned. "Not the view."

He opened his mouth to speak, and then her meaning dawned on him. "Follow me."

The next morning, they joined the entire Wyatt family for a Christmas morning breakfast then took their places around the fireplace in the parlor to open gifts. The Wyatt grandchildren—all fourteen of them—were running around and exclaiming about their gifts while the adults watched.

Lizzie settled next to Zeke and smiled at Pearl, Deacon's wife, when she joined them. "I'm so happy for your news," she told Lizzie. "Babies are the best."

"Are you saying we need another?" Deacon called from his spot beside the fireplace where two of their sons were climbing on his shoulders.

"Four is plenty unless you're planning to give up your Senate seat and stay home with me to corral them," she responded. Then she turned to Lizzie and reached over to pluck something from her hair and hold it out to inspect it. "Is that straw?"

Lizzie felt heat rising in her cheeks. Zeke didn't help the matter when he laughed. Oh, but she loved this man, and she didn't care who knew it.

She reached over and kissed him. Again. Like she planned to do for the rest of her life.

 **Kathleen Y'Barbo** is a multiple Carol Award and RITA nominee and bestselling author of more than one hundred books, with over two million copies of her books in print in the US and abroad. A tenth-generation Texan and certified paralegal, she is a member of the Texas Bar Association Paralegal Division, Texas A&M Association of Former Students and Texas A&M Women Former Students (Aggie Women), Texas Historical Society, Novelists Inc., and American Christian Fiction Writers. She would also be a member of the Daughters of the American Republic, Daughters of the Republic of Texas, and a few others if she would just remember to fill out the paperwork that Great-Aunt Mary Beth has sent her more than once.

When she's not spinning modern-day tales about her wacky southern relatives, Kathleen inserts an ancestor or two into her historical and mystery novels as well. Recent book releases include bestselling *The Pirate Bride,* set in 1700s New Orleans and Galveston, and its sequel, *The Alamo Bride,* set in 1836 Texas, which feature a few well-placed folks from history and a family tale of adventure on the high seas and on the coast of Texas. She also writes (mostly) relative-free cozy mystery novels for Guideposts Books.

Kathleen and her hero in combat boots husband have their own surprise love story that unfolded on social media a few years back. They make their home just north of Houston, Texas, and are the parents and in-laws of a blended family of Texans, Okies, and one very adorable Londoner.

To find out more about Kathleen or to connect with her through social media, check out her website at www.kathleenybarbo.com.

THE BRIDE OF BASSWOOD HILL

by Gabrielle Meyer

Dedication

To one of my youth pastors, Chas Norman. Twenty-four years ago, on a trip to see Billy Graham preach, you asked each student what we wanted to be when we grew up. I hesitantly told you I wanted to be an author, and without skipping a beat, you pulled a scrap of paper out of your pocket and asked if you could have the first autograph. Your confident belief in my dream has not been forgotten. Thank you for speaking into my life.

Dear Reader,

In my story, the fictional estate of Basswood Hill is modeled after the real property in my hometown called Linden Hill. The mansions at Linden Hill were built by lumber barons in the 1890s who were affectionately called The Pine Tree Bachelors by the locals. Eventually, both men married and went on to have children. They left a lasting impact on our community to this day, and the property is now run as a conference and retreat center and is open to tours.

My personal connection to Linden Hill came from the years my father was the caretaker for the property. My family and I lived above the carriage house, and I grew up playing along the banks of the Mississippi River, drawing my love for history from the beautiful homes on the hill. Though this story is a work of fiction, I took a great deal of inspiration from the estate.

I first created Alex, Noah, and Julia in my novella *The Tale of Two Hearts* in the *Of Rags and Riches Romance Collection*. It has been a pleasure to return to Linden Hill and to give Alex a happily-ever-after. I hope you enjoy reading this story as much as I enjoyed writing it.

Happy reading,
Gabrielle Meyer

Chapter 1

St. Paul, Minnesota
August 1900

Charles Frederick Alexander had only been to Swede Hollow one other time in his life—and he had regretted it every day since. Alex, as his friends called him, looked out the pristine windows of the carriage at the squalid living conditions of the Italian and Swiss immigrant homes. Half of the houses were leaning precariously to the side, and most were missing windows, shingles, and siding. The poverty in this neighborhood was so extreme, the city didn't even bother to tax its inhabitants.

The carriage door opened, and the driver stood with his spotless top hat perched high upon his head. "We've arrived, sir."

Alex surveyed the dismal house before him. "Are you sure this is where Alberto Bellini lives?"

"Quite sure."

How was it possible? Alberto had been one of the finest wood-carvers in St. Paul, decorating the largest homes in the state. He had overseen all the woodwork in Alex's father's home. How could he live in such a place while adorning one of the grandest mansions on Summit Avenue with his talent? It didn't seem possible.

Leaving the comfort of the carriage, Alex stepped into the muddy street, trying to avoid a puddle filled with horse droppings. Alberto's two-story clapboard home had never been painted, but it had all its doors, windows, and shingles, and was not leaning like some of the others nearby. But those were the only positive attributes Alex could give to the home. Sewage flowed by in nearby Phalen Creek, and garbage was strewn in the yards and alleys between the houses. The stench filled his nose and made his eyes water.

"Thank you, Terrance." Alex moved away from the carriage and toward the house, shaking the grime from his polished shoes, his mind on the older gentleman who inhabited the building. Alberto had not only been a friend but had become like a grandfather, teaching Alex valuable life lessons. The Italian gentleman had mentored him in ways Alex's father had never thought, nor cared to, while teaching him the art and skill of woodworking. But it had been years since Alex had seen his old friend, and now it might be too late.

Alex lifted his gloved hand and knocked on the thin door.

He glanced around the neighborhood and tried not to let his feelings show. Things had deteriorated drastically since the last time he had come to the hollow as a child. Originally, it had been settled and built by the Swedish immigrants to St. Paul in the 1850s, but as they slowly left, it had become inhabited by the Italians and Swiss. When Alex had come before, he'd been there to see his Swedish friend Hans Johnson.

Regret still stung from that last encounter with Hans. Alex should have been braver and more courageous to stand up for his friend. The only way he could live with his actions that day was to pass them off as the result of being young and immature.

But Alex had known better then—and he knew better now. There was no reason to treat anyone poorly just because of where they were born.

The door opened, and a beautiful young woman looked out at Alex, uncertainty in her gaze. She held the door like a shield, half of her body hidden behind it.

Alex removed his bowler. "Pardon me," he said quickly. "I thought this was Alberto Bellini's home."

He started to step away, but she opened the door wider, putting up her hand. "Wait. You've come to the right home." Her Italian accent was thick as her words tumbled out with starts and pauses. "This is Alberto's home."

The woman was young and very slender. She wore a red hand-kerchief over her thick brown hair. It matched the red bodice laced up the front over a white blouse. Under her white apron she wore a long black skirt.

Alex had traveled the world over but had never laid eyes on a more stunning woman. He stared at her for a moment longer than he should but could not find the words to speak. Who was she? Alberto had come to America alone. Was she a neighbor there to check on him?

"May I help you?" she asked.

"I just returned from Paris," he explained, "and I've only just heard about Alberto." He swallowed, hoping he wasn't too late—ashamed he hadn't come sooner. "Is he still alive?"

Intense sadness clouded the woman's eyes as she nodded. "*Sì*, but he is very ill."

Empathy and compassion filled Alex. It sliced through him, reaching deep within his heart. He felt her pain, knew it profoundly as his own. Alberto had meant a great deal to him too.

She studied him, her eyes traveling over his well-tailored suit to the handsome cab waiting. Did he look as foreign to her as she did to him?

"Would you like to see my grandfather?" she asked.

Her grandfather? Alberto had spoken about the son and grand-daughter he'd left in the Italian village in Switzerland where they lived, but Alex had never thought he'd meet her.

"Your grandfather spoke of you often—and very fondly," Alex said. "I'm—"

"Mr. Alexander?" she asked.

He nodded, surprised she knew his name.

The first hint of a smile appeared. It made her dark brown eyes sparkle. "He has told me much about you in his letters, ever since I was a little girl." Appreciation tinted her words. "He says you are the grandson he never had."

Guilt tugged at Alex. Why had he waited so long to see his old friend? "And he is the grandfather I never had."

"Please come in." She opened the door wider and moved aside. "He will be very pleased to see you."

Alex stepped over the worn threshold and into the main room of the house, sorry his feet were so dirty. He tried finding somewhere to wipe them.

"Do not worry," she said with a smile and a nod at his shoes.

The inside of the house wasn't any nicer than the outside, but here Alberto's beautiful wood carvings were on display in all the handmade furniture and various figurines. They made the room feel warm and welcoming, reminding Alex of the man who had created them.

"He's upstairs," she said.

Alex followed her up a narrow set of stairs and into a single room under the eaves of the roof. In the corner, a man lay on a sagging bed, his thin frame outlined in the light blanket over his body.

"I'm afraid he does not have much time," she whispered and then knelt beside the bed. She took Alberto's hand. "*Nonno*, you have company."

Alberto's eyes fluttered open, and it took a moment for him to focus on his granddaughter's face. "My Sofia," he said with a weak smile.

"Mr. Alexander has come." Her voice was filled with love. "He is here to see you."

"Alex?" Alberto looked beyond Sofia, pure joy radiating from his face. He reached out to Alex with his other bony hand. "My grandson has come home."

Alex moved to the other side of the bed and knelt by Alberto's side. He set his bowler on the floor and took the wood-carver's hand. "*Ciao*, Alberto. It has been too long, my friend."

Alberto's hair was completely white and the wrinkles in his face had deepened, but the light in his eyes had not faded. He pulled Alex's hand to his mouth and kissed it. "It is never too long between friends. I am happy you have come."

"So am I." Memories of his time with Alberto returned to Alex, filling him with some of the sweetest and most important moments of his life.

Alberto's breathing was labored and shallow, but he seemed to be filled with renewed strength as he looked between Sofia and Alex, his eyes glowing with purpose. He drew their hands together and pressed them to his heart. "I have prayed ceaselessly that God would bring Alex to my side before I died."

"Hush, Nonno," Sofia said. "We will get you well."

Alberto shook his head. "God is calling me home, but I prayed He would not take me until Alex came again."

A mixture of awe and disquiet filled Alex. Had God really answered the older man's prayers? Was that why Alex's father had summoned him home earlier than expected from Paris? Alex hadn't planned to come home for several more months. He hadn't even had a chance to speak to his father about why he'd been called home. Terrance had picked Alex up from the train station and told him Alberto was sick, so Alex had decided to come to Swede Hollow. He'd deal with his father, and the emergency that had prompted the telegram, later.

Alex's knuckles brushed Sofia's as Alberto held their hands over his chest.

"I saved for years to bring my Sofia to America," Alberto explained to Alex. "But now that she is here, I cannot care for her like I should."

"Nonno—"

"I do not know what will become of her," Alberto said, ignoring his granddaughter, fear and anguish in his eyes. "This is no place for her to live."

Alex couldn't agree more. It was no place for anyone to live. If he had known this was where Alberto lived, he would have done something for him sooner.

"But she has no one and nothing," Alberto told Alex. "Her father died six months ago, and she is unmarried."

"Nonno." Sofia shook her head, mortification coloring her voice.

"She has no money, or reason, to return to Switzerland." Alberto watched Alex closely, passion deepening his voice. "She is a woodcarver and has learned from her father, who learned from me. But I fear she will not find work as a carver. If she is fortunate, she might find work in a mill or as a housekeeper—but that is not the life for my Sofia." He smiled at his granddaughter. Love poured from him with each word he spoke. "My Sofia should live like a princess, enjoying the finest things in life. Does she not look like a princess?"

Alex nodded, unable to speak.

Tears streamed down Sofia's soft cheeks unchecked. "Nonno, you should sleep," she whispered. "You will upset yourself."

Alberto turned to look at Alex, his love for Alex just as strong and powerful as if they were real flesh and blood. "There is no man on this earth I trust or respect more than you, my grandson. I have prayed God would spare me until I could ask you to marry Sofia and care for her once I am gone."

The request, spoken so gently and with so much trust, left Alex truly speechless. He glanced up and met the gaze of Sofia Bellini.

Shock and alarm filled her eyes as she shook her head. "Nonno, you cannot ask Mr. Alex—"

"I have never asked for anything," Alberto said to Alex. "I have saved this great request for the thing that is most important to me in the world. My Sofia."

Alex was a confirmed bachelor. At the age of twenty-eight, he had spent his entire adult life avoiding matrimony—and having a great deal of fun in the process. As the heir of one of the largest fortunes in America, there had been no end to the women paraded about for his choosing. Eager debutantes across the country had vied for his attention—and failed. The only woman he'd ever loved, Julia Morgan, had married his best friend and business partner. It wasn't that he didn't want to get married—he'd simply not found anyone who had intrigued him enough to consider such a thing—aside from Julia.

Until now.

Sofia shook her head, more tears slipping down her cheeks. "I will be fine. I will find a way."

"You are a strong woman," Alberto said to his granddaughter. "But you should not face this world by yourself. I do not want you to suffer for one more day. That is why you came to America. I love you too much to leave you here alone."

Sweet affection filled Sofia's gaze as she looked upon her grandfather. They had not had much time together, being separated by a vast ocean for most of Sofia's life, yet the bond they shared was strong.

Something deep and powerful shifted in Alex's heart as he watched Alberto and Sofia and the great love they had for one another. Alex had never felt, or been shown, such love and affection from his parents. How was it possible that these two people, who hadn't been together in years, could be so close? He didn't understand it, but he craved it with every breath he took. He longed for a family of his own, one where he could give and receive unconditional love.

Suddenly a sense of confidence filled Alex that this was God's will. That Sofia Bellini was the woman Alex had been waiting for his whole life. He didn't know why—or how—but he knew. Not only did he have an overwhelming peace about Alberto's request, but he wanted to honor his love for Alberto by doing this for him.

And if Sofia Bellini could ever look at him with the love she showed for her grandfather, Alex would consider himself the luckiest man on the face of the earth.

There would be obstacles—more than Alex cared to think about—but he was certain it was the right thing to do. Alberto Bellini had been the most important man in Alex's childhood. Even though Alex wasn't proud of everything he'd done in his life, if it hadn't been for Alberto, Alex wouldn't know God, and he probably would have chosen a much more rebellious and troubling path.

But he hadn't—and he owed it to the man lying in the bed. If he could ease Alberto's passing and give him the assurance he needed to die in peace, he would.

"If Sofia is willing," Alex said gently, looking up to meet the woman's gaze, searching for her feelings on the matter. "I will marry her."

Sofia inhaled as she studied Alex, shock and concern tightening the lines around her mouth.

Alberto smiled and nodded. He laid Alex's hand on top of Sofia's and then placed his hands over theirs. "It is good, my children," he said. "Very good, indeed."

Sofia Bellini stared at the handsome man across from her, her thoughts and emotions too frayed to resist her grandfather's shocking request. She couldn't find the words to respond—not only because her grandfather had asked, but because Charles Alexander had just agreed.

What kind of man agreed to marry a complete stranger?

And what kind of woman went along with the ridiculous plan?

A desperate one? If that was so, then Sofia was exactly the kind of woman who would marry a stranger.

Yet Alex wasn't a complete stranger. Grandfather had spoken of him so often in his letters, Sofia felt like she already knew him—but that didn't mean she was ready for marriage. Grandfather saw only the best in people. Was there a side of Alex her grandfather had ignored?

"I do not have much time," Grandfather said to Alex. "Take Sofia to the courthouse and get a special license this very afternoon."

"Nonno." Sofia shook her head and pulled her hand away from her grandfather and the stranger. She couldn't let this happen. She stood, needing space from both of them. "I cannot marry this man. I do not know him." And she was so far beneath him, she was not even fit to shine his shoes. He was refined and elegant. The suit he wore was probably more expensive than all the clothes she'd ever owned in her life. She was a simple peasant from a southern province in Switzerland, only three weeks off the boat—and he was heir to a vast American fortune.

Under normal circumstances, she wouldn't even be qualified to work in his home as a scullery maid.

"Hush, Sofia," Grandfather said. "You know Alex."

No. She didn't. She knew of him, but that wasn't the same thing.

Alex also stood, bringing his hat with him. He held it in one hand as he met Sofia's gaze.

His eyes were the bluest she'd ever seen—but it was the kindness and compassion in their depths that drew her the most. He was handsome, yes, but Gianni had been handsome too—and look how that had ended. His good looks had deceived her into believing he was good on the inside too, but he had broken her heart and left her ashamed and embarrassed.

And three months pregnant.

"Miss Bellini," Alex said gently, "may I have a word with you?"

Sofia glanced at her grandfather, who had closed his eyes and appeared to be resting peacefully.

She nodded and then walked across the room.

Alex's footsteps echoed behind her, matching the beat of her troubled heart.

"I know this is sudden," Alex said quietly. "And you are probably scared and uncertain."

No more than she had been for the past three months—though, at least here in America she did not have to lower her eyes in shame when she walked down the street.

At least not yet.

"I have utmost respect for Alberto," he continued. "I would do anything for him."

Even marry his pregnant granddaughter? Would he be so quick to offer marriage if he knew she had been ruined by another man?

He swallowed and ran his hands around the brim of his hat. "It would be an honor to make you my wife."

Sofia's breathing was shallow, and the room began to tilt. She pressed one hand to the doorframe and the other to her turning stomach. The sickness had not bothered her often, but it threatened to bother her now.

Without a word, he placed his hand around her waist and helped her to a chair nearby. She took a seat, and he squatted next to her.

"Are you unwell?" he asked.

She took several deep breaths, thankful the dizziness passed once she was seated. "I am fine. A little shaken is all."

He watched her for a moment, compassion and uncertainty in his face. "We will not do this if you are not sure."

"Why would you marry me?" He was handsome, wealthy, and if her grandfather was correct, extremely good. Why wasn't he married already?

He didn't speak for a moment as he glanced over his shoulder to where Grandfather slept. When he looked back at Sofia, gratitude warmed his face. "I owe my faith, and much of the limited wisdom I possess, to Alberto. He was the first person to teach me what unconditional love truly means. He taught me compassion, courage, and responsibility. I do not know who I would be today if it wasn't for him." He studied her, shaking his head. "If you are anything like him, I would be a fool not to marry you."

Courageous and responsible were two things Sofia was not. She dropped her gaze, ashamed at the truth. "I am nothing like my grandfather."

"I do not believe that. I see the way you love and care for him. I believe you are more like him than you even realize."

Grandfather's breath rattled in his throat, causing Sofia's heart to gallop. He did not have much time left—and then where would she go? She couldn't stay alone in Swede Hollow, and she would be unemployable as soon as her pregnancy was noticeable. Then what would she do? Gianni had promised to marry her, but then his father had learned about their relationship and convinced Gianni that Sofia wasn't good enough. When Sofia told Gianni about the baby, he refused to acknowledge their child, already moving on to the next woman who caught his fancy. His father, the president of their village council, had threatened her if she ever stepped foot in Lugano again. She suspected she was not the first of Gianni's indiscretions.

Was it wrong to accept Alex's proposal? What would he do when he learned she was pregnant? Would he turn her out as Gianni had? He'd have every right.

Grandfather's breathing became normal again, and the tension in Sofia's shoulders eased just a bit.

"If you're worried about the—marriage," Alex said slowly, "I would not expect. . ." His words faded away, but Sofia understood his meaning. She would not be required to consummate the marriage. It would be in name only—a marriage of convenience. If that was the case, could she walk away if necessary?

"My home is a hundred miles northwest of here," he continued. "It's a grand home, with servants who would see to your needs. You would want for nothing."

Except love. She would want for love.

"I would do anything for Alberto," he said again. "I wish I could do more."

Sofia hated being on the receiving end of charity. She had never taken anything for free in her life, and she wasn't about to start now. Perhaps he could hire her as a maid, instead?

"Sofia?" Grandfather called for her.

She stood and went to his side again.

"I'm here, Nonno."

"Will you grant my final request and marry Alex?" He looked

up at her, fading quickly. "I cannot die in peace until I know you are taken care of."

"Perhaps Mr. Alexander will give me a job instead."

"No." Grandfather shook his head. "You should be a bride, not a maid. I want to know you will be cared for, no matter what happens."

How could she say no?

Tears gathered in her eyes, and she knelt beside her grandfather. "Of course," she said. "I will do this thing you ask."

Grandfather smiled. "Go now, before it grows too late. Come back when you are married. I will be here waiting."

Would he still be alive?

She leaned in and placed a kiss on his cheek.

He laid his hand upon her head and then said to Alex. "Come, my grandson."

Alex went back to the other side of the bed and knelt once again.

Grandfather took both their hands, as before, and placed them together over his heart. "The Lord bless thee, and keep thee both," he said to them. "The Lord make His face shine upon thee, and be gracious unto thee. The Lord lift up His countenance upon thee, and give thee peace."

"Goodbye, Nanno," Sofia said, her tears running down her cheeks.

"Goodbye, my Sofia. Remember I love you."

She knew he was saying goodbye for good, and he did not want her to stay and see him die.

"Goodbye, Alex," Grandfather said. "Take good care of my Sofia."

"I will. You have my word." Alex rose and walked around the bed, where he offered his hand to Sofia. "Shall we go? My carriage is waiting. We will come back here the moment we're done."

Sofia nodded and allowed him to help her stand.

They looked as different as two people could look. He was tall and fair, with light eyes and expensive clothing. She was small and dark, with brown eyes and peasants' clothes. What would people think when they arrived at the courthouse?

As they left her grandfather's room, she turned to look at him one last time.

Grandfather smiled and nodded. She returned his smile, though she didn't feel like smiling.

She led Alex down the stairs and out of the house.

The carriage was waiting, and just as she suspected, the driver's eyes grew huge when Alex motioned for him to open the door for her.

Sofia took a deep breath. She would marry Charles Alexander for her grandfather's sake, but she would find a way to earn her own income, and when she was ready, she would annul the marriage and make a way for her and her child.

It was the only option she had.

She could not bear to bring Charles Alexander shame or embarrassment when people learned about her baby.

Chapter 2

A moonless night enveloped Alex and Sofia as the carriage came to a stop under the porte cochere at his father's mansion on Summit Avenue. A single light glowed from Father's office window, but the rest of the house was dark. No doubt the staff would be asleep this late at night. Alex hoped he and Sofia could enter without disturbing the whole house, because it would only hasten the questions that were sure to arise.

"Thank you," Sofia said quietly in her lilted accent from the other side of the carriage. "For all you've done."

"I wish I could have done more."

It had been a long, emotional day. After their very brief wedding at the courthouse, they had returned to find Alberto had peacefully passed away. It had taken several hours before the undertakers were able to come, and then a bit more work to pack up the few things Sofia had wanted to take to remember her grandfather. Alex had asked if he could have Alberto's Bible, which he held reverently in his hands now. It was soft from use, its pages and cover well loved over the years.

Terrance opened the door, and Alex stepped out. He turned and offered his hand to Sofia. A lantern from the carriage flickered and highlighted her high cheek bones. Fear and uncertainty radiated from her eyes as she hesitated inside the dark interior.

"I will not let anything hurt you," he said gently. "You have my word."

She studied him for a heartbeat and then took the hand he offered.

Her hand was small and delicate. She did not wear gloves or have any of the adornments of the women he knew—but he'd never seen a more elegant or graceful lady. He marveled at the way she held herself on such a hard and trying day.

The reality that she was his wife washed over him like a tidal wave, taking him unaware, and he had a sudden urge to protect her. He had promised not to let anything hurt her, yet the man inside the house would be the first in line. Alex knew his father's feelings about the lower classes all too well. He would employ them, but he wouldn't associate with them. Wasn't that why Alex had witnessed Hans's beating all those years ago in Swede Hollow? His father wanted to make an example of the boy and threaten Alex that the same thing would happen to any friend Alex played with that didn't meet his standards.

Unease washed over Alex as he wrapped his wife's hand around his elbow, pulling her closer. He rarely interacted with his father anymore and preferred to keep it that way. But it wasn't always easy to avoid him, since his father was also his boss.

When he was nineteen, Alex had moved a hundred miles northwest to Little Falls, Minnesota, to manage the White Pine Lumber Mill, the largest mill in the United States. It was just one of a dozen mills owned by the Midwest Lumber Company, which his father had started with several business partners before Alex was born. Alex and his friend, Noah Walker, had been running the mill for nine years and had enjoyed great success—not to mention a reputation as the most eligible bachelors in Minnesota. They'd even been nicknamed the White Pine Bachelors.

Because of their success, Alex had been able to invest some of his wealth in the development of an automobile company. He and one of his partners, Elijah Boyer, had been in Paris at the World's Fair to exhibit their vehicle. They had broken several speed records and had gained a great deal of attention.

But then the telegram had arrived, demanding that Alex return to St. Paul immediately. An emergency concerning the mill would need Alex's attention.

So here he was.

With a new wife on his arm.

And a lot of explaining to do.

Terrance pulled the carriage away, leaving Alex and Sofia alone.

"I hope to take you inside without disturbing everyone," Alex explained. "I will show you to a guest room, and hopefully you can rest. I'll send a maid to you in the morning to see to your needs."

"A maid?" The night was dark, but Alex's eyes had adjusted and he could make out her form. She shook her head. "I do not need a maid."

She would, for so many reasons he couldn't begin to explain tonight. "Terrance will bring your trunk into the house so you will have it in the morning. The maid will help you dress for breakfast, and I will introduce you to my father then." They hadn't had much time to discuss all the particulars, and until he knew what emergency had called him home, he wasn't sure what to tell her. "After breakfast we will discuss the rest."

They would hold Alberto's funeral tomorrow morning, and then, as soon as possible, he wanted to return to his home at Basswood Hill to get Sofia settled. He hadn't been there since May and missed his house on the banks of the upper Mississippi River.

She didn't protest further, so he went to the front door and rang the bell. It would chime in the butler's room and hopefully wouldn't be heard by his father. If he could avoid a meeting with him tonight, he would.

They waited for several minutes, and then the electric light above the door turned on and the door opened.

"Mr. Alexander," the butler said as he pulled his arm into his suit coat. "We expected you hours ago." He paused as his gaze landed on Sofia. Questions crossed his brow, but he didn't ask them.

Alex would have to introduce Sofia sooner than later. "Thomas, I'd like you to meet my wife, Mrs. Sofia Alexander."

Thomas's eyes grew wide as he looked at Sofia again. She still wore the red handkerchief over her dark hair and the red bodice over the white shirt. No doubt she was a complete surprise to Thomas—for more than one reason. "We had no idea. Your father didn't tell us."

"He doesn't know himself."

Thomas moved aside and offered a slight bow. "Congratulations, Mr. Alexander. It is our privilege to welcome you and your wife home."

A few, low-lit wall sconces cast shadows over the grand entrance. Alberto's expert carvings were everywhere in the hall, on the furniture, in the trim, and even in the heavy doors.

Thomas closed the front door and nodded at Alex. "I will awake the staff to see to your—"

"Please don't," Alex said quickly. "We're both exhausted and would prefer to go to sleep."

"Of course." He nodded. "Your room is ready for you."

Alex glanced at Sofia, recalling his promise to her earlier in the day. It might cause some tongues to wag, but he'd not make her feel uncomfortable by forcing her to share a room. It wasn't uncommon for married couples to have their own rooms, but usually they were connected by a shared door. Alex's room did not share a door with any others. "Mrs. Alexander will take the room next to mine."

Thomas nodded and then glanced down the hall toward Father's study. "Your father is waiting up to speak to you. He said he'd like to see you the moment you arrive."

Father would be angry with the delay, no doubt, and doubly so when he knew why. There was no use trying to ignore him for the night.

"Please show my wife to her room," Alex said to Thomas. "I'll go see my father."

Sofia stood motionless beside Alex, and he could only imagine her discomfort. She was a complete stranger to this home. He hated to leave her but had no choice. He handed her Alberto's Bible and said, "I'll see you in the morning."

She accepted the heavy book and followed Thomas, casting a glance over her shoulder once on the way up the grand staircase before they disappeared out of sight.

Alex took a deep breath and walked down the hall toward Father's office.

"Come in," Father said even before Alex knocked. "I've been waiting for you."

Opening the door, Alex stepped inside.

His father sat at his desk, his back rigid as usual as he wrote in a ledger. "Take a seat." He didn't even look up to share a greeting. "We have much to discuss, and it cannot wait another moment."

Alex removed his bowler and sat next to Father's desk, his

muscles stiff with unease.

Father took a few more seconds to finish whatever he was writing and then he set his pen down and finally glanced at Alex. "Where have you been? I sent Terrance after you hours ago."

"I heard that Alberto Bellini was close to death so I had Terrance take me to him."

"Couldn't that have waited until a more convenient time?"

"Death waits for no man." Alex looked down at his hat. "He passed away."

"I asked you to shorten your unnecessary trip to Europe because something has come up." Father didn't bother to mourn Alberto's death for even a moment—but what did Alex expect? "As you know, Midwest Lumber has tried to acquire North American Lumber for years, but the Robertsons have resisted the sale—until now. Mr. Robertson has finally considered our offer, but he has requested a visit to one of our mills to see how we operate our business before he makes a final decision. The board has chosen your mill in Little Falls, since it is our largest and most successful."

The news was better than Alex anticipated. If Midwest Lumber acquired North American Lumber, they would become the largest lumber producers in the world. Alex could use the boost in his salary to invest more heavily in his automobile company, which was his real passion.

"Mr. Robertson and his wife, along with several of our board members and their wives, will arrive in Little Falls three days from now, in advance of the lumberjack festival." Father spoke with little emotion. "You, Noah, and his wife will host the guests for the week. If anything goes wrong, it will be on your shoulders." He stared at Alex. "So, make sure nothing goes wrong. The sale depends upon this visit."

"They'll arrive in three days?" Alex asked.

"Is there a problem with that?"

How would Alex prepare Sofia for her first social responsibility in just three days? Hosting several guests would be a major undertaking, even for the most experienced hostess. No doubt she'd be overwhelmed.

"Not exactly."

"Noah and Julia have been preparing for weeks. Your staff was alerted, and they have been preparing as well. Your only concern will be the bookwork. Make sure it's up to date and in good order."

The bookwork was the last of Alex's concerns at the moment.

"I will arrive with the board," Father continued, "to make sure everything runs smoothly." He rose. "I'm tired. I will see you in the morning." He started to walk toward the door.

Alex also rose. He could wait for morning to say something about Sofia, but then he risked one of the staff telling his father first. It was best just to get it over with.

"There's something else." Alex gripped the brim of his hat, praying for favor—though he doubted his father would grant it. "I'm married."

Father paused and turned to face Alex. For the first time in Alex's life, his father looked at him with what appeared to be pleasure and approval. "Wonderful. I've often said it would benefit you professionally to have a wife. She will assist Julia in entertaining our guests. I'm sure there will be teas and luncheons for the ladies while we tour the mill and conduct our meetings."

Alex nodded, though he couldn't imagine throwing Sofia into a bevy of socialites so soon.

"Where did you meet her?" Father asked. "Paris? Do I know her people? Was she there visiting the fair?"

"No." Alex shook his head, uncertain how to tell his father the truth.

Father frowned. "If you didn't meet her in Paris, then where? London?"

"I met her here, in St. Paul."

"Here?" Father walked back to Alex. They stood eye to eye, and his father stared at him. "I don't understand. Did you meet her here and then reconnect with her in Europe?"

"I just met her today."

Father's face became devoid of emotion. "You're jesting with me, Charles." His father was the only person who called him by his given name. "You've only met her today and you're married?" His voice rose a notch. "Who is she?"

"Her name is Sofia. . .Bellini. Alberto's granddaughter."

The clock in the hall struck midnight as Father's chest rose and fell. He worked his jaw back and forth and lowered his chin. "Have you lost your mind?"

"She recently arrived from Switzerland and has no one else. Alberto asked me to care for—"

"This is outrageous, even for you." Father's voice rose higher and higher. "You cannot be married to my wood-carver's granddaughter. It's not done. You have a responsibility to your wealth and class to marry well."

"She's the one I've chosen." Alex spoke slowly and evenly. "It was the right thing to do."

"The right thing?" Father's face turned red. "You will undo this thing, Charles, immediately. I demand you annul the marriage. We'll pretend it never happened."

"I have married her, for better or worse. I will not annul the marriage."

"You ungrateful, spoiled child. You're doing this to spite me, aren't you?"

"I'm an adult, Father. I'm almost thirty years old. I have chosen

240

to marry Sofia, and that choice is mine alone. It has nothing to do with you."

"You are a member of the Alexander family." His father raised his chin and puffed out his chest. "And with that privilege comes great responsibility. What will our peers think of you marrying a dirty immigrant?"

"She's not dirty," he said through gritted teeth, "nor do I care what my peers think."

"Your peers are responsible for your place in society."

"I care little for society."

"I'm painfully aware." He narrowed his eyes. "I've warned you about associating with the lower classes, Charles. They are good for labor and nothing else. If we allowed them, they would drain our resources and drag us down to their level. This girl will be your ruination."

"I have married her, and I will stay married to her," Alex told his father, ready to defend his decision—and his wife—regardless of what it cost him. "I already care very deeply about her and her welfare."

"You are a stubborn fool." Father shook his head and looked Alex over from head to toe, disgust in his glare. "If I cannot be rid of her, then I will make demands—ones you cannot deny if you want to keep your position with Midwest Lumber."

Was Father threatening to fire him? If Alex didn't have his income from the mill, he would be forced to close down his automobile productions—and he couldn't, not when they were so close to success.

"We will say this woman, whatever her name is—"

"Sofia."

"We will say she is from a wealthy European family and you met her in Paris—"

"Father, I will not lie, and I cannot ask Sofia to lie—"

"You will do as I say, or you will lose everything—your job, your home, and your investments." His words, spoken with so little emotion, cut Alex to his core.

If Alex didn't have a home or a job, how would he honor Alberto's request to take care of Sofia?

"If she makes any blunders, we will blame it on her European upbringing, do you understand?" Father didn't wait for Alex to respond. "Mrs. Robertson is related to Mrs. Caroline Astor of New York. Wealth, status, and old money mean everything to them. Mr. Robertson inherited his lumber business from Mrs. Robertson's father. If she does not approve of our family, this acquisition will not proceed. Do I make myself clear?"

Alex despised the social confines of his peerage. He was thankful to live in Minnesota, far removed from the constraints of New York and people like Mrs. Astor and Mrs. Robertson. But, like most expectations in his social group, he couldn't prevent them from invading his life.

"Yes."

"Good." Father continued to the door but stopped one more time. "At the first light of day, I will speak to the housekeeper and have her oversee outfitting your new *wife* for her role."

"We intend to bury her grandfather tomorrow morning and then leave for Little Falls."

"She will be outfitted before she leaves St. Paul—and I will not permit her to dress in mourning while our guests are here. I do not want her to let on that her grandfather has just died. That will put a somber pall on the entire venture."

How would Alex tell Sofia she couldn't wear mourning for her grandfather?

"You will return to Little Falls the day after tomorrow," Father continued.

"She'll hardly have time to settle in before our guests ar—"

"And she'll have no one to blame but you."

Father didn't say good night, but simply left Alex standing alone in his office.

Alex had made a promise to Alberto to take care of Sofia, and he'd made a promise to protect Sofia from getting hurt. He'd keep both promises, come what may.

Sofia Bellini Alexander stood in front of the full-length mirror, alone for the first time since she awoke early that morning. After they had buried her grandfather, she and Alex had returned to his father's home, but there hadn't been time to discuss the future before maids and seamstresses had descended upon her. She had endured hours of poking, prodding, and primping and hadn't been given many choices, though she couldn't complain about the clothing that had been selected for her. The only complaint she had was when she was told she couldn't wear mourning clothes to honor her grandfather's passing.

Now, with the dinner gong still vibrating in the lower hall, she stared at her reflection, uncertain if she liked what she saw—and more eager than ever to speak to Alex. How would she ever repay him for all these expensive things? Surely they had cost a small fortune. Dozens of gowns, for every conceivable occasion, had been selected for her. There were also hats, gloves, jewelry, shoes, jackets, hair accessories, and more.

How did they expect one woman to use all those things?

She took several deep breaths as she inspected her reflection. Her dark hair was styled in a high pompadour with a gray ribbon encircling her head. The ribbon was the exact same color as the silk evening gown she'd been tucked into for supper. It was one of the most exquisite things she'd ever seen, though nothing at all like the clothing she'd always worn. It was soft and flowed in waves to a long train behind her. Lace dripped from the bodice and sleeves. Her black gloves ran up to her elbows, and she had been given a long necklace of beautiful pearls, with matching pearl earrings.

What she saw before her in the mirror was stunning—but looked nothing like the reflection she'd gazed upon for the past nineteen years of her life.

A knock at the door made her jump.

"Yes?"

The maid who had been with her for most of the day entered. "Dinner is served, ma'am."

Sofia hadn't had the pleasure of meeting Alex's father, but that was about to change. She just hoped she could speak to Alex before she saw Mr. Alexander.

Leaving the relative safety of her room, Sofia followed the maid to the head of the stairs.

"The drawing room is to the right, at the bottom of the staircase," the maid said with a curtsy and then left her side.

Sofia gripped the handrail and started down the stairs.

A door opened in the main hall, and a moment later Alex appeared near the foot of the steps. He looked up at her and blinked several times, his face alight with wonder.

Heat warmed Sofia's cheeks at the look of admiration in his beautiful blue eyes. He was pleased with her appearance, which made her happier than she expected. Until then she hadn't realized how much she wanted to please him.

She stopped on the bottom step and met his appreciative gaze with one of her own. He looked handsome in his evening suit, with his dark blond hair perfectly styled, and his shoes shining.

"You're stunning, Sofia." He blinked several times. "I'm speechless."

"The clothes." She lifted the hem of the gown and shook her head. "They are too expensive. I cannot repay you."

"You do not need to repay me. They are a gift—a wedding gift."

"But I will not need them—later."

"Later?"

"When I have enough money to care for myself." She studied him, afraid he wasn't understanding her English. "It was not right for my grandfather to ask you to marry me. I will find a way to pay for myself and will go back to Switzerland." She had some distant relatives she could call upon if she needed. It wasn't what she wanted, but if it meant she could raise her child in safety and without fear, she would do what was necessary.

He studied her for a few moments. "Is that what you want? To return to your homeland?"

Sofia dropped her gaze, afraid he might see the truth and feel obligated to keep her. "Yes."

"I will not make you stay against your will," he said quietly, almost as if he was disappointed. "But I do not want you to feel like you must leave either. When I married you, I intended it to be forever." He waited for a moment, and when she did not reply, he continued. "If you want to leave, I will pay for you to return to Switzerland, but I'd really like it if you could stay long enough to help me."

"Help you?"

He explained to her about his father's business and about the visit in the coming days. "This acquisition is very important to my father's company, so we will have to do our best to please the Robertsons."

She nodded, willing to do anything for this kind man who had helped her.

"But. . ." He sighed. "My father does not want them to know you and I just met. He asked that we pretend we were acquainted in Europe—and that you come from a wealthy European family."

Sofia frowned and shook her head. "I do not understand."

Pain sliced through his gaze. "My father is all about appearances, and in his social circles old money means everything. He's afraid—" Alex struggled to explain, but realization finally dawned on Sofia. His father was embarrassed that she was a poor immigrant. Of course. He'd be concerned that it would not look good—especially for this important business transaction.

Sofia put her hand on Alex's arm, wanting to reassure him. "I understand."

He shook his head. "I'm sorry. Truly I am."

"It will be all right." She lifted her chin, ready to be strong and supportive. "I will try my best. For you."

He smiled. "And I will make sure you get back to Switzerland—or wherever you choose to go—and that you are taken care of, if that is truly what you desire."

"But, what about all these clothes and—?"

"They are a gift. You do not need to trouble yourself over them." He studied her with his confident and caring blue eyes. "I want you to have them."

Then it was settled. Sofia would pretend to be from a wealthy, prominent family in Switzerland and help Alex in the coming weeks—and he would ensure her safe return to her extended family.

He offered his elbow to her. "Shall we go to dinner? My father is waiting."

She took his assistance, mindful of her new role, and walked with him to the ornate dining room at the end of the hall. He smelled of sandalwood and was tall and strong beside her. She had never felt so important—or so out of place—as she did on his arm.

Mr. Alexander was already seated at the head of the long table. The room was decorated in dark walnut trim. Sofia smiled at all the beautiful, intricate carvings, feeling her grandfather's presence in this foreign place. Even though she couldn't mourn him with her clothing, she could honor his memory with her thoughts and prayers.

The butler and a footman stood at attention near a side table laden with food.

"Father?" Alex brought Sofia to the side of the table. "I'd like you to meet my wife."

Mr. Alexander stood and looked Sofia over from head to toe. "She'll do for our purposes, I suppose."

Alex's jaw tightened, and he said again, "Father, I'd like you to meet my *wife*, Sofia Alexander."

Mr. Alexander stared at his son, an unspoken threat in his gaze.

"If everyone is to believe we're a happily married couple," Alex said, barely controlling his tone, "you will need to treat her as a valuable member of our family."

Bowing, Mr. Alexander nodded once to Sofia. "Welcome to my home, Sofia. I trust you've been treated well."

Until this moment.

"Yes, thank you." She forced herself to sound more confident than she felt, and couldn't meet his gaze.

Alex pulled a chair out for Sofia to sit at his father's right hand, and then he walked behind his father's chair and took a seat directly across the table from her. When he was finally settled into place, he gave her a warm, encouraging smile.

If everyone in Alex's social circle was like his father, she'd need all the encouragement she could get.

As the footman brought out the soup course, no one said a word.

Mr. Alexander watched every move Sofia made. It caused her hands to tremble and her stomach to turn. The smell of the fish soup only made her more nauseated. She allowed the footman to pour it into her bowl, but she couldn't force herself to put the spoon into her mouth. She couldn't even look at it.

The babe within her would not let her forget her past mistakes, nor would men like Mr. Alexander. He was so much like Gianni's father, Sofia wondered if meeting this family was more punishment from God for her indiscretions. If Mr. Alexander could run her out of his home this moment and threaten her not to return, she was certain he would.

But it was Alex, who sat across from her, that gave her hope. He was nothing like Gianni—but if forced to choose, would he choose to please his father over protecting her, as Gianni had done?

Only time would tell.

Chapter 3

The first glimpse Sofia had of Basswood Hill made her catch her breath. Sunshine dappled through the large trees on the long driveway up to the mansions. To her right was a pool house and tennis court, and straight ahead were two beautiful homes. The one on the left was dark green, and the one on the right was white.

She sat next to Alex in his Duryea, an automobile that had been modified for him the year before, and loved the feel of the wind in her face. The drive from St. Paul had taken them almost four hours, but she didn't mind. She enjoyed the unhindered view of Minnesota's diverse countryside from the comforts of the vehicle.

"I'm almost sad that our ride is at an end," Alex said to her as he maneuvered up the drive. "Now we must face the real world again."

And the real world was rarely kind to her.

They hadn't been able to talk on the ride with the wind and the rumble of the motor making it too loud to hear each other. But Sofia had come to realize that despite all the trouble and uncertainty, Alex made her feel safe. He was a stranger, taking her to a strange place, but she felt protected and cared for.

"Your trunks should have already arrived at the train station," he said. "I telegraphed ahead for someone to retrieve them for you. Hopefully they've already been brought to your room."

He pulled the automobile to a stop in front of the white home. It was three stories tall, with black trim, thick leaded glass, and several dormers, bay windows, and tall gables. "The green home belongs to my good friend Noah Walker and his wife, Julia." Alex lifted his driving goggles off his face and removed his hat. "You'll like Julia. I sent her and Noah a telegram, and they should be expecting us."

At that moment, the front door of the green mansion opened and a young couple stepped out. The man was tall, with dark hair and a well-trimmed beard, but it was the woman who caught Julia's attention. Her light brown hair was piled high on her head, with tendrils softening her pretty face. She wore a pink gown—but it was the evidence of Julia's pregnancy that made Sofia pause. She should have felt thankful to have another woman in the same condition—but Sofia wasn't free to discuss her pregnancy. She'd rather no one knew, especially Alex. It was hard enough to know others would frown upon her pregnancy. She couldn't imagine seeing Alex's disappointment in her too. She wanted nothing more than to be done with this impending visit and then be on a boat back to Switzerland before anyone found out the truth.

"There they are now." Alex stepped out of the automobile and went around to open the door for Sofia. He offered her his hand and helped her climb out of the high vehicle.

Sofia wore a wide-brimmed hat with a driving scarf. She smoothed her new dress and forced herself to smile.

"Welcome to Basswood Hill," Julia said even before they stopped in front of Alex and Sofia. Julia's smile was so open and inviting,

Sofia couldn't help but warm to her. "I'm so happy you've come." She took Sofia's hand in both of hers. "We were shocked when Alex sent his telegram, but we couldn't be happier for him."

"Noah and Julia, I'd like you to meet Sofia." Alex made the introduction, though it wasn't necessary, since Julia put her arm around Sofia and started walking her toward the white mansion, talking eagerly.

"I've taken the liberty of preparing a meal for us tonight," Julia said to Sofia. "So you and Alex can join us at our house, and you won't need to worry about anything this evening. We'll get you settled in, and then when you're ready, I'll tell you all the plans that have been made for the Robertsons' visit."

Sofia glanced behind her and found Alex and Noah following them.

Alex smiled at Sofia.

"Your trunks have already been delivered," Julia continued. "They came about an hour ago. I'm sure you'll be anxious to see your new home, so I won't keep you long." She stopped at the base of the steps leading to the front porch and looked toward Alex. "I'm sure Alex would like you all to himself, so we'll just head back to our house. Feel free to come whenever you're ready."

Noah took his wife's hand and drew her toward him. "My wife tends to babble when she gets nervous or excited. Please forgive her, Sofia."

Sofia smiled. She did the opposite when she was nervous, tending toward silence. It was nice to have someone fill the quiet space.

Julia's cheeks turned pink as she lovingly set her hand on her swollen stomach. "I'm just very eager for you to like us, Sofia. We've waited a long time for Alex to bring home a wife." She looked up into Noah's face, and he smiled down at her. She looked back at Sofia. "I'm excited to hear all about your courtship and romance. I'm sure there's a wonderful story behind your marriage."

"I suppose that will have to wait for a bit," Alex said abruptly. "I'm sure Sofia is tired. I'll show her into the house, and then we'll come by later on."

Julia waved as her husband walked them back toward their house.

"They don't know?" Sofia asked. "Are we to be the only ones who know the truth?"

"I trust Noah and Julia. I'll tell them as soon as I can." He walked up the steps and opened his front door. "But, for now, I'd like you to see your new home."

Her new home for the time being anyway. It was hard to believe that she would be the lady of such a fine, elegant mansion—even if for a couple short weeks. In Switzerland she and her father had lived in a simple two-room cottage. It wasn't large or spacious, but it had been clean and weatherproof.

"After you." Alex opened the door, and Sofia climbed the stairs to step into the enclosed porch.

White beadboard covered the walls, with thick leaded windows encircling the entire room. There was a beautiful view of a nearby pond with ducks flapping their wings on the water. Comfortable furniture and several plants gave the room a welcoming feel.

Alex pushed open the heavy oak door that led into the foyer. He smiled as she walked past him.

The house wasn't nearly as fancy as his father's back in St. Paul, but it was well built and beautiful in its own way.

"It's desperately in need of a woman's touch," Alex admitted. "Noah and I had our homes built a few years ago, but he and Julia married right before his was finished. She was able to decorate their home to suit her taste." He shrugged and set his driving goggles on a nearby table. "I decorated the best I could, but—"

"It's lovely." She ran her fingers over the fine woodwork and admired the thick woven rug under her feet. A wide staircase sat at the back of the room, and a parlor opened up to the left.

It was hard to imagine that he might be self-conscious about his home. She'd only dreamed of such a place.

"There's more." Alex moved to the parlor and motioned for her to join him.

She walked through the parlor, which boasted a large brick fireplace and two matching reading alcoves on either side, and into a hall with a water fountain on the wall. Straight ahead was a dining room—but the room to her left made her catch her breath.

"It's a music room." Alex watched her closely. "Do you play music?"

The room was so much grander than its name suggested. It was large enough to hold a ball, if Alex so desired. It was painted a soft creamy color, with white trim and dark wood floors. Windows on three of the walls looked out at the large property, and in the distance, behind the house, Sofia caught a glimpse of the Mississippi River.

"I play the piano," she said. "Though, not well."

A grand piano sat in one corner of the room. Its shiny, wooden surface gleamed in the light from the window.

"This is a beautiful room." She shook her head. The room was at least six times larger than her home in Switzerland. "I can hardly believe you live here."

"I'm happy you like it." Alex didn't look at the room but watched Sofia. "I do hope you enjoy staying here—even if it's not for long."

She couldn't hide the smile that warmed her face. "I will."

He studied her, just as he had when she'd come down the stairs yesterday, as if he was seeing her with new eyes. "I knew I'd enjoy showing you my home—but I didn't realize how much it mattered to me what you thought of it, until now."

A door opened somewhere within the house, and a moment later four individuals filed into the music room. Two of them were women in black gowns with white aprons, and two were men in dark suits.

Alex greeted each of them with a smile and a few simple words, asking how they had been in his absence.

"Thank you for taking care of the house while I've been away," Alex said to the group at large. "I imagine it's come as a surprise that I brought a wife home."

The staff glanced at Sofia.

"I'd like to introduce you to my wife." Alex stood next to Sofia. "This is Mrs. Alexander."

No matter how many times she heard it, it didn't seem real.

"Sofia, this is Mr. Yankton, the butler, and Mrs. Stevens, the cook." He motioned to each of them. "Christopher is the footman and driver, and Ruth is the housemaid."

"How do you do?" Sofia asked each of them.

"There wasn't time to find you a lady's maid," Mrs. Stevens said to Sofia. "So, we hope it will be all right for Ruth to see to your needs until you can find one yourself."

Sofia couldn't imagine having a lady's maid all to herself. What would she do with her? "It's fine. Thank you."

"If there's anything you need, ma'am," Mr. Yankton said with a slight bow, "we are at your disposal, both night and day."

Sofia nodded, unsure how to respond to such a thing. Ever since her mother had died when she was eight, Sofia had been the one to care for her father and her home. It seemed strange to think there were four people at her beck and call.

"Mrs. Walker has made plans for your supper," Mrs. Stevens said. "I've been working with her on the upcoming visit and will go over all the food details with you in the morning, if you so wish."

"Yes, of course." Though she hoped Julia would take care of all the details. She didn't know the first thing about hosting a party.

"Will that be all?" Mr. Yankton asked Alex.

"Yes. Thank you."

The group left the room, and Sofia let out a breath she didn't know she'd been holding.

"You did very well," Alex said with a smile. "There's nothing to it, really."

It was easy for him to say. He'd been raised this way.

Sofia, on the other hand, had a whole lifetime of knowledge she'd need to learn almost overnight.

Raised in a wealthy European family, indeed.

Sunshine beat down on his shoulders as Alex walked the short distance from his home to Noah's. He'd left Sofia to rest and told her he'd come to collect her for supper in a few hours. He should be at the office, looking over the ledgers he'd left in his assistant's care for the past five months—but he needed to tell Julia and Noah the truth about his marriage, and the sooner the better.

Not only would he tell them the truth, but he'd ask them for advice. He would annul his marriage to Sofia if she desired to leave, but he didn't want her to go. Not only had he promised to care for her, but he knew it would cause a scandal. That was the last thing he wanted for his family, friends, and business to endure.

He rang the front door and was shown into the parlor by Noah's butler. Within moments, both Noah and Julia appeared.

"Why didn't you bring your wife?" Julia asked as she came across the room and received a kiss on her cheek by Alex. "I'm eager to know her better."

Julia's obvious pregnancy had come as a shock to Alex. Neither Noah nor Julia had mentioned it before he left for Paris, nor had they told him in the letters they'd exchanged over the months. Though Alex had graciously stepped aside when Julia had decided to marry Noah, Alex couldn't deny the pang of jealousy that filled his heart at seeing their obvious love match.

It was something he'd always longed for. When he'd married Sofia, he had hoped they would come to love one another the way his friends had—but with her desire to leave, he doubted he'd get the opportunity to try.

"Why didn't you tell me about the baby?" Alex asked.

Julia's face glowed with joy as she smiled. "People don't speak about such things, Alex."

"Not even among good friends?" he asked with a wink for her as he shook Noah's hand. "When is the wonderful occasion?"

Julia set her hand on her stomach. "In the beginning of October, if all goes well."

"Why don't you have a seat?" Noah asked Alex.

"We want to know all about Sofia." Julia took her husband's assistance as she lowered into a chair.

"And your time in Paris," Noah added.

"But first Sofia," Julia insisted.

Alex took a seat across from them and couldn't help but notice the way Noah held Julia's hand in his. If truth be told, Alex had gone to Paris to distance himself from this newly wedded couple as much as he had gone to pursue his automobile venture. Agreeing to marry Sofia had been one more way to assure himself he had moved past his feelings for Julia. Seeing them now, content and about to become parents, he realized his feelings had indeed changed. He wanted them to be happy.

"She's so lovely, Alex." Julia shook her head in amazement. "Quite possibly the most beautiful woman I've ever seen. Wherever did you meet her?"

"And how did you convince her to marry you?" Noah asked in good-natured teasing. "That's the more important question."

"That's why I've come to see you without her." Alex let out a sigh. "My father insists we tell everyone we met in Europe, but the truth is we met in Swede Hollow two days ago."

Noah and Julia stared at him.

"You met her where?" Noah asked.

"Her grandfather was Alberto Bellini, the wood-carver. Before he passed away, he asked me to marry her."

Noah's mouth dropped open. "You're jesting."

Alex shook his head. "Sofia just arrived in America a few weeks ago."

"But I saw the way she looked at you," Julia said with a frown. "It's very evident she cares for you."

"As soon as the acquisition is complete, Sofia hopes to return to her family in Switzerland." Alex hated to admit the truth. "She doesn't want to stay."

"But why not?" Julia looked from Noah to Alex. "What could await her back home that would be better than staying?"

"She did not wish to marry me but did so only for her grandfather." Alex looked down at his hands. "I imagine she's feeling overwhelmed and simply wants to return to what she knows."

"Can you not convince her to stay?" Julia asked.

"Let Alex be," Noah said to his wife. "He's a grown man. He'll do what's best."

"But there must be a way." Julia leaned forward to address Alex. "Make her fall in love with you, and then she will not want to leave."

"If only it were that simple." He smiled. Hadn't he tried to make Julia fall in love with him? "I have told her I don't want her to leave, but I won't force her to stay. She's agreed to endure this farce for my father's sake, but when it's all over, she's free to go."

"Then it will have to be a group effort," Julia said with a nod. "We'll all show her that staying is the best thing for her."

"Don't you think it would be wise to leave well enough alone?" Noah asked his wife.

"Not in this situation." Julia shook her head. "Sometimes we need a little reassurance when making life-changing decisions. We will offer Sofia the reassurance she needs."

Alex continued to smile at Julia. "I appreciate your enthusiasm, but if Sofia does not want to stay, I will not try to coerce her."

"I'm not speaking of coercion." Julia's blue eyes lit with surprise at his statement. "We need to show Sofia that the life you have to offer is better than anything waiting for her in Switzerland."

What *did* await her in Switzerland? Was there a man there whom she was pining after? If that was the case, how could he compete with someone who held her heart?

"Why do you want her to stay?" Noah asked Alex. "You couldn't possibly be in love with her so soon."

"And why not?" Julia asked. "Perhaps it was love at first sight."

Julia was ever the optimist and a romantic at heart. Those were two of the many things he liked about her.

"There are several reasons I want her to stay," Alex replied.

"Is love one of them?" Julia asked.

It should be strange to speak to Julia about love, but she was a good friend above all else, and always had been.

"I cannot deny I'm attracted to her, and I care very deeply for her well-being." He thought about the way Sofia made him feel when he was near her and the desire he felt to see her when they were apart. But was that love? "I hardly know her, but what I do know, I like very much—and I long to get to know her better."

"It's a spark," Julia said with a sigh. "And that's all you need to start a forest fire."

Noah laughed and shook his head. "Let's not speak of forest fires, my love. Lumber is our business, after all."

"But it is enough," she insisted. "You will grow to love her, and I know she will grow to love you too. You just need to have the time and space to fall in love."

"It might be very difficult, given the circumstances." Alex stood and walked to the fireplace where Julia and Noah's wedding photo sat on display. He longed for the kind of marriage his friends enjoyed, and he sensed there could be something very special between him and Sofia if given the chance. He'd felt it from the moment they'd met.

"Make the opportunities," Julia insisted. "Find the time to get to know your wife, and then woo her."

It wouldn't be easy, but the alternative wasn't very appealing.

"An annulment never looks good," Noah said. "For your personal reputation or your business. If you can avoid it, I would highly recommend staying married." He brought Julia's hand up to his lips and smiled at his wife. "It's a very enjoyable adventure."

"It can be," Julia said with a grin for her husband. "If it's the right person."

Alex tore his gaze from his friends and looked out the window at his home next door.

He would find a way to woo and win his bride, and he would do it before the Robertsons' visit was complete.

It would be his only chance.

Chapter 4

Sofia couldn't rest even if she had wanted to. The house, the grounds, the staff—it was all too much to take in. Even the room was beyond anything she had ever hoped or dreamed about. It was wallpapered in a soft, creamy color with delicate pink flowers. She wondered who had chosen the coverings, because it didn't look like something a man would select. A small sitting room in the back looked out over the tree-covered hill for which Basswood Hill was named, and the sparkling river lay beyond that. Grape arbors, a gazebo, and stone pathways crisscrossed the property.

Everything was so lovely and well maintained. Why had Alex chosen to leave this place and go to Paris? What had drawn him away?

A soft knock at her door brought Sofia's head up from her palm where she'd rested her chin as she admired the view out her window.

"Yes?" she asked.

"It's Alex." He paused. "Have I awakened you?"

"No." She rose and crossed the room, her heart picking up speed at the sound of his voice. Why had he come now? She didn't expect him for hours.

The thick rug felt marvelous under her stockings. She had taken off the new shoes because they had pinched, and changed into an afternoon gown. Her maid had suggested she put on a nightgown to take a nap, but Sofia had never napped before in her life and didn't plan to start now.

She opened the door and found Alex standing in the hallway. He was looking down at the floor but glanced up with a bright smile. He looked genuinely pleased to see her again.

Her heart caught in her throat at the look in his eyes. He was so handsome and strong, and he'd been so kind, how could she not like him?

Did he like her too? He must, though he hardly knew her. If he did get to know her, and knew her past mistakes, would he still look at her that way?

"Have you had enough time to rest?" he asked.

"I haven't had time to nap since I was a child," she confided. "I don't know how to be idle. I've kept my father's house and worked with him as a wood-carver from the time I was eight years old. I cannot abide being useless."

"You're far from useless, Sofia. Your roles have just shifted. You'll need to use your energy for different things now."

She wasn't sure she wanted to do different things. She was good at keeping house and carving wood. Those were the things she knew and was confident performing. She did not know how to host parties and entertain guests. She did not belong in this world.

"I brought you a gift." He lifted his hand, and it was then that she noticed he held something.

"I do not need more gifts." She shook her head. "I have more things than I can ever use."

The light in his eyes dimmed and he pulled back his hand.

Immediately, she felt remorse for her words. If he wanted to give her a gift, who was she to tell him no?

"It's not like the other things," he said slowly. "It's actually nothing useful—I just thought you might find it interesting."

"I'm sorry." She looked down at her hands and couldn't bring herself to meet his disappointed gaze.

"I loved and respected your grandfather more than any man I've ever known." His voice was full of deep emotion. "He taught me important lessons about life and love and faith. But he also taught me how to carve."

She looked up at him then. "You're a carver?"

"I'm not very good, but I do love to carve wood, and I've spent many hours trying to perfect my craft, though I'll never be as good as Alberto." He held out his hand again and turned it so it was palm side up.

In his hand was a small, delicate flower carved out of basswood. It was not elaborate or intricate, but it was still very beautiful in its simplicity.

"This was the first thing Alberto taught me to carve." Alex smiled down at the flower. "He told me that basswood was the best wood for beginners and that as my skill improved, so too would the wood and tools I used. He said that anything worth doing would require a great deal of work, patience, and dedication." Alex turned the flower over, revealing an identical pattern on the other side. "I've improved since I made this flower, but I still keep it to remind me of where I started and how proud I was when I completed this."

"It is very good for a beginner." Sofia smiled. "It looks very similar to my first carving, and I remember my father teaching me the very same thing. I suppose my grandfather taught him as well." She loved knowing that she and Alex had something more in common.

"Alberto left a very important legacy." Alex took Sofia's hand in his own and met her gaze. "I can only hope and pray I do the same." He placed the flower in the palm of her hand. "I'd like you to keep this as a reminder of your grandfather—and of me."

Sofia's heart expanded, and a wave of emotion washed over her. "Thank you," was all she could manage to whisper. Of all the beautiful and elaborate gifts he'd already given her, this was the most precious.

They did not speak for a moment, but then Alex said, "May I take you out for the afternoon? I'd like to show you around town and take you to the mill and my office, if that wouldn't bore you too much."

"Will we drive in the Duryea?" She couldn't hide the excitement in her voice.

He grinned. "If you'd like."

"I'll be ready in a moment."

"I'll meet you outside."

She rushed to get ready, not bothering to call her maid for help. In less than ten minutes, she stepped outside in the riding dress and hat she'd worn earlier that morning.

Alex waited beside his automobile, but it was his footman and driver, Christopher, who sat behind the wheel.

"I thought it would be more pleasant to ride beside you in the back," Alex explained. "And have a chance to talk as we take our tour."

Sofia nodded, enjoying the thought of sitting beside him, listening to him. She loved the rich timbre of his voice and the cadence of his words. It sounded so foreign to her ears.

He helped her into the back seat and climbed in beside her. It was a tight fit, and his leg was pressed up against hers, but she didn't mind in the least.

Christopher put the vehicle into motion, and they drove out of the estate and onto a main thoroughfare. The motor was loud in the front of the automobile, and it would be difficult for Christopher to hear them, but Sofia had no problem hearing Alex right beside her.

"Do you miss your homeland?" Alex asked.

"I miss many things about home," she conceded, "but I love America. I wanted to come here since I was a little girl. It is everything I thought it would be and more." It was exciting and so very big.

"Why did you choose to come now?"

She looked down at her stomach, which would not hide her secret for much longer. How did she tell Alex the truth—without telling him the whole truth?

"When my father died, my grandfather insisted I come."

"How long has your father been gone?"

"Six months."

"You did not come right away?"

She had fallen in love with Gianni and had thought she'd stay in Switzerland as his wife. That had been the plan, until his father had changed Gianni's mind. "There were things I needed to prepare."

They passed houses and businesses, people going about their work and play. The downtown was busy and crowded. Beautiful green lamps lined the streets, while large plate glass windows reflected the brilliant sunshine. Two- and three-story brick buildings boasted every type of store imaginable.

Alex didn't speak as they passed through town, but he did wave at several people. Curious gazes turned their way as groups gathered to chat and speculate about her, no doubt.

They crossed a bridge spanning the Mississippi River, and he showed her the massive mill with the countless logs stacked in the yard. She marveled at his industry. He became animated as he explained how the enormous logs were chopped in the forests during the winter, put into the river in the spring, and floated to the mill by men called river rats who jumped from log to log, breaking apart jams and overseeing their transportation. Once they arrived at the mill, they were sawed, stacked on trains, and then shipped all over the world.

He spoke about his childhood, his work at the mill, and his passion for automobiles. He told her about his time in Paris and his love for the Olympic Games. He asked her about her childhood, her father and mother, and her village in Switzerland. They spent several hours touring the town and countryside, all the while talking. Her conversation with Alex was effortless, and she found herself telling him things she'd never shared with anyone else.

Everything, except for Gianni.

Somehow, in a very short amount of time, she felt she knew the man beside her better than she knew almost anyone else. He was not afraid to share his hopes and dreams, his fears and weaknesses, or his confidence and knowledge.

And all the while, he sat close to her, smiling into her eyes with excitement.

As they pulled back into Basswood Hill, Sofia felt both exhausted and exhilarated.

"I hope I haven't bored you." Alex opened the door and held out his hand to help her alight.

"Of course not." She couldn't imagine ever being bored in his company. "I enjoyed myself very much. I learned a great deal today. Thank you."

"Have I left enough time for you to dress for supper?"

She shrugged. "I have only dressed for supper one other time."

He laughed. "I will meet you in the foyer in half an hour, and we can walk over to Noah and Julia's together."

He walked her into the house, and she left him at the top of the stairs to enter her room.

As she closed the door, she paused, suddenly realizing that after everything Alex had shared, he'd failed to tell her one very important thing.

She had no idea if Alex had ever been in love before. And she wondered if he had simply forgotten to talk about it—or if he had avoided telling her because it was too painful to discuss.

Chapter 5

A brisk rain poured down on the gravel drive as Alex and Noah stood just inside Noah's front porch waiting for the two black carriages to come to a stop. Inside the conveyances, Alex's father would be riding with Mr. and Mrs. Robertson, as well as one of the board members. In the other carriage would be two other board members and their wives, each of them expecting to be entertained for the week.

"Are you ready?" Noah asked Alex.

"Not even a little." Alex had hardly slept the night before as he'd pored over the company ledgers long into the early morning hours. When he finally went to bed, he'd laid awake, thinking about his wife and the time they'd spent together. Sofia had shared openly about her childhood and her family, but she'd said very little about past relationships or the reasons she'd finally come to America. He had a feeling there was something she wasn't telling him, but he couldn't begin to guess. He had tried getting her to trust him where her heart was concerned, but the pain in her eyes and voice suggested she'd been hurt far more than her words let on and it would take a great deal of time and patience to get her to open her heart to him.

He didn't know if he'd have the time it would take.

The drivers jumped down from their seats to open the doors, while Alex and Noah stepped into the rain with umbrellas to assist the ladies into Noah's home.

"Welcome to Basswood Hill," Alex said to the lady he assumed was Mrs. Robertson. "We hope you'll enjoy your stay."

"I had hoped for a better welcome than this," Mrs. Robertson said as she lifted the hem of her dark gown and hurried alongside Alex to the front door. "This mud will ruin my dress."

Alex could hardly control the weather, so he didn't comment.

When she was safely inside the house, he returned to the second carriage. The door was open, and a much younger woman sat there grinning. "Hello, Alex."

Annabeth Cummings.

"Are you just going to stare, or help the poor girl to the front door?" Annabeth's father, J.T. Cummings, sat across from her, a smile on his face. "She's been looking forward to this visit for weeks. Don't make her sit out here in the rain."

"Yes, of course." Alex held out his hand, and she took it, stepping close to him under the umbrella.

"Are you surprised?" she asked.

"Quite. I thought your mother was accompanying your father this week."

"She hasn't been feeling well, so Papa asked me to come instead." She looked up at him, her large blue eyes wide and expressive. "I thought perhaps you and I could get reacquainted."

The two of them had been close at one time, and Annabeth had assumed they were courting. When Alex said he wasn't interested in marrying her—or anyone else at that time—she had been crushed. Thankfully, it looked as if time and distance had helped her forget that she'd been angry at him.

He walked her around a puddle, and she simply laughed. "I do miss being a child and having an excuse to play in the mud. What do you think Mrs. Robertson would do if we stopped to make a mud pie? Would she die of mortification?"

"That would be my guess." Alex smiled with her and showed her into the house, several fond memories returning to him of his time with Annabeth.

The men entered next, everyone speaking at once. Alex and Noah asked how their ride had been and asked after their welfare.

Annabeth stayed close to Alex's side as she laughed and spoke to the two other ladies in their party.

"My wife has refreshments waiting in the parlor," Noah said to the group as he motioned for them to move into the house. "Won't you follow me?"

The eight newcomers continued to chat as they walked through the entrance and into the front hall.

Alex's father put his hand on Alex's arm and held him back, just enough to whisper. "Where is your *wife*?"

"She is with Julia in the parlor, waiting for our guests."

"If she ruins this for us, I will be very angry, Alex."

"Sofia will ruin nothing."

Father let out a deep breath. "We're courting a calamity here. If she makes one wrong step, Mrs. Robertson will stop everything."

"She won't." At least, she wouldn't on purpose. Alex knew Sofia understood the gravity of the situation and would do everything in her power to make a good impression.

"Welcome to Basswood Hill," Julia said as everyone entered her beautiful parlor. She glowed as she smiled at their guests.

Alex walked around the group and met Sofia's worried glance with a reassuring smile. She was as lovely as ever in a blue afternoon gown, her thick, dark hair styled in an intricate series of twists and tucks. He stood next to her and took her hand, as much to appear a happy couple as to give her a bit of confidence. He would not leave her side, and he hoped she knew that.

Noah also stood next to his wife. Julia had been raised in a wealthy family in New York. She'd been taught all the manners and etiquette befitting her lifestyle. She was as gentle and natural as could be.

"I believe there are some introductions to be made," Noah said to the group at large. "All of you know my wife, Julia, but I don't believe you know Alex's new wife, Sofia."

Annabeth's gaze narrowed on Alex and Sofia, her eyes traveling the length of Sofia's gown from head to foot. While the others stepped forward to formally greet Sofia, Annabeth stood back until she was the last to extend her hand to Alex's new wife.

"I can hardly believe someone finally caught the last White Pine Bachelor." Annabeth briefly shook Sofia's hand and then stepped back again, a cunning smile on her face. "I had it on good authority that Alex was still single." She glanced at her father with a pointed look. "This must have happened recently."

"Very recently," Alex said. "Just—"

"Just before he returned to America," Father interjected. "He met Sofia in Paris while she was there visiting the World's Fair with her family. They were not planning to marry so quickly, but when I called Alex home, he didn't want to leave Sofia, so they were married there and waited to surprise me when they came home this week. They are planning a more formal party to celebrate their nuptials. You will all be invited, of course."

Sofia glanced at Alex, concern tightening her brow.

"Quite the newly wedded couple," Mrs. Robertson said with

a pleased smile. "And who are your people, Sofia? Perhaps I know them. I've traveled extensively in Europe."

The concern in Sofia's eyes turned to panic.

"The Bellinis," Father spoke up again. "Surely you've heard of Marco Bellini? He's one of the largest silk producers in Lake Como, Italy."

"Oh. Silk." Mrs. Robertson nodded, appreciation in her voice. "How lovely." But then she frowned. "I don't believe I've had the pleasure of making Mr. Bellini's acquaintance, though I toured Italy just last year."

Sofia offered a shy, quiet smile to Mrs. Robertson but did not respond.

"We'll have to rectify that soon," Father said with a tight smile. He then raised his eyebrows at Noah and Julia. "Now that everyone's been introduced, perhaps our guests would like some refreshments."

"Yes, of course." Julia's cheeks filled with color, obviously embarrassed by Father's words. It was the hostess's job to make everyone comfortable, after all, and she had been nervously watching the introductions unfold.

Julia indicated for the two footmen to move away from where they stood near the door. One had a tray of beverages, and the other had a tray of sandwiches. They began to walk between the guests as Alex led Sofia off to the side, away from the others.

"You're doing a marvelous job." He tried to give her a reassuring smile.

"I am afraid I'll ruin everything for your family." She spoke softly, her worried eyes seeking Alex's approval.

Warmth filled his chest at the concern she felt for his family and business. It couldn't be easy to go on with this charade, but she was doing it for him. He would do whatever was necessary to keep her safe and comfortable. If it were up to him, he'd make them all leave so she could have space to adjust to this new lifestyle.

He briefly touched her soft cheek, a tender smile on his lips. It wasn't hard to show her affection, or to pretend he was truly in love with her. She was easy to like and even easier to be with. There was no guile or pretense, no hidden motives or agendas. She was simply Sofia, the wood-carver's daughter—and Alex's wife.

"I must confess," Annabeth said as she glided up to Sofia's side, a water goblet in hand, "I fully intended to come here and claim Alex for myself." She smiled demurely, though there was a hardness in her eyes that Alex didn't like. "But now I will have no choice but to make you my dearest friend, Sofia. It must be difficult to come to a new country and to learn new customs and traditions." She looked at Alex. "Though, having such a handsome and wealthy husband must make the difficulty easier to bear."

Sofia looked from Annabeth to Alex, indecision in her gaze. No doubt she was unfamiliar with women like Annabeth Cummings who were used to the games played by women in their social circles. It wasn't unusual for a compliment to be laced with an insult or accusation.

Alex could never abide such behavior, and now that it was turned on his wife, he hated it even more.

"Sofia has much to learn," Alex said with respect tingeing his voice. "But I've never known a lovelier, kinder, or more selfless woman, and I have no doubt she'll learn everything she needs to know very quickly. But, more importantly, she'll fill my home with joy and laughter, regardless of where she was born."

Sofia studied him, her brown eyes glowing with something warm and grateful. He couldn't stop himself from smiling at her, hoping the admiration he felt was shining from his eyes for everyone to see.

"Well." Annabeth lifted her chin, too well mannered to reveal her real feelings. "I do hope we can be friends, at the very least."

It was Sofia's turn to grace Annabeth with a radiant smile. "Of course, and perhaps while you are teaching me about your ways, I can teach you about mine."

Annabeth raised her eyebrows, as if learning about another culture was something she never considered, nor had the desire to undertake. "Wouldn't that be nice? Perhaps, if I had learned more about Italy before Alex left America"—her words were syrupy sweet—"he might have been interested in staying right here and succumbing to my charms." She laughed as if she were joking.

Sofia didn't respond for a moment, but then she slipped in closer to Alex's side, her hand still in his, and continued to smile at Annabeth. "I suppose we'll never know."

Alex loved having Sofia so close, and he loved even more that she was staking her claim on him—a prospect he didn't mind in the least.

Maybe there was hope for her to stay after all.

Sofia wasn't sure if it was the unborn child inside her or the pressure of being on display all afternoon, but she was utterly exhausted and close to tears. Keeping up false pretenses in front of so many strangers, especially Annabeth Cummings, had been very difficult.

She slipped into her bedroom, even though the sky still held a hint of color. The guests were enjoying evening entertainments at Noah and Julia's home, but she had left, complaining of a headache. Alex had asked if he might escort her back to his house, but she had insisted he stay with his guests.

Now, as she closed her bedroom door behind her and leaned against the hard surface, she let out a weary sigh. At least here she could be herself, with no one to impress or convince.

"Mrs. Alexander?" Ruth, the maid, stood just outside the door, always at the ready. "Would you like me to help you undress and prepare for bed?"

Sofia had tried sneaking into the house so the staff would not know she was home. She had no wish for the girl to help her, but the gown she wore was so exquisite and so complicated, she conceded that she would never be able to get out of it on her own.

Opening the door, Sofia took a step back. She forced herself to smile. "Thank you."

Ruth entered and immediately began helping Sofia undress. In no time at all, Sofia was out of her corset and in a soft nightgown with a robe tied around her waist. Ruth put all Sophia's things away and then came out into the room again, hesitation shadowing her face.

"Is something wrong?" Sofia asked her.

Ruth didn't lift her gaze. "Nothing, ma'am."

On instinct, Sofia wrapped her arms around her body, as if she could shield her growing child from unwanted shame and ridicule. Had the maid somehow discovered the truth? But how?

Ruth dipped with a curtsy. "Will that be all?"

"Yes."

The maid nodded and then left the room.

Sofia looked down at her stomach. It was just as flat as before, though there were other changes in her body that she had noticed. Had Ruth guessed the truth, or was Sofia being paranoid? If Ruth did suspect, would she speak about it to the other servants? What would happen if they started to spread the news? Everyone would assume the child was Alex's, and with such a recent marriage, there would be speculation about his character. He didn't deserve to have rumors circle about him. He was too honorable.

It was another man who had dishonored her.

"Sofia?" Alex knocked on the door. "May I come in?"

Her pulse started to thrum at the sound of his voice and the intimate position she was in, standing in her bedroom in her night-gown. But as her husband, it wasn't indecent for him to come into her room.

Without a word, she went to her door and opened it for him.

Worry lines etched between his handsome brows. "I couldn't stay at Noah and Julia's knowing you weren't feeling well. Is there any-thing I can get for you? Perhaps some headache powder?"

The setting sun sent pink, orange, and lavender streaks across the sky, lending a soft glow to her room and his dear face. She had not yet turned on her lights, and now, in the dimming shadows, the space around them felt cozy and warm.

"I told you not to worry about me," she said softly. "You should not have left your guests because of me."

A rueful smile tilted his lips. "Truth be told, I was happy for a reason to leave. I'll return later to escort the Cummings and my father back." He leaned against the doorframe, his gaze taking in her appearance, appreciation in the depths of his eyes. His voice was low when he spoke. "But, for now, I'd rather be here."

Heat climbed up her neck and into her cheeks while pleasure settled into her belly. She should have dropped her gaze, but she couldn't tear it away from Alex. He looked so handsome in his eve-ning suit. She'd never met a man who was more confident or sure of himself. She had loved watching him with the others. Though she herself had never felt more out of place, standing in his shadow seemed to hide her from the others' view.

The room was growing darker by the minute, so Sofia left the door and went to a lamp near the bed. She flicked it on, wanting to invite Alex in to her small sitting room to watch the last of the day's sunshine that had come following the rain. But was it wise to invite him into her room and take the risk that she might invite him into her heart as well? She could not find a single thing to dislike about Charles Alexander. On the contrary, every day she found more and more to love about him. The longer she stayed in his presence, the harder it had become to deny her feelings.

"May I come in?" he asked, his voice tentative. "There are some things I'd like to discuss. Or would you rather I leave you to sleep?"

Her heart fluttered at the idea of spending time alone with him again. Who was she to deny his request to speak to her? She owed him so much more than she could ever repay.

Besides, she wanted him to stay.

"You may come in." She turned on another lamp and then offered him a smile.

He entered the room and followed her into the adjoining sitting room. Windows encircled three sides, giving them a perfect view of the property and river.

The sitting room was still overly warm from the day's heat. Alex waited until Sofia took a seat on one of the lounge chairs, and then he paused. "Do you mind if I remove my coat?"

She shook her head. How could she, while she sat there in her nightgown?

Alex removed his coat and hung it over the back of his chair.

The room was small, so the chairs were close and his presence was all-encompassing. She could hardly think of anything else as he sat beside her, looking out at the property.

Neither one spoke for a moment. As each second passed, Sofia grew more uncomfortable. What did he have to say to her? Would it upset her?

"What would you like to discuss?" she finally asked.

He turned, his blue eyes so vibrant and full of life.

In that moment, she could no longer pretend she didn't have feelings for him. They had grown quick and sure, despite her best efforts to keep her heart safe, but they were there.

"First, I wanted to tell you I'm sorry about Annabeth," he said.

Sofia shook her head. "It's not your fault." She had tried not to let the other woman's words hurt her, but they had. It was clear she had hoped to win over Alex and had not anticipated his marriage. But her opinions about Sofia were not completely wrong. "I am the first to agree with her that I do not belong here."

Alex frowned. "That's not true." He reached across the short divide between their chairs and took her hand. He'd done it several times that day, but all of the other times had been in front of others, for show. Now, here, alone, it was for a different reason all together. "Sofia, I don't know how to explain this, but since you arrived, I've never felt more at home here at Basswood Hill. Not only do you belong, but I want you here."

"You're the only person who feels that way. Your father does not want me—"

"It is not my father's choice." He lifted her hand to his lips and placed a gentle kiss there.

A tingle ran up her arm and went straight into her heart. She felt as if her chest would burst with the pleasure of his touch.

"Miss Cummings does not want me," she said a little quieter.

"It is not Miss Cummings's choice either," he said just as quietly, placing another kiss on her hand.

She swallowed, her breath coming quickly. "If Mrs. Robertson knew the truth, she would not want me either."

He looked up at her, his eyes filled with emotions she couldn't begin to identify. "It is most definitely not Mrs. Robertson's choice."

His words, though powerful enough to convince her that she did, in fact, belong at Basswood Hill, did not reflect the reality of the situation. If he could not see the truth, then she would have to see it for both of them. Not only was she a poor immigrant, but she was carrying another man's child. When the news came out, it could ruin Alex's reputation and his possible acquisition—not to mention his respect and admiration for her. She could not let that happen.

She removed her hand from his and clasped her hands on her lap. She did not meet his gaze but looked down at her newly polished nails. They were yet another reminder that she was only pretending. She'd never had polished nails before.

"What is wrong, Sofia?" he asked. "Why don't you want to stay here. . .with me?"

It wasn't that she didn't want to stay. She did. More now than ever before. Could it be possible that this man could truly want her? But it didn't matter even if he did. She knew what was best for him—knew what would happen if she stayed and he learned her secret. She would make the choice to leave now before either one was hurt.

"I don't belong." She shook her head. "And if you cannot see that, then I will have to remind you every chance I get. You need someone like Julia—"

He rose from his chair so unexpectedly, Sofia stopped speaking.

Alex went to the window, one hand resting on the back of his neck as he stared outside.

He was quiet for so long, she finally rose and went to stand by him. "Have I said something to upset you?"

Alex shook his head, but Sofia knew she had. Why would he be upset at the mention of Julia—unless. She studied his profile. Had he been in love with Julia? Her heart broke for him as she recognized the truth. It must have been awful when Julia chose his best friend—and even more difficult to be neighbors and to see them every day. Was that why he had gone to Paris? To get away?

"I'm sorry," she whispered, suddenly understanding so much more about Charles Alexander. He'd been rejected by Julia, just as

Sofia had been rejected by Gianni. She couldn't imagine how hard it would be to see Gianni every day, knowing he loved someone else.

The last thing she wanted to do was upset Alex even more. "I simply meant—"

"I know what you meant." He finally turned and looked at her. "Julia is Noah's wife. I do not want someone like Julia." He caressed her face with his gaze. "I want someone like you." He paused, his voice lower than before. "I want you, Sofia."

She caught her breath as he took her into his arms and placed a gentle kiss on her lips.

The kiss was so unexpected and so marvelous, Sofia was powerless to pull away. Instead, she met his kiss and returned it, surprising herself with the depth of her feelings.

But her feelings scared her. She had given her heart away to Gianni too easily. She couldn't do the same with Alex. "I'm sorry." She finally pulled away, shaking her head. She shouldn't have responded to his kiss so eagerly.

"You have nothing to be sorry about." Alex watched her closely. "You're my wife, Sofia. If I could, I would kiss you like that every day for the rest of my life."

His words made her feel weak with longing. The desire to say yes to him was on the tip of her tongue, but she could never do that to him. Ultimately, she would hurt him.

He reached for her again, but she pulled back, putting space between them. "I cannot," she whispered.

He didn't move as he frowned. "Why not?"

She wanted to tell him about the baby, wanted him to understand, but she knew nothing good could come of it. She couldn't expect him to happily take on another man's responsibility.

"Are you in love with someone back home?" He was still

studying her, as if he could see into her very soul. "Do you want to return to him?"

Did she? She wanted to forget about Gianni, but the reminder of his love—and betrayal—grew in her womb.

"No, I do not want to return to him." Of that, she was certain. "He would not take me back."

"Then you are in love with someone else."

Sofia shook her head. "Not anymore."

"Then what is it? What aren't you telling me?" He took a step closer to her, and she shied away again. He stopped. "You can trust me."

"My head is beginning to hurt again," she said, unable to look him in the eyes. "I'd like to lie down and rest."

He stood there for another heartbeat, and then he lifted his coat off the back of the chair. "As you wish."

Alex left the sitting room but paused in her bedroom and turned to look at her as if he might say something, but then he took a deep breath and left.

Sofia's legs grew weak, and she lowered herself onto the lounge chair. It would only become harder, the longer she stayed at Basswood Hill.

As soon as possible, she would leave Alex behind. He deserved so much better than what she had to offer.

Chapter 6

No matter how hard he tried, Alex could not keep his mind on his task. He had spent the day touring the mill with his father, Noah, Mr. Robertson, and the two other board members. They had walked through every part of the operation, starting at the sorting works where men separated the logs that flowed down the river from the logging camps in the spring. There they sent the white pine logs to the mill and pushed the others further downriver to the other mills along the way. After the sorting works, they had gone to the millpond where the logs waited until they could be hauled up the conveyer belts to the mill and either run through the massive saws or stacked in the yard until they could get to them.

Now, as the group sat at the table in Alex's office and looked over the impressive numbers, he breathed a sigh of relief. The day was almost done and he could soon return home to the woman who had kept him distracted all day. Sofia.

"Everything looks marvelous," Mr. Robertson said with a

contented smile. He closed the ledger and pushed it toward Alex. "Well done."

"Thank you," Alex said. "We've been running this mill for nine years now, and we're doing more sales than ever."

"I can see that." Mr. Robertson stood and put his hands on his rotund belly. "If my stomach is telling the truth, I believe there will be a meal waiting for us back at Mr. Walker's house very soon." He set his hat on his head, his affinity for food evident in almost everything he did. "I believe I've seen all I need to see today."

The others also rose, smiles all around.

"We will spend tomorrow with our employees at the lumberjack festival," Noah said to the men. "There will be competitions and events to enjoy, and it will give all of you an opportunity to speak to the men who work for us."

"I look forward to the day," Mr. Robertson said as he walked out of the office.

"Charles and I will join you soon," Father said to the group. "Go ahead without us. We'll follow in Charles's car."

Noah led Mr. Robertson and the board members out of Alex's office, closing the door softly behind him.

Alex took the ledger off the table and put it back in its place on his desk. He didn't meet his father's gaze as he made himself busy, not wanting to know why his father had stayed behind to speak to him.

"Everything seems to be running smoothly," Father finally said.

Could it be that simple? Didn't his father have some criticism to offer?

"I believe Mr. Robertson is pleased with what he sees." Alex turned and leaned against his rolltop desk. "It's been an exceptionally good year for our company."

"I wasn't talking about the mill, though I'm relieved to find everything in good condition. I've often had my doubts about how you and Noah run this operation."

Alex crossed his arms and chose to overlook his father's comment. There was usually no point in contradicting him. "What are you talking about then?"

"Sofia." His jaw was set. "For the most part, she keeps to herself, and for that, I'm thankful."

"She's deathly afraid to speak up." Alex hated watching her shy away in conversation with the others. He sensed that if given the right atmosphere and situation, she would have a great deal to share. In private she spoke freely with him because she wasn't afraid to be herself.

"And rightly so." Father walked over to a filing cabinet and ran his finger over the surface. He looked down at the dust in disdain. "Only a few more days now and the acquisition will be as good as done. I hope Sofia can continue to stay out of trouble." He glanced up at Alex. "I suppose we'll need to put plans in place for the wedding celebration. Mrs. Robertson will expect to get an invitation."

Alex didn't meet his father's penetrating gaze. "There won't be a need to plan a celebration."

Father stopped his inspection of Alex's office. He paused and stared at Alex. "Why not?"

Alex took a deep breath. "She's planning to return to Switzerland as soon as the others leave."

"Return to Switzerland?" Father walked toward Alex. "For how long?"

"Indefinitely."

He came toe to toe with Alex, forcing Alex to meet his gaze. Anger seethed from his father's face. "A divorce?"

"An annulment."

"I forbid it."

"You were the one who wanted it to begin with."

"Before anyone knew about the marriage. Now it's too late."

"I cannot force her to stay when she does not want to be here."

"It will ruin you, Charles, and it will stain our family and business."

Alex tried to step away, but his father would not move, forcing Alex to stay where he was. "It might hurt for a while, but it won't ruin us."

"This is a small town, and people do not accept these things lightly here." Father's chest rose and fell. "One misstep and our working relationship with these people, and with our clients, could be compromised. I will not allow you to make such a mistake."

"I will not force her to stay."

"What have you done wrong? Why would someone in her position not want to stay?"

"I've done nothing wrong." At least, that's what he'd told himself. There must be something else pulling her away—but what? How could Alex fight against an enemy he couldn't identify? "She wants to return to her people."

"Then change her mind. Give her whatever she wants. You made the mistake in marrying her. Now you must deal with the consequences. Do not allow the situation to become even more detrimental to our family."

"I'm trying."

"Try harder."

"She feels out of place."

"Because she is." He drew closer to Alex. "She is not one of us and never will be. The most we can hope is for her to fade into the background."

Anger tightened Alex's chest. "She should never have to fade into the background. How will she ever fit in or be one of us if everyone continues to treat her so poorly?"

"You have no one to blame but yourself, Charles. It's not everyone else's fault that she's a dirty immi—"

"We were all immigrants at one time." Alex stood to his full height, which was several inches taller than his father. Heat gathered under his collar. "And she's not dirty or undeserving of our respect and admiration."

His father was finally forced to step back.

Alex adjusted his lapels and walked toward the door. He paused and looked back at his father. "And the only way to convince her to stay is to treat her with love and kindness. She will always feel low and underserving if you treat her poorly—but I will not. I cannot relegate her to the background of my life either. Sofia wasn't meant to blend in. She was meant to stand out, and that's exactly what she will do."

He pulled the door open and left his office. He was tired of his father and others in his social set treating those who were less fortunate with contempt and disdain. It was people just like Sofia who had helped to make Father wealthy. If it wasn't for the hard work of the hundreds of immigrants they employed, they would have no one to operate their mills, serve their food, or care for their needs.

And it was time he did something about the disparity. Maybe he couldn't change things for the masses, but he could change things for Sofia.

"I'm so very sorry about Annabeth," Julia said to Sofia as she walked beside her along the riverbank path. "She's a woman who knows what she wants, and when she doesn't get her way, she can be. . .difficult."

Difficult was a kind word for the way Annabeth Cummings had treated Sofia during the luncheon they'd just endured. The woman had been shrewd and sly, trying to draw personal information out of Sofia under the guise of friendship.

But she had failed.

"She is only disappointed," Sofia said, trying to give Annabeth the benefit of the doubt.

"You're too kind." Julia smiled. "But I think that's why Alex likes you so much."

"Likes me?" Sofia's cheeks grew warm at the thought.

"Of course he likes you." Julia's eyes twinkled. "Perhaps it's even love."

The other ladies had decided to nap after lunch, but Julia told Sofia she wanted to stretch her legs and asked if Sofia wanted to see more of the property. Sunshine rippled on the river as it flowed past, and a soft breeze blew off the surface of the water, offering a bit of respite from the heat—and from the embarrassment that warmed Sofia's cheeks.

"He does not love me," Sofia said, thankful she could speak freely with Julia. "He hardly knows me."

"He speaks very highly of you." Julia placed her hand on her rounded stomach, her gaze soft and gentle. "What he has seen and what he knows, he likes very much. Besides, do you not believe in love at first sight?"

Was it possible? Sofia didn't know, but she couldn't deny her own feelings for Alex had grown quickly. Perhaps it was possible.

"Did you fall in love with Noah at first sight?" Sofia asked.

Julia's cheeks were dimpled as she looked out over the river. "I came to Little Falls because I inherited my father's shares in the Midwest Lumber Company, but I had heard horrible rumors about Noah and Alex and was determined to remove my investment if the rumors were true. So I met both men under the impression that they were the lowest sort of humans."

Sofia couldn't imagine Alex being a bad person. He'd shown her nothing but kindness. "What happened then?"

"I met both Noah and Alex, and they were determined to convince me otherwise." She giggled and shook her head. "Before I arrived, Noah's mother suggested the best way to deal with me was for one of them to marry me."

"Is that why you married Noah?"

"No." She pointed to a stone bench built into the riverbank and guided Sofia to sit with her. "Noah and Alex are very competitive, so before I arrived, they started to fight about who would have to deal with me. But once I arrived, they—" She paused and looked down at her hands.

"What?" Sofia asked.

"I'm embarrassed to admit the truth."

"It is all right." Sofia wanted Julia to be truthful with her, wanted to know what had happened between Alex and Julia.

"After they met me, they began to compete for my affections." Her cheeks became even pinker than before. She motioned to the mansions on the hill behind them. "They had just started building their homes, and even that became a competition to see who could build them bigger and better—all while trying to impress me."

Sofia couldn't even imagine having such extravagant wealth being spent on her behalf. "Were you impressed?"

"Yes and no." Julia shrugged. "I wasn't impressed with all the money they spent, or that their competition almost destroyed their friendship and business."

"But it didn't." Sofia was glad of that. "And you found that they were good and honorable and trustworthy?"

"Yes. Both of them impressed me with their character and values. I learned that all the rumors I had heard were lies, meant to destroy them and their business. Society can be a cruel place to reside."

Sofia knew that very well. "How did you choose between them?"

Julia's blue eyes were so bright and full of joy. "It wasn't easy, but I followed my heart, and it led me to Noah."

"And Alex?" Sofia knew how it had ended—but there was a part of her that needed to know everything. "Why did you not choose him instead?"

"Alex is very dear to me. He is selfless, generous, and so very kind." Julia turned in her seat so she could face Sofia. "But I do not care for him the way I do for Noah. I knew there was another woman for him—I just didn't realize she was halfway around the world." She shook her head in amazement. "Isn't it wonderful how God brought you together?"

Sofia wanted to ask a question she was certain she already had an answer for—but she had to know. "Does Alex still love you?"

"No." She put her hand on Sofia's arm. "I don't believe he ever did. I think he was driven with the need to beat Noah, and maybe he's been envious of our happiness, but I always knew that Alex's heart did not belong to me." She gently squeezed Sofia's arm. "Because God was saving it for you."

Sofia looked down at the folds in her gown. "I do not deserve his heart."

"Of course you do." Julia bent her head, so Sofia would look at her. "Do not throw away your chance at true love and happiness. Do not convince yourself that you are undeserving. Truth be told, we're all undeserving. But no matter what is in our past, and no matter what some people may think or say, each of us deserves to be loved. If God loves you, then why shouldn't Alex?"

Could it be true? But what about her past mistakes?

Julia rested her hand on her stomach again. Her baby would be welcomed and loved and celebrated. There would be no shame or embarrassment at the child's birth. Yet the child Sofia carried would come into the world already burdened with all those things. Sofia wanted desperately to tell Julia the truth, but it wouldn't make things better. In fact, it might make things more complicated.

The wind blew a gentle kiss over Sofia's face and ruffled the hem of her gown.

"I want you to know something, Sofia." Julia met her gaze and didn't waver. "Alex has had dozens and dozens of women fawning over him for the past decade. He could have chosen any one of them from Minnesota to Paris—but he chose you, and he wants you to stay."

"He had little choice. My grandfa—"

"He had a great deal of choice in the matter." Julia's voice was full of assurance. "I have watched Alex get out of any number of predicaments over the years. If he had wanted, he could have stalled until it was too late. But he chose to marry you." She smiled. "I do believe he fell in love at first sight."

Even if it was true, it didn't mean Sofia was good for him.

"Enjoy his love," Julia said, taking Sofia's hand in her own. "Embrace it, and no matter what, do not let it go." She nodded. "I might be a little selfish when I say this, but I do hope you stay so we can become good friends. I've always wanted a sister, and you are the closest thing I've ever had."

"I've never had a sister either." It had only been her and her father for the majority of her life.

"I do hope you'll consider staying." Julia finally stood. "Don't let people like Annabeth Cummings dictate who you love or where you live. Life is too short to worry about what people think. The only opinion that should matter is Alex's." She motioned toward the path leading back to the house. "Shall we?"

Sofia walked beside Julia, trying to believe everything the woman said, but a part of her still had doubts. It was easy for Julia to tell her not to worry about Annabeth, or people like her, but Julia didn't know what it was like to be an immigrant—or to be poor. Even if Alex wanted her to stay, which she was beginning to believe—it could mean disaster for everyone and everything he held dear. How could she be the cause of that? If she had the choice, shouldn't she try to protect him from calamity?

In only a few days their visitors would leave and Sofia could return to the life she used to lead.

But how would she go back to a life of poverty after living like a fairy-tale princess? Perhaps, she should just let herself enjoy the next few days. What would it hurt? All too soon, it would come to an end. For now, she would savor every moment.

Chapter 7

The weather could not have been better for the lumberjack festival. Alex sat on wooden bleachers that had been hauled to the edge of the White Pine Mill Pond for spectators to watch the many different competitions. At present two lumberjacks were competing in the log rolling event. Two men stood on a twenty-inch round log, trying to maneuver their feet to make the log spin and toss their opponent into the water. Both men were expert river rats, having years of experience on log drives down the river. Their feet were fast and sure, and their balance was amazing.

"How marvelous," Mrs. Robertson said as she watched the men turn the log first this way and then that, water splashing against their feet. "I remember watching my father drive logs down the Hudson River when I was a child." She looked at Alex, her face shaded from the sun under a pink parasol. "Did you know my father started his career as a river rat in New York? He saved for years and then built his first sawmill in Ohio when he was thirty-three. Within ten years, he had the largest lumber company in America." She glanced at Alex's father briefly. "That is, until your father and Noah's father started Midwest Lumber."

"I didn't know that about your father." Alex hadn't stopped to wonder about how American Lumber had started.

"My father was the first on that side of my family to be born in America." Mrs. Robertson turned her gaze on Sofia next. "But he made the most of his opportunities. He married my mother, who was a descendant of one of the original Dutch settlers to New York."

Sofia sat with Julia and Annabeth, taking in the activities with just as much interest and enthusiasm as the others. Her brown eyes glowed with excitement, and for the first time since Alex had met her, she seemed completely at ease. He smiled when she smiled, loving the way the sun shone off her fetching hat. She was lovely—and when she turned and caught him admiring her, she gave him a gentle smile and his heart did a little flip.

"Your wife is very beautiful," Mrs. Robertson observed.

"I agree." Alex couldn't hide the appreciation in his voice. "I was taken with her the moment I met her."

"I can see why." The older woman nodded with approval. "It's a very rare gift to marry a woman with beauty *and* connections. You are a fortunate man."

Sofia didn't have a single connection in the world, but that didn't matter to Alex in the least. It didn't even matter that she was breathtaking, though he couldn't deny that he loved to look upon her. What mattered to Alex, and always had, was a woman's heart. From the moment he saw Sofia's devotion to Alberto, he had known what was in her heart, and that had attracted him more than anything.

Mrs. Robertson lifted her chin just a notch as she watched the log rollers, though she was still present in the conversation with Alex. "It was my great disappointment that Mr. Robertson and I could not have children."

Alex looked away from the older lady, somehow feeling that he was intruding upon her personal life, even though she had invited him into it.

"We did not have a son, or even a daughter, to inherit the family business," Mrs. Robertson continued. "That is why we have decided to sell it." She finally looked back at him. "I wanted to meet you and Noah, and your wives, because you are the next generation. You will take Midwest Lumber into this new century, and someday your children will continue the legacy. I want to make sure I am handing my father's business off to worthy successors."

Alex placed his hand over his heart. "It would be an honor to continue your family's legacy."

She nodded. "I believe you."

One of the lumberjacks slipped and fell into the water. The crowd cheered for the winner, who jumped off the log and into the pond. He gave his opponent a helping hand, and then the two men grinned and made their way out of the water.

"Our family and business have always been above reproach," Mrs. Robertson said to Alex when she stopped clapping. "I would not hand over my inheritance to just anyone. My husband is concerned about the business side of things, whereas I'm more concerned about the social implications."

Alex nodded, his pulse picking up speed. Did she have something to say against Sofia?

"I have enjoyed spending time with Julia and Sofia," Mrs. Robertson said. "Both ladies have impeccable pedigrees and reputations. I couldn't ask for more."

Alex hated to deceive Mrs. Robertson, but his father had given him no choice. "I'm happy to hear it," he said with little emotion. Sophia was from a fine family. Yes, they were poor in money, but they were rich in honor, compassion, and love. He wished those were the things by which Mrs. Robertson judged a person's worth.

Everyone began to disperse, so Alex helped Mrs. Robertson from the bleachers to join the others. He was thankful when she turned her attention to someone else.

"I do believe our lunch is ready," Julia said to their party, her face shaded under her own parasol. "If you'd like, we can make our way to the picnic area."

Father offered Mrs. Robertson his arm to lead her to lunch. Alex caught Sofia's gaze and smiled. They had been with the group since they left Basswood Hill that morning, and he was looking forward to a few moments by her side. She looked so happy and content, and he was eager to find out why.

As he moved toward her, Annabeth intercepted Alex and wrapped her arm through his. "How kind of you to escort me to lunch," she said.

It would be rude for Alex to put her aside, so he tried to communicate his disappointment to Sofia with his eyes. She simply nodded and took the arm Mr. Robertson offered.

"You know," Annabeth said as they left the millpond and moved toward a copse of trees along the riverbank a short distance away, "I've always considered myself a good judge of character. Most people feel comfortable enough with me to share intimate details of their life."

Perhaps that was why she had a reputation for being one of the biggest gossips as well. He couldn't imagine sharing anything personal with her.

"But I have learned nothing new about Sofia," she said, "other than what you and your father have told me." She lifted a gloved hand to her chin. "I can't decide if it's because I've lost my touch or because she's hiding something from you."

Alex and Annabeth were in the middle of the group as they walked over the uneven ground. Thankfully, Mrs. Robertson was at the head with Father, but any of the other guests could hear her if they were listening close enough.

"You don't need to worry on my account," Alex said with a forced chuckle to ease the moment. "Sofia is hiding nothing from me."

"But how would you know?" she asked. "Isn't that the point of hiding?"

He took a steadying breath, his anger rising swiftly. Annabeth was trying to cause trouble, and he needed to put a stop to it immediately. There was no use in niceties any longer.

"Please refrain from making accusations against my wife. It is not fair nor becoming."

"Accusations?" She lowered her hand to her throat. "I was simply curious."

"There is no need for your curiosity." He motioned toward the sawing competition, ready to change the subject. Two teams of lumberjacks were sawing through a massive white pine log at least five feet in diameter. "Are you enjoying the activities?"

"Don't say I didn't warn you," Annabeth said under her breath, all pretenses gone from her tone.

Hundreds of people had come out for the day's festivities with their families. Many of them worked for the White Pine Lumber Company, though some were other citizens from town. Bankers, lawyers, pastors, and grocers mingled side by side, their own picnic lunches being spread out to enjoy.

The group finally arrived at the picnic site where Julia's staff had prepared an impressive lunch. Three checkered blankets were on the ground under the poplar trees. Fine china was set out with silverware, linen napkins, and glass goblets. As everyone began to find a seat, Alex left Annabeth and went to his wife.

His heart sped up at being near her, and when she greeted him with a smile, everything else faded away. "Are you enjoying the day?" he asked her.

"I love it." Her face shone with happiness. It warmed Alex to the core. "I've never seen such competition before."

"There will be more this afternoon," he promised. "And we haven't even gone to the craftsmen's tents." He was excited to show her the wood-carver who was demonstrating his skills today. "I'm sure you will find much to entertain you."

She allowed her eyes to wander over the crowd gathered on the banks of the Mississippi River and let her gaze rest on the town across the way. Contentment relaxed her facial features.

"Do you like it here?" he asked her, his voice low—expectant.

"More and more every day. Minnesota is just as my grandfather described it." She smiled to herself. "I almost feel as if I've lived here all my life."

An ember of hope kindled in Alex's chest. He would not press her about staying now, but it did his heart good to hear her say such things.

The others had found their spots. Julia and Noah sat alone on one blanket, and Julia patted a spot next to her. "Join us?" she said to them.

Alex took Sofia's hand and led her over to the blanket. Father entertained the Robertsons while Annabeth and her father visited with the other board members.

Julia and Sofia conversed easily with one another as they discussed the festival and dined on cold fried chicken. Julia shared details about some of the people sitting around them, pointing out friends she thought Sofia might enjoy meeting.

Sofia was animated and comfortable as she spoke. Something had shifted within her, something that Alex liked a great deal.

As Sofia turned to Noah and asked him about his family, Julia met Alex's gaze and lifted her eyebrows in excitement.

Alex sent her a questioning gaze, wondering if she had been the reason for Sofia's newfound ease.

Julia simply smiled and then joined in on the conversation again.

No matter what Julia had done or said, Alex was happy that Sofia was finally fitting in.

With a full belly and a light heart, Sofia held Alex's hand as they walked through the vendors who had come to the festival. They had left the others behind at the picnic and been content to wander, with no particular direction or purpose but simply to enjoy the day.

"Noah and I started this festival the first year we arrived in Little Falls," Alex said as they stopped to look at furniture made with white pine lumber. It was built by a local craftsman with an incredible gift. "We wanted a way for everyone in the community to come together and have some fun, but also to see how the mill affects their daily lives."

Everywhere they turned, someone was doffing a cap or offering a curtsy to Alex. They treated him and Noah like royalty, and, she supposed, it was only natural. The mill employed more people than anyone else in town, and if it hadn't been for them, the town would be half its current size. Their respect and admiration for the "White Pine Bachelors," as she'd heard so many people call them, even though they both were now married, was strong. But Alex's esteem for his employees was just as deep. It didn't matter who he spoke to, whether it was the lawyer they employed or a lowly river rat who ran the logs, Alex treated each one with the same regard.

Sofia watched, quietly storing everything inside her heart.

"This is the one I've been waiting to show you." Alex gently tugged on her hand, and she happily followed him to the end booth where an old gentleman sat surrounded by beautiful wood carvings. At his feet were piles of wood chips, and in his hand was a figurine of a lumberjack about a foot tall. The details in the piece were magnificent.

The man caught sight of Alex and immediately rose. "Mr. Alexander!"

"Hello, Mr. Poletti." Alex extended his hand. "It's good to see you again. Thank you for coming on such a short notice."

"It is my pleasure." The corners of the man's brown eyes were wrinkled from smiling. "I am so sorry about Alberto. I did not know he was ill. He was a good man. One of the very best. I count myself blessed to have known him. I was sorry to hear he passed and could not be here today."

Alex smiled at Sofia, which drew Mr. Poletti's attention. "This is my wife, Sofia."

Mr. Poletti removed his hat with his free hand, revealing a balding head. He bowed with great reverence. "It's a pleasure to meet you, Mrs. Alexander."

"The pleasure is mine."

His eyes grew wide at the sound of her voice. "You are from Switzerland, no?"

He recognized her accent so quickly? "Yes," she said with a grin. "Lugano."

"Lugano?" His eyes grew even wider. "I am from Paradiso, on the other side of the bay." He shook his head in wonder, but then he frowned. "And Alberto, he was from Lugano too, no?"

Sofia nodded and smiled, liking this man immediately. "Alberto was my grandfather."

"Ah!" He set the figurine down and took her gloved hands into his own. He kissed the backs of her hands several times and then squeezed them. "Alberto's little Sofia?" He laughed. "He spoke of you so often I feel as if I know you already. Alberto and I worked together for years. He dreamed of you coming to America, and here you are." He stood back and looked her over. "*Bella, bella,* you are so beautiful, just as Alberto said."

"*Grazie.*" Her cheeks grew warm from his praise. "Thank you."

Mr. Poletti then looked at Alex, his expressive eyes filling with even more excitement. "Alberto must have been so happy and proud to have you as his grandson."

Alex glanced at Sofia. She nodded, her heartache over losing her grandfather mingling with the joy she knew he had taken at her marriage to Alex. "My grandfather was very pleased," she said.

"He was the best wood-carver in America." Mr. Poletti nodded with complete confidence. "He taught me more than I ever taught him."

"He also taught my father," Sofia said. "Who taught me."

"You carve wood?" Mr. Poletti asked.

"Sì."

He lifted up a piece of basswood and a carving tool. "Would you like to make something?"

Her fingers itched to carve again, but now was not the time nor the place. All around her people mingled while talking to vendors and admiring the products. What would people think of her if they saw her carving wood like one of the vendors?

Guilt immediately assailed her. Was she looking down on Mr. Poletti because he was a vendor and she was supposed to be a lady? Shame weighed heavily on her heart.

Mr. Poletti's expectant smile dimmed, and he set aside the wood. "I'm sorry to have asked, Mrs. Alexander."

"No." She shook her head, not wanting him to feel bad when it was her fault. "I'm honored to be asked."

His smile returned and he patted her hand. "Maybe another time?"

Sofia nodded. "I would like that, very much."

Alex watched Sofia closely, and she wondered if he had guessed at her response. She'd never met someone who was so aware of her thoughts and feelings as her husband.

"It was nice to see you, Mr. Poletti," Alex said, shaking the man's hand. "Thank you again for making the time to come to the festival and showcase your work."

"I will be at the Minnesota State Fair in a couple weeks," he said. "Perhaps you will come?"

"I love the fair." Alex took Sofia's hand in his. "I'd love to show it to my wife."

In a couple of weeks? Wouldn't she be on a ship, sailing back to Europe in a couple of weeks?

"Have a good day," Mr. Poletti said as he returned to his stool and took up his figurine.

Sofia waved and followed Alex, her hand in his.

They were at the end of the vendors' booths, and just beyond them were the banks of the Mississippi. Sofia didn't ask where they were going as he walked her to the riverside. She was just happy to be out of the crush of people and have a few moments alone with him.

A gentle breeze blew across the water, and Sofia closed her eyes. She took a deep breath, savoring the smell of the water and the moist earth.

"You seem happier," Alex said to her. "I love watching you enjoy yourself."

She opened her eyes and met his gaze. He held her hand, but she had the desire to press herself close to him, to feel his strength and affection. He would embrace her without hesitation, of that she was certain, but she didn't want to give him false hope.

"I am happier," she said. "I've decided to allow myself to savor these days here. With you."

The joy in his eyes dimmed. "Then you're still set on leaving?"

"I think it's best."

Alex reached for her other hand and drew her to face him. "What if I think it's not? What if I think the best place for you is right here with me?"

Her heart fluttered and pleasure raced up her arms from where he touched her, but those feelings were fleeting. She knew, better than anyone, that it didn't matter how much she loved someone. It was never enough. Her love for Gianni had not been enough, so how could her love for Alex be enough?

Sofia sighed. "I don't want to discuss this again. The day is too beautiful to ruin with these things." She gently squeezed his hands. "Can we just enjoy the time we have left?"

"I would enjoy it so much more if I knew you were staying."

She looked down at their hands. His were so large and powerful, capable of great and important things. "I must do what is best for both of us," she said, forcing herself to smile. It was her turn to tug Alex. "Shall we rejoin the others? It must be time to return home and prepare for the party." That evening Julia and Noah were hosting a dance in honor of the Robertsons' visit. Dozens of people had been invited to attend. There was still much to prepare.

He came willingly, though there was a heaviness to his step that hadn't been there before—and Sofia knew she had no one to blame but herself.

Chapter 8

Moonlight sliced across the river, its beams rippling over the water as it gently glided south. Alex stood on the veranda of Noah and Julia's home, leaning against the railing, watching the river. He never tired of this scene. Never tired of the constant flow of water or the abundant wildlife that shared the river with them.

But tonight, not even the beauty and majesty of the river could settle his heart. Behind him, in Julia and Noah's ballroom, dozens of friends and neighbors had assembled to dance and be merry. Sofia was in the midst of them. She had proven to be an excellent dancer and had been more at home in her dancing slippers than anywhere else. Not only was she a good dancer, but everyone had wanted to meet her. Word had already spread through town that Alex had married, and now was their opportunity to finally meet the woman who had captured his heart.

Her dance card had filled up almost immediately. She'd reserved three dances for Alex, the most he could expect, but she had given away the others. Already he'd danced with her twice, loving each moment, but now he would have to wait until the last dance of the evening to hold her in his arms again.

He turned his gaze from the river and looked through the glass doors and into the ballroom. It wasn't hard to locate her among the others. She wore a beautiful green gown, and her thick hair was pinned up in countless curls. She laughed as she wove around the ballroom with one of the clerks who worked in Alex's office. The man was young, handsome, and single. And he was besotted by Sofia—as were a dozen other men in the ballroom. How could they not be? She was the most magnificent creature ever to grace their city.

One of the doors opened and Noah appeared. "I thought I'd find you out here."

Alex turned back around to look at the water again. "I came out here to be alone."

"My wife sent me looking for you. She noticed you left quite a while ago and said several people have been asking for you. She won't rest until you've returned to the dance."

"I'd rather not deal with everyone tonight."

Noah leaned on the railing beside Alex. They had been best friends from childhood, though their good-natured rivalry had threatened to come between them more than once. Their friendship had stood the test of time, though, and had come out on top.

"Sofia looks like she's finally having a good time," Noah mused. "But I know you well enough to know that something isn't right." He paused for only a moment. "She's still planning to leave, isn't she?"

Alex straightened. "I don't know what I can do to change her mind."

"Seems kind of strange, doesn't it?" Noah casually crossed his arms. "You've spent the past ten years fighting women off, and now the one woman you want doesn't want to stay."

"Ironic, isn't it?" Alex used his hand to knead the back of his neck. "Maybe that's why I want her even more. She's the first woman who didn't throw herself at my feet upon learning who I was."

"An appealing prospect."

"It's more than that." Alex shook his head, feeling completely incompetent. "She's everything I'd ever want in a wife. I'll never meet another woman like her—I don't *want* to meet anyone else."

"It's not hard for me to see you're in love." Noah smiled. "And, if my eyes don't deceive me, I'd guess Sofia's in love with you too."

"Then why won't she stay?" Alex's frustration continued to mount. If Noah had come to offer encouragement or sound advice, he wasn't hitting his mark. He was only making things worse.

"Have you asked her?"

"She says she knows what's best for me."

"What does that mean?"

"She thinks she's not good enough."

"That's ridiculous."

"I know. She thinks if someone finds out who she really is, it will ruin my reputation."

Noah rubbed his closely trimmed beard. "Have you told her that getting an annulment will be even more detrimental?"

Alex shook his head. He hadn't, partially because he didn't want to guilt Sofia into staying. He wanted her to stay because she wanted to be here, not because she was obligated.

"Try talking to her again," Noah said. "Tell her you love her and you want her to stay."

The music ended, and the couples on the dance floor started to go their separate ways.

"I'll go speak to her and tell her you're out here." Noah didn't wait for Alex to respond, but returned to the ballroom and walked up to Sofia. He said something to her, and she looked toward the veranda.

Alex's pulse picked up speed as she moved toward the door. He had never told a woman he loved her, not even Julia. What if she rejected his love?

The lights from the room silhouetted her body as she turned the doorknob and stepped out onto the veranda. He struggled to see her face, but he had already memorized her movements and the way she carried herself. She was grace and elegance and everything else that was lovely and feminine.

He didn't wait by the railing for her to come to him. Instead, he met her in the middle of the veranda and took her hands into his, turning her slightly so he could see her face from the reflection of the lights in the ballroom. They were all alone as the next piece began to play. It seeped out into the night, wrapping them in a gentle cocoon.

"You look lovely tonight," he finally said, his words just above a whisper.

She smiled, her eyes filling with a hint of pleasure—but then they clouded over. "Where have you been? I've been looking for you for over an hour."

"I came out here to be alone and to think." He motioned for her to follow him, and they went to a bench looking out at the river. It was hidden in the shadows and would offer them privacy. "Sit," he said. "You look tired."

She touched her brow with her gloved hand. "I am feeling a little tired."

"All the excitement from the past few days?"

Sofia didn't respond but simply nodded.

They sat close on the bench, their legs pressed together. He held her hands, not wanting to let her go until he had shared his heart. No matter what happened, he couldn't let her go without a fight.

"I had Noah call you out here because I wanted to tell you something."

She studied him in the dim light. "Yes?"

He couldn't just blurt out his feelings, but he didn't know how else to convey the depth of his love. He put his hand on the side of her face and brushed her velvety-soft cheek with his thumb.

She didn't pull away or flinch at his touch. Instead, she continued to watch him, her eyes fluttering for a heartbeat as he ran his thumb over her lips.

"Sofia, I'm in love with you. I think I've been in love with you from the moment I saw you standing in your grandfather's doorway." He leaned his forehead in to touch hers. "You've captured me, heart and soul, and I cannot abide to think about you leaving."

She didn't speak, nor did she move.

"Say something, my love." He pulled back to look into her eyes.

Tears had gathered, and one slipped down her cheek.

"What is this?" he whispered as he wiped it away with his thumb. "Why are you sad?"

"I'm not sad," she said. "I'm in love with you too."

His heart soared like never before, yet there was no joy in her words. "Why are you not smiling?"

"Because I don't believe it's enough."

"We're in love with each other." He couldn't hide the incredulity from his words. "How could that not be enough?"

She touched his cheek, sadness filling her eyes. "I loved someone once, very much, and he said he loved me too, but when things became hard, he left me all alone."

Alex pulled his wife into his arms and held her close. How could someone ever leave her side? "He was a fool."

"He was a man, pressed on every side by forces he could not control."

"There is nothing in this world that could drive me from your side, Sofia." He pulled back to look into her eyes. "I love you more than anything. If you'll have me, I'll spend the rest of my life proving that love to you." He kissed her then, every bit of his love pouring out of his heart and into their embrace. Her lips were soft and sweet, and he became lost in the pleasure swirling around them.

She responded to his kiss and wrapped her arms around him, pulling him tighter.

"Promise me you'll stay," he said as he kissed first one cheek and then the other. "Promise you won't leave me."

"I want to stay, Alex." She slowly pulled away from him as she shook her head. "But I cannot."

Reality crashed back down upon him. "I don't understand."

"Given time, you would."

He doubted he would ever understand. He loved her. She loved him. He wanted her to stay, and she wanted to stay. What else was there to understand?

"I know what is best for you, Alex."

"No." He shook his head, both desperation and frustration deepening his voice. "I know what's best for me, and it's you. It will always be you. I am not the man who hurt you. I would never leave you."

Something flickered in her gaze, and it gave Alex a bit of hope.

She nibbled her bottom lip and slowly nodded. "You're right. You aren't the man who hurt me."

He pulled her into his arms again. "I would never hurt you, Sofia. You are as dear to me as my own life."

She clung to him, as if she believed it was true for the very first time. "Before you make any promises to me, there is something I need to tell—"

"Alex?" A woman's voice called out to him from the ballroom doors.

It was Annabeth.

"Alex, your father has asked for you to come immediately."

Alex sighed. "We will have to continue this conversation later." He smiled. "When we have a bit more privacy."

He stood and offered his hand to his wife. She hesitated but then took it and rose to stand beside him. He kissed her one more time before he smiled down at her. "Shall we go back?"

Sofia wiped at her tears. "There are things we need to discuss."

"And we will." He lifted her hand to his lips and kissed it gently. "Later." He wrapped her arm around his and led her to the ballroom doors.

Annabeth held the door open for them. "Your father is making a speech and asked for you to join him."

Alex held Sofia's hand and smiled at her just before they entered the ballroom.

She returned the smile, and for the first time, he allowed himself to hope that she would be by his side for the rest of his life.

The final strains of the waltz reverberated off the stringed orchestra as Sofia followed her husband to the front of the ballroom to join his father.

Mr. Alexander stood stoically as he watched the dancers come to a halt. He had been cool and indifferent to Sofia for the whole visit, and she didn't expect anything to change now. They had shared nothing more than simple greetings, but she had no wish for more. She knew exactly what he thought about her, but she was choosing to believe Alex when he said it didn't matter what everyone else thought. Alex loved her, and that was enough.

More than enough.

As long as he still wanted her after he learned about the baby.

Alex smiled at her again, the depths of his love revealed in the warmth of his gaze. Oh, if only she could be worthy of that love. For the first time, she had hope that maybe she could be. Maybe their love was real and true. Perhaps she'd mistaken the feelings she had for Gianni as love. She had been blinded by her feelings and had done the unthinkable, believing he had her best in mind, when all he'd thought about was himself.

Alex was different. What she felt for him was different. He had put her above himself and had risked everything to marry her.

"Excuse me," Mr. Alexander said. "May I have your attention, please?"

Sofia stood close to Alex's side, her hand nestled firmly inside his. She had wanted to tell him about her pregnancy under the light of the moon, when they were declaring their love, but Annabeth had intruded on the moment. The truth would put Alex's love to the test, and she could only hope and pray it would survive. As soon as possible, she would pull him aside and tell him.

The room quieted and everyone turned their attention to Mr. Alexander.

"I have an important announcement to make, though I feel it's a bit redundant by now."

Everyone chuckled politely, their attention shifting to Alex and Sofia.

"I would like to formally announce the marriage of my son Charles to his wife, Sofia."

Applause erupted, and Alex turned his gaze to Sofia. He grinned, his hope and adoration almost too much for her to look upon. He thought she was pure and wholesome—how would he look upon her when he learned otherwise?

"In the coming months," Mr. Alexander said with one of the first smiles Sofia had ever seen on his face, "we will plan a formal party to celebrate their nuptials, as well as the acquisition of North American Lumber. You will all be invited to my home in St. Paul."

More applause resounded in the room.

"The acquisition has been agreed upon?" Sofia asked Alex over the clapping.

"Yes. The Robertsons made their formal offer just this afternoon, and our board accepted." He couldn't contain his happiness as he spoke to her. "All that's left is the legal paperwork, which will be done later this week in St. Paul, and then it will be official."

"How wonderful." A twinge of pain suddenly tightened her belly, catching Sofia unaware. She hitched her breath, conscious of the room of people watching, and tried hard not to wince.

"Are you all right?" Alex asked, concern wedging between his eyes.

The pain passed and she let out the breath she'd been holding. She felt a cold sweat on her brow, but she managed to nod. "I'm fine. Just a little warm and tired."

"Would you like something to drink?" he asked.

"That would be nice."

The orchestra began to play again, but their guests did not return to the dance. Instead, they came up to Alex and Sofia, pushing in around them to congratulate them.

There was nothing else to do but stand there and accept their well-wishes. She forced a smile on her face, but another cramp seized her abdomen, and this time it was low and throbbing.

Panic overwhelmed her. Was something happening to the baby?

No matter where she looked, she could see nothing but people. They swarmed in and out, their voices loud and unyielding.

Sofia suddenly felt herself swaying, and she reached to try to stop herself from falling. The faces around her became filled with concern.

"Darling?" Alex spoke close to her ear, but she could not focus on his face.

The pain continued to increase, and she could do nothing but whimper. Her head began to spin, and she stumbled, but Alex was by her side, and he scooped her into his arms.

She wrapped her arms around his neck and buried her face into his shoulder.

"Dr. Harrington." Alex called for the doctor in a panicked voice.

"Right behind you," the doctor said.

Everyone moved aside as Alex rushed Sofia out of the room.

"Put her in our bedchamber," Julia said as she appeared by Alex's side. "The room at the top of the stairs and to the right."

Sofia was thankful she had not passed out, but she was afraid she still might. The pain continued, and all she could think about was the baby. She moaned with the discomfort. Had she somehow wanted this to happen? How many times had she wished she wasn't pregnant? She had told herself it would make her life so much easier—yet, now, the thought of losing this unborn child brought the deepest grief she'd ever felt. Guilt pressed against her chest, and she began to pray that God would spare the baby.

"Sofia," Alex whispered against her ear. "What's wrong? Where does it hurt, my love?"

"My stomach."

"Perhaps it's appendicitis," the doctor said somewhere close at hand.

Doctor Harrington opened the bedroom door and turned on the electric light. Alex lowered Sofia onto the bed and then knelt by her side.

"You'll need to leave while I examine your wife," Dr. Harrington said as he rolled up his sleeves. "It shouldn't take long. I'll call you in when I'm done."

Alex nodded and then placed a kiss on Sofia's brow. "I love you," he said.

He rose and left the room.

"Now," Dr. Harrington said, "what seems to be the problem, Mrs. Alexander?"

Sofia didn't want to tell the doctor the truth, but she would do whatever it would take to save her baby.

She couldn't look him in the eyes as she whispered. "I'm pregnant."

The doctor didn't miss a beat. "I'll have someone come in to assist you into a nightgown so I can examine you."

He went to the door and asked Julia to come in. Gently, and without any questions, Julia helped Sophia change into one of her nightgowns, concern on her face. When they were done, Julia slipped out of the room again so the doctor could return. He sat beside her on the bed to start palpating her stomach, but he paused and studied her face.

"I would guess you are at least three months along."

She swallowed and nodded.

He asked her a few more questions concerning her general health, her pregnancy, and the pain. Dr. Harrington was kind and gentle, his gray hair a testament to the years he'd been a physician.

"My best advice is to get plenty of rest," he finally said. "Hopefully the cramping will stop and you can carry the baby to full term." He studied her for a few more moments. "I'm assuming most people do not know about your pregnancy yet?"

She shook her head. "No one knows."

"Not even your husband?"

"No."

He frowned and sat on a chair beside her. "So then, you did not marry because you were expecting?"

It was a relief to finally share her burden with someone, even if it was a stranger. She knew her secret would be safe with him, and because of that she was free to tell him the truth.

"Mr. Alexander is not the father. I was pregnant before I met him." She began to cry, her tears streaming down her temples and into her hair. "I did not mean to hurt him, or anyone else. I did not wish for any of this to happen."

"There, there, sweet child." Dr. Harrington took out a clean handkerchief and placed it into her hand. "No matter how big our mistakes, God is even bigger. What the enemy intended for evil, God can use for good." He smiled and patted her hand. "Help God turn this into something good, for you and the baby."

She nodded and wiped her face. "Do you think the baby will be all right?"

"Only time will tell. If you're experiencing cramping and nothing else, then you should be just fine. But heed my advice and stay off your feet for a few weeks and call for me if you experience any other symptoms." He stood. "Your body will take care of the rest."

He placed a blanket over her. "I will call your husband in. I think you and he need to have a talk."

One of the last things she wanted to do while being forced to stay in bed was have such a difficult conversation with Alex.

But she was done with the secrets. She was ready to live in the light again, and if that meant risking his love, then that's exactly what she would do.

Chapter 9

Alex paced in the hallway outside Noah and Julia's bedroom. His two friends waited with him, concern deep in both their gazes.

"Everything will be fine," Julia promised Alex. "She didn't look ill earlier today. Perhaps it was something she ate."

Alex wanted to believe Julia, so he tried to smile for her sake.

"Dr. Harrington is the best in the business," Noah assured everyone standing there. "He will have her better in no time."

"What's taking so long?" Alex asked. "He said it wouldn't take much time to examine her."

"You'd rather he be thorough, wouldn't you?" Julia asked.

"Of course."

Father appeared on the stairs with Annabeth and the Robertsons.

"How is she?" Mrs. Robertson asked. "We didn't know there was anything wrong until we saw you leave the ballroom with her in your arms."

"The doctor is in there now." Alex stopped pacing. "I appreciate your concern."

Annabeth came to stand by Alex's side. "I'm so sorry this happened. Is there anything I can do to help?"

"No." He shook his head. "Thank you. As soon as the doctor is finished examining her, we will know more."

"What kind of complaint did she have?" Mrs. Robertson asked. "Perhaps I could give the doctor some advice."

Alex doubted Mrs. Robertson could aid the good doctor, but who was he to tell her such a thing?

"She looked so happy and content today," Annabeth mused. "Who would have guessed she was ill?"

"It came on quite suddenly," Alex said, wishing they'd all leave.

"At the festival, she was just as energetic and lively as the rest of us." Annabeth sighed. "I guess one can never tell what's truly going on under the surface."

Mrs. Robertson nodded her agreement.

"For instance," Annabeth said to Mrs. Robertson. "Did you know that Sofia isn't the daughter of a silk maker?"

"What?" Mrs. Robertson frowned.

Alex took a step forward, his heart rate escalating.

"I overheard her speaking to a wood-carver this very afternoon." Annabeth had the face of innocence as she spoke, but Alex knew exactly what she was doing. "She said her father and grandfather were wood-carvers, and she's not from Italy, but from a town called Lugano in Switzerland." Annabeth turned to look at Alex. "I'm pronouncing it correctly, am I not?"

"What is she talking about?" Mrs. Robertson asked Alex. "Is this true?"

Father's cheek muscles twitched as he watched Alex, anger and loathing seething from his eyes.

There was no use trying to hide it anymore.

"It is true," Alex admitted. "Sofia just arrived in Minnesota a few weeks ago. She came to live with her grandfather who was a woodcarver and one of my dearest friends. But Alberto died, and Sofia had nowhere else to turn."

Mrs. Robertson's eyes grew wide. "You didn't meet her in Paris?"

"No. I just met her last week."

She put her hand to her chest, shock registering across her face. "Are you not married?"

"We are married," he assured her. "We were married last week. The day we met."

"My gracious." Mrs. Robertson pulled out a fan and began to pump it close to her face. "It's all been a lie."

"I love her," Alex said, as if that should explain everything. "She is just as lovely and kind and good as she appears. That is not a lie."

"But we were led to believe she was from a family of distinction." Mrs. Robertson stared at Father, accusation squinting her eyes.

"She is from a family of distinction," Alex said. "Her grandfather was the most honorable man I've ever met."

"Which is more than I can say about any of you." Mrs. Robertson pursed her lips and then lifted her chin. "In light of this information, I do believe we will need to reconsider selling our company."

"Please." Alex stepped forward. "Do not deny Noah and Julia this opportunity because of me." He despised himself for bringing this upon his friends. "They are worthy of your goodwill, even if I am not."

Mrs. Robertson looked at each of them, one by one, and then snapped her fan closed. "I am retiring for the night. I will give you my final decision in the morning."

She walked down the hall, her husband close on her trail, and disappeared into one of the bedrooms.

"I suppose I should return to the party." Annabeth spoke as if she had done nothing out of the ordinary. "I'm having a lovely time." She moved past Father on her way down the steps.

"I told you you'd regret your hasty decision to marry that girl," Father said.

"The only thing I regret is that I live in a world that does not value her for her heart and her character." Alex shook his head. "Sofia had no choice about her parentage any more than I did—yet she is worthier to live this life than I am."

Father didn't bother to respond but simply turned and left the hall.

Julia put her hand on Alex's shoulder. "I'm so sorry," she said.

Alex looked from Noah to Julia. He would have given everything up in an instant for Sofia, but he couldn't do that to his friends. "I'm the one who is sorry."

Noah shook his head. "Don't be. You're only doing what I would have done if put in your position."

The bedroom door opened, and Dr. Harrington met Alex's gaze. "Is she going to be all right?" Alex asked.

Dr. Harrington glanced at Noah and Julia and then back at Alex. "I believe so. I've told her she needs to rest for a few weeks, but after that, she should be just fine."

Relief made Alex weak. "What's wrong with her?"

The doctor glanced at the Walkers again and then said to Alex, "She'd like to see you, son."

His words, which were so simple, were weighed down with something heavy.

Alex didn't wait to see if he had more to say, but left everyone and went into the bedroom.

Sofia was in a nightgown, lying on the bed under a quilt. She opened her eyes, and that's when he saw she was crying.

Closing the door, Alex walked across the room and knelt beside his wife. He ran his hand over her forehead, smoothing back her dark hair.

Another tear ran down her cheek.

"Are you in pain?" he asked.

She shook her head. "It's better now that I'm lying down. I think I just overdid things today."

"I'm happy you're feeling better." He smiled, trying to get her to smile, and put his hand on her cheek. "Why are you crying?"

Sofia closed her eyes and buried her face in his hand.

"What is it? You can tell me." Fear tightened his chest. Hadn't Dr. Harrington said she'd be fine in a few weeks?

She swallowed and met his gaze. "I have something to tell you— something that may change everything. I tried to tell you earlier."

He couldn't imagine what she could tell him that was so dire. "Whatever it is, it will be fine. I promise."

Her lips trembled as she took his hand away from her face and held it. "I'm pregnant."

"Pregnant?" He frowned, the word not making any sense to him. "What are you talking about, Sofia?"

"Before I left Switzerland." She let out a breath. "I thought Gianni loved me. I thought he would marry me. He made so many promises, but then his father learned about us, and he convinced Gianni he could find a better wife." She wiped at her tears with her free hand. "When I told him I was expecting a child, he turned around and walked away. I was left alone, with no one and nothing to turn to, so I came to America."

Confusion clouded Alex's mind as he pulled away from Sofia. He stared down at her, and for a moment he wondered what else she might be keeping from him.

But the look of pain and remorse in her beautiful eyes told him she was telling him everything there was to tell. Empathy filled his heart—empathy and anger. How could a man turn his back on both Sofia *and* his child? How could a man leave the two most precious things in the world to fend for themselves? And what kind of man would have placed Sofia in this position to begin with?

"I'm so sorry," he whispered as he took her into his arms and held her against his chest. His voice caught in his throat as emotion swelled inside him. He had every right to be angry with Sofia, but he felt only compassion. Her remorse and sorrow were so deep, there was no question that she regretted her past mistakes. It was not his job to punish her or withhold the forgiveness he had to offer. It was the very same forgiveness God had offered every time Alex humbled himself before the Lord.

She grasped his lapels and wept into his coat. "I'm sorry, Alex. I'm sorry that I am not the woman you thought you marr—"

"You are exactly the woman I thought I married."

"But I'm not—"

"You are dearly beloved," he said gently. "And highly favored." His heart broke for Sofia, and he grieved for what she had endured. "You are my wife," he said as he pulled back and wiped her tears once again. "And nothing will ever change that. I love you more than life itself. When I offered you my name, I also offered you my unconditional love."

"I will bring you shame and embarrassment."

He ran his thumb over her cheek, marveling at how completely he loved her. "You and the baby will bring me love and joy all the days of my life. Nothing you could do would embarrass me, Sofia. From this day forward, this child will belong to both of us, and we shall carry whatever may come together. You no longer have to carry this burden alone."

Love radiated from her eyes as a tremulous smile tilted her pretty lips. "Does this mean you want me to stay?"

He smiled. "I never wanted you to leave."

"Not even now?"

"More than ever, I want you to stay."

She wrapped her arms around him and hugged him close. "Then I will stay by your side for the rest of my life."

He returned her embrace. "To have and to hold from this day forward, for better for worse, for richer, for poorer, in sickness and in health, to love and to cherish, till death us do part."

"I do," she whispered.

Epilogue

Basswood Hill
May 1901

Sofia sat on the blanket on the upper lawn of Basswood Hill, thankful for the warm sunshine and the budding trees. Tiny green leaves and little green stems poked out of hiding after the long, cold winter, offering a promise for the summer yet to come.

"Isn't it amazing how quickly the babies are growing?" Julia mused as she sat next to Sofia and held her son under his arms. Little Gideon Walker was now eight months old and had the deepest dimples Sofia had ever seen. He grinned, his first two teeth budding out like the leaves all around. His smile was wet and full of joy.

Baby Grace lay in Sofia's arms, fast asleep. At the age of three months, she was just beginning to find her personality. Her giggles were infectious, and Sofia found she could spend hours simply watching her daughter. Even now, as she slept so soundly, Sofia found it difficult to take her eyes off her. She was perfect in every single way.

Just a few yards away, Alex and Noah played tennis, their white

321

trousers and white shirts reflecting the brilliant sunshine. It was a beautiful Sunday afternoon, one similar to the others they'd shared with the Walkers over the past ten months. But now, with winter behind them, there was a whole new world for the babies to explore.

Christopher, the Alexanders' footman, approached with cookies and lemonade on a silver platter. Sofia took a glass from the servant and offered him a smile. It had taken her several months to learn how to live the lifestyle Alex provided, and though she still enjoyed doing many tasks on her own, she'd accepted her position as the mistress of Basswood Hill. Even though it had been hard to adjust at first, she knew her role in her home and the community was important not only to Alex but to everyone who lived in Little Falls.

Alex and Noah finished their game and joined their wives and children on the blanket, breathing heavily from the exertion.

"I'll beat you next time," Noah promised Alex. "Next Sunday, same time, same place."

Alex sat beside Sofia and put his hand on Grace's downy head and then kissed Sofia on the cheek. He laughed at Noah. "I beat you last Sunday, and I'll beat you next Sunday as well, but if you want to put yourself through the pain, I'll oblige you."

Julia rolled her eyes and handed Gideon off to his father, who lifted him high in the air, eliciting a giggle from the chubby little boy.

"I almost forgot to tell you about the letter we received at the office on Friday," Alex said to Sofia, taking a glass of lemonade from their footman with a nod of thanks. "The Robertsons are enjoying their grand tour of Europe. They were in Brienz, Switzerland, when they wrote."

"Some of the finest wood-carvers in the world live in Brienz." Sofia had visited there with her father when she was a small girl. It was in the center of Switzerland, north of Lugano.

"How are they enjoying their retirement?" Julia asked.

"They seem to be having a wonderful time." Alex rested his elbow on his raised knee. "Mrs. Robertson told me, once again, how pleased she is that her father's company is in our capable hands."

After the Robertsons had learned the truth about Sofia's heritage, Mrs. Robertson had seriously considered rescinding her offer, but it was her husband who had reminded her that her grandfather had been an immigrant to America. If he had not been given the opportunities from his adopted homeland, which were offered to his son as well, Mrs. Robertson would not have a company to sell. She had finally agreed, and the acquisition had gone on as planned.

Sofia wished Alex's father had been as understanding. Though he was civil and acknowledged Sophia as his daughter-in-law, he had not shown her any warmth. But Alex often reminded her that his father didn't share warmth with him either. Their visits were few and far between, and it seemed his father was content with that arrangement. As for Sofia's pregnancy, they had kept it quiet, for the most part, and very few people raised their eyebrows when Grace had arrived six months after their marriage. The beautiful brown-eyed baby girl had been born into the center of a devoted family with an affectionate father who never once looked upon her as anything but his.

A gentle breeze ruffled the tops of the trees, drawing Sofia's gaze to the heavens and thoughts of her grandfather who had brought her and Alex together. Almost a year ago, when she had found herself pregnant and alone, she had no hope of ever finding redemption or joy again. But God, in His infinite and mighty power, had orchestrated a series of events that had brought her and Grace into Alex's loving arms. They had been given a new name and a new future. One man's rejection had led to another man's unconditional love. She had everything her heart could ever desire, but more importantly, her daughter would carry the same legacy. There would be no burden of shame or embarrassment on Grace Alexander's life. That was the greatest gift Alex had given to Sofia and their daughter.

Grace stirred in Sofia's arms and opened her beautiful eyes to look up at her mother and father. A sleepy smile widened her toothless mouth, and she immediately reached for the necklace Sofia wore.

"Look who's awake," Sofia said as she lifted her daughter up for the others to see.

Gideon took notice of Grace and reached for her from his father's arms. Noah set Gideon down on his tummy, and Sofia held Grace close for him to admire. The babies stared at one another, as they often did when put side by side, but this time they both smiled. Gideon reached out and, ever so gently, took Grace's pudgy fist into his hand. He didn't pull or push, but simply held it—and then tried to put her fist into his mouth.

Sofia glanced at Julia and shared a smile.

It would be fun to see what the years would bring.

After a few more minutes, Gideon began to yawn, and Julia and Noah took him into their house to put him down for his afternoon nap. They waved at Sofia and Alex before stepping inside.

Alex stood and stretched and then took Grace into his arms. He offered his hand to help Sofia off the blanket, and then he put his free arm around her waist to walk his little family into their home.

Before they opened the door, Alex stopped and placed a kiss on Sofia's lips.

She pressed into him, and he held both her and Grace in a hug.

"I will never tire of saying this," he whispered. "I love you."

"And I will never tire of hearing it," she said with a smile.

Dr. Harrington had been correct when he said that no matter

how big one's transgressions were, God was even bigger. She'd seen it firsthand as the Lord had taken her mistakes and used them to produce something beautiful, as only He could.

He'd given her hope and a future.

With a contented smile, she stepped into the house with her little family, happier than she'd ever been in her life.

Gabrielle Meyer lives in central Minnesota on the banks of the Mississippi River with her husband and four young children. As an employee of the Minnesota Historical Society, she fell in love with the rich history of her state and enjoys writing fictional stories inspired by real people and events. Gabrielle can be found at www .gabriellemeyer.com where she writes about her passion for history, Minnesota, and her faith.

ECHOES OF THE HEART

by Amanda Barratt

Dedication

In memory of the 146.
You are not forgotten.

Soli Deo gloria

Chapter 1

July 9, 1909

Send these, the homeless, tempest-tost to me,
I lift my lamp beside the golden door!

The golden door," Aileen O'Connor whispered, her words lost in the blur of sounds around her. The suitcase handle in her left hand bit into her damp palm, her sister Meggie's fingers wrapped around her right. Before them, on her own little isle amid an ocean of blue, stood the Statue of Liberty—proud and crowned, holding a torch aloft, as if to say, *I'm watching over you. I'm lighting your way.*

Ellis Island. Would this golden door, this America, welcome them as Lady Liberty did, with a kind face and an outstretched hand?

Now was not the time to be pondering the answer. She must see them through inspections first.

America must be a first-class place indeed. They didn't let just anyone set foot on her shores. One had to be proven first.

And Aileen hadn't scrimped and saved and crossed an ocean to be turned away.

For hours they waited on the ferry, while boats ahead of theirs disgorged their passengers. Though her ankles throbbed, she refused to move from her place by the railing. Sun beat down, sparkling off the water. The back of her dress stuck to her skin. Seagulls circled overhead, squawking raucously.

She glanced at Meggie. Her fifteen-year-old sister clutched a valise, her thin frame pressed against the railing.

Though doubtless as hot, thirsty, and tired as Aileen, Meggie smiled. The gesture transformed her pale features into sweet loveliness. "It'll be grand to be on land again."

And away from all these people. Aileen could scarcely turn around without brushing against a fellow passenger. Languages blended in a high-pitched babble of syllables and cadences. Russian. Italian. Yiddish. They'd made the crossing mostly with fellow Irish. Now, separated onto different ferries, she picked out few familiar faces. Instead, those nearby were outwardly as different from each other as could be imagined. Inwardly though, she guessed, their hearts all beat with one refrain. A single word, over and over.

America.

A woman in a kerchief clutched a squalling infant in her arms. Three bearded men in hats spoke quietly in Yiddish. An Italian family watched over their children, who perched on a trunk. Their mother kept a close eye on them, weary and watchful, her rounded middle announcing another member would soon be added to their family.

Finally, it was their turn to disembark. They queued up behind the Italian family.

"It looks like a palace." Meggie's eyes sparkled. "They're greetin' us like royalty."

"Just walk in like you are, and we'll be all right," Aileen whispered, trying to bolster Meggie's courage as well as her own. Beneath her dress, her heart beat hard and fast. She swallowed back the dryness in her throat.

They filed off the ship and onto the quay. Uniformed officers shouted in multiple languages.

"Form a line! Please, keep in line."

The family ahead of them struggled with their bulky trunk, sweat glistening on father and son's foreheads as they bore it between them. Behind them a baby wailed.

Was the immense brick building ahead meant to frighten or invite them? It did indeed look like a palace, with its domed turrets, arched windows, and massive front doors. An American flag billowed in the breeze.

Shuffling toward it, clinging to her worn suitcase, surrounded by a horde of others with the same worries, hopes, and dreams as she, seemed to reduce them each from human beings to packages laid out for processing.

Aileen glanced down at the tag pinned to the collar of her blouse, stating the name of the ship she'd crossed on, her name, and her number on the ship's manifest.

Packages indeed.

She lifted her chin. If that was what one must be to enter America, she'd gladly be thought of as a package.

Meggie's fingers found hers and squeezed as they entered an echoing room. Hundreds of voices, clattering footsteps, men in uniform keeping order. The noise rang in her ears, making her want to press her hands against them and hear only the peat-scented wind moaning over Erin's cliffs.

In the muddle of languages, she made out one official saying in English that they must leave their baggage to be picked up after they were processed. Around them the same words traversed in Russian, Italian, Yiddish. Couples eyed each other anxiously, clinging to bags and cases.

Aileen pressed her suitcase against herself. She'd guarded it jealously during the two-week voyage. Who knew what sort of folk might be lurking nearby, waiting to steal it?

"Should we leave it?" Meggie whispered.

Around her, everyone else set down their luggage, prodded along by officials.

Aileen swallowed. Nodded. "We'd best." Rule breakers would likely be frowned upon, perhaps not be allowed to continue through processing. Reluctantly, she set down the suitcase, Meggie placing the valise beside it.

"Form a line! Men on this side, women on the other. Hurry up," the officials called, urging them onward. One shoved a stoop-shouldered older man, making him stumble. Aileen stared down at her cracked leather boots. What was the point of this fine building if they were to be treated like cattle once inside?

The line dragged forward, up a flight of stairs. Aileen watched as those ahead trudged upward. At the top, men and women in white coats surveyed each person's ascent.

A weeding out, that's what this was. She'd done the same herself in the garden plot back home, ripping out the inferior, letting the strong remain.

Urgency thrumming through her, she turned. Meggie's eyes stood out against her pale, sweat-dampened face. They hadn't had anything to eat or drink for hours.

"Pinch your cheeks and bite your lips," she murmured. "And when you walk up the stairs, step lively."

Meggie nodded. Aileen bit her lower lip hard and pinched her cheeks to make the blood come. Her knees shook when it was their turn up the stairs, but she kept her head high and her step sure. She didn't dare glance behind to see how Meggie fared.

Upstairs more lines snaked forward. Minutes passed. Babies cried. The room stank of sweat, soiled nappies, and too many desperate people.

Aileen took a shaky breath, letting her eyes fall closed. Of all the times to feel lightheaded. Mam's words echoed in her ears.

"In all my born days, I've never met a lass as stubborn as my Aileen. If she sets out to do a thing, that's what will be done, for sure and certain."

What she'd set out to do was make America their home, hers and Meggie's. And she'd dredge up every speck of stubbornness she owned to make it happen.

She watched as those ahead were inspected. A tall young doctor surveyed each woman in turn, unwrapping shawls, fingering heads. Most were sent onward to the next line. The doctor wrote something in chalk on the coat of an elderly woman with hunched shoulders, and one of the assisting nurses pulled her aside. The little Italian girls passed inspection, but the doctor took one look at the pregnant mother and marked *PG* in a brisk sweep of chalk. She too was taken aside.

Before Aileen could look to see where the woman was being taken, her turn came.

The doctor couldn't have been above twenty-five, only a handful of years older than herself. It gave her small satisfaction to see he too was suffering in the heat.

"Unbutton your blouse," he said, voice a monotone. Her fingers shook. She tried to make them move faster, tried not to fumble over the small loops. He would think she had something wrong with her. That her hands always shook. He wouldn't know she'd never so much as taken off her shoes in front of a man.

Wretched buttons. She'd worn her Sunday best, and it had a mile of small black buttons down the front. She undid what she hoped were enough. Her cheeks flamed.

The doctor pressed an oval disk to her exposed skin. The metal was still warm from the person before her. "Deep breath."

How could one breathe deeply under such scrutiny?

Next, another doctor, gloves sheathing his hands, pushed his fingers into her upswept hair. She forced herself to stand still, not mind the fact that her blouse hung half open in a room jammed with people. She didn't have lice. She and her sister were clean, healthy people.

But had she said this, she doubted he would have paid her heed.

She wanted to wait for Meggie, but the nurse motioned her onward to the next line. She pulled her blouse together with both hands. At least the doctor had not marked her.

She breathed a sigh of relief when Meggie again stood behind her. Her cheeks were red, and she looked near tears.

"Never mind it." Aileen helped her sister do up her buttons. "We'll soon be out of here."

The line shuffled forward. She finished Meggie's buttons then did her own. She looked up from slipping the last one through its loop just as the person in front of her moved away.

"Hold still." The white-coated doctor held a buttonhook, the very kind she'd used on her boots that morning. His hand flashed out, and pain seared the tender flesh under her eyelid as he flipped the skin upward. She bit hard on her lip to keep from crying out. As he moved to do the other side, she jerked back involuntarily. He grabbed her chin in one hand.

"It will be easier if you don't fight it."

Gritting her teeth, she endured the procedure a second time.

"On you go."

Dazed and blinking, she stumbled forward into the herd of people. This time she waited for Meggie.

"What was *that* for?" Her sister blinked and rubbed her eyes.

"To make sure we have healthy eyes, I guess," Aileen said as they followed their group into a vast room separated into rectangular squares by iron-pipe railings. Like cattle pens. High half-moon-shaped windows let in sunlight. At the front of the room, affixed to the second-floor balcony, hung an American flag. A banner saluting those who had made it this far.

A middle-aged woman in uniform tapped her on the shoulder. "If you'll come this way, please." A smile softened her features. "Just a few questions and you'll be on your way." She directed them through the crowd to one of the pens. Thankfully, benches lined the small square. Aileen sank onto one, motioning Meggie to do the same. The odor of garlic emanated from the man next to her, but she scarcely minded it, luxuriating in the relief of being able to rest her aching feet. At intervals officials called out names, and groups marched to one of several desks.

An hour dragged. The benches around them emptied. It wasn't difficult to discern the fates of those being questioned. Some left the desk with giddy smiles, a lightness to their steps. Others slumped their shoulders and were led away.

They'd pass. Surely they had to pass.

Were she in the habit of praying, now would be an opportune time. Meggie likely was doing just that. She still had faith. But God hadn't seen fit to help their family in Ireland. If He had, Mam would be here beside them as they'd planned. Instead, she and Meggie had stood in a windswept churchyard while Mam's wooden coffin was lowered into the earth beside Da's. Ten years ago a farming accident had taken Da, and three months ago Mam had sickened with fever, passing a week later. Aileen had done what she always had: forged ahead. She'd gotten them this far through her own good sense. It couldn't fail her now.

No one spoke much outside their family groups. The man reeking of garlic was replaced by an olive-skinned young man and woman in colorful garb. They held hands, as if their solidarity could anchor them. The young man whispered something, and the girl nodded.

Aileen couldn't help but envy the woman, to have a man at her side during this ordeal.

Instead, she and Meggie were utterly, truly alone in this room of deafening clamor, sharp accents, and every so often, a cry of raw despair.

So much humanity, such deep suffering. All had fled their homelands in search of something better. It wasn't difficult to discern the meaning behind the frantic words uttered in garbled languages. Dreams were dashed, hopes crushed.

Ellis Island. A land of promise for some. Of tears for others.

"O'Connor."

They made their way to the front of the room. A thin-faced man sat behind a tall oak desk, a ledger spread in front of him. Aileen tried to walk proudly. Would her show of bravado fool him into thinking she was a fit American? Or would he see straight through her to the scared lass of twenty that she was?

"Name?" The man peered up at her behind owlish spectacles.

"Aileen O'Connor."

"Place of birth?"

"Ireland. County Mayo."

"Your destination?"

Destination? The word fumbled in her mind for a scrambled moment. "New York City."

"Marital status?"

"Single."

"How much money do you have?"

She'd been warned about this on the boat by a man coming over for the second time. You had to have twenty-five dollars to be allowed into America. She didn't have twenty-five dollars. Few folk in her village had ever *seen* twenty-five dollars.

She swallowed. "I have enough to live on for a little while. And. . .I will work hard to earn more."

If he asked her how much she did have, she'd already decided she would say it was sewn into the lining of her petticoat and she couldn't get it out to count it.

Thankfully, he didn't ask.

No, she'd never been in jail. No, she wasn't an anarchist— whatever that was.

"Do you have a job?"

The fellow passenger had also told her the law didn't allow you to have a job lined up before arrival. But they also didn't allow anyone in whom they suspected would become a burden on the state.

Perspiration trickled down her back. "No. But I've got relatives who will help me find one as soon as we're settled."

He grunted and made a notation in the ledger.

"Are your relatives waiting for you?"

Aileen nodded. She'd sent a letter to Uncle Emmet before their departure, giving the name of their ship. They'd arrived right on schedule.

"My uncle will be waiting." She made an effort to pronounce the *g*. Americans didn't say "waitin'."

The man paused, stamp hovering over a piece of paper. Behind the tilting spectacles, he seemed to be taking her measure. Aileen straightened her shoulders. Her breath stuck inside her lungs.

He stamped the pass and pushed it across the desk.

"Collect your luggage then go down the center flight of stairs. The pier to New York is just outside. Next," he called.

Aileen waited while the inspector interviewed Meggie. A group hustled past her, nearly knocking her off her feet. She backed away, eyeing Meggie, willing her not to say anything daft.

If her sister was rejected, both of them would be on the next boat back to Ireland.

Take us both, America. Please, take us both.

After what seemed like an eternity, Meggie hurried toward her, clutching her stamped paper to her chest. Aileen's lungs expanded in a sigh of relief.

Meggie grinned. "Let's get out o' here, before they change their minds." Her sister's tone was thick with remnants of the old country.

A lady in the baggage room helped them find their luggage and pointed them to the exit. Following others, they clattered down a narrow flight of stairs. Excited voices mingled with eager footsteps.

Aileen pushed open the door, ushering them into late-afternoon sunlight, and took a deep gulp of briny ocean-scented air.

Everywhere people were laughing and crying and greeting each other. Many of these families had likely not seen each other for years, separated by the cost of obtaining a ticket.

Aileen smiled as a father picked up his two wee daughters, swallowing them in his strong arms. The little ones snuggled against their father's chest, giggling as his mustache tickled their cheeks. She could scarce remember a da's strong arms, a love like that.

"I don't see him. What if he's not here, Aileen?" Meggie's voice was tinny.

"It's been eight years. We look so different, it'll take him a while to find us." But Meggie's words added fuel to the fire gathering tinder inside her own chest. She tried to conjure a memory and pair it with one of the faces in the crowd. A head of thick dark hair, like Mam's. A chiseled jaw and a man of few words.

She searched each face. . .the dark-eyed Italians, the pale-haired Swedes, the many nationalities she couldn't place.

He wouldn't forget them. He had to be here somewhere.

"What if he forgot about us?" Meggie asked.

An official approached. "Pardon me, miss. Are you looking for someone?"

"Our uncle." Aileen tried to sound confident.

"You're welcome to wait here. But you're not allowed off the island until your relatives arrive to fetch you. Regulations." Before Aileen could answer, he'd already moved through the crowd. Families made their way through the line leading to the New York ferry.

Time dragged. The suitcase pulled on her arm; her fingers ached. Groups boarded a ferry and it steamed away, waves churning up froth. How hard would it be to sneak on? Join a crowd and just walk on?

Beside her, Meggie looked close to tears.

"Aileen? Aileen O'Connor?"

Aileen turned. An older version of the man she remembered walked toward them. He wore a brown vest and matching trousers. In the past years he'd lost some of his hair and gained several inches of girth that filled out the vest until the buttons strained.

"Uncle Emmet." Relief washed over her.

His ruddy features eased into a grin as he hugged them in turn. "Welcome to America, girls."

As they joined the line for the ferry, she glanced behind at the dwindling group framed by the huge buildings of Ellis Island. She hoped she'd never have cause to see it again. Now that she'd arrived, she had no intention of going back.

"We're here, America," she whispered as they stood on the deck. A breeze stirred the strands of hair at her nape as she propped her arms on the railing, staring at the high buildings on the New York shoreline. "We're here."

Chapter 2

A week later

*Y*ou've got to earn, girls, Uncle Emmet had said. *Our place is too crowded for the two of you. You'll need rooms of your own.*

After a week of sleeping wedged between Meggie and her two small cousins on a sagging mattress scarcely fit for one, Aileen couldn't agree more. Her own job, their own place—that's what she wanted.

She'd be doing her best to get them the first today.

America. Where everything moved at top speed—people, carriages, the wheels of life.

"How will we know which is the Asch Building?" Meggie's cheeks were pinker than usual from the pace they'd been keeping, strands of honey hair curling around her cheeks.

"Uncle Emmet said it was ten stories tall. You'd have to be daft or blind to miss something that large." Aileen smoothed the piece of paper covered with Uncle Emmet's scrawled directions in her sweaty palms. They passed Washington Square Park.

It was a world away from the Lower East Side, where humanity lived crammed together like pickles in a barrel. An impressive stone arch framed the entrance of a spacious park carpeted in lush grass. Couples strolled its graveled paths or stood beneath shade trees. The women wore wide-brimmed hats bedecked with silk, feathers, and masses of flowers.

A throng of girls breezed past, handbags swinging, laughter and chatter echoing in their wake. Aileen peered at the directions.

"They look so fine," Meggie whispered. "Just look at those fancy blouses they're wearing."

"Shirtwaists." Aileen quickened her pace as they started down Washington Place. "They're called shirtwaists. I've told you that. We'll be earning our living making them, so you'd best remember. . ." Her words trailed off.

There was no mistaking the Asch Building, even if a stream of girls hadn't been making their way toward it. Ten stories of impenetrable brick reached toward the sky. Advertisements for clothing companies ran up along the building's corner.

"We're working *here*?" Taking a wobbly step back, Meggie craned her neck and stared.

"If we're late, we'll not be working anywhere." Aileen tugged her sister's hand and pulled her along. She couldn't let Meggie see she too had been affected by the size of the building. In Ireland, cliffs plunged toward the sea, formed by nature. In America, this massive structure was the work of man. A monument to the power and riches of its builder.

A line of women stretched onto the street. Aileen and Meggie took their places at the end of it. At intervals several of the girls disappeared inside and the rest moved forward.

The two girls ahead talked softly, heads bent together. Aileen couldn't help but contrast their creamy white shirtwaists, tailored skirts, and fashionable hats with her and Meggie's unadorned dresses and narrow-brimmed straw hats.

This factory must pay well for its workers to dress in such finery. Of course, she was under no delusions about affording elegant things for herself and Meggie. They needed a place to sleep and food on the table. Everything else would have to wait.

One of the girls turned. Though her clothes added to her appearance, she would have been a striking young woman regardless. Her thick black hair was piled beneath her hat, and her vivid dark eyes stood out like gemstones.

"Good morning," she said, voice tinged with a slight Italian accent. "I'm Rose Colletti. And this here's Ida Eidelman." Ida was dressed more simply, and tendrils of light brown hair wisped free beneath her smaller hat. When she smiled, a gap showed between her two front teeth.

"I'm Aileen O'Connor. This is my sister Meggie."

"First day here?" Rose asked.

"Yes. Our uncle told us. . ." Aileen's words faded as they reached the front of the line and joined the throng rushing to enter the building. Everyone crowded into a metal cage, and the iron doors closed shut. Aileen found herself pressed against the wall near the back, surrounded on all sides by bobbing hats and rustling skirts.

A jolt shook the floor. Aileen's stomach lurched as they rose upward.

"What?" Rose laughed. "Never been in an elevator before? Don't worry, most of us hadn't before we started here. You'll soon get used to it. We all did."

"Is it safe?" Meggie's eyes were wide.

"It's a modern marvel," Rose said. "The whole factory is."

"Not that that stops the bosses from working us past our time and docking our wages," Ida muttered, arms folded across her chest.

The iron doors opened and everyone spilled out. The huge room buzzed with activity. Talking. Laughing. Chairs scraping as girls took their places in front of rows of sewing machines. Men stood at long tables covered with piles of fabric. Dozens of windows let in morning sunlight.

"We'll put our hats in the cloakroom, and you can report for duty." Rose breezed through the room, waving and calling out greetings. Aileen followed, grateful to be with someone who knew what to do. They hung their hats on hooks in the cloakroom and returned to the main room. Rose marched up to a man standing by one of the fabric-covered tables. He wore a brown vest over a white shirt. The buttons of the vest strained against his rotund middle.

Rose cleared her throat. "Mr. Marchetti, sir."

Mr. Marchetti turned. His beetle-like eyebrows rose.

"This is Aileen and Meggie O'Connor." Rose glanced at Aileen.

Deep breath.

"Our uncle, Emmet Moore, was here to see you, sir, about a job for us. We were to report to the eighth floor for employment." Aileen tried to use fancy words, to sound smart, to keep the Irish from seeping into her syllables. Rose hurried away and took her place at one of the machines.

"Ah, yes." Aileen tried to follow Mr. Marchetti's heavily accented Italian. "You girls sew?"

Aileen nodded. "Yes, sir. I have experience using a sewing machine."

"Excellent." Mr. Marchetti's mustache lifted with a thin smile. "And you, young lady?"

Meggie blinked. Sewing had never been her strong suit.

Mr. Marchetti leaned in. Meggie backed away. Standing next

to her sister, Aileen smelled the overpowering odor of garlic on his breath.

"Ever used a sewing machine?"

Face red, Meggie shook her head.

"We've no need for inexperienced girls on this floor. Go to the ninth. They'll use you snipping threads."

Meggie's gaze sought Aileen's. She looked like a frightened fawn. Panic vised Aileen's chest. She'd expected to work beside her sister so she could be there in case Meggie needed help.

But if this was what it took to get work, they had no choice.

"Go. I'll see you later." Aileen gave her sister a little push. She steeled herself against the sight of Meggie, arms hugged across her chest, walking toward the elevator. She needed to focus on her own work. She turned back to Mr. Marchetti.

"You'll be a learner today. No pay."

"But I'm skilled with a sewing machine, and I'll be working—"

"No pay," he repeated. "If you do good work, we'll give you a time card tomorrow and put you on the payroll. There's an empty place beside Rose Colletti. Hurry up. Power starts in a few minutes." Without another word, he walked away.

Well, I guess you don't get far arguing with him.

She pressed back a sigh. One day without pay wouldn't be that bad. They'd see what a fine seamstress she was and give her a time card tomorrow.

Yet the injustice of a day's work with no pay stung.

Most of the girls were already seated at the machines. Men at long tables bent over layers and layers of filmy material with sharp-looking blades in hand. Patterns hung on wires above the tables like strings of streamers. She tried not to think about the stares of the others as she walked to her seat. Rose threw her a quick smile.

Throat dry, Aileen stared at the gleaming black machine. She recognized most of the parts. Still, the slender, shiny needle seemed to wink at her with a menacing glare. Cut pieces of the creamiest cloth she'd ever seen filled a basket to her right. She picked up one.

"You'll be sewing the back and half of the front of the shirtwaist together. Straight seam. Easy as falling off a log. Just don't make a mistake." Rose's perfect forehead crimped, a darkness entering her eyes. "They dock your pay then."

Aileen nodded. She was about to ask "how much" when a low din filled the room. The floor trembled.

So this is what Mr. Marchetti meant about the power. It sounded powerful, like a great beast running rampant through the room. Heads bent to the machines, needles flew through fabric.

"Push down on the treadle when you're ready to start. After that, the machine runs until you let up."

"You mean, no need to keep working the treadle. . ."

"Like I said." Rose grinned. "Modern marvel." She pressed the treadle of her machine and began sewing with intense concentration.

Aileen bit her lip and picked up the fabric. It felt like a waterfall in her hands.

Sew a straight seam. Sew a straight seam, and don't ruin the fabric.
Nothing else mattered.

The new girl stared at the machine like it might gulp her up and eat her alive.

Out of the corner of his eye, Lorenzo Favero watched her. She sat beside Rose, gaze riveted on the sewing machine, every ounce of concentration focused on keeping the fabric sliding smoothly. Her forehead crimped, and her lower lip was tucked between her teeth.

During his four years as a cutter at the Triangle Waist Company, he'd seen many a newcomer enter its doors. One could always tell a greenhorn. They had a look about them, wide-eyed and jumpy. Dazzled by the vastness of the factory and scared stiff they'd fail at the job. They were the ones who jabbed their fingers with the lighting-swift machine needles, who spent the first few weeks with docked pay from the mistakes they made. Who left at the end of the first day looking as wrung out as a washrag and as wilted as three-week-old flowers.

Usually Lorenzo let them sort themselves out. He was a cutter after all, one of the most skilled and highly paid employees at Triangle. He'd no need to concern himself with a new sewing machine girl, who was usually taken in hand by her neighbors.

But from the moment she'd walked onto the factory floor, he'd noticed something about her. A spark, a determination. . .and yet a fragility. It made him want to go up to her, put his arm around her, and say, *It'll be all right. We've all been where you are.*

"Favero!" Mr. Marchetti's voice boomed behind Lorenzo. From the sound of it, his boss wasn't any too happy.

He turned. "Yes, sir."

"Do we or do we not pay you wages for thirteen hours of work?" Marchetti's brows lowered, two salt-and-pepper beetles meeting in the middle of his forehead.

"Yes, sir." He flashed a grin he hoped was conciliatory.

The brows disapproved. "Then is it too much to expect you to *give us* thirteen hours of work?"

"No, sir."

"Get to it then."

"Of course. Right away, sir." Lorenzo turned toward the cutting table. He pulled a pattern off the line and positioned it over the layers of filmy lawn. Marchetti harrumphed and walked away.

Lorenzo shook his head with a rueful half-smile. As one of

Triangle's best cutters, he was in little danger of losing his job. He'd an eye for the work, knew how to position the patterns on the fabric so the least amount of yardage was wasted. And he could complete double the work in the time it took a less-experienced cutter to fulfill a day's quota.

Yet he'd best work quickly today to avoid Marchetti's ire. If there was one maxim at Triangle, it was *Every worker is replaceable. Dispensable.*

Beside him at the cutting table, already wielding his knife over the fabric, Jacob Levin gave a quick glance up from behind round spectacles.

"What has you so distracted?" he asked as Lorenzo placed the final pattern atop the fabric and surveyed the intricate puzzle of pattern pieces he'd created.

"Who says I'm distracted?" He picked up his knife and chose where to make his first cut—the back of the waist. Carefully, he pressed his left palm down on the pattern, wielding the knife with his right hand, guiding it along the outside of the metal-edged pattern piece.

"I do. You've been staring at the girls like you're meshuga. Which one's caught your eye?"

"Not your Ida, if that's what you're worried about."

"It better not be Ida. Or you'll find yourself flat on your back in a dark alley." Jacob's tone was teasing.

Marchetti passed by their table, halting the conversation before Lorenzo could come back with "that we should both live so long to see the day when you could put me flat on my back."

Machines hummed in an endless droning, like hundreds of bees buzzing around his head. It was a sound one grew used to, eventually stopped noticing. But to the young woman with cinnamon-hued hair, it would be unfamiliar. Like so much else in this strange universe she'd stepped into.

He turned, blade in hand, gaze falling on her again. A knifepoint of pity sliced him.

Truly a shame someone as lovely as she had stepped into a place where endless shirtwaists would become her world.

Chapter 3

By the time the bell sounded at noon, signaling a break for lunch, burning pain knotted the muscles in Aileen's neck and shoulders. The power stopped, and for the first time in hours, the machines stilled. She straightened from her bent position and massaged the back of her neck with cramped fingers.

Talk and laughter rang out freely as the workers spilled toward the cloakroom, likely to collect their lunches. She realized now, stupidly, she'd brought nothing for her and Meggie. Her empty stomach gurgled. The thought of working until 8:00 p.m. without anything to eat increased the lightheadedness already hovering in her periphery.

"Come on." Rose tapped her on the shoulder. "We'll go upstairs to fetch your sister, and then we'll have our lunch together."

Aileen stood on wobbly legs and gave Rose a grateful smile. Though she hadn't brought anything to eat, she could at least sit and get to know the other girls. They took the elevator to the ninth floor. The factory floor there was much the same as on the eighth, except without the cutters' tables. Long rows of sewing machines and tables covered in piles of shirtwaists filled the space. Most of its occupants had already left, though a few remained at their machines, eating their lunches and talking among themselves.

"There she is." Rose pointed to a table in the back. Meggie sat in front of it, the only person remaining. Aileen wove through the room, followed by Rose. Meggie bent over a piece of fabric held in one hand, snipping stray threads with a pair of silver scissors. A basket of completed shirtwaists sat to her right, a pile of unfinished ones to her left.

Meggie looked up. Her face was pale, her eyes wide. "Aileen." She blinked rapidly, as if holding back tears.

"Come on," Aileen said. "We're going to have lunch with Rose."

Meggie shook her head, and bent to her work again. "I can't," she whispered.

"Of course you can. Don't be silly."

"No. I really can't. The foreman said I didn't 'fulfill my morning quota.' So I have to keep working." Meggie's hands shook as she snipped threads from the finished shirtwaist.

"But that's not right!" Aileen's voice escalated. They couldn't do that. Meggie had worked hard, she was sure of it. Of course one wouldn't be as productive as an experienced worker the first day on the job. The bosses had no right to expect that.

She turned to Rose, who stood silently, a look of sadness on her face.

"It's the way of it, I'm afraid."

"Then. . .then I'll stay with her. I'll help her."

"No." Rose shook her head. "If you do that, the foreman will think she's not capable. She'll lose the job then. I'm sorry, Meggie." Rose gave her a sympathetic smile. "We'll see you at the end of the day." She tugged on Aileen's arm. "Let's get something to eat before we lose our chance."

Aileen just stood there staring at Meggie. A sense of utter help-lessness washed over her at the sight of her sister's too-pale face, the tremble in her hands, the quiver in her lip.

She'd move heaven and earth to keep Meggie safe. But if she wanted them to keep their jobs, she could do nothing.

Powerlessness was worse than physical pain.

"Come, Aileen."

This time she let Rose lead her away. At the door she glanced over her shoulder. Meggie sat at the table piled with shirtwaists, turning the fabric in her hands, snipping threads. Alone.

Aileen's throat tightened, and she dragged in a breath. As the elevator fell, she barely noticed the sensation of being carried from floor to floor.

On the eighth floor, she followed Rose into the cloakroom, and Rose grabbed her lunch pail. Amid the chattering voices and milling young women, they returned to their machines where they pulled out their chairs and sat. Across the room, she glimpsed Ida in con-versation with two girls and a bespectacled young man.

Rose opened her lunch pail and pulled out a square of something wrapped in brown paper. Hands limp in her lap, Aileen watched her open it. Saliva gathered in the roof of her mouth at the scents of bread and cheese.

Carefully, Rose broke the sandwich in half.

"Hey, Rose."

Aileen pulled her gaze away from the sandwich. A tall man stood behind Rose's chair.

"Hey yourself, Lorenzo." Rose's dimples flashed.

"And who is the lady?" Eyes the color of coffee with cream met hers.

Aileen's cheeks flushed.

"Aileen O'Connor." Rose flattened the brown paper and placed her sandwich on it. "Started here today."

"Welcome to the Triangle Waist Company, Miss O'Connor. Lorenzo Favero at your service." He bowed, grinning when she looked up. It was the kind of grin that could coax a skinflint into handing over his wallet and saying thank you for the privilege. Utterly, unabashedly charming. Brown hair, thick and curly, tumbled over his broad forehead. Stubble darkened his chiseled jaw. He wore a white shirt with thin black suspenders, shirtsleeves rolled to the forearms—

And she'd stared at him much too long.

"I'm pleased to meet you." As she tested the American phrase, his grin emerged again. She gave herself a mental shake. She wasn't the sort to be won over by a handsome face.

"Aren't you going to eat your lunch, Aileen O'Connor?" In his accented Italian, her name sounded different. Lilting, but in an unfamiliar, musical way.

She opened her mouth to say something—she honestly didn't know what—but Rose beat her to it. "I was just about to offer Aileen some of my bread and cheese." She smiled at Lorenzo.

"Well now, that will never do. You need every bit of that sandwich for yourself, *Signorina* Colletti. Or else your lovely self is liable to blow away in the next stiff wind. If you'll permit me, I can supply the deficiency. One moment." Lorenzo Favero turned and headed toward the cloakroom. Her gaze lingered on his broad shoulders, the offhand grace with which he strode through the room, before, for the second time in her brief acquaintance with Lorenzo Favero, she forced herself to look away.

Rose bit into a corner of her sandwich.

Aileen leaned toward her. "I'd rather not."

"Not what?" Rose set her sandwich on the brown paper. Little ringlets of dark hair curled around her cheeks.

Her own face flamed. "Eat his food. It was kind of him to offer, but it wouldn't be proper."

"Look." Rose lifted her sandwich. "I've known Lorenzo for four years. He's almost like a brother to me. It's wise of you to be cautious. Gracious knows New York's crawling with scoundrels. But though he lays on the charm rather thick, Lorenzo is more honest and honorable than most men I've known. You won't compromise yourself if you let him share his lunch. His mama certainly packs him enough."

She sensed, rather than saw, Lorenzo return. Chair legs scraped as he pulled up a seat beside hers. She caught a waft of a fragrance piquant and unfamiliar as he shifted his chair toward hers. He reached into the pail and unwrapped a hunk of crusty bread and a chunk of meat that emitted a rich, spicy smell.

He couldn't fail to hear her stomach growl.

He halved both the bread and meat, placed them on one of the brown paper squares, passed it toward her, then uncapped and handed her a jar of water. Their fingertips brushed as she took it.

"Ladies first." That smile again.

The fabric dust floating in the air had dried her throat to near rawness. Before she could think better of it, she lifted the jar to her lips. Water ran down her throat in a soothing stream, blessedly cool. She gulped more. Droplets trickled down her chin and splotched the front of her dress. Cheeks flushing, she handed him the jar and wiped her mouth. "Thank you. But I can't take anything else from you."

"Why not?" He picked up his half of the bread and bit into it, jaw working as he chewed.

"Because then"—she swallowed—"I'd be in your debt. And that wouldn't be fitting."

He shrugged. "If you want to starve and let that food sit there, that's your business, I guess. But come eight o'clock, you'll be wishing you'd taken me up on it." He bit off the end of the sausage-like meat.

She stared at the bread and meat, their scents teasing her. Fresh bread. Spicy meat speckled with herbs.

She would eat a few bites and sneak the rest up to Meggie. Surely she'd have time before their break was over. She should have packed them something. Then she'd not have to accept the offering of a stranger.

But it would do her nor Meggie any good if Aileen starved herself to the point of fainting.

Tentatively, she picked up the bread and took a bite. Its crusty exterior and pillowy softness made her close her eyes with the goodness of it. When she swallowed and opened them, she found Lorenzo studying her.

"Good?"

She nodded. "Yes." She paused, the next words lodging in her throat. "Thank you."

"You're welcome," he said quietly, strands of hair falling into his eyes as their gazes held. "And there's no debt."

As she looked into his face and read the kindness there, the hardness inside her that the years had calloused over shifted a minuscule amount. A fraction of an inch. She sensed it.

And it scared her.

With unrest bubbling below the surface of the factory, the last thing he needed was to insert himself into the life of a stranger. Yet whatever inexplicable compulsion that had struck him the moment Aileen O'Conner walked into the factory continued to draw him.

Why this urge to help her? Was it because he knew firsthand the realities of life as a newcomer? He and his sister, Silva, had been the first of their family to leave Italy in 1903. He'd been sixteen. Silva, two years older, had gotten them jobs at a sweatshop—work that made Triangle seem like a trip to Coney Island. Often they'd worked eighteen-hour shifts to finish an order, crammed into a crowded tenement room with other workers, knowing that if they ruined an order or missed a day of work, they'd be replaced in the blink of an eye.

He remembered Silva, dragging herself to work, face flushed with fever, a hacking cough deep in her lungs. The bone-chilling winters with never enough money for heat. The hunger, as gnawing as it had been in Italy. The drive to seek opportunity in this land that was apparently filled with it. The despair when opportunity proved as elusive as finding a single gold brick on any American street.

At first, he'd done easy work like basting, his clumsy fingers struggling even with that. After he'd mastered it, he'd asked around, figured out where the money was. Cutters were a valuable commodity, especially those who wasted the least amount of yardage. So he'd learned fast and become a cutter at another sweatshop. The money he and Silva earned paid the way for his mama and younger brother, Giuseppe, to journey to America. Lorenzo had applied for a job at Triangle, and been accepted—doggedly determined to provide for his family so Giuseppe could attend school and become something better than a factory slave.

Their padre had planned to join them. But the eruption of Mount Vesuvius had stolen that dream—and Padre's life.

The bell shrilled, signaling quitting time. Lorenzo sucked in a sharp breath, shoving the images aside. He made one last cut and swiped scraps into the bin beneath the table. The machines stood silent, workers clogging the factory floor, eager to leave the shop behind and return to homes and families.

"See you tomorrow." He tossed Jacob a grin.

"Ah, tomorrow. You come much too soon," Jacob said in an exaggeratedly dramatic voice.

Lorenzo shook his head and chuckled, heading to the time clock to punch out before making his way to the single-file line queuing up to exit the factory. A watchman stood by the door, and each girl opened her handbag for inspection. When did the bosses think they'd have time to steal something, that's what he'd like to know.

Still, the practice continued, a misery for weary bodies at the end of a thirteen-hour workday.

Finally, he passed the guard and strode through the door. He descended the narrow stairs, the footsteps of those behind him clattering in his ears, and exited onto Greene Street—factory employees weren't allowed to use the main entrance that opened onto Washington Place. Outside he waited, hands in his pockets, watching the workers spill from the doors, heading off in various directions.

He shouldn't be standing here waiting for her. Yet. . .he was.

Minutes passed. Summer twilight fell over the street, bathing the ten-story Asch Building. He drank in fresh air. The Asch Building was only a short walk away from Washington Square Park where shade trees sheltered manicured paths and women with parasols strolled on the arms of men in bowler hats. Here humanity didn't dwell crammed like canned sardines in rooms with paper-thin walls, where every time one stepped onto the street for a breath of air, they instead breathed in the filth and waste of their neighbors. On the Lower East Side, perhaps the only thing more difficult to find than gold was solitude.

Lorenzo shifted. The tide of workers had subsided to a trickle, yet Aileen hadn't emerged. Nor had Rose, unless they'd somehow gone ahead of him.

A group exited the Asch Building. Rose walked beside Aileen, their heads tipped toward each other as they talked quietly. A younger girl with honey-blond hair and a wispy build trailed a step behind them.

Aileen noticed him before the others. He registered the exact moment their gazes locked. She blinked. The long day at the factory had left her worn, with tendrils of hair escaping from their loose upsweep to fall around her face and neck. Still, she was *bellissima*. Truly beautiful.

Rose waved and hurried toward him, handbag swinging. Aileen and the other girl followed more slowly.

"Lorenzo. I'm so glad you haven't left yet." She gave him a slightly quizzical look, as if to ask why. He wasn't fond enough of Triangle to hang around the place after quitting time.

"Why? Are you in need of a knight in shining armor to escort you to Bleecker Street? I know how the crowds of handsome swains flock at your approach." He tossed her a wink, and she rolled her eyes.

"If you think I can't hold my own against any crowd of handsome swains, you're softer in the head than I thought, Favero."

Lorenzo stole a glance at Aileen. She didn't smile and looked almost uneasy. Or perhaps he was reading too much into her expression. Studying her far too closely.

"Then is there some other way I might be of service?"

"Aileen and her sister are looking for a place to live. They've been staying with her uncle, but he hasn't room to keep them much longer."

Aileen pressed her lips together.

"And you know how renters tend to cheat newcomers if they think they can get a few extra pennies out of them. I'd offer them a place with me, but we're already eight to two rooms. So if you know of a respectable family looking for a couple of boarders, well, you'll be my hero for life."

Bless Rose Colletti. For all her flirtatious ways and high-spun dreams, she was one of the kindest people in the city of New York. He'd seen her shepherd many a new girl at Triangle. Once, they'd been newcomers together, helping each other find their footing.

"It's all right, Rose." But Aileen looked at him as she said it. "We don't need Mr. Favero's help. Meggie and I will start looking for a place tomorrow."

The way she said it—so all-fired independent—dug beneath his skin.

"If you wouldn't mind telling me, when do you expect to do that, working from seven in the morning until eight at night? Of course, you have Saturday afternoon and all day Sunday, but at that rate it could take a couple of weeks."

In a way, he admired her independence. But at the same time, he knew where stubbornness could lead, the poor decisions one could make as a result, and the dangers that could ensue.

Aileen swallowed. "That really isn't any of your business, now is it?"

He reached up and rubbed the back of his neck. "Seeing as Rose here has asked me for help, it kind of is. And as a matter of fact, I do know of a place. My sister Silva lives in the same building as me and my family. She and her husband have been wanting to take in boarders to help with the rent. They haven't got much, a mattress in the front room, but they're decent people who'd charge you a fair price and give you meals besides."

"And they live on Bleecker Street, same as me," Rose said. "We could walk to work together."

Aileen paused. Seemed to be waging a battle. Trust or not to trust. Risk or not to risk. She weighed her options carefully, it seemed, more so than some greenhorns who'd jump at any kind face or helping hand. Life had done this to her, as it had hardened him.

A longing rose within him. For her to realize he could be relied on. For her to trust him.

"It would be nice not having to walk to the factory alone," Aileen's sister said quietly.

Aileen blew out a breath. "I suppose we could at least try it. Would they be ready for us to move in tomorrow night?"

Hoping Silva wouldn't give him a verbal tanning for agreeing without her consent, he nodded. "Tomorrow night would be just fine."

Chapter 4

September 11, 1909
Two months later

S*trike.*
 The word had started as a whisper, a ripple. The ripple had turned into a wave.

The wave was well on its way to becoming a flood.

Aileen sat at her machine, guiding the fabric as the needle flashed through it in a dizzying blur of up-and-down. The machines could sew hundreds of stitches per minute. And hundreds of stitches per minute were what their operators were expected to produce.

Day after day, the same routine. Up at five thirty to wash and dress, gulp down breakfast, then dash down the street to the Collettis' to meet Rose. Walking to the factory, no matter if the skies were clear or pouring rain, hurrying to punch her time card, all the while thinking, *Don't be late. Never be late.*

She'd heard what happened to those who were late, even ten minutes. Docked half a day's pay. Rarely did her own pay envelope contain the promised amount. Always they were being docked for something—a minuscule mistake, lagging behind on their quota. Charged for the needles they used, thread, electricity, space in the lockers in the cloakroom. Of course, no one paid them extra when the foremen shortened their lunch break or set the clock back at the end of the day, making them work longer.

At the end of the first week, Meggie had made nothing at all. Apparently the factory was doing her a favor by letting her learn on the job.

The nightly searches where they had to open their handbags in front of the guard. To use the lavatory one had to ask. When permission was granted, no one was allowed more than one minute. A few seconds more and the foreman would be banging on the door, shouting.

Aileen pulled the stitched piece free, added it to the pile in the trough in front of her, then picked up the next set of pieces.

She well understood why Ida and some of the others whispered that dangerous word.

Strike.

They were weary of the unfairness, the prosperity of the bosses, the workers' inability to have a say about wages and job conditions. Already Ida had urged Aileen to join Local 25, a union group started by the International Ladies' Garment Workers' Union.

Local 25 wanted to take a stand.

The bell rang, signaling lunchtime. Aileen rose, pushing back her chair. She stretched, rubbing the stiff muscles in the back of her neck, arching her lower back, then headed toward the cloakroom to collect the pail Silva had packed for them last night.

Aileen crowded into the elevator. In minutes she stood in front of the Greene Street exit to wait for Meggie, Rose, and Ida. On sunny days, they headed to the park to eat their lunch beneath a tree and relish the fresh air. On rainy days, they sometimes pooled their pennies and went to a nearby café for a cup of tea. Often Lorenzo came too. He always paid the bill.

As a cutter, taking home twenty dollars a week as opposed to the six dollars sewing machine operators made, he could afford to.

Rose, Ida, Meggie, and Ida's sweetheart, Jacob, hurried toward her. Beside them, laughing with Meggie, walked Lorenzo. He grinned at Aileen, a look of devil-may-care abandonment that tingled through her to her toes. Cheeks flushing, she looked away.

"Ready?" Rose called.

They fell in step together and walked the short distance to Washington Square Park. The air nipped with the beginnings of autumn—the glory time before cold set in and reminded one that winter was coming. They hurried past the stone archway entrance that always reminded Aileen of the gateway to a palace, and settled themselves on the grass beneath a shade tree.

Aileen opened the lunch pail and pulled out the meat and cheese sandwiches Silva had packed, handed one to Meggie, then unwrapped her own. Lorenzo sat, back flush against the tree, head leaning back, eyes closed. He opened one eye and caught her looking at him.

A roguish grin tugged the corners of his mouth.

She looked away and busied herself with her lunch.

"Clara Lemlich got beat up last night." Ida leaned forward, hands fisted atop her skirt.

"What?" Rose lowered her sandwich, eyes widening.

Ida nodded. "They're still picketing at Leiserson's." Since August, Ida had talked of little else besides the big walkout—seven thousand workers from various factories had gone on strike. Despite the uncertainty and the bosses' refusal to bend to the workers' demands, the strike continued. Fiery twenty-three-year-old Clara Lemlich was at the center of it. "Clara had finished her shift on the picket line and was on her way to the union office. Two thugs attacked her and left her in a back alley. She got terribly bruised and broke six ribs."

A chill traveled down Aileen's spine. "Who were the men who attacked her?"

"Clara thinks they were hired thugs, paid to beat her up. The bosses are scared because their workers haven't returned to the shops, and they know the influence Clara has. They meant to intimidate her. To get her to back down."

"But she won't, right?" Jacob swallowed a bite of his sandwich. Aileen hadn't even tasted her lunch.

Ida gave a bitter laugh. "Not a chance. If anything, Clara's more determined than ever now. For the bosses to resort to tactics that low needs to be met with resistance. Every worker has the power to change the tide of the labor industry." Her eyes sparked. "But only if we join together. A united voice, rising so loud they won't be able to ignore it."

The words coursed through Aileen. With that determined glint in her gaze and passion in her voice, Ida could be on a union hall platform herself, giving speeches like Clara.

"Do you think it will come to Triangle?" Meggie asked. "The strike, I mean."

"It will if Local 25 has anything to say about it. Already there's been talk, plans. Harris and Blanck need to know their workers aren't just going to lie down and let themselves be trampled."

"What will it mean?" Aileen was almost afraid of the answer.

"Living on ideals, that's what it'll mean." Lorenzo polished an apple on his pant leg. "Hunger. Cold. Picket lines. For weeks. Longer maybe. Until either the bosses give in or everyone goes back to work." He looked up, eyes darkening, strands of hair curling over his forehead. For once he wasn't joking.

"Will you join the strike?" Ida asked, challenge in her gaze.

Lorenzo bit into his apple, cheeks bulging as he chewed. He swallowed, regarding Ida. Aileen watched him, wondering what his answer would be. Though Lorenzo had slipped into their group, often joining them for lunch, walking home with them to Bleecker Street, he was still a cutter. In some ways, an outsider, because he was paid more and was part of Triangle's most valued class of workers.

Slowly, he nodded. "I'll join the strike. Because I know not to support it is a vote for the bosses, men like Harris and Blanck who think themselves so powerful they won't even acknowledge their workers with so much as a 'good morning.' But I won't relish it. It'll mean hard times for all of us. We'll need backbones of steel if we've any hope of getting the bosses to agree to our demands." He stared out across the park, voice quiet. "I wonder if we truly know how long and difficult a struggle it will be."

Ida picked up her lunch pail and stood. She stared down at Lorenzo, features tight, nostrils flaring. Just looking at her sent a thrill through Aileen. That kind of passion was nothing less than electric. "If there's anything survival in America has taught us, it's how to have hearts of iron. Backbones of steel."

September 27, 1909

"What happened at the meeting?" Hands in his pockets, Lorenzo walked alongside Aileen and Rose on the way to the factory, Ida and Meggie following behind. Morning sunlight slanted from the sky, and the air still bore the fresh scent of last night's rain. A motorcar drove by, sleek and gleaming.

"Oh, it was quite something." Rose spun in a little circle, facing him and walking backward for a few steps. "Clinton Hall was packed. Well over a hundred Triangle workers attended. 'On behalf of every worker, we demand equality!' " She punctuated her words with a flourish of her hands. " 'Our voices must be heard!' "

"Careful there, Sarah Bernhardt." Lorenzo grabbed her arm before she walked into a lamppost.

"The meeting was a serious matter." Ida spoke up. "We're discussing how best to organize ourselves."

"Obviously Mr. Blanck and Mr. Harris agreed with Ida." Aileen's lips tweaked in a wry smile. "Somehow they got word of the meeting, and that's what all the fuss was about on Friday."

"The little speech they gave on the factory floor, you mean? Rambling about how great their own so-called Triangle Employees Benevolent Association is. Threatening to fire anyone organizing a competing union." Lorenzo shoved his hands into his pockets.

"Like that would stop us now," Ida said. "On Friday, several of us went straight to the union office after work." She fell into step beside him, skirts fisted in her hands. "If you feel so strongly about it, Lorenzo, why weren't you at Clinton Hall?"

"My mama needed help with a few things." His excuse sounded lame, but it was true. His family meant everything to him. If the strike happened, it would hurt them. Could he blame himself if he wasn't eager to jump on top of a soapbox and demand it start tomorrow?

They neared the massive Asch Building. A crowd gathered outside the Greene Street exit.

Lorenzo's gut tightened.

"What's going on?" Aileen's brow furrowed.

Ida brushed past them, half running toward the Asch Building. The crowd grew, becoming a teeming, shifting mass. Voices escalated.

He turned to the girls. "Stay here. I'll see what's going on." He pushed through the crowd, elbows shoving into him, handbags knocking against his shoulders. He flashed a glance behind him.

Aileen followed, shoving her way forward. Her hat tilted at an awkward angle over her eyes as she fought to reach the front.

When they did, they paused, standing side by side, staring at the building. Chains roped off the entrance. A sign hung on one door: *FACTORY CLOSED.*

"What does it mean?" Aileen's words were almost lost in the din.

He met her gaze. "It means the bosses are trying to intimidate us. To assert themselves as the masters they believe themselves to be."

Her jaw jutted forward. As the crowd pressed in around them, she stepped closer. He caught the fragrance of soap and lavender. "Then they don't know the sort they're dealing with, now, do they?" Her Irish accent lilted over the words.

One corner of his mouth tugged upward. "No, I expect they don't."

A voice lifted above the fray. Lorenzo glimpsed Ida standing near the front of the building. Hair straggled down her cheeks and her eyes blazed. "Everyone, we must strike now!" she shouted, sweeping her hands in an expansive gesture to encompass the crowd. "Not a one of us must set foot on the factory floor until our terms are met and our conditions granted. Anyone who wishes to join the ILGWU must wait no longer. Strike must be the word of the day!"

"Strike." The word became a crescendo, a chant, passing through their ranks like a baton. "Strike!"

Something brushed his fingertips. Aileen's hand. He took it, wrapping his own around her slight, calloused fingers. Surprisingly, she didn't pull away but squeezed back.

Holding fast.

In a world falling to pieces.

Chapter 5

October 4, 1909

The picket line.

    The front lines in this battle for justice and equality.

Aileen stood shoulder to shoulder with Rose and Ida in front of the Asch Building, autumn wind seeping through her thin coat and stinging her cheeks. Overhead the sky was pellet gray. Her empty stomach cramped beneath the banner tied toga-like over her shoulder.

TRIANGLE WORKERS ON STRIKE.

They'd been on strike for a week, picketing outside the factory in shifts. Afraid of what might happen to her gentle sister on the picket line, she'd signed up for extra shifts to cover for both of them. Meggie remained at home with Silva, while Aileen spent hours each day on the picket line.

The leaders of Local 25 deemed it best that only women work the picket lines, as they'd attract the most sympathy from passersby. Lorenzo volunteered part-time at the union office and worked part-time washing dishes and peeling potatoes at the restaurant where

Silva's husband was employed. Lorenzo had refused to draw union pay and for now was eking by. As they all were. As they all would continue to do. For as long as it took, everyone said.

The aching question was: *How long would that be?*

Most passersby gave them a wide berth. Occasionally someone stopped and spoke to them. The union leaders had been clear about the rules for picketing. *Wear your best clothes and present a neat appearance. Don't shout or harass passersby. Present your views calmly and logically.*

"Almost time for the scabs to arrive." Ida's cheeks were blotchy with cold. She wore her hair scraped back from her face, making her cheekbones more pronounced. Unlike some of the others, she didn't seem to mind the cold. Ida seemed to possess an inner fire that kept burning no matter the opposition.

As if on cue, a group of women neared the factory. Blanck and Harris had paused production for barely a day before hiring new workers. Scabs.

Today some of those in the crowd looked different. Women in gaudy dresses with painted lips and rouged cheeks. Like the sort who sold their bodies to men. Surely they weren't the newest factory recruits.

Aileen searched the faces of the replacement workers. Likely most of them were simply hungry and trying to provide for their families by taking any job available. She'd heard Blanck and Harris were wooing replacements with increased wages and free cake during lunchtime.

Did the replacement workers realize the depth of their actions? That by working for the bosses they inhibited progress that would mean betterment for all?

"Don't work for them," Ida called. "Join our strike!"

"We're not just doing this for us." Aileen caught the eyes of a girl about Meggie's age. She shivered in the cold and barely met Aileen's gaze. "Our strike is for the rights of all workers!"

"Please!" Ida took a step forward. "Don't go in there."

The crowd separated. The prostitutes marched forward, walking right up to the picket line. The odor of cheap perfume and stale sweat tinged the air.

"Shut up, the lot of you!" The makeup the woman wore didn't hide the hardness in her face.

It happened in a blur. A clenched fist flashing out. A sickening thud.

Ida crumpled to the ground.

The women descended upon them. Shoving. Hitting. Clawing. For a second, Aileen stood frozen, the sounds of shouting, crying, and swearing blurring around her.

Suddenly pain blared through the flesh of her upper arm.

Her attacker held a hatpin. The woman's face contorted in an ugly sneer.

"Blasted strikers." She raised the hatpin again.

Aileen ducked. The woman missed.

Breath heaved from her lungs. Someone hit her on the head. Her vision blurred. As she went down, she saw her fellow strikers through the haze. Fighting. Falling.

The woman dove on top of her. Air left Aileen's body in a whoosh. The woman's weight pressed down as she raked her fingernails across Aileen's cheek. The metallic taste of blood trickled over her lips. Her head jarred hard on the cold pavement.

"No!" With a shout, she grabbed hold of the woman's ear, pulling as hard as she could. The force startled her attacker, and Aileen shoved her away, clambering to her feet.

A police wagon drove up and parked. Men raced out. Whistles shrilled.

Rescue.

The uniformed officers burst upon the fray, breaking up the fight with their batons, pulling the prostitutes away from the strikers.

One of the policemen grabbed Rose. Blood trickled down her cheek, and her left eye was swollen shut. "You're under arrest." He grabbed her hands, yanked them behind her back.

Arrest?

Aileen ran over, blood dripping down her face. Rose turned her battered face toward Aileen. Fear emanated from her friend.

"You can't arrest her. She did nothing wrong. They attacked us. We committed no crime."

The policeman's gaze narrowed at her. His mustached mouth was set in a thin line, his eyes stony beneath his cap. "The whole lot of you are under arrest."

"What for? There's no law against striking in an orderly fashion, which was what we were doing, until those. . .those women set upon us." Her voice rose, her aching hands fisted at her sides.

The policeman raised his baton. "Shut up. Or I'll club you myself. Believe me, it would be a pleasure with the way you've all been disturbing the peace." He shoved his face toward hers, gaze daring her.

Her chest hurt to suck in a breath. She swiped a hand across her face, her fingers coming away bloody. She lifted her chin and glared at him, saying nothing.

In minutes, the police rounded them up and loaded them into the darkened van. They sat on benches that wrapped the interior, guards interspersed between them. Most of the girls looked down at their laps, as if in shame. Someone cried softly.

The van started up, leaving Triangle behind. Through the small barred window, Aileen watched the towering Asch Building fade from view. Ten floors of modern progress. A testament to the indomitable rich.

Fear spidered clammy fingers down her spine.

Aileen looked away from the window. Across the aisle sat Ida. Her nose was bent at an odd angle, and her cheeks bore the tracks of fingernail marks. Hair tangled against her cheeks. She met Aileen's gaze.

The defiance simmering there bred the same in Aileen's chest. *We will fight. We will go down fighting.*

⌒

The cell stank of urine. Somewhere, water dripped from the ceiling, landing on the floor in a steady *plink, plink, plink.*

"It must be raining outside," Rose whispered. She sat against the wall, arms wrapped around her knees.

"Must be." Aileen stared at the grillwork of iron bars across from her, the prison hallway beyond. They'd been locked up for hours. She'd lost count of how many.

"What do you think will happen to us?" Rose's voice sounded small, leeched of its usual drama. The dim light cast shadows over her swollen-shut black eye.

Aileen leaned her head against the cold cell wall. A sigh fell from her lips. "I don't know." She wanted to say they'd be released, that someone would come for them, but was that the truth? The past hours seemed like a nightmare. One she fought to wake up from but couldn't.

"It'll mean hard times for all of us. We'll need backbones of steel if we've any hope of getting the bosses to agree to our demands. I wonder if we truly know how long and difficult a struggle it will be."

Lorenzo had known it even then.

Tears pressed against her eyes. Against her will, one fell, salt stinging the wounds on her cheek.

Doubtless when he heard of their arrest he'd be frantic. He

worried about her, going out on the picket line every day. Though he never said it in words, she sensed it in his eyes as he stood in his apartment doorway, gaze following her as she descended the stairs.

What of Meggie? The sister she'd vowed to protect, promising Mam as the fever sapped her life away that she always would. What would happen to Meggie if Aileen was sentenced to imprisonment?

The ache in her chest had nothing to do with her injuries and everything to do with the pain of fear. Of anger. Of defenselessness.

Oh Mam. I'm sorry. I didn't mean for this to happen.

"But is it worth it? Really worth it?" It was Mam's voice, as loud as if she sat beside her on the cell floor.

Aileen closed her eyes, wrapping an arm around Rose's trembling shoulders, leaning her head against her friend's.

Yes, Mam. It's worth it. Someone has to show the world that what we're fighting for is simply human decency. Somehow, we must show the world. . . .

～⊙

"Arrested!" Lorenzo rounded on the woman behind the desk at the union office. "All the girls who picketed this morning?"

The woman nodded. "I'm afraid so. They were attacked by a group of"—red crept across her face—"indecent women. Likely, someone hired them to disrupt the strike. The police arrived and arrested the girls. The other women were permitted to go free."

He'd stood in the doorway only this morning, watching Aileen leave for the picket line. She'd worn the hat she'd bought last month—her first American purchase, and her worn coat. She looked so young, descending those stairs in the gray light of dawn. Yet he'd seen the determination in her gaze grow since the strike began.

Dear God, please, Aileen. Protect her. And the others, Rose, Ida. . .

A desperate clamor started in his chest.

"Where have they been taken?"

"The Tombs prison," the woman said wearily, face pinched.

"Is anything being done to help them?"

Sympathy entered her gaze. "Is one of the girls your wife?"

He swallowed, shaking his head, the word *wife* lodging inside him. "But I know several of them."

"Representatives from the union are on their way to the prison to pay their bail." She checked the watch pinned to her shirtwaist. "They should be there by now. It took them a while to collect the funds."

He leaned forward, placing both hands on the desk. "Thank you." He turned and strode from the office.

"I hope your friends are all right," the woman called after him.

The streets bustled with late-afternoon activity. A boy plodded past, loaded down with a bundle of fabric almost as large as he was. A *shlepper*, delivering goods to some sweatshop. A fancy motorcar drove by, a uniformed chauffeur in front, an elaborately dressed woman in the back seat.

"Bunch of stiffs," Lorenzo muttered, shoving his hands in his pockets.

He walked as fast as he could, running part of the way. In the past, he'd have taken the trolley to get there faster. But he could no longer afford such a luxury, even at a time like this. Every cent he made had to be counted and saved. There was no way of knowing how long the strike would last, how hard the coming winter would be.

Finally, he reached the massive gray stone prison building. He paused, bending double, catching his breath. A creak. A guard opened the door.

At the sight of them, anger, sharp and raw surged through him.

A dozen girls, faces bruised, dried blood on their cheeks, several supporting their comrades, trudged out.

"Aileen!" He called her name, the word pulled from him by a force beyond his control.

She looked up. She cradled her arm, and deep scratches etched her pale cheeks. "Lorenzo," she breathed.

He went to her. She gazed up at him, and in her eyes he read the misery of what she'd endured today. Gently, he put his arms around her. It wasn't meant to be anything more than a quick embrace. Yet she relaxed against his chest and inhaled a long sigh of a breath. The softness of her, the smallness of her in his arms. . .

She stepped away, averting her gaze. Several of the other girls had already drifted away, and he watched them make their slow, painful way down the street. Rose hung behind. A dark bruise marked her swollen eye. Still, she smiled at him, and he rested a hand on her shoulder. "Let's go home."

They nodded, and he lent an arm to each as they moved down the street, leaving the prison behind.

Chapter 6

November 22, 1909

She was tired. Plain and simple. She had taken the morning and late afternoon shifts on the picket line, the wind knifing through the threadbare fabric of her coat while slush seeped through a hole in her shoe. She'd taken to hobbling like an old woman because of the chilblains on her feet. Her knuckles were swollen from where the policeman's baton had struck her last week, and her hands were red and cracked from the bitter cold.

Still, the strike continued.

The last place she wanted to go tonight was Cooper Union for a meeting. She wanted to lie on the mattress next to Meggie with the quilt pulled over her head and relish the rare sensation of warmth. To sleep and forget about the cold and her empty belly and the strike. When she slept, sometimes she returned to the Ireland of her childhood, to Mam crooning a lullaby in her lilting voice, to Da's hearty laugh and strong arms.

When she slept, there was no reality.

"Are you going to the meeting tonight?"

She looked up at her sister's voice. Meggie bounced Silva's infant daughter, Lucia, on her hip. If Aileen had been on speaking terms with the Almighty, she'd have asked God to specially bless Vito and Silva Romano. Though they could hardly afford to, they'd allowed Aileen and Meggie to continue living in their apartment for a much reduced rate since the strike had begun, and still fed them meals. For her part, Aileen ate the smallest portion possible, just enough to keep up her strength. Already guilt drove at her for taking advantage of this young couple's kindness.

"I probably should." She got up from the mattress, wincing at the pain in her feet, and slowly made her way across the apartment floor.

Meggie followed her. "Lorenzo said you could walk with him. He should be by soon to pick you up."

"Oh," was all Aileen said as she slid her arms into her still-damp coat and did up the buttons with unwieldy fingers.

"Can I come?" Meggie shifted her grip on baby Lucia.

"I don't know." Aileen smoothed a hand across her hair, patting down flyaways. She hadn't bothered replacing the hat she'd lost in the fight. "There's going to be a lot of people and noise—"

"You don't let me do anything!" Meggie's voice rose. "No picketing or union office work or meetings. All I do is stay in this blasted apartment day in and day out. I'm not a baby, Aileen. Girls younger than me are at the center of the strike, and I'm sick and tired of being left out."

For a second, Aileen stared openmouthed at her sister. Something inside her that had long been at the breaking point snapped.

"So you want to be cold, colder than you've ever been in your life, so cold your hands and feet never stop aching with it? Stand for hours while people point and whisper but mostly look away and act like you don't exist? You want to be beat up by the coppers?

Hauled into jail, where you hope someone will come and pay your bail? Or maybe you'd like to be sentenced to Blackwell's Island for a week, like what happened to Annie Kenowitz, where you slave in a workhouse alongside thieves and common criminals? This strike isn't some grand adventure. It's terrifying and horrible and—" Her voice cracked. She clamped a hand against her mouth, shaking.

Meggie stared at her. Drew in a shaky breath. "But I want to be a part of it." Her voice was quiet. "I'm tired of being safe and protected while other girls risk the picket lines. Didn't I join the strike, same as the others? Please, Aileen. Don't stop me from doing my bit."

At the look on her sister's face, the fight drained out of her. She'd thought she was doing what was right for Meggie by protecting her. But this was America. Not a country paved in gold, but one that required hardship and sacrifice and risk out of each of them. Meggie wasn't too young to learn the realities of such things.

She sighed. "All right. You can come to the meeting. But don't be getting your hopes up about the rest."

"Thank you." A smile wreathed Meggie's face. She looked so young and girlish, pretty as a china doll. Still, within her sister was stronger stuff. It was time to test her mettle.

"Oh, for the love of the saints, just get your coat." Despite her weariness, she smiled back.

The key jiggled in the lock, and then the apartment door opened. Lorenzo and Silva came in.

Everything within her heightened at the sight of him, came to life beneath the numbing dullness brought on by her day. His dark hair tousled by the wind, his eyes bright in his tanned face. His half-smile as their gazes came together.

She couldn't, wouldn't name whatever lay between them. But that didn't mean she didn't hold it close and let it water the parched places of her heart.

Silva took off her coat and reached for Lucia. "My *preziosa bambina*." She nuzzled her daughter's cheek, whispering to her in Italian. She looked up, cheeks pink from cold, dark eyes smiling. "Thank you for watching her."

Meggie smiled. "I'll be going with you to the meeting, if that's all right." She looked up at Lorenzo. "Aileen said I could."

Lorenzo nodded. "Fine with me." He turned to Aileen. "Ready?"

They left the apartment, steps turned toward Cooper Union, only a few blocks away from the Asch Building. Darkness coated the sky, their path lit by streetlights and the glow from the buildings they passed. She moved closer to Lorenzo, their shoulders almost brushing, his body heat bringing a measure of warmth against the chilly air. They hadn't touched since the day she'd been released from prison. But even now she still recalled every nuance of his arms around her, the even cadence of his heart against her ear. Then, for the first time in a long while, she'd felt safe. Protected. Cared for.

They reached Cooper Union, the imposing redbrick building blazing with light, people pouring toward it in a steady tide. Ida had told her the great President Abraham Lincoln once gave a speech denouncing slavery in its auditorium.

"We need our own President Lincoln," Ida had said. *"Someone to speak against the slavery of the modern age."*

Thousands packed the basement auditorium, and she was grateful Lorenzo led the way through the crowd and found them three seats in the middle. From her seat between Meggie and Lorenzo, she scanned the vast room. Most of those in attendance were women, young like herself. Local 25 had distributed thousands of circulars, calling for a union meeting to discuss issues citywide. Ida had told her she'd volunteered to be one of the runners, carrying word of the speeches to nearby meeting halls if the crowd overflowed. And it had. People flooded the auditorium, standing along the walls, squeezing into every available space. At least a hundred crammed the stage, almost all men. The important guests—columnists, ILGWU leaders, and somewhere, the president of the American Federation of Labor himself, Samuel Gompers. Those on the platform wore suits and looked well fed. They'd not been standing in picket lines week after week, enduring the cold and hunger, the beatings by strikebreakers and policemen.

What could they really know about the battles happening at the factories on strike?

The speeches began. One after another, men took the podium and spoke. They were skilled orators, she'd give them that. Yet what did their words honestly mean? What action did they propose to back them up?

An hour and a half later, she turned to Lorenzo. "They don't seem like they know what they really want," she whispered. "Half of what they're saying is strike, the other half not now—we're not ready. How is that supposed to help us? If we at Triangle have been holding out for over two months, why can't everyone?"

Lorenzo nodded. "Mr. Gompers is about to speak. Let's see what he has to say."

A rotund man in a trim dark suit and spectacles walked to the podium. Applause thundered through the auditorium as the audience rose, giving him a standing ovation. Aileen stood and clapped with the rest. Maybe this celebrated leader would finally give them what they were hungry for. A plan to grab hold of.

Gompers bowed and held up a hand. "A man would be less than human if he were not impressed with your reception. But I want you men and women not to give all your enthusiasm for a man, no matter who he may be. I would prefer that you put all of your enthusiasm into your union and your cause."

A little thrill jolted through her.

"I have never declared a strike in all my life. I have done my share to prevent strikes, but there comes a time when not to strike is but to rivet the chains of slavery upon our wrists."

Finally. She glanced at Meggie. Her sister's eyes were wide and full of awe. They exchanged a grin.

"Yes, Mr. Shirtwaist Manufacturer, it may be inconvenient for you if your boys and girls go out on strike, but there are things of more importance than your convenience and your profit. There are the lives of the boys and girls working in your business."

Aileen leaned forward, breathing in air stuffy with the scents of too many bodies packed together. *Call us to action.*

Minutes passed as Gompers continued. ". . .I say, friends, do not enter too hastily. . . ."

Hastily? What? Didn't he know the Triangle workers had been on strike for weeks? Wasn't this meeting supposed to be about calling a general strike, all factories united in a single front against the bosses? The girls who'd worked the picket line had come out tonight in the cold, bone-weary, for this?

She listened to the remainder of his speech in a haze. Applause filled the auditorium as he made concluding remarks. He told them to strike, eventually, when they couldn't get the manufacturers to give them what they wanted.

Ida always said the manufacturers had never given them anything close to fairness.

"They call these union meetings?" Lorenzo muttered with a look of disgust. "As in everything else, it's the leaders who get to talk. Working men and women are, as usual, supposed to sit and listen. But if the union wants to represent us, there should be words from one of us."

She couldn't agree more. Others nearby began to stir, as if they too were disappointed.

A man stood at the podium, introducing the next speaker, some-one called Jacob Panken. Her head ached, her stomach gurgled. She'd hardly eaten today.

A young woman stood up and shouted something in Yiddish. Aileen gasped. Clara Lemlich. She'd seen her once when she'd visited the Triangle picket line. Clara had encouraged them to keep sticking together, her words galvanizing them for days afterward.

"What did she say?" Aileen turned to Lorenzo. "Could you understand it?"

He nodded. "I've picked up some Yiddish. She said 'I want to say a few words.' "

The men on the platform stared at her as Clara walked forward. She looked like a schoolgirl in her white shirtwaist and dark skirt, a man's necktie around her neck. She looked young, as young as the girls on the picket line, a slip of a thing who couldn't be over five feet tall.

"Get her on the platform!" someone shouted. "Let her speak her piece!"

Clara hurried down the crowded aisle. Those nearest the stage helped her onto the platform. Mr. Panken and the man who'd been introducing him stepped to the side, looking discomfited, almost annoyed.

A hush fell over the auditorium as Clara stepped in front of the podium. For an instant, she swept her gaze across the audience. Aileen caught her breath. Clara began to speak in Yiddish, the words coming fast, impassioned.

"Quickly," she whispered to Lorenzo. "Tell me what she's saying."

" 'I have listened to all the speakers. I have no further patience for talk, as I am one of those who feels and suffers from the things pictured.' " Lorenzo stopped. Cheers exploded in the auditorium, applause, shouting, stamping of feet. He looked directly at Aileen.

"She said, 'I move that we go on a general strike.' "

A cheer burst from her own throat, and she jumped to her feet, palms stinging. This! This was what they'd been waiting for. Finally, the voice of someone who understood.

The applause roared for minutes. When it died down, the man who'd introduced Mr. Panken stepped forward. "Do we have a second to the motion?"

Applause shook the auditorium.

The sensation surging through the room was more potent than electricity. It surged into her own weary body and funneled in strength.

Again, the man tried to quiet the crowd. "Please, vote carefully. Think before making a decision. If you fear hunger, cold, and suffering, have no shame in voting against the strike. And if you vote in favor"—he paused—"you are sealing a pact to struggle until the very end."

Behind him, Clara's eyes burned, her chin raised as she surveyed the crowd. Asking wordlessly if they stood with her, one girl to countless others.

"Do you mean faith?" he shouted, raising his right hand. "Will you take the old Jewish oath?"

In a single wave, thousands raised their right arms, voices filling the auditorium in a unified storm. Aileen raised her right hand along with the others, as did Meggie. Whatever this was, it was powerful. More than that, it meant action.

Lorenzo leaned in, whispering the words of the pledge. " 'If I turn traitor to the cause I now pledge, may this hand wither from the arm I now raise.' "

A half a beat later than the rest, she murmured the words, heart stirring with every one.

I will not turn traitor. I will not back down.

~⊙

December 25, 1909

"The Uprising of the 20,000," the papers called it. At first it had been an electric, fervent thing. Especially when wealthy women championed their cause in droves, backing them with press and pocketbooks. The police still arrested strikers, but now matrons of the ilk of Alva Vanderbilt Belmont and Anne Morgan turned out in their furs and velvets to lend support. When Rose was arrested and hauled to night court, Mrs. Belmont, who'd run out of cash after paying bail for several girls that night, looked the judge right in the eye and asked if he'd kindly accept her Madison Avenue mansion as surety. It was valued at $400,000, she said.

The bowled-over judge had naturally agreed.

Not to be outdone, Anne Morgan hosted a lavish tea, where her well-heeled guests listened to strikers recount their experiences. Ida had been one of the speakers, returning with tales of how the wealthy ladies gasped when a young Italian girl said her boss had gotten a priest to tell his workers they'd be sent to hell if they joined a strike. And only a few days ago, motorcars had paraded down Fifth Avenue, strikers and society women sitting side by side, the cars bearing signs: STRIKERS SEEKING JUSTICE. VOTES FOR WOMEN. The women supporting the strike were also ardent suffragettes.

Progressive young college girls had joined forces with the society matrons. Some even walked the picket line. In a way, Aileen was grateful. The police were less likely to use violence when they might unwittingly do so against a society girl. Yet most of these privileged young women seemed to have little concept of the realities of the strike. After a few hours in the cold, they returned home to hot meals and warm beds, while the strikers starved and shivered.

Many owners of smaller shops had caved in the first two days of the general strike, granting their workers better wages, fewer working hours, and a closed shop—a union-only factory. Triangle had not been one of them, and so far there were no signs of contrition from the Harris and Blanck faction. Yet with the tide of publicity in favor of the strikers and their socialite supporters, surely they'd have to agree eventually.

Aileen stood at the window, staring out at the swirling snow from behind frosted panes. The Romanos and Faveros had celebrated Christmas in a meager fashion, but what they lacked in gifts and feasting, they made up for in warmth and laughter. After the meal, Lorenzo, Silva, and Vito had sung a traditional Italian Christmas carol. Listening to the melody sung in Lorenzo's rich voice had made unexpected tears start to her eyes. Tears that threatened even now. She drew in a shuddering breath.

Oh Mam. Will the pain of missing you ever go away? Somehow the joy and love around her only added to the ache inside her heart. An emptiness that threatened to consume her.

The door creaked open. She turned, expecting to see the Romanos and Meggie returning from the festivities at the Faveros. Lorenzo emerged from the shadows. A half-smile settled on his lips.

"All alone?"

She nodded. "I wasn't feeling much like a party."

He moved to stand behind her. Together they stared out at the snow-covered street. She'd never seen so much snow. Momentarily carpeting the filth of the Lower East Side in purity. Falling like white ash from the heavens.

She turned, tilting her head to look up at him. "That song you sang. What was it?"

" 'From Starry Skies Thou Come.' " Stubble shadowed his jaw, and she smelled the fragrance of candied fruit on his breath from the panettone they'd had for dessert.

"What are the words in English?"

He gave a shrug, a little smile. "Well, it goes something like this:

From starry skies descending,
Thou comest, glorious King,
A manger low Thy bed,
In winter's icy sting."

Though not raised in song, the emotion in his voice remained.

"O my dearest Child most holy,
Shudd'ring, trembling in the cold!
Great God, Thou lovest me!
What suff'ring Thou didst bear,
That I near Thee might be!"

He stopped. A tear trickled down her cheek, her shoulders trembling. Wordlessly, he rested a hand on her shoulder. She averted her gaze. What must he think of her, falling to pieces over a few words?

Why was she? Was it him, the timbre of his voice, his nearness? Not entirely. The words stirred something within her, undoing the emptiness. They told of the Christ Child, come down from heaven as an infant. As a Savior. "Is it true?" Tears wet her cheeks as she looked up at him in the semidarkness. "That He loves us?"

"I believe it is," he said simply.

"Yet there's so much suffering everywhere. If He loves us, why doesn't He help us? In Ireland, the priest said those who were rich were so because the Lord favored them. That seemed horrible to me. What made God love someone else more than me? Is it because of something I've done or failed to do?" She'd never voiced these thoughts to anyone, keeping them hidden behind the shield of her own self-reliance. But Lorenzo's unadorned words, "*I believe it is*," had pulled them from her.

Lorenzo shook his head. Sighed, as if gathering his thoughts. "What that priest said. . .that's not the way of it at all. I don't know why some want for nothing while others lack, but it has nothing to do with God's love. Christ Himself was born into a poor family from a humble village. For Him to show preference to the rich would mean He'd be turning against His earthly family. He would never do that. In His time on earth, He cared for the poor, and He still does. On the cross, He offered himself for all of us. He offered Himself for you."

Lorenzo's words, spoken in a gentle voice, made more tears rush to her eyes. *"He offered Himself for you."*

Would the glorious King who'd come as a holy Child answer her with love?

Oh, she wanted this. To put her trust in something beyond her own abilities and believe in Someone other than herself.

She wiped a hand across her face then inhaled a long breath.

"Would you show me?" Her voice was soft and a bit broken. "Would you show me how to ask Him?"

Lorenzo's throat jerked. "It would be my honor."

There, by the window, on the floor of a New York tenement, snow falling softly outside, she found what it was to have no fear in surrender.

Chapter 7

January 1910

Aileen lay on the mattress, hair splayed like threads of flame across the pillowslip. For two days, she'd worked the picket line while battling a cough and fever, although she'd only admitted it after Lorenzo found her crumpled at the bottom of the stairs in a heap of exhaustion.

He could scarcely bring himself to tell her the news.

Her eyes fluttered open, her gaze fixating on him. She struggled to sit up, and he knelt to help her, propping her up with pillows, her skin too warm through the thin fabric of her nightshift. Her collarbones protruded sharply, the hollows in her cheeks grown more pronounced as the winter ground on.

"What happened?" Her voice was raspy.

How could he tell her?

"You did attend the meeting?"

Across the room, Silva stirred a pot at the stove, baby Lucia cradled in one arm. His sister murmured soothing words to Lucia, who was feverish too, as she worked.

He nodded. "I attended it, yeah."

Her gaze narrowed. "What aren't you telling me?"

He scrubbed a hand across his jaw. Blew out a breath. "The union officers presented Triangle's proposal. They agreed to give us shorter hours and better wages and to reemploy those who participated in the strike."

"What about the closed shop?"

He shook his head. "They won't do that. Blanck and Harris firmly refuse to recognize our union."

Her eyes fell shut. For a long moment, she said nothing, Silva's bustling at the stove the only sound. "What happened then?"

"There was a vote. Almost unanimously, everyone refused to return to a factory where the union isn't recognized."

"Then we keep striking." A cough spasmed her thin frame. She leaned forward, breaths heaving until it passed. She looked up, eyes stark in her pale face. "If we hold out long enough, they'll agree to our terms. Eventually they'll have no choice but to bend."

He didn't want to admit, even to himself, that the months of suffering had been in vain. That despite the picket lines, the publicity, the brutal attacks, they'd eventually be forced to go back to work under management who could alter rules and wages on a whim. Better wages and shorter hours were a good thing, but only in a factory that hired solely union employees and recognized union officers as having a voice. Otherwise, six months or a year from now, what would prevent the promised wages and hours from being taken away in the time it took for a boss to snap his fingers? And if someone dared protest, the bosses would give them the boot and hire some obliging greenhorn who just wanted a job.

"You don't think so, do you?" Blast it all, but he hated that tone in her voice. Day after day, she'd left for the picket lines with a firm set to her shoulders. Now she looked crumpled. Broken.

He shook his head. "I don't know."

"What should we do?" Her voice rose. "Go back to work? Apologize for the inconvenience we've caused? 'Oh, I'm sorry, Mr. Blanck. I'll bow and scrape and slave at my machine, while the only rules anyone's required to abide by are yours.' The rights of workers are at stake here, and not only at Triangle. At factories all over the city, the bosses will be looking to Blanck and Harris to see what terms they settle on with their workers. We owe it to those workers, to ourselves, not to give up." She held his gaze. "I won't give up." She lay back against the pillows, face chalky, as if the effort of speaking had sapped the remainder of her energy.

"Rest now." He laid a hand on her shoulder, let it linger there a moment. "When you're well, you can fight again."

She nodded and closed her eyes. He stood. For a long moment, he stared down at her, hands in his pockets, heart twisting with emotions too numerous to name.

She wasn't the same frightened girl who'd arrived at Triangle that long-ago first day. She was brave and strong and full of so much passion.

If only he could mend the world and make it right for her.

February 8, 1910

The strike was over.

January had been hard and bitter. After the initial proposal was voted down, many society women withdrew their support, saying the strikers should be content with what the factory owners had offered. Though the picket lines and passing out of pamphlets continued, everyone had grown tired. Sick. Cold. Hungry.

Desperate.

When the bosses again met with the union leaders, it had all been settled.

They'd achieved a 12 percent increase in wages and a fifty-two hour workweek. No longer would the factory dock workers for the use of needles, thread, and other petty materials.

But Triangle and other large factories refused to implement a closed shop.

Aileen sat at her machine, the rasping whirr of hundreds of needles a din in her ears. Upon their return to the factory, they'd transferred her and Ida to the ninth floor. Though Aileen was glad to be near Meggie, who'd been promoted from snipping threads, she missed sitting near Rose and catching a glimpse of Lorenzo at the cutters' tables.

The strike hadn't been for nothing. They'd stood strong and gained concessions—many smaller factories were now closed shops with good unions. Fewer hours and better wages would benefit them all, and it would be fine indeed to start bringing home a pay envelope again.

Still, there would be no recognized union at Triangle.

She slid another sewn piece into the center trough and picked up an unsewn one from the pile. As she did, she stole a glance at Meggie, who sat at her machine, the pale skin of her neck exposed, strands of honey hair wisping around her face.

When she and Meggie had arrived in America, she'd never imagined they'd become involved in something as bold as a strike. But she'd thought her dreams about America would come true, that hard work would lead her to more than days as a human machine.

Now the strike had ended, and she must move on with her life, such as it was. Find joy in the good and seek God for strength to endure the rest.

Lorenzo's face filled her mind. His gentle hands helping her sit up while she'd been sick, his frame sitting on the edge of the mattress as he wiped her hot forehead with a damp cloth.

Truly, she'd not reckoned to find a man with a heart as tender and steadfast as his.

Another piece into the machine. The rhythm and flash of the needle. The push of her hands as she guided the filmy fabric through.

And as she sewed, she thought of him.

Chapter 8

May 1910

Her shirtwaist was the shade of pink roses, matching those in her cheeks. And he couldn't go a minute without stealing a glance at her as they walked through streets tinged with twilight.

They weren't engaged like Jacob and Ida, who were getting married next month. They weren't even courting. He had to remind himself of this. They were going to the dance hall together only because Rose had invited them.

He could scarcely believe Aileen had said yes. Usually she attended night classes with Meggie and Ida or spent evenings with the Romanos. Now that they worked on different floors, he saw her less. Never mind that he went out of his way to see her more, leaving his apartment at the same time as she so they could walk to Triangle together, waiting for her outside the building to walk her home. But Meggie was always with them, usually Rose too.

Tonight it was just the two of them. And he intended to make the most of every moment.

"Did I tell you how nice you look?"

"Yes, you did." She smiled. "But I confess I like hearing it again all the same."

"Your shirtwaist isn't from Triangle, is it?"

She shook her head. "I bought it at Macy's. I don't think it came from Triangle. It doesn't look like it anyway, and we would know."

He shoved his hands into the pockets of his freshly pressed gray trousers. "It's strange, isn't it, when you think about it. We buy things without really knowing where they come from or how they're made."

"I wonder if we still would if we knew the conditions they were made in." She sighed, her forehead furrowing. "If only there were some way of labeling things, letting the customer know the workers who produced an item were treated fairly. Even if the finished product cost more. I'd rather save up or go without than think someone was paid too little or treated unfairly making something I bought." She lifted her skirt to step over a puddle. "And now you're probably regretting going out with a girl who doesn't know how to keep serious thoughts from her head for even an hour." She made a rueful face.

He chuckled, shook his head. "Not at all. I don't mind, really."

"You might if I start in on votes for women." She grinned.

He shrugged. "Why shouldn't women have the vote? They have to abide by the laws, same as men. The women I know are some of the most committed citizens this country has. If a woman can be imprisoned for a crime, shouldn't she also have a say in electing those who control the legal system?"

"I couldn't agree more." She paused. A giggle escaped. She shook her head. "I give up. We can't do it. We can't not have a serious conversation."

She looked so beautiful when she laughed. It was good to leave the winter behind. Then they'd striven and stood united and comforted each other but rarely laughed.

They approached the brightly lit dance hall. Music drifted from the open windows, jaunty and carefree. Girls in bright hats and fresh shirtwaists walked arm in arm with their beaus. Even the air seemed to anticipate the evening ahead, smelling of fried food from the nearby restaurant and summer wind. And garbage, but that was a New York staple.

"I don't know about you, Signorina O'Connor"—he shot her a grin—"but the only thing I'm serious about right now is dancing."

City lights bathing her face and hair, she laughed again, reaching for his hand and twining it in hers. "Let's go then."

Chapter 9

February 13, 1911
Nine months later

Standing in the doorway of the apartment, Lorenzo took in the sight of his mama sitting at the table. Graying black hair hung in a loose braid down her back. Lamplight framed her face, softening the deep-set lines and creases. She bent over one of Giuseppe's socks, holding it to the light as she darned.

Mama had always been there, even in the lonely days when it had just been him and Silva, struggling through the first years in America. Her presence had remained in his heart, memories of her guiding him through the hardest moments. Always, she'd been the center of their family, her arms encircling them in love, her hands piecing together the broken, her keen eyes noticing when one of her children was in distress. "*Sit*," she'd say, briskly motioning them to a chair. "*Trouble shared is trouble halved. So talk.*" They'd talk, and she'd listen, her gaze never leaving their face. Then she'd dole out her wisdom, which usually included a scattering of Italian proverbs and, when her sons' trouble was the result of their own stupidity, the verbal equivalent of a swift kick in the rear.

Lorenzo's chest ached with the love swelling there.

She turned, noticing him. "Lorenzo Favero! Are you trying to frighten an old woman into having a heart attack?"

A smile eased across his lips. "No, Mama."

"Then come into the light where I can see you. It is late. Did they keep you so long at Triangle?"

He crossed the room. "I went for a walk after work." He rested one hand on the back of the kitchen chair opposite her. "Mama, can I talk to you?"

She laid aside her darning egg and folded her hands atop the table. "Of course, *mio figlio.*"

Chair legs scraped as he pulled out the chair and sat facing her.

A smile softened her face. "It has been a long time since you asked that. As a little boy, you were always wanting to talk. Pulling on my skirts with some story, wanting me to listen to you or answer your questions. I often despaired of getting any work done. Ah, but I miss those days. My chattering little boy."

He smiled, remembering it too.

"So what is on your heart? Or do I even need to ask?" She gave him a knowing look.

"What do you mean?"

She shook her head, as if he should already know. "A mother's eyes see her children better than anyone. I have watched how you look at Aileen. And how she looks at you."

His face warmed, and he stared at his folded hands. "Yeah. . .um. . ."

"I know you love her."

It was like he was ten again and she'd told him she knew he'd been the one sneaking bits off the platter. "How do you know that?"

She smiled, lamplight casting a golden glow on her face. "It is easy. You look at her like your padre looked at me every day of the twenty-three years we shared together."

His throat tightened. It was easy to think of his mama only in that role. But she was a woman too, who'd loved a man with a booming laugh, eyes that crinkled into slits when he smiled, work-hewn arms, and a humble faith. Their love had given three children life, and he'd witnessed their devotion on both the good days and the hard ones.

"If Aileen and I ever have a family, I want to be as devoted a husband to her and as good a padre to our children as he was."

Tears misted her eyes. "Well, what are you waiting for? Speak to her. My mama always said, 'When a friend asks, there is no tomorrow.' But I think the same applies to love."

"I'm going to ask her tomorrow. On Valentine's Day."

She nodded. "That is good." Then she stood. "Wait here. I have something for you." She bustled into the adjoining bedroom she shared with Giuseppe. He waited, listening to the familiar sounds of the building—footsteps, voices, a baby crying—the front room still fragrant with the scent of spices from the evening meal.

Mama returned, carrying something wrapped in a handkerchief. She placed it on the table in front of him and resumed her seat. "Open it."

He hesitated.

"Go on."

Carefully, he unfolded the fabric. A simple gold band lay nestled in its center. He picked it up, held it to the light. "Mama. . .this is your ring."

"And your nonna's before it was mine. Now it is yours."

He held the ring in his palm. As a boy, he'd rubbed his fingertip over the rounded edge while they held hands during family prayers. "But I can't take this."

She reached across the table and laid a hand against his cheek, her touch both gentle and strong. "I want you to have it. To give it to her as a symbol of your love. Your nonno and nonna's names are engraved inside. Your padre showed me when he gave it to me. Two generations of Favero women have worn this ring. It is hers now."

Tears pricked his eyes, but they were born of joy. Of love. Of the promise of a future. "I love you," he whispered.

Her smile held a trace of wistfulness. Perhaps she remembered her own engagement, the man who'd slid the ring on her finger so long ago and who had not lived to see his son take a bride. "I love you too, mio figlio."

◈

February 14, 1911

The Lower East Side was no fairy tale. Yet Lorenzo Favero could still make a girl feel like a princess.

He made *her* feel like a princess. And in a brown suit jacket, hair curling over his forehead despite having started out the evening slicked back, she could imagine no finer prince.

They'd walked to Lombardi's on Spring Street and ate slices of crispy pizza, rich with flavorful sauce and gooey with cheese, then to a nearby shop for vanilla ice cream drizzled with hot fudge. As usual, they'd talked and laughed, but something about Lorenzo's behavior seemed different. Tense, in a subtle way. When she'd questioned the reason for such an extravagant evening, he'd said it was because of Valentine's Day, and she deserved to be spoiled.

They walked back to Bleecker Street, stars carpeting the jet-hued sky overhead, their breaths pluming from their lips in the cold. Lately he'd taken to holding her hand on their walks. But tonight he didn't claim it. Nor did he strike up a conversation. They usually talked about everything, the night classes they both were taking, their childhoods, hopes and dreams for the future. She folded and unfolded her fingers at her side. Had she done something to upset him? Or was something else on his mind?

She decided to ask him. He'd never hesitated in answering her plainly before. As they walked, she angled her face toward his. "Are you all right?"

His brow creased. "Of course. Why?"

"I don't know. You just seem a bit. . .quiet."

He shoved his hands into his pockets. A beat passed. He swallowed. "There's something I have to say."

Her heart accelerated. He looked serious. Too serious. And he didn't say anything. Just. . .stared at her. Gone was the confident man who'd strode across the factory and shared his lunch, the one who'd fought during the strike and helped her not to give up afterward. The man beside her now looked uncertain, nervous.

He must have something horrible to tell her. Was he sick? Had he decided to leave New York? Determined he didn't want to see her anymore?

Whatever it was, she couldn't bear that look on his face. She put on a brave smile and took a deep breath. "You know you can tell me anything."

"I know," he said quietly. "All night I've been thinking about how to best put this into words so it comes out just right. I'd planned on saying it earlier, during dinner, but there were all those other people around. It just didn't seem right."

Now she was really worried.

"Please, Lorenzo. Just say it." She hadn't meant to sound anything but encouraging, yet her tone came out brisker than she intended.

He took a deep breath. Shook his head. "Not here. We'll go somewhere. Washington Square Park. We. . .we can take the trolley

400

so we don't have to walk."

Oh, this was too much. She stopped in the shadow of a closed storefront, turned to face him. Wind blew strands of hair into her face. "For the love of the saints, Lorenzo Favero, just spit it out!" She paused, collecting herself. Whatever it was, he didn't deserve her temper. "What I mean to say is, you've been on edge all evening, and I'm starting to worry. Whatever terrible thing you have to tell me can't possibly be worse than the suspense of waiting for it."

He frowned. "Terrible thing? You think I've something bad to tell you?"

"With that look on your face, I can't imagine it's good."

They stood, facing each other on the sidewalk. In the distance came the sound of voices, the brisk stride of footsteps, the honking of a horn. He cleared his throat. "Signorina Aileen O'Connor."

Well, that was formal. "Yes?"

"There's something I've wanted to ask you for a very long time."

"Yes?"

He reached out, clasped her hand, and lowered himself to one knee on the sidewalk.

She gasped. "Lorenzo, what are you doing? It's filthy down there. Get up!"

He shook his head, a grin tugging at the corners of his lips. "I can't. Not until I've asked you to marry me, which I can't do if you keep interrupting me."

Her breath fled her lungs, her world stilling, stopping, centering on a single point. Him.

"Asked you to marry me. . ."

"Very well." Her smile trembled at the edges. "Go ahead."

"Okay." His grin deepened, a dimple appearing in the crevice of his cheek. "So here's how it stands. I'm a cutter at Triangle. Currently I make twenty-two dollars a week. I arrived in America with one suitcase, and I still don't have much more than that. I don't even have a place of my own, but I will get one. I can't promise fine things, at least not yet. I can't even promise a life away from the Lower East Side, though I surely hope that will happen someday."

She started to nod, to tell him none of those things mattered, to say yes, but he shook his head with a chuckle. "I'm not finished yet. That was just the beginning."

She gave a little laugh.

"So though I can't offer you those great things, at least not right away, this is what I can offer. My heart, to belong to no other but you. My hands, to work as hard as they're able to take care of you and Meggie and any other family we might have. And my love, from now until my last breath." He swallowed. "Even if you don't say yes, that last one will still be yours, because I can't imagine loving anyone but you."

Tears filled her eyes.

"Oh, and one more thing." He reached inside his pocket. "I've got this too." He held up a small gold ring that shone beneath the streetlights. "It was my grandmother's. My grandfather had their names engraved inside. And it belonged to my mother. Both of us, me and her, want you to have it now." He paused.

She could scarcely form a single word, what with the tears sliding down her cheeks and the tightness in her throat. The depth of what he promised had well and truly undone her. Shaken her world in the most complete of ways. "Yes." She laughed shakily, swiping her free hand beneath her eyes. "Yes, *Signor* Lorenzo Favero, I accept your proposal. And in return I offer you my heart, to only ever be yours, my hands, to work right alongside you, and my love forever."

His eyes widened. "Are you sure?"

She smiled. "You didn't need to do all that to convince me. I would have said yes no matter what." While he'd been talking, she'd been too focused on him to notice anything else. Now, out of the corner of her eye, she saw several pedestrians giving them curious looks. A few had even stopped to watch. "But please, get up off the street. We're attracting attention."

He grinned. "Perhaps the straitlaced Americans need a lesson in *amore*," he said, accent thick. He stood, the knees of his trousers soaked with slush and who knew what else. Yet as he took a step toward her, all thoughts of that fled. His face was but inches away. Separated from hers by less than a breath. Her limbs went weak at the look in his eyes, a look that repeated every single one of his words. He trailed his hand across her cheek, framed her face with both hands. "Did I say I love you?"

"You said enough," she whispered. "More than enough."

In the next instant, their lips met, their breaths melded into a single refrain. She wrapped her arms around him, standing on tiptoe to pull him close.

This is a dream. I'm dreaming. Not standing on a New York street on Valentine's Day being kissed breathless by the man I love.

Yet as he kissed her, long and leisurely, so utterly it surely did instruct a few Americans as to the meaning of amore, she let herself be swept away.

In the rightness that was everything about this man, this moment. And this love.

Chapter 10

March 25, 1911

Five minutes to quitting time on a Saturday afternoon had never been so full of promise. Tomorrow he'd put on a suit, walk to Father Esposito's church three blocks away, and marry his Aileen.

Lorenzo stood at the cutting table. He finished cutting out a bodice piece and hung the pattern on the wire strung above his table.

Come on, clock. Hurry up already.

He'd never known an afternoon to drag so long. He had to get home to grab the remainder of his belongings and take them to the apartment on Sullivan Street.

The apartment he and Aileen would share after tomorrow. His throat went dry. At long last, there need be no more nightly good-byes at her apartment door.

"Be careful you don't cut your hand off with that thing."

The voice at his elbow made him start. Jacob stood by his shoulder, a twinkle in his eyes. "That's not funny, Levin."

"Did I say it was funny?" Jacob made a mock serious face. "I just happened to notice a certain cutter's mind has been far from Triangle today. Thinking of his upcoming trade of carefree bachelorhood for the shackles of matrimony, hmm?"

"Come on, knock it off. You didn't see me giving you any grief before you married Ida. Besides, I thought you said marriage was the best thing that ever happened to you."

"Ah, and it's true." Jacob grinned. He hung a stray pattern on the wire above the table. "And speaking of marriage, I have reason to expect another consequence of that happy institution to visit Ida and me before the year is out."

"You don't mean you and Ida. . ."

Jacob's grin all but split his cheeks. "Will soon have an addition to our family."

"Why, that's great." Lorenzo clapped a hand to his friend's shoulder. "Congratulations, old man. To both of you."

"Thank you. I expect it won't be long before I'll be offering the same congratulations to you and Aileen." Jacob winked.

A few tables away, a group of cutters stood talking. One of them put a cigarette to his lips, exhaling a plume of smoke.

"They really ought to quit that," Lorenzo said under his breath, making another cut through the layers of lawn. The sharp slicing sound blended with the noise of the end of the workday, foremen hurrying with piles of finished pieces in their hands, shipping clerks bustling in with clipboards and order requests, a burst of laughter from the group of cutters.

The quitting bell rang.

Finally.

Lorenzo focused on the fabric, finishing the last cut. Around him, workers tidied their stations before heading out for the day. Already a line had formed at the Greene Street door. Waiting in the queue was the last thing he wanted to do today.

Jacob pushed scraps through the slot into the bin below the table. "You know, both of us will start getting pretty dull, being old married men and all. In five years, we likely won't recognize—" He stopped.

Lorenzo looked up. One of the cutters grabbed a water bucket from a window ledge and tossed its contents onto the pile of scraps beneath a table. Great. Mr. Bernstein would be spitting mad when he heard—

In a flash, the flame leapt. Lorenzo spied a pail on another window ledge, grabbed it, and raced toward the fire. He threw the water onto the flames and sprinted across the room for another bucket.

"Fire!" someone shouted.

"More buckets." Bernstein's voice. "Quick, men!"

Water sloshed against the edges of the pail as he navigated through the maze of cutting tables. Flames darted upward, licking at the hanging patterns, lapping up the layers of lawn spread across the table. The force of the heat shocked him as he tossed the water over the blaze.

Bernstein shouted for more buckets. Jacob grabbed at the patterns, trying to yank them down. Lorenzo tore at several. Heat from the metal edges scorched his hands. Flaming patterns fell. Burning particles of fabric floated in the air.

"Stop!" He grabbed the back of Jacob's coat. "It's too late."

The line of burning patterns collapsed like a row of dominoes.

The flames sped forward, as if the bucketfuls had been no more than drops. Smoke choked the air. Screams. Shouts. Girls crowded the aisles, jostling each other, making for the exits. Lorenzo coughed, the air searing his lungs. Flames consumed the table.

The hoses. They needed to get the hoses.

He pushed through the crowd, reaching Bernstein. "Mr. Bernstein." He gasped. "The hoses."

Bernstein turned, wild-eyed. "They're bringing them." Two men broke through the crowd, hauling a long snake of a hose. One of them pushed it into Bernstein's hands as he jumped onto one of the tables. "Is it open?" He turned the nozzle, aiming the hose at the flames.

In a second, water would rush free and extinguish the blaze.

Choking on the smoke, Lorenzo waited.

Bernstein swore. "Why isn't it working?" He yanked at the nozzle, twisting it. Nothing happened.

"There's no pressure," Lorenzo shouted. Flames crackled. The windows popped. Glass shattered.

Bernstein threw down the hose and jumped off the table. "We have to get everyone out!" He ran, grabbing the girls, herding them toward the elevators, shouting at them to get out.

There wasn't time to think. Panicked girls screamed, pushed, flooding down the narrow aisles between the rows of tables toward the exits.

Burning fabric particles landed on his clothes and hair. He batted them away, barely noticing the pain. In a nearby aisle, a girl lay, face tilted to the side, body motionless. He bent over her. Was she. . .?

She blinked, gaze cloudy.

"Come on." He pulled her up with him, her body limp against his, and dragged her through the crowd toward the Greene Street stairs. Dinah Lipschitz, the bookkeeper, sat at her desk, shouting into the phone. The Greene Street elevators descended, leaving dozens standing by. Lorenzo fought forward, supporting the girl.

"Get out. Go now!" Mr. Bernstein shouted, gesturing toward the Greene Street doors.

The tide of people flooded toward the stairs, the girls stumbling over their skirts. Sparks glittered on their upswept hair, their clothes. They ran, coughing in the thick smoke. The girl in his arms slumped against him. He shook her hard. "Come on. Wake up. You've got to get out of here."

"I'll take her." Rose stood at his elbow, backdropped by a haze of smoke. "Quickly. Help the others."

Lorenzo handed the limp girl over to Rose. She draped the girl's arm over her own shoulders and stumbled toward the Greene Street stairs.

He turned. A woman careened wildly, arms pinwheeling as she ran. Her hair flamed behind her as she shrieked and screamed. She turned. Their gazes caught. Terror shone in her eyes. The scent of charred hair, burning flesh. It smelled like death.

He sucked in a breath. His thoughts went to his padre, caught in the conflagration as Mount Vesuvius exploded in a rain of molten lava. His eyes white against his charred face, his lips moving in a silent plea.

Burning alive.

At long last, the quitting bell rang. The hum of the power slowed then stopped, the rasp of the machines silent for the first time in hours. Chairs scraped the floorboards, clattered against the tables as girls stood and pushed them in.

Aileen rose, stretching her back. She glanced across the aisle at Meggie and smiled to see her sister chatting with a friend. Girls laughed and talked as they headed for the exits, cloakroom, or washroom. Aileen made her way toward the cloakroom, steps light. She barely heeded the way the wicker baskets beneath the tables in the narrow aisles snagged at her skirt, or the long line of girls ahead of her. A few minutes earlier, Mary Leventhal, the pretty young forewoman, had handed out pay envelopes. Aileen had slipped hers in her skirt pocket as Mary smiled and offered congratulations.

Mrs. Lorenzo Favero.

Such beautiful words. She couldn't wait to call them hers.

In less than twenty-four hours, she would no longer have to wait. The weeks of planning would be over, and she'd begin a new life with the man she loved.

Thank You, Lord. Truly, I am overwhelmed by Your goodness to us.

She reached the cloakroom and headed to the lockers to get her pocketbook and lunch pail. She needed to collect Meggie and hurry back to Silva's. Vito had found a set of kitchen chairs secondhand and was renting a wagon to bring them to the new apartment.

Across the room, a pretty brunette sang in a sweet, clear voice, doing a little twirl in front of the mirror.

"Ev'ry little movement has a meaning of its own. . ."

The girl looped arms with her friends, the hit tune blending with their giggles as they hurried out of the cloakroom, singing as they walked.

With a grin, Aileen joined in as she followed them out into the main room.

"Ev'ry thought and feeling by some posture can be shown,
And ev'ry love thought
That comes a stealing
O'er your being must be revealing. . ."

She unclasped her pocketbook and pulled out her time card.

A scream ripped through the air. Aileen spun.

"Fire!" a woman shouted.

Across the room, glass shattered. Flames burst in through the windows. People screamed. She stood frozen as fire roiled into the room, a ball of writhing color billowing across tables piled with shirtwaists.

Meggie. Her sister's name galvanized her, forced her feet to move.

Her heart thudded and her breathing came fast as she pushed her way through the girls jamming the aisles, craning her neck for a glimpse of her sister's blond hair.

The aisles were too crowded. She scanned frantically for another way. Hiking up her skirt, she climbed onto the nearest table and jumped to the next. She stumbled, nearly fell. Gasping in the smoke, she kept going, clambering from table to table.

One. Two. Three.

She reached the table where Meggie sat. Empty. "Meggie!" Smoke scraped her lungs, her shouts coming hard, frantic. Her sister had to be here.

God, please.

Flames devoured the tables, rising higher. Mocking her.

Suddenly she glimpsed a form huddled beneath the table. She climbed down, skirt hefted to her thighs. Meggie crouched beneath the table, shaking, tears welled up in her eyes.

"Aileen." She sobbed the word. "I thought you'd left—"

"Come on." Aileen grabbed her sister's hand, pulling her up with her. Flames lapped greedily, engulfing the tables, coming closer. Smoke darkened the air, burning her chest with every breath. "Back over the tables."

"I can't," Meggie whimpered, gaze riveted on the spreading blaze.

She grabbed her sister's shoulders, looking into her eyes. "You have to."

Terrible seconds slid by. Somehow they made it over the tables. Crackling filled her ears. Ash floated downward. Her mind blurred. She needed to think. Girls thronged the windows. One climbed out, reached back in to help the girl behind her.

The fire escape...

Should they go there too?

No. It would be full already. Wouldn't hold everyone. She grabbed her sister's hand and pulled her toward the Washington Place elevators. Dozens of workers crowded near the elevators in a seething pack. Nearby, girls pressed against the door to the Washington Place stairs, pushing against it, pounding it with their fists. Holding tight to Meggie's hand, hemmed in by the crowd, she struggled to breathe. Flames bubbled across the row of tables they'd crossed a minute ago.

Heat. Such blinding heat.

The elevator appeared. The crowd surged toward it. Girls hurtled through the doors, shoving others out of their path, cramming in. The car seemed so small.

Aileen pushed forward, pulling Meggie with her. Seconds. Seconds before the elevator filled and began its descent.

"Come back," a girl cried, clawing at the doors. "Please, come back for us!"

"What are we going to do, Aileen?" The light cast eerie shadows over Meggie's face.

"They're going to come back. And we're going to be on that elevator." Could Meggie even hear her over the shouts and cries?

She'd get them both on the elevator. She had to.

Lorenzo. The eighth floor. Had the flames spread from there? Was he even now trying to reach her? *Oh, let him stay far away from the ninth floor.*

She couldn't think about him, or about anything beyond this second.

Huddled around the door to the Washington Place stairs, girls fought to open it. A young man grappled with the knob, shoved his shoulder against it. Aileen fixated on him as he pushed, face red, muscles straining.

Why won't it open? Do they want us all to burn?

When it didn't move, he ran headlong through the crowd, toward the windows. Flames divided the room, licking higher and higher.

Surging. Across the room, a girl plunged into the flames. Whether she ran or was shoved, Aileen couldn't tell. Fire encircled the girl's body, feeding on her hair, her skirt. She let out a piercing scream and flailed wildly.

In the next instant, she fell to the ground. The air crackled.

Oh dear God. Dear God.

Aileen pulled her gaze away.

Would the elevator come back for them? Or was waiting here the most futile thing she'd ever do? They were surrounded, squeezed into the center of the crowd. She couldn't have gotten them through without shoving those around her down or aside. No one wanted to move anywhere but forward. And where else was there to go?

Smoke clogged her lungs, swirling in an impenetrable fog. Flames whipped through the air, their dry heat scalding. Closer. Coming closer.

Only minutes. That's all they had. Then the fire would be upon them.

The elevator emerged, the cable car visible through the smoky darkness. It stopped. Perhaps for the last time. Those in front banged and clawed at the door. It opened. People pushed, screamed, surging into the car. The motion of those behind her drove her forward, Meggie's hand gripped in hers.

Forward. Just a few more steps.

"Please," a man shouted from inside. "Don't overload it, or we'll all die!" His words sounded far away, an echo. A girl plowed past her into the car. Meggie's hand in hers was sweaty.

Keep going. Keep—

Someone shoved her from behind, pushing her inside the elevator. A slipping. Meggie. Their hands had broken contact. Frantic bodies crushed around her from all sides.

This wasn't panic. This was desperation, raw and feral.

"Meggie!" Blood roared in her brain. She couldn't move, pinned by those pressed against her. She fought to raise her hands, to push aside the obstructions in her path.

The elevator operator grappled to close the doors.

"No!" she screamed. "My sister! Stop! Wait! Meggie!"

The doors closed.

On the other side of the iron slats, she glimpsed Meggie. Standing in the crowd of women, tongues of fire surging toward her. Her sister's eyes were wide against her pale face, her mouth open as if she shouted something. Light flickered in an otherworldly glow.

I've got to get out. I have to go to her. Even if I die with her, I can't leave her.

"Let me through," she screamed, fighting to push the women in front of her aside with the force of her body. "I want to get out!"

The elevator began its descent.

Meggie's terrified face. Her skirt billowing in the suffocating air. Her hands outstretched, reaching toward her. Grasping.

For someone who wasn't there.

"Aileen!"

Did she hear it, or did she only imagine it? Her sister's voice, shouting her name through the choking smoke.

Some seconds last a lifetime.

Some seconds steal a life.

Chapter 11

Lorenzo spied something on the floor—someone's coat. He grabbed it, raced toward the woman. She ran, flaming hair streaming behind her. As if fire were something she could outrun.

He shoved her to the ground and jumped on top of her, smothering the blaze with the coat. She jerked beneath him, screaming. He beat out the flames, warring against them. When he withdrew the blanket, she lay limp, the remnants of her hair hanging in charred shreds. Burns puckered one side of her face. Her lips parted. A breath. She was alive.

He scooped her up, carried her toward the crowd rushing through the door to the Greene Street staircase. Smoke choked him. He coughed, gagging on the acrid taste. A man ran past him. "Hey!" Lorenzo shouted.

The man turned. Beneath his newsboy cap, his eyes were round with fear.

"Please." Lorenzo gulped, heaving a breath. "Take her down, get her somewhere safe. I've gotta help the others."

Without a word, the man took the girl, carrying her against his chest, following the crowd down the stairs. Seconds hazed together as Lorenzo pushed the remaining women toward the stairs as they screamed and batted at the sparks falling on their hair and clothes. "Go, go!" Flames barreled toward the Greene Street stairs. An inferno. He couldn't see across the room to the Washington Place door. All he could see was a wall of rising fire.

Aileen.

In the single second it took to think her name, he changed from a machine working by rote, feeling nothing but urgency, to a man desperate, driven.

The ninth floor.

I have to get to the ninth floor.

In the fog of smoke and falling ash, he made out Mr. Bernstein shouting at Dinah Lipschitz who still sat at her desk, clutching the phone.

"Fire!" she screamed, voice hoarse.

She's trying to warn the other floors.

"I can't get anyone on the ninth floor," Dinah cried.

"For mercy's sake!" Mr. Bernstein's swarthy face was black with soot. "Those people don't know."

"What should I do?" Dinah gripped the phone.

"Go." Bernstein dragged Dinah up from her chair and pushed her toward the Greene Street stairs. "Save yourself."

She ran, body bent into itself, through the smoke and down the stairs. Flames curled around the legs of her desk, consuming the wood.

"Mr. Bernstein." Gasping from the smoke, he could barely yell the words. "The ninth floor. I'm going up there."

"I'm coming with you." Bernstein sprinted toward him, skirting the flames. Lorenzo flung himself through the Greene Street door, Bernstein at his heels. Smoke stung his eyes.

Aileen. I'm coming, my love. I'm coming.

Up the stairs, into the ninth floor vestibule. *I'm coming.*

The force of the heat pummeled him. A wall of fire blocked the door to the factory floor, a raging blaze burbling up from a barrel of machine oil. Flames whipped, searing the air.

God, please. No. No.

"It's too late." Bernstein heaved the words. "We can't get in there. Tenth floor."

He stood motionless. He'd run through the flames. Yes. That's what he would do. He could do it.

My Aileen. My Aileen is in there.

"Move, Favero!" Bernstein shouted. "We can't help those people."

Tearing his gaze away from the roaring flames, Lorenzo ran back toward the stairs. Smoke blinded him. He couldn't see what was ahead. A rushing, like waves crashing against rock, filled his ears. If the tenth floor was blocked, then what?

They'd be trapped.

He ran blindly, groping up the stairs. Finally, they broke through to the tenth floor, pushing through the door.

Smoke filled the tenth floor, flames pouring through the windows. It hadn't spread like on the other two floors. Not yet. Bernstein barreled past him.

Lorenzo bent double, gasping for breath.

Aileen. Meggie. Ida.

Enough.

People rushed this way and that, like rats in a maze, shouting, running. But where? Across the room, Mr. Blanck held a little girl in his arms, another clinging to his leg. His daughters. The man stared vacantly as flames poured into the room.

A woman darted from window to window, screaming. In a flash, she leapt out. Just. . .jumped. Here one instant, gone the next.

A sound tore from his throat. Lorenzo looked away. A man in a suit stood on a desk, trying to break a skylight with his bare hands.

"The roof!" Bernstein shouted. "We can get out that way. Everyone, follow me."

The little girl standing next to Blanck whimpered. Her father didn't seem to hear her. As people fled toward the stairs to the roof, Lorenzo ran to them. Another man rushed over, carrying a ledger under his arm, coughing in the thickening smoke.

"Mr. Blanck," said the man. "Come. We're going up on the roof."

Blanck hardly seemed to hear him. Standing in his burning factory, he'd ceased to be the powerful owner. Now he looked stricken. Paralyzed.

The child cried harder, trembling. Lorenzo picked her up. "Hey, there." Somehow he made his voice gentle. Her large red hair bow was askew, her face scrunched as she sobbed. "Shhh. It's okay. I've got you."

The man dropped the ledger and took the other child from Blanck's arms. "Come, sir." He tugged at Blanck's sleeve. Mutely, Blanck followed. The room darkened with choking smoke, flames an iridescent glow. Bernstein shouted to the man still pounding at the skylight, swearing at him to get down.

Flames poured in on the side of the room closest to the Greene Street stairs. To get to the stairs and the roof, they'd have to go through the narrowing path. Go fast.

"Hold on, little girl." The child clung tighter to his neck. "It's going to be okay."

Bernstein had a woman in his arms, her body limp as if she'd fainted. The crowd rushed into the stairwell. "Quickly," someone shouted. "It's coming in through the window."

Fire blew through a broken window in the stairwell. Black smoke swirled. Footsteps clattered as those ahead ran past through flickering flames.

Dear God, help us.

He yanked his shirt from his pants, cocooned the little girl inside it, shielding her body as best he could.

Then he ran.

Heat scalded him.

Hell. I'm running straight into it.

Inches away, fire whipped through the broken window. He kept running, clutching the little girl, wheezing from the smoke.

Don't stop.

Quicksand. Was there quicksand? It mired his legs, pulling him down, down, down. He sensed somewhere he was burning. His eyes stung.

Run, mio figlio. Run. Padre's voice, close as a whisper.

He broke through. The roof. Air. Daylight. He dragged in a breath, yanked open his shirt. Blanck's daughter looked up at him. He'd feared she'd be burning, but she wasn't. He set her down and beat at the sparks on his clothes and hair. Workers staggered onto the roof, gasping, slapping the sparks from their bodies.

A young woman ran toward him. "Mildred!" She knelt beside the little girl. "There you are, my darling." She threw her arms around the child then looked up at him. Her hair hung in half-pinned tangles around her face, and her skin was gray with ash and soot. "I'm their governess. I lost sight of them in the confusion. Your daddy's over there." She pointed to where Mr. Blanck stood, holding his other daughter. "Thank you," she said.

He nodded and let the woman take the little girl back to her father. He looked up at the sky. Pale blue and soft clouds tinged with rising smoke.

The roof offered only temporary safety. Soon the flames would reach it too. He crossed the expanse and moved toward the edge. Glanced down.

A sheer drop plunged ten stories down.

His stomach churned, and he backed away.

Two buildings loomed to the north and west, their rooftops roughly fifteen feet higher than the Asch Building, one a few feet taller than the other. Both so close a person could almost climb onto their roofs, if not for the difference in height. One belonged to New York University. On his way to work, he'd seen students hurrying through its doors, young men around his own age dressed in suits and carrying books beneath their arms.

If someone lowered a ladder, they could scale it onto one of the buildings. To safety.

He scanned the crowd. If someone could crawl up the side of one of the buildings, reach the roof, and get help, they'd be rescued. He'd do it.

He crossed the roof, heading toward the towering wall of brick.

As he reached it, he saw men on its roof, lowering a ladder.

"We'll help you up," one shouted as the ladder descended. Young men in suit coats. University students. The ladder settled into place, and one of the young men climbed down.

"Come over here," Lorenzo called, waving those nearest forward. "We'll help you up the ladder." Smoke fogged the air, thickening. Another student hastened down the ladder.

"Let's get them up." He had sandy hair, his pinstripe suit crisp. He looked like he'd never done a day's work in his life. Yet his voice was confident and steady.

"This way." Lorenzo guided a girl toward the ladder, steadying her as she climbed the first few rungs. A minute passed as she ascended. She reached the top, and the waiting students pulled her onto the roof. Time stretched as they worked to ferry those who'd escaped the tenth floor onto the roof of the adjoining building.

A second ladder had been lowered on the opposite side of the building, and he glimpsed climbers scaling the rungs, skirts billowing around them. Smoke plumed thicker, and flames licked onto the roof, funneled from the airshaft. An encouraging look, a boost, and he let go as another young woman ascended, clambering in her long skirt. As he helped them up, he glanced quickly into every face. Some were unfamiliar. Some were acquaintances.

None was Aileen. And there was no time to ask if anyone had seen her.

Roughly, he shoved emotion aside.

Finally, only he and one of the students remained. The student motioned to the ladder. Nodded. "After you."

Lorenzo climbed the rungs, hazily aware of the pain in his burned hands. He gained the top. Hands reached to pull him onto the roof. He clambered to his feet.

For a long moment, he stood near the edge, shoulder to shoulder with young men who'd not have looked twice at him yesterday, staring across as smoke consumed the Triangle Waist Factory.

The second the elevator stopped, its occupants spilled out in a universal mass of panic. Aileen didn't care about the people pushing past her, shoving into her to flee the car, didn't even notice. She rounded on the elevator operator, a young man with dark hair.

"Go back up. Right now. Go!"

He shook his head, gaze sorrowful. "It's too late, miss. I'm sorry. We'd never make it. The flames were already coming through the shaft."

"My little sister is up there." A feral darkness possessed her body.

She came at him, shoving, punching his chest, backing him against the elevator. "Go back up, or so help me I'll—"

He shook his head, doing nothing to stop her from hitting him. "If I knew I could make it back down, I would. I'm so sorry." Tears filled his eyes. His throat jerked.

Roughly, she turned away and left the elevator. Through a haze, she saw people running through the lobby, women, firemen. Girls stood in groups weeping. Two ran to each other, calling out "Mary!" "Celia!" They flung their arms around each other's necks and cried. The front door, the one leading to Washington Place, stood straight ahead.

Air. She needed to breathe. To get away from the voices and people.

Somehow those ordinary thoughts, those simple needs, bolstered her enough to approach the door. A policeman stood guarding it. She tried to walk past him, but he stepped in front of her.

"You have to stay inside, miss."

She stared at him. Oh, she was so heartily sick of policemen. A blurred memory—Meggie stumbling up the apartment stairs after a day on the picket lines, cradling her arm to her chest, mumbling, "Copper," when Aileen asked what had happened.

Now, she gritted her teeth, seething. "Get out of my way!"

His eyes widened. In the second it took for him to register her words, she slipped past him and onto the street. Firm ground. Sky. Air. She gulped it in. It still tasted of smoke. She stood on the pavement, taking deep breaths. The noise of fire engines clanging and street sounds surrounded her.

Then she ran—past firemen hauling a hose and past two policemen—blocking out any voices that might try to stop her. Fire wagons sat parked near the sidewalk, their horses snorting and stamping in fear. A huge crowd had gathered across the street. They stared up at the Asch Building, transfixed.

Aileen stopped, lungs pinching as she coughed. Flames crackled, lapping through the windows. Within the building, the fire raged. Rooted to the ground, she stared at the windows of the ninth floor.

Then she saw her. The girl, climbing onto the window ledge, flames at her back. She stood poised, looking down at the crowd. Her skirts swirled in the smoke and wind. A ladder had been raised against the side of the building. At the sixth floor, it stopped. Impotent. A group of firemen held nets, angling them below the window.

Aileen stifled something. A cry? No. It hadn't come from her.

She couldn't look.

She couldn't look away.

The girl spread her arms, birdlike.

And jumped.

The sound the woman's body made as it struck the net was one she would never forget. Finality. It was the sound of finality. A dull thud, a ripping as the impact tore the net from the firemen's hands, and the girl plummeted through. Red bled from the place where she fell, her form crumpled and twisted. Two firemen picked her up, lifted her between them, and placed her body on the sidewalk.

More girls appeared in the windows, their faces startlingly pale against the sea of fire at their backs. They climbed onto the sill—a threesome. Arms around each other's shoulders, they stood on the sill only a moment.

Their skirts billowed as the three of them fell together. Floating gently at first, then the terrible sound of their bodies striking the net. Tearing through it. Plunging to the ground.

Others followed, more and more of them. They perched on the windowsills, faces upturned to the sky as if drinking in air that was fresh, smokeless. But they only stayed a moment before jumping, grabbing aimlessly toward the ladder as they passed. One girl's hair flamed behind her, burning all the way down. Like a comet falling from the heavens. When she fell, the firemen turned their hoses on her body before carrying her to the pile. They'd stopped using nets. They had no more.

Aileen wanted to move, to leave this place, but her feet wouldn't obey. As if she saw herself from outside, she noticed her body shook. Trembled like she had a fever. But she could do nothing about that either.

A man appeared in the window. Jacob.

No! Don't!

The shout lodged in her throat.

From his place inside, he helped a girl onto the ledge, steadying her carefully. He held her out, away from the building, arms supporting her shoulders. For an instant, she dangled, suspended by only his hands.

He let her fall.

Seconds of silence.

A hollow thud.

Those around Aileen, even the men, wiped tears from their cheeks, sobbed, and turned their faces away from the unfolding horror.

She could neither join them in their tears nor turn her face aside.

Jacob guided a second girl onto the ledge. Like the first, she didn't struggle. As if letting a man drop her nine stories down was as natural as letting him help her across a slippery street. How had it happened? Had they begged him to do this for them, too afraid to jump themselves? Had he offered?

As before, he held her away from the building and let her fall.

Another girl appeared in the window. Her skirt was blue. Her hair, light brown.

Ida.

"I'm not going to be working at Triangle much longer."

"Going to start your own uprising somewhere else?"

"No." A smile transformed her face, made it glow. "I'm going to raise our little boy or girl to know a different world than this."

Had it been only hours ago, only lunchtime?

No, not lunchtime. A lifetime ago.

Ida took her husband's hand as he guided her onto the window-sill. His touch as gentle as he'd always been with her. A bridegroom, even now. She turned and put her arms around him, their lips meeting in a soft and tender kiss.

This is a nightmare. Ida and Jacob are going to have a baby, seven babies, with half-grins like Jacob's and bold spirits like Ida's. This isn't happening.

Aileen couldn't watch the rest. Yet in her mind, she saw it anyway. Ida, arms wrapped around her body, cradling the child in her womb, as the distance of nine stories and the span of ten seconds dissolved a beautiful life. The promise of another.

Before she looked up, she heard the second thud.

Jacob.

His too-still body lying on the pavement inches from his wife. Neck bent at a sickening angle, hand outstretched. Almost touching hers.

Aileen's world spun, the sky, the smoke billowing from the Asch Building, the faces around her melding into a blur. She blinked, tried to stay upright, tried to open her mouth and call for help.

Then all at once darkness closed around her.

Chapter 12

For fifteen minutes, they kept them in the lobby of the New York University building. A policeman came and told them it wasn't safe to go outside. Twice Lorenzo insisted he had to leave, that there were people he needed to look for. Aileen. Meggie. Rose. Jacob. Ida.

The policeman wouldn't let him. For once, Lorenzo saw kindness in the gaze of a member of that profession. More than kindness. The man looked stricken. Overwhelmed.

"They're falling. We can't let anyone out until its safe."

"Falling? The flames?"

The policeman shook his head. "Bodies. They're jumping from the ninth floor."

The words sluiced through him with the full force of unspoken implications. "But there are people out there, right? Firemen. . .men with ladders, nets?"

"The ladders only go to the sixth floor. As they fall, the bodies are breaking through the nets."

"But they are trying."

"They're doing everything they can."

Lorenzo turned away and asked no more. He crossed the room and sat against the wall, knees drawn up, staring at his burned and blistered hands. The other survivors from the roof talked among themselves, asking questions, recounting what had happened. He didn't need to. He pulled out his battered pocket watch, opened it.

Five o'clock. The quitting bell had rung at four thirty.

An eternity had passed since then.

Finally, they let him go. The street was dusky with smoke and crowded with people. He moved toward the Asch Building, searching for Aileen's red hair and pink shirtwaist, Meggie's blond curls and cream shirtwaist.

Shirtwaists.

He cursed them.

Smoke still clouded from the Asch Building, but from what he could see, no flames. The structure itself looked untouched.

Of course. Of course it was. After all, the building was fireproof. He remembered Jacob telling him long ago, saying how great it was to work in a modern American factory.

"They don't let you burn."

Didn't they?

The sight of the bodies piled in front of the building drove the breath from his lungs. From a distance, they looked like bundles of fabric lumped together. But as he drew closer, their forms became distinct. Rows upon rows. Stacks upon stacks. Two policemen stood by, guarding them. A photographer snapped pictures.

Water from the hoses puddled on the sidewalk. It had a strange pinkish tinge.

Bile rose in his throat.

He walked toward the policemen.

"I'm looking for some people." His voice came out hoarse and scratchy. He cleared his throat. "Aileen and Meggie O'Connor. Rose Colletti. Jacob and Ida Levin." There were others. The cutters he swapped jokes with, Dinah, the Italian girl with the gap between her teeth who always smiled at him as she took his finished pieces to run them to the operators. But he'd start with those.

"Are you a relation?" the younger officer asked.

"Aileen O'Connor is my fiancée. The rest are friends." To him, a second family.

"And you suspect they might be. . .?" He made a vague gesture toward the bodies.

It hurt to breathe. He glanced at the pile. A slender arm poked out, wrist limp. A bracelet with green beads was clasped around it. Somewhere out there was a person who knew the owner of that bracelet. She was someone's daughter, sister, sweetheart. Now, she lay in a pile of others like her. Different women but with a common fate.

"I don't know."

"They'll be moved to the Charities Pier on Twenty-Sixth Street. It should be open by tomorrow. Go home, lad." The man's accent was Irish, like Aileen's. "If they don't return. . ." He swallowed, left the rest unfinished.

Go there.

Lorenzo turned and walked away, head bent. Voices merged around him, a medley of languages. English, Italian, Yiddish.

As the sky grew gray, their common cadence joined them as one. "Lorenzo!"

He looked up. Rose ran toward him, hair in tangles around her soot-smudged face. She threw her arms around him, hugging him fiercely. "Oh, thank God."

He hugged her back, and then she drew away. He read her face, searching for answers. "Aileen?"

427

Tears trickled down the grime coating her pale skin. His heart stopped. The flames he'd seen on the ninth floor mingled with Aileen's face, the memories converging.

His mind became an empty, howling thing.

"Aileen is. . .all right." Rose gulped. "But Meggie. . ." She buried her face in her hands.

Aileen was alive. For a second, a surge of something like hope, life, filled him.

Before crashing to his boots.

Meggie, smiling and sweet-faced. The little sister he'd never had. Only last week she'd pulled him aside after Sunday dinner, blushing. *"Lorenzo, could you tell me? How do I know when a boy likes me?"*

"Where. . .where's Aileen?" Somehow—from where, he didn't know—the words came.

She pointed toward a building across the street. "Over there. She fainted. I found her after she came to. They told me she was in the crowd as the people were. . .coming down."

"Does she"—his tongue wasn't working right—"know?"

Rose nodded, drawing in a deep breath. "She told me."

Together they crossed the street. Among the masses of people, he glimpsed Aileen sitting against the side of a building. "I told her I should take her home, but she wanted me to stay and look for you." He barely registered Rose's words, something else about her wanting to go home and reassure her parents, and was that all right? He said something back, yes, she should go home.

As he approached, Aileen looked up, eyes holding his. Her hair hung limp around her face, and her clothes were covered in soot.

She was alive. She'd been spared.

He wanted to put his arms around her and never let go. The realization that he'd found her penetrated his consciousness, but a portion of his mind wouldn't believe it. He'd seen the flames on the ninth floor, heard the policeman's words about those who'd jumped from the windows.

His thoughts wouldn't organize themselves. Was this what doctors meant when they said someone was in shock?

Somehow he had to gather himself and be strong for her.

He knelt beside her. "My love."

"Lorenzo." Her voice was fragile. She reached up, touched the side of his face, eyes wide and as disbelieving as his own must be. He put his arms around her, holding her against himself, hers twined around his neck. For a long moment, they stayed there, kneeling on the street and holding each other. Not weeping or speaking or doing anything but registering the sensation of the warmth of the other, each quiet breath.

He didn't move. Let her be the first to draw away. When she did, she sat back against the side of the building, eyes never leaving his. "Meggie. . ." She stopped. Unlike Rose, she didn't cry. She just sat there, that single word hanging in the air between them.

"I know," he said gently, afraid the wrong words would shatter her. "Rose told me."

"Jacob. Ida."

He'd lost count of how many times that day shock and grief had punched the breath from his body. How many more would follow before its end?

He blinked. How was it possible only this morning he'd walked with them to the factory, Ida and Jacob arm in arm, whispering together as if they had a special secret? How could it be that less than two hours ago he'd clapped a hand to his friend's shoulder while Jacob grinned his golden smile? What was the last thing Jacob had said to him? When had it been? He remembered Jacob beside him, fighting the fire, and then. . .the confusion and smoke. Had his friend been somewhere on the eighth floor, struggling for his life, while Lorenzo had worked to save others?

I'm so sorry, old man. I'm so sorry.

All around them came the sounds of the frantic, the grieving. He stood and held out his hand to her. Right now it was all he had to offer. Words, those syllables that once flowed from him freely, now seemed as worthless as the smoke threading the air. She took it and stood.

Leaning on each other, they moved down the street, making their way home.

Aileen opened her eyes, turning her face slightly. Lorenzo's head rested against the back of the sofa, his eyes closed, his arm around her shoulders, warmth radiating from his body.

Where? Why?

Then she remembered. Everything.

She pushed herself to a sitting position. They must have fallen asleep on his mother's sofa. Another memory, foggier than those of yesterday, surfaced.

They were to have been married today. How lovingly they'd planned for this day, how eagerly they'd anticipated it.

Yesterday's events had been neither planned for nor anticipated.

Right now she was too tired to add this new loss alongside the others.

He looked peaceful sleeping beside her, lashes dark against his skin, face framed by the pale light of dawn. She didn't want to wake him. If only she could lean against him, close her eyes, and forget everything. It would be easy, such a lapse into forgetfulness.

But she could not.

She owed Meggie that much, at least.

He opened his eyes. She watched the same transformation come over his face, the seconds of blissful forgetfulness, then the slamming force of memory. Her heart broke more for him than for her. She could let herself feel for him. She couldn't for herself.

"We have to go."

He scrubbed a bandaged hand across his jaw—his mother had tended both of them last night, saying little, silent pain in her gaze. "Yeah. There's going to be a lot of people." He stood. "Do you want something to eat first?"

She shook her head.

Minutes later, after Lorenzo knocked on his mother's door and told her where they were going, they made their way down the street. Above the tenement buildings, the sun rose, streaks of gold, ochre, and red.

The colors of fire.

She jerked her gaze away. Though the city stirred with its usual sounds, they seemed subdued, as if all of New York knew what an ordinary Saturday in March had become. Her footfalls echoed in her ears, and she wrapped her arms across her chest, not because she minded the physical cold but because she had nothing else to shield herself with.

Though nothing could protect her from what lay ahead.

All too soon, they approached the pier on Twenty-Sixth Street. The line stretched far back from the immense iron-framed yellow building. Hundreds of people. Men, women, even children. Standing alone or in little clusters. The scent of the river met her—water and salt.

They took their places at the end of the line, side by side. His hand found hers, and she grasped it—the warmth of his fingers, his bandaged palm.

Two hours passed. In fits and starts, the line moved forward as police escorted groups into the building. The waiting queue was silent, too silent for New York. This ordinary street had become a funeral line.

Lorenzo turned to her. He'd not spoken since they'd left the apartment. Perhaps he did not know what to say, or perhaps he sensed how cheap and immaterial words had become.

Tender sorrow filled his eyes as he looked into hers. "There are some things that once seen cannot be unseen, Aileen. You don't have to do this."

"No." She shook her head, breathing deeply. "I do. She must be. . .identified." Could it really be her voice speaking such hard, sterile words? *Identified.* It made Meggie sound like an object. Not the sister who loved laughter and the nickelodeons and playing with baby Lucia, who'd joined the picket lines with fierce-hearted courage.

The movement of the line cut off her thoughts as they filed through the doors. Her hand shook, clasped around Lorenzo's, but she didn't let go.

The high-set lights were dim, as if in an attempt to veil the stark-ness of it. Pine coffins circuited the room in a double row, starting at the door. Boards propped up each head so the faces were visible, though a sheet cloaked the rest. Sulfur from the lights and brine from the river mingled with an odor she couldn't define. Then she realized. It was the scent of death.

The line shuffled forward, footsteps and murmured voices the only sounds in the weighted silence. She forced herself to look into every face. Some were peaceful, as if they merely slept. Others bore the marks of pain, their expressions cast in a grimace.

Somewhere in this room was Meggie.

God help me. I don't want to see my sister here.

She recognized familiar faces from the factory, fellow workers whose names she didn't know. The brunette who was always fluffing her bangs in front of the cloakroom mirror. Now they lay matted against her skin, her vivid green eyes closed. The older Jewish woman who always wore a button-down brown coat—she had it on even now—and sometimes sang softly in Yiddish when the foremen weren't within earshot. *If only I'd taken the time to learn their names. Then I could identify them.*

What of those who had no families to perform this service for them? These faces, these girls in pine boxes, had been part of the landscape of her life. Yet she'd not known their names, had never spoken to them beyond casual greetings. Now it was too late to do even this for them.

The bodies closest to the door looked to be the ones who'd suffered the least damage and could be most easily recognized, perhaps to spare those searching from having to proceed further along the line if it wasn't necessary. The deeper into the room they went, the more disfigured the faces and bodies became—battered, burned. Farther down the line, a wrenching keening broke the silence.

The rending of a soul.

A policeman hastened to where the woman stood gazing into the box. He held a lantern up to illuminate the face, questioning her quietly. She responded in a garbled voice, tears streaming down her cheeks. Another policeman penciled the woman's answers in a notebook.

A touch against Aileen's back. She turned. Lorenzo met her eyes, and she read there what he did not need to say with words. For a long moment, she clung to his face with her gaze. His hand against her back was strong, steadying, gentle.

Then she looked into the face of the girl in the coffin.

My Meggie. My sweet, sweet girl.

The left half of her face had been badly burned, but somehow the right was almost untouched. If she looked only at the right side, Meggie seemed to be sleeping. As she'd been the first time Aileen

433

saw her, an hour after Meggie's birth. The moment her sister's weight lay in her arms, a fervent protectiveness rose up inside her. Meggie had been as small as one of her dolls, so fragile. When she'd blinked wide blue eyes up at Aileen, a powerful love, one that shifted the orbit of her world and centered it on this precious bundle wrapped in pink, had filled her so intensely, tears welled up in her eyes, though she'd been only five. She'd bent her head near her sister's ear and whispered, *"I'm your sister, Aileen. And for sure and certain, you're safe with me, Meggie lass. If you're scared or sad or lonely, as sure as Ireland is green, you'll always have me."*

Aileen released a gasping breath.

"You'll always have me. . . ."

She pushed back everything—the fear that shook her legs to the point of collapse, the sobs rising hard in her throat—and bent over the coffin. Gently, she brushed the back of her hand across the undamaged side of her sister's face. Her skin was cold, her body so very still. Yet Aileen let her hand linger there.

"I love you, Meggie O'Connor," she whispered.

There were so many things she wanted to say but couldn't. Thoughts and emotions she hadn't even begun to sort through and couldn't bring herself to voice. She gave what she had, and what she had were those five simple words.

"Miss?"

Still bending over Meggie, she turned and looked into the face of a policeman who stood beside Lorenzo.

"Is this your sister?"

"Meggie," she said, voice serrated. "Meggie O'Connor."

"And you're her next of kin?"

She nodded. The policeman said something about claiming the body, releasing it for burial, but his words ran together in her mind. Lorenzo nodded, speaking to the policeman. Then the officer walked away, leaving them alone while others filed past.

She stood facing him. He looked utterly broken, his curly hair tangled, traces of soot still evident on his haggard face. "I. . ." He swallowed hard. "I have to keep looking. For Jacob and Ida. He doesn't have family here, see. Somebody has to. . ."

She nodded, gaze falling once more upon her sister.

"Aileen, what's love like?"

"It's not like in the dime novels, Meg, all sighs and roses and moonlit walks. It's hard and scary, because life is. But it's real. And when it's real, you know you've found someone to journey beside, no matter where that journey takes you."

"I'll go with you." From where she found the ability to say it, she didn't know. Nor how she would gather the strength to continue this walk of loss.

But she would.

She would not let him walk alone.

Chapter 13

The night of Meggie's funeral, Lorenzo found Aileen sitting on the fire escape, arms wrapped around her knees, staring out at the darkened street. She'd not broken since the fire, except for a moment when she first saw Meggie. But she'd gathered herself, walked beside him as they searched for, found, and identified the bodies of Jacob and Ida Levin, attended their burial alongside him, and stood beside her sister's newly turned grave pale and dry-eyed.

She needed to break. Yet he knew what it was to fear grief, to shrink back into the safety of keeping emotions trapped inside one's chest rather than releasing them and, in doing so, risk shattering oneself.

He sat beside her on the tiny platform, resting his bandaged hands on his knees. She turned. In the faint light, her features were pale, her gaze hollow. For long minutes, neither of them spoke. His throat ached. He'd give his own life to bring her sister's back. There was nothing worse than watching the suffering of someone as close to you as your own heart, powerless to do anything to mend it.

God, show me what she needs.

"I don't want to rush you," he said quietly. "I just want you to know I'm here if you need to talk or cry, whatever you need. You don't have to do it alone."

For several minutes, she didn't seem to have heard. She didn't speak or even look at him. He wanted her to talk to him, to show him what she was feeling, to cry in his arms. But if she wasn't ready, he had to wait with her and for her until she was. That was the crux of commitment. Waiting. Staying.

He stared out at the city, the lights in the buildings across the street. How many across New York battled grief on this cold March night? He'd read in the papers the death toll had surpassed 140. Two girls had survived the jump from the ninth floor. One was still alive in a hospital, the other had lived only a few hours.

"Why did God take my sister?" She spoke without looking at him, voice soft.

Was she talking to herself, or was it a question she meant him to answer? What words could he find that wouldn't come out like weightless platitudes?

God, help me.

"Why didn't He protect her? Was it because of me?" She faced him now, and he saw it in her gaze. The cracking in her veneer. "I didn't stop to think about anybody else but her. Not Ida or any of the other girls. I just wanted to make sure she was safe. I should have shoved her in front of me in the line for the elevators instead of holding her hand. I should have determined to stay behind. Then maybe she'd be here right now. I've been playing it through my mind, every minute. Why didn't I do it differently? It's my fault that I'm here and she's not. It's my fault."

He swallowed. The emptiness in her voice tore at his heart. "It isn't your fault, Aileen. It happened so fast. Do you think I haven't thought the same? Rose told me Jacob went up to the ninth floor once he saw the fire couldn't be put out. I should have gone too. Then maybe I could have saved you both." Those weren't the words he'd meant to say. Yet they were the ones that came to him. "Maybe we'll always live with regret, but carrying the burden of wishing we'd made a different choice won't bring those we love back to us."

"But why didn't God stop the fire? It says Christ told the waves to be still, and they were. The people who died, they were decent human beings." Anguish filled her eyes. "If anyone deserves to be punished, it's those who live in luxury off the profits of workers who are paid next to nothing. Not girls of seventeen who just wanted a small amount of goodness out of life. They weren't asking for yachts or diamonds, just a little bit of joy. Was that too much for them to ask?" Her face crumpled. "Was that too much for them to have?" A sob shuddered from her throat.

And the shattering came.

He pulled her into his arms, cradled her against his chest, and let her cry. He didn't whisper that everything was going to be all right. Silva had done that when they got the news about their padre, and he'd jerked away from her. Everything wouldn't be all right. There was loss. There was a void. Nothing was all right.

Don't stop the storm. Hold her through it.

Where the words came from was as inexplicable as when he'd heard his padre's voice as he ran through the fire. Yet the truth of from whom they came washed through him like cooling rain.

Time passed. Her keening subsided into quiet sobs then into silence.

"Thank you," she whispered, the remnants of her tears glistening on her cheeks. "Knowing you're here has given me a solace I do not deserve."

He slid his arm around her shoulders. "And as long as God allows, I'll be right here."

"After all this," she whispered, "you still trust Him?"

He exhaled a breath. Did he? Was it trite to answer yes? What if he'd had to walk along that line of coffins and find Aileen among the faces? His mother, Silva, young Giuseppe? Would he trust still if he lost everything, left with only Christ to cling to?

God, help me to show her.

"I don't trust because it's easy. I trust because He's good." He met her eyes. "The fire. . . that was a horrible thing. There's still so much we don't know about how it happened and why so many died, but I know it had a lot to do with a lack of consideration for the workers. Things that might not have happened if we'd gotten our union. I guess there'll be an investigation and we'll learn more. Maybe change will come because of it. But that change won't bring back the lost, and it won't heal the grief felt by their families. Life is broken, Aileen. It's hard."

Images of Jacob and Ida's battered bodies, of the child they would never hold, of his padre stolen by Mount Vesuvius and the grief in his mama's eyes rose before him. "Jesus told the waves to be still, and they were. But sometimes the waves aren't still and the storms don't stop. Yet in the midst of it, He's there, holding us through them. He has an eternity in store, no matter what this earth brings. There are no storms in heaven. For Meggie there's only joy and love and peace, just as there will be for us someday. I don't know why God didn't stop the fire, why we lost Meggie. But it wasn't because of you."

Again, they sat in silence, looking into darkness.

"Is it all right to ask God why?" Her voice still shook, but there was a new steadiness there too.

"I think we wouldn't be human if we didn't. It won't be easy going forward. But you don't have to do it alone."

"But what if something happens to you?" She pressed her lips together as if holding back another wave of tears.

What if something happens to you, my Aileen? Then how will I go forward?

Words his mama had said not long after Padre died filled his mind.

"Never, never will I call myself alone."

"If something happens to me, you still won't be alone. Even in her last minutes on earth, Meggie wasn't alone. God was right there with her." In the midst of the flames. At the peak of the darkness.

A trace of peace filled Aileen's face in the midst of tear tracks and shadows. "He was with her," she murmured. "I sense it."

He cupped her face with one hand. "We are never alone." He let the words soak into his own heart, past the loss, sorrow, and emptiness there, a gift to himself as much as to her. "You are never alone."

A month later

Aileen stood with her hand around her husband's in front of the simple headstone as the setting sun slipped below the horizon.

MARGARET GRACE O'CONNOR

1894–1911

RESURGAM

She turned to Lorenzo, smiling through a mist of tears. "She would have loved everything about today."

He nodded, wind riffling his thick dark hair.

"After your mama finished my wedding dress and I put it on, Meggie told me I looked like a princess, and she begged me to let her try it. At first I almost didn't. But now I'm glad I did. She looked so beautiful, twirling in front of the mirror." She sighed, but it was out of memory, not regret.

Though loss still severed her heart, though she woke in the night shaking with tears, she'd reached the beginning of something like healing. Begun to cry and laugh and remember her sister as the gift she'd been. "She's dancing now," Aileen said softly. "I know she is."

Silence fell in the empty graveyard. A hallowed stillness as they both remembered. She withdrew her hand from Lorenzo's, stepped forward, and knelt beside the grave. She lifted the flowers she carried to her nose, inhaling their sweet, pure fragrance then placed them next to the headstone.

"There was joy today, Meggie," she whispered, resting her palm against the grass, the blades brushing her fingers. "I wore our dress and married Lorenzo, and it was as beautiful as you said it would be." She inhaled a shaky breath, eyes falling closed, her sister's face filling her mind. Laughing at Rose's theatrics. Lifting her chin and saying she was old enough to join the strike. Twirling in a dress that was too big for her, while her eyes shone. "For sure and certain, I love you, little sister."

Then she rose and looked up at the man who stood a few paces away watching her. She walked toward him, the tendrils of hair that had escaped from their pins blowing in the breeze. She drew in a deep breath. "I'm ready."

He held out his hand, and she slipped hers within his. The setting sun gilded his dark hair, outlined the angles of his handsome face. Her husband. The man who would walk beside her through whatever the future held, cherish her heart, and point her to the One who could heal it.

Together they walked away, through the twilight-hued streets of the city that had become home. They reached Sullivan Street and their apartment door. He turned to her, a crooked smile unfurling. She laughed as he lifted her in his arms and carried her inside. There he set her down in the center of the room.

"I love you." Wonder filled his gaze as he regarded her.

"I love you too," she whispered, her heart full with the sweetness of how truly she meant those words.

He bent and kissed her. A kiss that spoke of the tender treasuring their love would always hold. It lasted far longer than any they'd shared yet, and he made every second count. Against his lips, she smiled.

"What?"

"Remember after you proposed when you said those straitlaced Americans needed a lesson in amore?"

A grin tugged at his lips as he nodded.

"Well, you're looking at an Irish lass who isn't so straitlaced, but who'd like to sign up for more of those lessons in amore."

"I think"—he kissed her again, long and lingering, a roguish glimmer in his gaze—"that could be arranged."

She wrapped her arms around his neck, looking into his eyes with a smile. "Good."

Since immigrating to America and meeting Lorenzo Favero, she'd lived and loved and been broken in ways that had forever changed her. Daily she prayed the loss had not been wholly in vain, that in the aftermath of a fire that had scarred and stolen from so many, a better future for workers would arise.

And she would fight for it with the man she loved beside her.

The future before them. The past an echo in their hearts.

Author's Note

This novella is based on the true story of a strike and a fire that changed America. From September 1909 through February 1910, workers at the Triangle Waist Company went on strike. What started as a few hundred workers taking a stand against injustices at the factories where they worked became an uprising twenty thousand strong across New York City. Workers in other cities, such as Philadelphia, also joined the strike.

Those who dared go on strike suffered hunger, poverty, and persecution from the police and hired strikebreakers. Hundreds were arrested, and many served sentences at the workhouse on Blackwell's Island. During a union meeting on November 22, 1909, twenty-three-year-old Clara Lemlich called a vote for a general strike to the overwhelming support of her audience. Notable society women and suffragettes such as Alva Vanderbilt Belmont and Anne Morgan took up the cause of the strikers, and newspapers filled pages with articles opening the eyes of readers to the injustices faced by factory workers.

At the beginning of 1910, the strike lost the support of some of the "Mink Coat Brigade" who were displeased when strikers refused to settle with their bosses without union recognition. To socialite Anne Morgan, insistence on union organization smacked of socialism, which as a banker's daughter she wanted no part in. By mid-February the strike ended. Some workers had succeeded in gaining union recognition, but owners of larger factories like Triangle refused to cede to demands for a closed shop. With few other options, the workers returned to their jobs. After the fire, many, including Clara Lemlich, stated the fire could have been prevented, or the scope of the tragedy minimized, had there been a union at Triangle. The locked doors to prevent workers from stealing petty items and the lack of fire drills and safety standards were issues a union would have addressed.

The Triangle Fire occurred just thirteen months after the strike ended. On March 25, 1911, a fire caused by a cigarette started in one of the scrap bins beneath the cutters' tables on the eighth floor. Feeding on the highly flammable atmosphere, the flames quickly spread. On the eighth floor, workers fled through the elevators or via the stairways that led to Greene Street and Washington Place. Those who sought refuge on the flimsy fire escape were killed when it collapsed under the weight of its occupants, crashing eight stories to the ground. Before it collapsed, a few workers used it to exit at the sixth floor.

By the time the fire reached the ninth floor, it had already consumed most of the eighth. On the ninth, it spread with devastating speed across the room occupied by 250 sewing machine operators— almost all women in their late teens and early twenties. Life-or-death decisions were made in a matter of seconds. Within minutes flames cut off the exits, and those who didn't make it onto one of the elevators were left with two choices—jump nine stories or be burned alive. Fifty-four jumped, including a young man who performed the only chivalry he could as he helped four girls to fall, including his sweetheart, whom he kissed and embraced before jumping himself.

Though firemen arrived on the scene with ladders, they only reached the sixth floor. The force of each falling body upon striking the nets equaled 11,000 pounds; thus the nets also proved useless. Twenty minutes after the fire began, 144 people—121 of them women—were dead. The youngest victim was fourteen. Two women survived the jump and were hospitalized, only to die from their injuries within days. Until September 11, 2001, no workplace disaster in the history of New York City claimed more lives than the Triangle Fire.

After the fire, owners Max Blanck and Isaac Harris were charged with manslaughter. Evidence pointed to their neglect of safety conditions, and worker testimonies stated the locked doors prevented escape on the day of the fire. When the verdict was reached, Blanck and Harris were acquitted due to a lack of evidence that they themselves *knew* the doors were locked.

The press coverage the fire received forced the American public to confront the conditions in which their mass-produced goods were made. The safety of factory workers was put under investigation, while reformers used the stories of those who died in the fire to spur action. We owe much of our workplace safety today to laws put in place following the Triangle Fire. New laws required high-rise buildings to have automatic sprinklers. Fire drills and fire extinguishers became mandatory. Doors were required to swing outward and remain unlocked during operating hours. Laws were enacted ordering proper sanitary conditions and benefits for workers who suffered injuries on the job. New mandates protected women from working more than fifty-two hours a week, and outlawed child labor.

But the privileges we enjoy today were bought with a price. Samuel Gompers, the first president of the American Federation of Labor, said it best: "Rarely does an opportunity arise for such legislative reform, but women had to burn first in order for this to happen."

Sadly, millions today continue to suffer dangerous working conditions and extremely low wages. On November 25, 2012, a fire at a garment factory in Bangladesh claimed the lives of over 117 people. Reading accounts of factory fires that have occurred in recent years offer eerily similar parallels to the conditions faced by the Triangle workers. In many cases, those endured today are even worse. Among others, the chocolate industry also presents its own set of sobering realities. By becoming informed consumers, choosing to boycott companies known for unethical treatment of workers, by researching the facts and speaking the truth, we can make a difference.

Speak up for those who cannot speak for themselves,
for the rights of all who are destitute.
Speak up and judge fairly;
defend the rights of the poor and needy.
PROVERBS 31:8–9 NIV

Blessings,
Amanda

To learn more about the Triangle Fire, I recommend the following resources:

American Experience: Triangle Fire, PBS documentary
Triangle: The Fire That Changed America by David Von Drehle
The Triangle Fire by Leon Stein